Graveworld Book II

The Gardens
Arcane

Ryan Z. Dawson

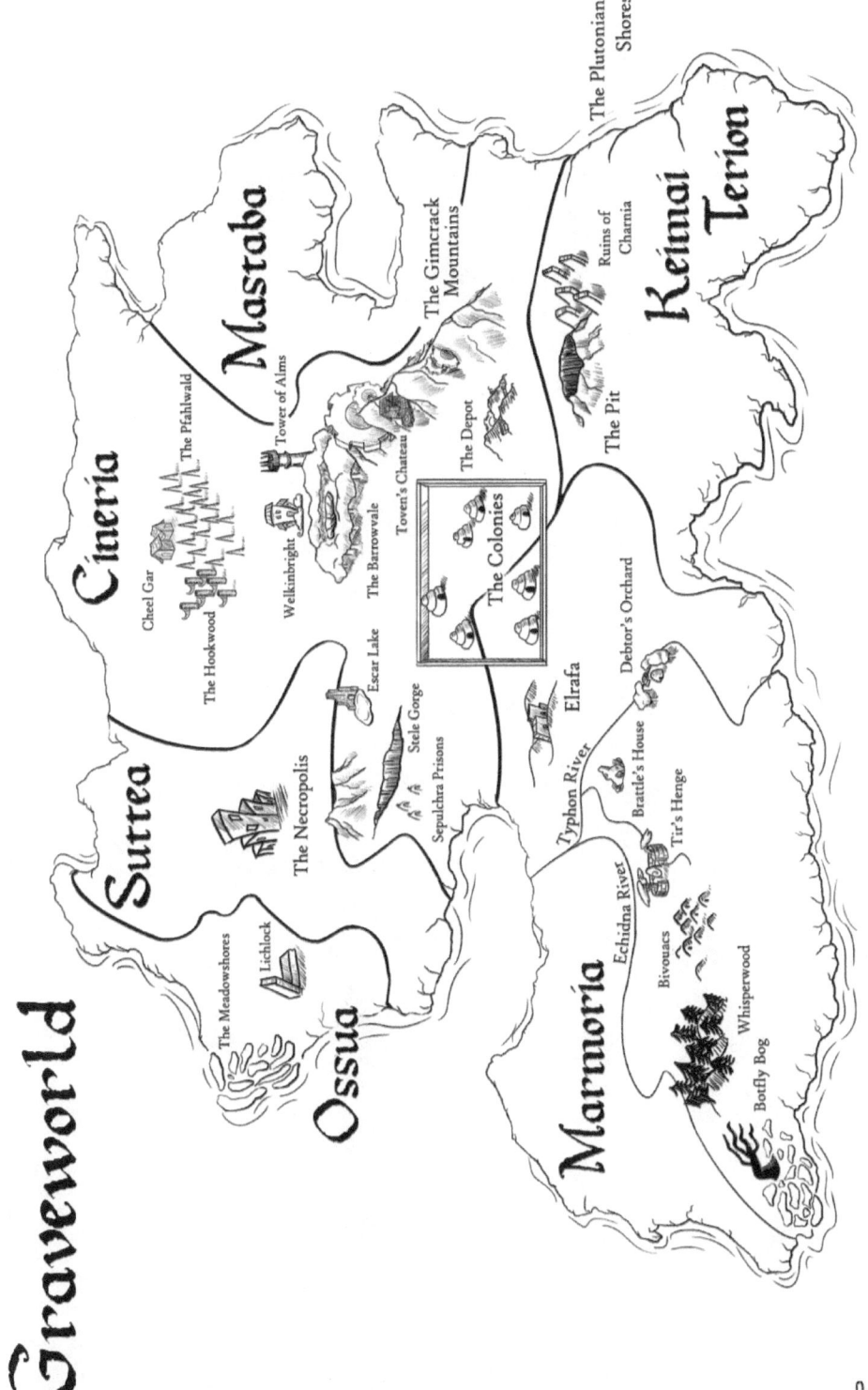

Graveworld

Cineria

Mastaba

Sutrea

Keimai
Terion

The Plutonian
Shores

The Pfahlwald

Cheel Gar

The Hookwood

Tower of Alms

Welkinbright

The Barrowvale

Toven's Chateau

The Depot

The Gimcrack
Mountains

Ruins of
Charnia

The Pit

The Colonies

Escar Lake

Stele Gorge

Sepulchra Prisons

Debtor's Orchard

Elrafa

The Necropolis

Lichlock

The Meadowshores

Ossua

Typhon River

Brattle's House

Tir's Henge

Echidna River

Bivouacs

Whisperwood

Botfly Bog

Marnoria

The Gardens Arcane

by
Ryan Z. Dawson

Edited by
Dara Rochlin
Buddy Wagner

Cover art by
Joshua Gilley

Inner illustrations by
Elizabeth Person
Rob Stepp

First Edition: 2018

ISBN 978-0-9907920-9-3

Dire Ninja Media
Live Oak, CA 95953

www.direninja.com

For Lisa, Johannes, Joe, and Rainbow.

Acknowledgements

Thanks to:

Dara Rochlin

Buddy Wagner

Josh Gilley

Robb Stepp

Elizabeth Person

(in no particular order)

"Ah, past the plunge of plummet,
In seas I cannot sound,
My heart and soul and senses,
World without end, are drowned."

"There Pass the Careless People"
-A.E. Housman (1859-1936)

Twenty-Six

The Gimcrack Mountains claw east into miles of shriveling woods and puckered foothills. They sit eerily still with nothing left to power the wounding machines at their roots. Storms brood over them, and strange shadows breed in their high passes. They seem to stare and to want, haunted by a restless anger. A new life is emerging in them where there was once only Toven's will. For two days' travel, Alan watches them giving birth to themselves. When the woods drop away and the ground flattens into salt, the mountains begin to move again.

"We've awakened something Toven's machines were keeping in torpor," Stag's Blood says, standing on the forecastle with his mane blowing around his shoulders. He is strong in the sun and shadow-lithe, looking healthier than ever. "I wouldn't want to cross those mountains now."

Alan is feeling stronger, too. For the first time, he feels something close to balanced. The sea of dead voices surges in his mind, swelling to new crests of harmony, and he is learning to hear them. Even when they speak nonsense, he listens intently. The Kingwatcher's bloom serves him as a moderator; helping to integrate the dead voices into Alan's other senses. He feels himself growing into a measure of certainty he could never achieve in the lands of the living, and the Mercy Gale feeds his new strength back in speed.

Even at clipping speed, it takes days to cross the saltpan. A low wall of crumbling hills hems it in to the south. Hills arise to the north, and tombs lean out of them to watch the Mercy Gale pass like shocked gossips. The ground is pocked with headstones and the pits of open graves.

Huge, winged things circle the ship at night. In the dead quiet just before dawn, they emerge from quagmires beneath the moon-silver sand and wind into the sky, curling their ophidian bodies as if to slither up the air. Then they follow the ship, drawn to her mast, hissing at it as they dip toward the weather decks. It's only after the Mercy Gale leaves the saltpan for higher, greener ground that they disappear.

Beyond the saltpan, the ground ripples up into a series of tiered meadows. The first are brown and salt blown, but they grow richer and stronger as they rise. The Mercy Gale picks her way up the greening hill with almost sapient care, and when she finally reaches the highest field, Alan and company look down from the main deck to see tall grass blooming around her feet.

Here, the wraiths set her down to rest. She curls her legs in tight against her hull and lets her keel down onto rich, giving earth. The descending whines deep inside her almost sound relieved after the long journey from Gimcrack.

It is a warm, windless morning. Alan and Brattle sit on the forecastle as the first sun is rising, letting the light stream over them. It runs like liquid citrine, filling the hollows of Brattle cheeks and chasing the shadows from the corners of his pearly eyes. Alan's heart aches for the feeling of sunlight on his face.

Stag's Blood is curled nearby, at the base of the gun. "Welkinbright was a fair and wonderful place, I hear," he says, "before someone took it away into the sky. That must have been a long time ago. I've not heard much tell of it."

"Very long," says Sophia from the point of the bowsprit. "And no one knows why it rose away."

"Some don't even think it exists," Brattle says, looking up into the cloud-flecked blue. "I know my Da didn't. I never gave it any thought. Do you think we'll see it soon?"

"I don't know," Sophia says. Her happy red light dims a bit toward purple. "It has been a very well-guarded secret, but we are nearly where the map says we should be. We should reach the precise spot tomorrow, I imagine — not that I'm much good at counting speed in knots. I wonder what we'll find when we gain the Deep."

"And what we'll do when we get there," Alan says. "To the city itself, I mean. 'Eternal Flame' is the only hint we've got."

"Pwysh's riddle," Stag's Blood says. "The best we can do is ask."

"Who lives there?" Brattle asks. "You said Toven married one of them? They must be umans of some sort."

"Sylves," Sophia replies. "Empyreal Fae. The oldest of us here. Words fail me to describe them. Only seeing them will suffice."

Noon comes with a sudden heat, and the wind remains reluctant. Alan and the others go below, and there they feel the Mercy Gale's engines start to stir again. The wraiths spur her awake gently, and she takes a long time to uncoil. By the time she is underway again, evening is bluing in the west.

They cross the last field under a cloudless night. Brattle rolls up against the wall, knees to his chin, back-to-back with snoring Stag's Blood. Alan stretches out in the companionway, content to wait there for the rest of the night in contemplation, but sleep steals over him unexpectedly. He feels it pawing at his edges while he meditates, a guilty animal begging his grace for abandoning him, and he barely recognizes it at first. Then he is wrapped in it, its face against his and its familiar weight on his chest. It is a light sleep, and it brings a gentle dream that he can't remember when we wakes alone in the stairwell.

Alan stretches and climbs the companionway toward open morning. For a moment, he feels old. He sees the ghost of who he used to be flitting like a moth in the mists of his mind. It recedes, and he doesn't follow it. By the time he reaches the weather decks, he is his new self again.

The Mercy Gale has stopped at the edge of a wide, green basin. Alan meets Stag's Blood and Brattle at the starboard edge of the main deck and looks down into its smoking heart. There is a forest of silver trees climbing out of it, their leaves quaking in a warm breeze. Fairy candles dance in clouds just beneath the canopy, leaving the whole wood glowing cornsilk blue.

"Is this the place?" Brattle asks.

"The Barrowvale," Sophia says. "At the bottom are the graves of the old-world kings, laid there by the first of Midion's sons at the new beginning of time."

"What's happened to it?" Stag's Blood asks.

There is a bare spot in the middle of The Barrowvale where trees have been knocked flat. The ground is churned up and trenched at the feet of enormous chunks of rock, and a great tangle of wood and metal is the source of the smoke that is rising from the clearing. There are similar wounds throughout the forest, and many of them are quite large. In the nearest and largest is an angular mass of stone that looks at least fifty feet tall. After staring at it for a minute, Alan realizes that it has windows. The rim around the far edge is what remains of a gable, and the debris strewn around contains several smashed stairwells.

"These are buildings," Alan says.

Sophia draws a harsh, ringing gasp. "Welkinbright buildings," she says. "The Empyrean City is falling from the sky."

"Where *is* Welkinbright?" Alan asks as they descend into the Barrowvale. "Too far up to see?"

"That would be my guess," Sophia replies, "if any of it remains aloft at all. This is not the whole city fallen down around us, though. I'm fairly certain of that."

They follow a faint path through the silver woods toward the first large clearing. Brattle leads, as he's the only one who seems to be able to see the path very well. Light slants through the canopy, diffusing into a golden spray in the lower boughs. Their way is dim, and shadows move in the woods nearby, following them.

"Toven's doing," Sophia says. She is sitting on Brattle's shoulder, much to his irritation. "I do not know how, but I feel him in this."

"We should reserve judgment until we've seen more," Stag's Blood says. "We can't pretend to know anything yet."

The forest is littered with rubble. Everywhere Alan looks, there is a split tree or a divot in the ground where a great hunk of stone has buried itself. They climb over shattered floors and tables lying in white splinters in the wrecks of whole dining rooms. Alan feels the dead here. They reach out across thousands of years, so thoroughly faded that they hardly exist anymore. He hears their kingly whispers and can't comprehend them.

"There aren't any bodies," he said. "That's got to be a good sign, at least. I can only feel the dead kings."

"I will take that comfort if it is all I can get," Sophia says. "What do the dead kings say to you, Alan, if I may ask? How do you feel them?"

Alan tries to let the new voices in, but they skirt him. They are careful. Whatever they have to say, it's clear that they're afraid to say it, and that they don't trust outsiders.

"They don't say much they'll let me understand," Alan replies. "Their voices in my head are like worries or doubts: they arise suddenly, and you can't squash them. Listening to them is like lying awake at night and being unable to quiet your mind. It's a challenge to learn to deal with it, but I'm making strides. These dead don't like me. They want to reach out, but I think want us to leave even more."

"They are the last things left of the old world, then," Sophia says. "I wish I could feel them like you do."

"Tell me about the old world," Alan says. "What happened to it?"

Brattle answers before Sophia can. "It died," he explains, "and it had to be resurrected. It came back without its spirit — you know how that works — so someone gave his spirit up to make it whole again."

"How does a whole world die?" Alan asks.

Stag's Blood replies from beside him, "slowly."

Brattle stops at the edge of the clearing. The others line up beside him and stand staring into the wounded space. Alan finds

13

the devastation difficult to take in all at once. The ground is strewn with silver bark. Grass is turned up in great swaths, exposing black earth and splintered roots. Every last stone of the fallen spire is cracked; it is a testament to the strength of Empyreal mortar that they remain stacked together. The spire's roof is nearby in a sprawling pile, its skeleton frame broken and crumpling under the weight of falling eaves.

"I am sick to see this," Sophia said. "What was it Toven sent you to do here, Alan?"

Alan shrugs. "He didn't know. Pwysh's note only says 'eternal flame'. Toven thought maybe I was supposed to extinguish it."

"A questionable conclusion," Stag's Blood says. "Look there. Maybe those two can tell us what happened."

There are gray-clad figures moving through the wreckage. They are tall and thin, with white flames flickering where their hair should be. Sadness follows them, a sick shadow, limping behind them to tug the gold-edged hems of their robes. Alan watches them fighting it and losing. They bow to pick things up as they make their way through the clearing, stopping often to talk with each other about what they find. When they see Alan and company watching them from nearby, they stand still, as if unsure what to do.

"I will speak with them," Sophia says. "They are uncomfortable with strangers."

"Ain't you a stranger, Soph?" Brattle asks.

"Let's take our chances," Alan says. "Nothing ventured, nothing gained."

They move into the clearing toward the staring figures. Sophia leaves Brattle's shoulder to address them, shining gold to match the rising suns.

"I humble myself before you, noble ones," she says. "I am Sister Sophia of the Sisterhood of M, and I represent the Mothers of the Necropolis on my first pilgrimage. My companions are Alan, Brattle, and Stag's Blood, and we have come to help the Empyrean City. Are you Welkinbrighters? Will you tell us what's happened?"

The gray fairies look at each other. They are very beautiful. Their features are soft and delicate. Both have the same wide-set, golden eyes and plump mouth, but the smaller one's nose is crooked. His ears are also taller and more pointed.

"Wretches of the underworld," says the smaller one. His voice is smooth and deep. He draws it like a sword from the sheath of his throat, balancing charity and doubt on its tip. "We will lead you out. We are turning all travelers away. Come with us."

"You'd turn help away in these dark times?" Stag's Blood asks, taking a step forward and angling toward the sylves to show his flank. "How long has the city been falling?"

"Do not address us again," the tall sylph says. "We are acting on strict orders, and we have no power to bargain on anyone's behalf."

"You could hear us out," Brattle says. The gray fairies pull deep frowns. "You ever hear of Pwysh? He sent us here. We're on his errand."

"We know of Pwysh, bogworm," says the smaller sylph. "We know that he wasted himself in your swamps, ministering to *lower animals*. And we know of the Sisters of M. But, no matter who you are or why you are here, you have no authority to defy us on our own land. You must abide, friend or foe. Dark times make foes of many."

Alan searches the fairies' faces. They command incredible power, and the light of grace in their faces intimidates him. Their clothes seem to shine. Even in their fear and sorrow, they are the purest beings he has ever encountered. He feels like a blotch on the world in their sight, but he screws up his courage and steps toward them.

"The fire of your hope is not out," he says, trying to summon some clout. "There are embers of it burning – I can see them. How long have they been dying? Who tried to extinguish the Eternal Flame? Was it Toven, the King of the North? Let us help you. You need allies."

"There are no allies," says the tall one. "There are only future enemies.

"Then you'd better arrest us," Alan replies, "because we're determined to prove you wrong."

The gray fairies look at each other again. The strange coils of their hair dance as a stiff breeze blows up from the west. It lifts ash and stone-grit into the air in a great curl, and Brattle sneezes.

"This is not for us to consider," says the smaller sylph. "We'll take you to our captain, since you've refused to leave. He will decide what to do with you."

The gray fairies lead Alan and company east across the Barrowvale. Where the woods run thin, flowers creep into soft mats of grass. Black stones stand in broad, green lawns, their mirrored faces bright with fairy lights. At the feet of red hills, they pass beneath a row of natural arches. The ground falls away from huge plates of striated stone that form a lip above the basin's precipitous eastern wall. From that vantage point, the full extent of the damage to the forest is visible.

"Is there anything like this in your sphere?" Stag's Blood asks Alan as they stand at the brink. Their guides are resting nearby, hands on their knees, heavy huge breaths. They appear unaccustomed to underworld foot travel. Alan pities them their weakness, though, even in their exhaustion, they are dazzling.

"There's usually an order to human spaces," Alan replies. "Even when they aren't entirely level, they follow careful lines. There's structure there, and more structure underneath. We tend to build deep. I didn't realize how clean and controlled it was until I was outside it, surrounded by pure wild. We can't build this way. We're too small. We don't have the scope."

"It's beautiful even with the city falling," Stag's Blood says. "There's something about the abject tragedy that's romantic."

Alan can see for a long way with the eyes of the dead to aid him. He looks out over copses of shivering birch and brown-grass hummocks sinking in drainage swamps in the north. In the far west, the woods thicken until not even deer can pass through them. Graves line the basin from side to side, and the bones caged within them are restless. He can see all of the Barrowvale through them, but, in the process, he takes on all their ancient anger. After a moment's looking, he pulls himself away and turns back from the edge.

"Almost there," says the taller sylph. They are ready to go again, though their cheeks are red from exertion. "Just up the hill to the Tongue now. No more stops."

Ahead of them, a rose-brown promontory emerges from the knots of stunted trees like a huge tongue. Weedy scrub grows on either side, and it is propped up against a smaller wedge of stone that strains beneath it like a frenulum. There is a coil of smoke rising from a camp near the Tongue's base, and Alan can see more gray-robed figures moving around a fire there as they near it.

"Ain't much use in this heavy air, are they?" Brattle laughs. The tall sylph looks back at him and frowns. Alan wants to recoil from that expression, but Brattle only meets the sylph's gaze and laughs again.

The climb toward the Tongue is short, but the suns are high, and Alan is sweating down his back when they finally reach the camp. Empyreal faces greet them, glaring from behind spears or bowstrings. Once there, and after they have made sure that the trespassers aren't going to flee or draw weapons, the gray guides take their places among the others of their kind while their captain approaches. Sophia starts to rise from Alan's shoulder to greet him, but Alan puts his hand up to stop her. Then he steps forward himself, and he meets the captain in the center of the camp as the circle of staring fairies closes behind him.

"We found these four near the southern edge," says the taller sylph from somewhere behind the small crowd. "They wouldn't leave."

"You must be the captain," Alan says. "I think you're just the one we want to see."

"Kelen," says the captain. Then he looks around for the taller sylph. "You didn't bind them?"

"We don't mean any harm, Captain Kelen," Alan says. "In fact, we're here to help. I'm Alan, and this is Brattle, Stag's Blood, and Sophia. We're friends of Pwysh and the Sisterhood of M. We just want you to hear us out. We want to talk about the Eternal Flame."

Kelen puts his hand on the point of his long chin. He regards each of Alan's companions with a wise and doubting eye and paces twice across the face of the rock, considering. He is old, and the white fire on his head is guttering. Lines run down his gaunt face to frame his frowning mouth. Alan watches him winding up; he can practically hear the gears in Kelen's head turning.

"Why?" he says, turning back to Alan. "We are hearing no one out. We are turning all away – even your Sisters, little Fetchlight. Your being here is a serious offense, and you speak of things that we keep secret from outsiders. Why should we hear you when we could throw you all from this rock?"

Alan wilts. He isn't sure how to face Kelen with courage, so he tries to imagine what a courageous person would do.

"Don't you want to do everything you can for your city?" Alan says. "Throw us if you're going to. But if you do and we could have helped, you might as well be throwing Welkinbright down there, too."

Kelen considers this with a nod and an enigmatic smile. There is tremendous sadness in his eyes. Alan wonders how long he's been away from his home in the sky.

"And what would your aid cost Welkinbright, spirit?" he asks. "What would you pry from our hands as we lay dying?"

Alan struggles to find an answer. He hopes that his fear and doubt show through him somehow. Finally, he takes a knee and bows to Kelen, saying, "What price is too high to restore the Empyrean City?

Kelen motions for Alan to rise with an amused smile on his face.

"You are new at this," he says. "It's almost funny. You would starve as a deceiver, Alan. Stop your shaking; I've found my mercy. Sit and tell us what you know. If the least you can do in this desperate hour is nothing, it will be no more than we have achieved so far."

Alan explains the situation as well as he can while Kelen and the others listen in motionless silence. He shows them the map and Pwysh's notes, and they pass them around slowly. None of them can read Pwysh's writing, but Kelen recognizes it.

"He lives in his code," the sylph captain explains, "even if it remains impossible to decipher. This is his work, beyond any doubt."

Stag's Blood and Brattle join in to help Alan flesh out the story. Sophia offers her perspective quietly, in awe of the Empyreals.

"I understand that Toven is no friend to Welkinbright," she says. "He is no friend to us either. He has gone into darkness and peril from which there is no return. Restored to its might, Welkinbright could stand against him."

"We were thinking it could've been him was responsible for the city starting to fall in the first place," Brattle says.

Stag's Blood adds to this. "Or someone in his service."

"We have pursued all avenues," Kelen says. The first sun is setting behind him. The second encircles him in its bright orb, leaving rays of light beaming around him. His pale skin becomes almost translucent, leaving webs of veins visible in the hollows of his cheeks. "The Clockwork King has been of little concern to us in this matter."

"You need to reconsider that," Stag's Blood says. "He spoke of the Flame, but he sent us here claiming that he knew nothing of it. How long has the Eternal Flame been out?"

Kelen stands. He hands Alan's papers back to Brattle and starts to pace the rock again.

"It is not out," he says with a sigh. "It is weakening. Dying. Its font is corrupt, and we cannot purify it anymore. Could Toven really have done this? He is not allowed in the Gray City. Annun brought him there against our wishes, and we all suffered for it."

He turns to look out over the Tongue. The wreckage far below is lit blue under clouds of fairy candles. Alan sees the hungry shade of sorrow hanging from his shoulders. He starts to slump beneath it.

"That was the Spire of Acherion," he says, his voice trembling. "The Silverbranch. And there was its court. There is no restoring age. Time is gone away through our hands, crumbling from the sky, irretrievable. Toven first appeared to us there, under silver arches, the first underworld fae we had allowed among us since the ascension. I'm not sure how much that means to any of you, though I'd expect a Sister of M to understand it best among the rest of the wretches. What do you have that will save the Empyrean Fire? What did Toven's blood know that Welkinbright does not?"

"Bell, star, and spirit," Alan replies. "Do any of those things mean anything to you?"

Kelen closes his eyes to think. Alan feels him searching himself. Lines cross his face, making him look ancient. His brows rise toward his forehead, where thin flames dance as white as bone.

"Take us to the flame," Brattle says. "If we can help, we'll do it there."

Kelen nods and straightens himself again. He sucks a faint sob through his nose and folds his arms to put his hands into the sleeves of his robe.

"There is panic in Welkinbright," he says, "and wild fear. It has taken all of us. Ascension is a gift. I am not qualified to give it."

"If we fail," Alan tells him, "you can throw us down here with the Spire of the Silverbranch. Let us fall with the rest of your city if we can't do anything to save it."

"These are dark times," he says. "I suppose we would do well to take whatever light we can."

Twenty-Seven

Alan sits back against the black monument and pushes his hands into his sleeve pockets. He has found a place in the silver wood where the dead run deep. They move beneath him in a pit of ancient vaults, a spiritual force greater than gravity. They call out through miles of mud and rock and rotten eons, confessing themselves, begging to be remembered, and he listens.

The dead do not despair. They don't hate the way the living do. Flesh masks subtleties of emotion that divorce from the physical lays bare. Death leaves spirits raw, hurt, and unable to cope with the change in living ways. Most grow into themselves, but many remain tethered to their physical lives. Despair is ripped away. Hate vanishes, leaving wounds of the spirit that only acceptance of death can heal, but some spirits are too injured to manage even that.

Alan sees those wounds in himself. *A slave to the physical*, Alan thinks. *I suppose I've been dead for most of my life.*

But there is another state. Behind death is a nameless, staring threat that all spirits fear – living or otherwise. Alan feels it at the corners of his perception, huge and dark, feeding him horror. It is strongest in the elder spirits because its hands are in them, teasing them apart slowly. They speak of nothing else, and Alan tries to shut them out. The others weave whispers of it into their confessions. It is the mouth of oblivion: a fading into nothing that awaits spirits who refuse their natural accession of new forms.

Alan listens to the kings of the old world ramble for a long time. They are happy to have him to talk to, and they aren't bothered in the least by the fact that he can't respond. The connection only goes one way.

What would I say to them? Alan wonders. *If I could put myself in their minds the way I let them into mine, what could I tell them about the living?*

It would be too dangerous. Oblivion is unstoppable. Alan has learned a lot about the dead voices, and he feels stronger in his magic now than ever before, but he knows that he doesn't have it in him to brave the jaws of that particular darkness.

Chills crawl up his spine, and he lets them come. They slip over his shoulders and down his chest, making him shudder hard and flap his hands. In fear, he can focus. When he looks out of himself again, it's almost night. Gloom is crawling over the Barrowvale, twisting its tendrils between the silver trees, and the fairy candles are waking above him. He stands and stretches, feeling invigorated.

"Are you finally back?" Sophia asks from a nearby rock. "I was worried about you."

"Yes," Alan says. "And thank you. I never know how long it's going to last. I haven't really been doing this very long, and this spot is strong. I was really in there."

Sophia nods. "Stag's Blood and Brattle came by with their kills; it looks as though they are set to eat for weeks now, though I wonder how they'll fit it all in that little knapsack. They tried to talk to you, but it was like you were asleep. They've gone up to the Tongue now to see if Kelen is ready yet."

She takes to the air. Alan holds out his hand, and she lands on it. Her light is indigo.

"Let's meet them," Alan says. "It's been three days. If the Empyreals haven't decided anything by now, we might have to force them."

"How do you plan to do that?" Sophia chimes.

Alan heads east from the heart of the woods. The Tongue is a few miles away. The path toward it winds through fields of monolithic ruin. The Empyreals left it picking through the rubble for survivors.

"I don't know," Alan says. "I'm hoping it won't come to that."

Brattle and Stag's Blood are near the Tongue, waiting at the curve of the path. Alan and Sophia meet them under a star-strewn sky, and the four make their way to the Empyreal camp as the moon rises.

"Good hunting here," Stag's Blood says. Pale light is falling through the screen of trees to the west. It shimmers in his fur as if caught there. "And we found another pack for all our meat."

"That was lucky," Alan replies.

"Ghouls' luck," Brattle laughs. "But we ain't got papers to wrap the cuts in – nor knives enough to butcher proper." He hands Alan their old knapsack. He is wearing a green haversack over one shoulder bandolier-style. Its strap is thick and beautifully beaded. "It's a kelpie's seabag, I think. Pulled it out of a little gray river to the north."

At the Tongue, the sylves are saddling cats and preparing to leave. When Alan and company arrive, they stop and muster into a circle, with Kelen in the center. He sits astride a rose-furred mount with feathers woven into its fur.

"We were about to ride out for you," he says as Alan enters the circle. Sophia is stuffed into his sleeve pocket. Brattle and Stag's Blood wait at the edge of the rock. "We are divided, and divided we shall remain. Faro and I will lead you to the Tower of Alms. The rest of my company will stay here and continue to work."

A sylph emerges from the crowd to take a place in the center beside Kelen. Faro is large and lean with dark eyes and a tall flame atop his head. He wears many rings on his thick fingers. His cat is as gray as his robes. The others frown at him. Alan recognizes the two sylves they met before in the back of the circle. They are no less beautiful for the pain and loathing on their faces.

"Come with us now," says Faro. "The sooner we are away, the better."

Night arrives glowing. Alan feels its weight on his shoulders. From the high eastern path toward the Tower of Alms he can watch it spreading through The Barrowvale. It blankets the trees to still their quaking. Its tendrils hunt down through the canopy, and the nightbirds fall silent for fear of them. It walks the woods and the high rim paths cloaked in star-silver, a cold-eyed stranger, the bare eye of the full moon glaring from its face. Night has a whole life here. It holds dominion over the strange and the secret; Alan feels it peering into him, looking for his fear, trying to expand its sphere of influence, and it's all he can do to resist.

"I miss the dead nights," he says to Brattle. "There's nothing here like simple emptiness. Even darkness has some substance – some weird life."

"Your sphere sounds boring," Brattle says. "We got more than just plain form to work with here. What good is safe? How can you live without bein' scared? Bad as it can be, I'll take the living twilight any day over whatever blank, sunless thing you call night."

The gray Empyreals lead on quietly. The forest gives way to clay and shale highlands. The Tower of Alms appears in the distance, bathed in moonlight, its upper levels lost in clouds. The ground flattens into a wide plateau, and the going is easy until they reach the base of the tower. There, Kelen calls a halt, and the group meets to talk before the tower's iron door while the Empyreal tie their cats to a post.

Kelen and Faro stand on the wide stoop, their hands motionless at their sides. Alan looks up the tower walls. There are lights in the many windows. Torches hang from the balconies, swinging in the light breeze that has kicked up from the west. Sophia sits on Alan's shoulder.

"The Iron Spire," she says in a tinkling whisper. "I never believed I would get to see it. I didn't expect it to be so high."

Alan nods and says, "I wonder who keeps the lights burning."

"The valravn will take us up," Kelen says. "Don't be afraid of them. And you must never come here again, or we will kill you. Do you understand? These ways are well guarded. Swear now or go no further."

"Of course," Alan says.

"We never had cause to come before," Brattle adds.

"I wish we didn't have to swear," Sophia says. "But I will if there's no other way. I have always wanted to see the Empyrean City."

"You shall," Kelen says. "For as long as it takes to see if you are worth her time."

"We are," Stag's Blood replies. "And when Welkinbright is saved, you may consider releasing us from our oaths."

Kelen and Faro nod, satisfied, but their faces are dark with worry.

"Up then," Faro says.

Kelen reaches into the front of his robe and pulls the chain of a necklace over his head. He grips the large, white key hanging from it in both hands and closes his eyes. Raising it to his lips, he kisses it and whispers three words. In a shimmer of light, a keyhole appears beneath the elaborate door pull. Kelen turns the key inside it, and Faro helps him haul the heavy door open. Its hinges sing, and powdered rust puffs down from the hinges.

A wide chamber opens beyond the door, its ceiling invisible. The floor is a round slab of sand-strewn granite, and there is a slight gap between its coped edge and the base of the wall. There is a shadow in the room; Alan can feel it watching them from the dark where the ceiling should be. It is heavy, and the air is hot under its weight. Fear has made a home here. As soon as Alan enters, it begins gnawing at him.

There are nine concentric circles of painted tiles radiating from the middle of the room to rim of the floor. Every eighth tile is marked only with a single symbol, but the others depict colorful scenes that, when studied in order, clearly tell a story. Alan stares at them as he follows the others into the room. They are staggeringly detailed and vivid despite the years of age on the surrounding stones.

Sophia is looking at the painted tiles, too. "These paintings are amazing," she says to their guides. "What is their significance?"

Faro sighs.

26

"Nothing," Kelen says, "if Welkinbright falls."

"It's the founding, isn't it?" Sophia continues. "I know some of these images. I have seen them in books. The plague of darkness and the lighting of the Flame. I love the old stories."

"I heard 'em in ancient graves," Brattle says. Old stones in my swamps been known to whisper. Witches' tales – the ravings of hags' cursed blood on the ground where their spirits are anchored: that's all I ever took 'em for. Wouldn't mind drinking from the source if you boys feel like springing."

"Hags' lies shall suffice," Faro replies. "Our stories are our own."

"This was the Tomb of the Child King," says Kelen. "Everything here honors him."

"Stand in the center," Faro says as Kelen shoulders the door closed. "Do you pray?"

"Thrice daily, as is our way," Sophia says. She flutters down to walk the cold floor, her inner light winking brightly. Shadows dance away from her, moving as she moves. "But my whole life is a prayer."

"And mine," says Brattle, "though not to any good gods. I don't kneel, if that's all right."

Stag's Blood walks a slow circle around the floor. His claws click on the stone as he flexes his toes. Faro kneels and watches him. Kelen approaches with a stick of incense, and Alan wonders where he got it.

"Not for a long while," Stag's Blood says. "Days get in the way, falling after one another. And then there is the terrible emptiness – the feeling that words and hopes will never be as strong as certain and direct action. But I will pray to honor you."

Faro closes his eyes and sits back on his heels. He holds up his hand, his first two fingers pointed to touch his forehead while his thumb rests on the bridge of his nose. Alan remembers playing guns with Allison when he was small. Kelen kneels and sets his incense on the floor. Smells rise from it as ribbons of color.

"And you, human?" Kelen says. "Whom do you pray to, if you do?"

Alan shrugs and shakes his head. It's all he can do; the admission won't come. He hasn't prayed since his finger-gun days, but he can't tell the room. It feels wrong to say anything.

"The Kingwatcher," he finally says.

"Minos keep you, then," Kelen replies, "and hear you."

With this, he tilts back beside Faro and puts his fingers to his forehead. Sophia leans down to press her cheek to the floor. Stag's Blood stetches beside her, his front paws out and his rump in the air. He flicks his tail as if counting out the meter of a song. Brattle looks at Alan with Sophia's shadows scudding across his face and his big eyes faintly glowing.

For a moment, Alan considers actually trying to pray to the Kingwatcher, but he gives up when he can't think of a way to start. The Seed of Minos is blooming in his mind. The Kingwatcher's voice winds through it along its tendrils, penetrating his inner dark at a whisper. He can't pray because isn't sure how to tell Minos from himself anymore.

The floor moves. With a sudden hissing, hollow scrape, it starts to rise up the wall, turning slowly as it ascends. Stag's Blood sprawls to keep his balance. Sophia nods on, praying in her jingling voice. When she has finished, she stands and pats white sand from her tiny hands, and the sylves rise with her.

"We are on our way," Kelen says. "It won't be long now."

Sand hisses pours over the edge of the floor to fall down the shaft. The slab moves without the aid of any machinery. There is a strong and persistent pressure beneath it, like a cushion of air.

"I've seen mountains dancing," Stag's Blood says, "and now stone slabs rising. This is impressive magic. Is the Flame its source?"

"It gives us much," Faro replies. Then he corrects himself. "It gives us everything."

"What did Toven want when he came to you?" Alan asks.

Faro hesitates for a moment before answering. "What happened didn't happen to us," he says. "It happened to the rich, and they always lie."

"Tell us their lies, then," Stag's Blood says. "Surely your gossip isn't sacred."

Faro looks to his captain. Alan watches them stare at each other. Light arcs between their faces, pulsing from one white-flamed brow to the other. Kelen turns his head, and Faro responds with a minute twitch of his upper lip. Alan realizes that he's watching telepathy.

"You weren't always so protective," he says. "What happened?"

Kelen takes a sip from a white flask. "Annwyn was the daughter of Aryn," he says, wiping his mouth on the bell of his sleeve. "She was dark and wild, and she found her life's fire in low places. When she might have soared, she wanted to crawl. When she should have been serving her king, she was debauching herself among the wretches, as she had an unnatural love of your kind. When she met Toven, she was ripe for his plucking, and he plucked. He married her, hoping to inherit the throne, but Aryn disowned her. There is no heir to inherit anything now."

"And there will be nothing to inherit," Faro says. His eyes are glistening with tears. "Our city falls, and we are powerless to stop it from within. Again, we look to wretches for help. I will live to see the last days of my country. I will diminish among you; I feel the poison of the underworld in my blood already. I have watched hope withering in such horror, and I am almost spent. I can bear no more desperation."

"I understand," Alan says. "I've been there. It's hard to reach into the dark again when all you've ever found there is pain, but sometimes that's the only thing you can do. Sometimes, that's where hope is."

Faro starts to respond. Alan can't meet his gaze; the pain in his eyes is terrifying.

"We are trusting you, aren't we?" he asks.

29

"This is Toven's work," Sophia says. "You must know that."

"All we know is that we want to undo it," says Kelen. "We will look for reasons when we have strength enough again for wrath."

The floor rises over open windows and recessed slits where gem torches burn. Alan tries to look out over the balconies when he can, but all he can see through the windows is deepening black. Faro kneels and starts to pray again, and Kelen relights the guttering incense in the white flame on his head. Alan sits and watches the wall slide down beneath the edges of the rising floor, and the full weight of what's ahead falls over his shoulders.

It descends in slow motion, like a blanket bellying out to drape itself over him. It might be a wonderful thing to smother himself in, but he can't afford it. He searches his strength instead, reaching for its depths, trying to find where it ends. To his dismay, there are no answers. There's only the rhythm of his steps and the windy echo in the stairwell.

Sophia walks the floor, looking at the painted tiles. Her light is brighter than Alan has ever seen it. Brattle follows her as if enchanted, and they say nothing to each other. Stag's Blood comes over to stand beside Alan, his footsteps unsteady. Alan can't help but chuckle at the sight of all that dark majesty staggering toward him.

"This place is all but a ruin," Stag's Blood says. "It had a heart once, but it's not beating anymore. You can feel the rot of sorrow creeping in. I don't like it."

"There's a certain beauty in that," Alan says. "A kind of romance – isn't there?"

Stag's Blood shakes his head. "Beauty like that isn't meant to last."

Kelen approaches them, his hands folded together. He is wearing a black ring. There are bruises on his knuckles. He nods to Stag's Blood, and then fixes Alan with a grim stare.

"My compatriots are utterly without hope," he says, "and I cling, perhaps beyond all reasonable justification, to every last scrap of it. I have never been another way. I tried to vouch for you to them, but I couldn't, and they abandoned me. I have no explanation for my trust in you. Now I wonder if I'm not as blind as they are.

"I've never needed to doubt, and I never have – even in the throat of doom. I have believed unwaveringly in Welkinbright's future until now. Now, I find myself at the edge of something that I thought went on forever, and I do not know how to be certain again. What will you do when we reach the Flame, human? What plan or power do you have to save us? Tell me. Tell me how my faith will be rewarded."

"Blind conviction is not enough for some things," Stag's Blood answers. "I *know* Alan's power. I believe because I've seen it. Let your faith fade if you must; in the meantime, wait."

Kelen purses his lips. Old lines frame his mouth – the dark scars of scorn held in check too long.

"Does the cat speak for you?" he asks. "Has he got your tongue?"

Alan shakes his head. "His opinion is his own," he says, "and I value it. I wish I had something prettier to say that would put all of your fears to rest – believe me. All I can say for sure is that Pwysh knew I could do this. It's not much, but if your faith has subsisted on nothing thus far, it should suffice."

"It will have to," says Kelen, lacing his fingers together behind his back. "How do you know the Swamp Wizard? Who are you to him?"

Alan looks at his feet. His shoes are ready to split. The laces are fraying apart, and the faux leather is peeling away from the uppers, showing white underneath. There's no answer there.

"Chosen," Alan finally says. "As for why, I have no idea. What about you? How did you know him, and did you know that he's dead?"

"No," Kelen says, toying with a smile, "but I am not surprised. He meant well, but he kept bad company. He came to us looking for something, and I never knew if he found it. He had a dark spirit with him. I wonder what has happened to it now that he is gone."

31

"What kind of spirit?" Stag's Blood asks. "What was it like?"

Kelen squares his chin and looks up at the approaching ceiling. The Tower of Alms is narrowing. Snow is blowing in from the windows above them. They will soon be at the top.

"Small," he says, "and barely there. Toven hated it, and he called it a writher. I was none too fond of it myself. The foul things wretches bring up from the underworld! Every day I spend among you, in the mud and the pits of your graves, I feel more and more polluted. Your world rots. That is its purpose, and that is why we ascended." He lets his smile loose at last, and it spreads across his face like a wound at the dragging tip of a knife.

"Ah," he goes on, "but Midion is not *your* world, Alan. Is it?"

Near the top of the tower, the first hints of light are rising in the eastern sky. Clouds creep in through the balcony windows with blue spheres chasing each other through them. The walls shine with condensation. As they finally reach the double hatch that will lead them out to the top of the tower, Brattle is mopping ice crystals from his brow. The moving floor slows and finally stops, resting on sheer force of will. Faro seems to be straining where he kneels. His face is pulled tight, and cords are beginning to stand out in his neck. He rises to help Kelen with the door, and his cheeks purpling with burst capillaries. Alan pulls his hood up and is quite comfortable in the depths of his robe.

"Do you need any help?" Alan asks him. "Are you all right?"

Faro only nods and tries to smile. "Faith moves mountains," he says, "but the sooner we are above, the better."

"How high are we?" Brattle asks, coughing. He crosses his arms to hide his shaking hands.

Kelen removes a key from the pocket of his robe and uses it to unlock the hatch. He and Faro fold the doors open, and the wind roars in from above.

"Up and into the cage," Kelen says. "We'll go higher still. Are you feeling sick?"

"He's a swamp creature," Stag's Blood says. "He's spent too long living too low to the ground."

Sophia tinkles her wings together angrily. "Nonsense," she says. "This is nothing a Conservator cannot withstand."

Brattle chuckles, shivering. "Conservator," he says. "*That* is nonsense."

Sophia's hopeful green light fades toward worried yellow.

"It will pass," Faro says. "We should have given you some mandrake to chew. It slipped my mind."

"You know by now that we don't entertain visitors often," Kelen says.

The top of the tower is a broad slab of white marble surrounded by a complex crown of black spires. There is an enormous, golden cage in the center of the roof, tethered to the spires by silver cords, with a beam across its top like a perch or a handle. The wind whips over the slab at screaming speed, banging the cage against the stone as if trying to whisk it away.

"Quickly," Faro says, all the strain now gone from his face. "And low."

With this, the gray fairies march off across the roof. The wind pulls at their cloaks, but it can't move them. They stand tall, side by side, unaffected by the blast.

Alan ducks into the wind to follow them, pinching his robe tight at his throat. Sophia slips into the pocket of his sleeve and clings there, shivering. Once he's sure she's safe where she is, Alan runs for the cage. His hood blows back, and his robe swirls up around his waist. He has to turn to keep it from turning into a sail. The wind snatches at him violently, and his shoes slip across the marble as it lifts him up onto the balls of his feet. Reaching the cage, he rolls into it through the bars and braces himself against the nearest corner. Faro takes a small horn from his belt and puts it to his lips to blow three short, clear notes. The wind rips them away almost immediately, and Alan has his doubts that anyone could have heard the sounds, but Faro blows no more. Instead, he stands beside Kelen to watch the northern sky. Stag's Blood arrives with his mane tossed around his face and Brattle close behind him. They clamber in to sit around Alan and watch the Empyreals waiting.

The last stars are winking out beyond the golden bars. Dawn pours over a wild, white sea heaped with high billows that shift with the wind. Sophia risks the climb up onto Alan's shoulder in an attempt to look out across the clouds, her heartlight glowing warmer than Alan has ever felt it.

"Beauty," she says.

"The shelf of a storm," Kelen replies, barely audible. "They will fatten and rain before the day is done."

A black shape appears on the horizon. Other shapes materialize around it as it draws nearer. It dips into the clouds and then rises again, undulating. It is a huge crow surrounded by a flock of smaller birds. It swings a circle around the tower, cawing, and Brattle covers his ears.

"Hanegal is coming," Kelen shouts. "He will take us up! Hold on to the bars!"

The crow descends in a flurry of huge wing beats. He grips the great handle on top of the cage and begins to pull, his cries deafening as he tugs against the silver cords. The raucous flock that arrived with him swirls through the spires. They gather around the ends of the cords in cawing knots, and the cords fall away as birds pull them loose from the cage's frame. When the last one is free, Hanegal lifts the cage into the air, tilting it crazily at first. Alan and Brattle cling to the bars as the cage swings. Stag's Blood tries to get his paws around something, but he can't grasp. He slides along the floor and hits the far side of the cage with a small yelp. Sophia clings to Alan's robe and flaps her wings as hard as she can until Hanegal straightens out again.

The Empyreals collect themselves. They barely rocked while the crow was swinging the cage. Kelen goes to Stag's Blood's side to help him up.

"Are you all well?" he asks, turning toward Alan and Brattle. "Hanegal is in an unusual hurry this morning. I'm troubled as to why."

Stag's Blood sits down to lick his paw. "Nothing broken," he says. "I wish I had your balance."

Kelen only nods knowingly at this. Then he turns and calls up to the crow, "The Shrine of the Flame."

Hanegal replies with a series of caws and the cage lurches as he adjusts his course. Alan gets to his feet and looks out at the clouds below. They are breaking and thinning out; he can see the forest through them. Great curved peaks appear in the northwest, crowned in glittering ice, up to their shoulders in clouds.

"You still wish for those dead nights, Al?" Brattle asks, knuckling up beside him. "Sure this sight don't beat 'em?"

Alan tries to fall in love with the world beyond the bars, but he can't. It's too far away and too deep in shadow.

"It does," he says to Brattle, "but something feels bad."

"There's a bird approaching," Faro announces. Alan and Brattle meet Stag's Blood at the door of the cage, which is held shut with seven silver latches.

"Who?" Kelen asks.

Alan searches the sky. He sees nothing in the mist ahead. Dawn is at its brightest now, with both suns up. The horizon is a line of blinding white.

"Gamley," Faro replies. "He is light and unattended."

"Coming to meet us?" Stag's Blood offers. The stony silence that follows makes Alan's heart sink.

"Coming to meet *you*," Faro snarls. "*We* are not Toven's enemies."

Kelen holds his hand out, reaching as if to touch the crow carrying the cage, but he can't reach. Nonetheless, Hanegal responds with a croak. "Hold fast, Honnie," Kelen says.

Now Alan sees Gamley. He is diving in from high above them, a meteor streak in the eastern sky dragging a faint tail of ice crystals. His wings are tucked, and he is wearing a red-crested helmet with a silver beakplate. The rising suns are behind him, and for a moment, he seems to hang motionless before them. Then he drops crazily, talons up and wings unfurling like black banners.

Brattle growls and squeezes the bars before him until his knuckles go white. Alan does the same, his stomach heavy with fear. Sophia wriggles into his sleeve and clutches the fabric there as hard as she can.

"Framer keep us," she says, and her heartlight turns black.

Twenty-Eight

How long has it been? Six months feels like a thousand years. Alan remembers the heft of his life, how he used to lean on it, and the years he spent defining himself by gravity. Now he is in freefall, high above himself, looking down at the speck of grief he has lived.

I thought I was the biggest thing in the world, he says to himself, *but I've been small, small, small. It's never too late to expand.*

Gamley hits the cage at full speed, and Hanegal tries to roll with the impact and loses his grip on the shining handle. The cage drops toward the clouds, spinning and turning over one corner, and Alan stiffens in anticipation of a crushing impact. He feels as brittle as a leaf. Raw, animal fear grips him, and he goes blank, unable to process it. He isn't conscious of reaching out through magic to slow their fall, despite the tremendous effort it takes. Only when Hanegal wraps his feet around the bars of the cage to catch it does he feel the drain on his power.

The cage is now on its side. Stag's Blood hits the bars again, but he's ready this time: he rights himself in midair and manages to land on his feet, though he winds up with his legs splayed oddly. Brattle lands on Faro, who spits and swears as he tries to regain his breath. Only Kelen has been able to maintain his grip on the bars. Hanegal flaps hard, trying to gain altitude as Gamley circles around for another pass. He pounds the air with his wings, leaving Alan's skull ringing.

Alan tries to land lengthwise across the bars. He bangs his shoulder and elbow hard, and something pops in his back when he comes down. Faro and Brattle hurry to help him up, each rubbing new bruises as they do so.

"I hope you can do that again," Faro wheezes. "He is coming back."

Alan is about to explain that he had only been acting on instinct when Gamley dives in again, his claws open to strike at Hanegal. The birds scream at each other, and Hanegal's escort mobs Gamley in a whirl, moving as if of one mind. Alan tries to reach out again. He stretches out his arms, his fingers splayed and his shoulder smarting. Power rushes through him, but, for all his fear, he can't find the same panicked strength that slowed the falling cage. All he can manage is a push that ruffles Gamley's wings and puffed collar.

Gamley flutters away for a moment, trying to find better footing. He clutches for the cage, nearly inverted, and attacks from beneath Hanegal while clinging to it. Hanegal shrieks as Gamley pierces his breast with powerful pecks. The silver beakplate flashes, tearing bloody wounds down Hanegal's chest and belly. Teary-eyed, Kelen rushes the cage as if to beat Gamley's talons away with his bare hands. Brattle stops him before he can hurt himself.

"Get him off Honnie!" Faro cries. "He'll kill him!"

Stag's Blood steps forward, pushing his huge head between the bars, and lets out a terrible, ringing roar. Flashes of red and white light explode around Gamley's head. The smaller birds disperse, cawing, and vanish into the cloudbed. The armored crow finally releases the cage and drops away to regroup, leaving Hanegal lame.

Kelen is in hysterics. Faro tries his best to console him, but he is barely shouldering the weight of mortal fear himself. Hanegal's wing beats begin to weaken, and his blood runs down through the bars of the cage to stain the gold. Death creeps over the crow, bigger than any sky, its cold tendrils winding toward the bird's failing heart, too. There are many prizes here: it touches the gray fairies where they are weeping, it winds into Stag's Blood's whipping mane, and it darkens Brattle's pearly eyes. It will claim them all, and soon. Alan's head fills with howls.

"That won't keep 'im gone," Brattle says. "Work your mojo, bony. I'll grab feather when the bird comes in. And Stags, give me another distraction."

"Right," Alan says, though he has neither any idea nor any inkling to ask what Brattle is planning. Instead, he turns his attention to Hanegal and the cold shadow stretching over him.

Stop, he tells the black threat. *Stay back and wait. I command you.*

The shadow shrinks. Alan feels it listening to him. Its attention is cold and horrible. The cage rocks, and he tries to center himself. Hanegal bleats incessantly, and he blocks out the sound. Death moves all around them, a billowing force he can almost see, blown broad on its own bitter wind. Alan lets the magic work inside him. It needs to strike its own balance between its will and his own. Every minute, he has been growing in it. Even with the midday sky wheeling around him Gamley rising again for another attack, he finds the calm to reach out and push death aside.

Hanegal's wounds are horrific. Alan wills the flesh to close, chanting "Knit, Knit" under his breath. He feels hot pain in broken bones as he presses their edges together. Blood wells up to wait in torn arteries, patient as the rising sun until it can gush again to the beat of Hanegal's strengthening heart. Alan can hear death raging in his head, and the voices he carries laugh back at it in mockery.

By your power, they jeer, *another life is spared.*

"Whatever you did," Kelen says to Alan, "it worked. Hanegal is flying right again, albeit a tad lopsided."

The crow caws his triumph. He rights himself, rises, and angles away to avoid Gamley's next dive. Alan relaxes, letting the magic and all his intense focus fall back into him. He would go to his knees if he could do so without falling through the bars. Instead, he sags on Kelen.

"How much further?" he manages to ask.

"We're past the sightline now," Kelen replies. "This is Welkinbright air. The city will soon be in sight."

"Just keep watchin', then," Brattle says. "Backs to me and you won't try nothing. Here he comes for his last pass!"

Alan looks north and his heart sinks. Gamley is streaking toward them, his wings opening. Gamley's talons glitter at the ends of his spread toes, each easily as long as Alan is tall. He knows that Hanegal is hurt, and he means to hit the cage again. Stag's Blood goes rigid. Alan braces himself against the cage ceiling, his every sinewy strained tight in fear. Sophia emerges from his sleeve, her heartlight blazing blue. Alan cups her in his hand.

"We're almost there," she says, pointing past the huge, black shape of the charging Gamley. "Look at the city, Alan! You're missing it!"

Somewhere, death takes up a laugh. Alan's spirit shrinks, but he does as Sophia says. Welkinbright appears behind Gamley, a perfect line of silver in a sun-strewn spray of mist. He can see bannered roofs and the heads of black lanes leading into the king's gardens. Bells are ringing in the south quarter, their voices clear and high on the headwind.

"I see it," Alan says. "It's beautiful."

Gamley screeches. His shadow falls over them, but he doesn't hit. Stag's Blood lets loose a thunderous roar, and Alan has to turn away from the lights that burst in Gamley's face. With the crow thumping its wings in confusion, Brattle draws his bright knife and leaps from the cage.

Sophia gasps. Kelen and Faro shout in vain. Alan reaches, but is too slow to stop him. Brattle lands high on Gamley's breast and grabs a fistful of feathers for purchase. He digs his heels into Gamley's flanks and starts pounding the bird with his blade. The elaborate helmet flips off Gamley's head, taking his beakplate with it. The crow rolls, and Brattle clings to land more strikes. He draws huge arcs of blood and feathers through the air on each backstroke. Panicked, Gamley flaps into a high spiral and vaults into the northern sky, taking Brattle with him. In an instant, both are gone.

Hanegal flies on toward Welkinbright. Alan waits in the tilted cage for Gamley to come down. The voices of the dead are utterly, horribly silent. Sophia climbs his robe to sit in the hollow of his shoulder, her head against his cheek.

"Onward," Faro says. "Injured, Gamley will return to the one who sent him."

"And Brattle?" Stag's Blood asks. He seems embarrassed to speak. The question hangs for a moment, as if trying to decide if it belongs in the hush.

"Trust not to hope," Kelen says. "And, in the meantime, wait."

Hanegal approaches Welkinbright at a careful pace. For a while, Kelen and Faro try to get him to turn the cage on its right end again, but he is either too hurt to comply or not greatly concerned with how he's gripping his cargo. Alan lies down across the bars as best he can and busies himself searching the crow's wounds in meditation. He is angry with his magic, and for a while, it won't respond to him. He reaches, and it recoils. With it beyond his control, he feels tiny and powerless again. This feeling sits in the pit of his stomach as a hollow pain, and he wonders for some time whether he might throw up.

Sophia sits with Stag's Blood, and they talk with the gray fairies as the suns climb to their burning noon. Above the clouds, their heat is pitiless. A fresh breeze tempers it, but it isn't long before Alan is covered in sweat. He lifts the hem of his robe a bit, exposing his belly in a vain attempt to find some relief. When Sophia approaches him through the air, a tiny bell swinging through the cage on bright pink wings, he is trying unsuccessfully to coax his magic awake to cool himself.

"You saved us, you know," she says as she walks lightly across his chest. "Twice. Do you feel that your magic failed?"

"I couldn't push Gamley away when it counted," Alan replies. "It didn't fail. It refused. It's been so capricious! But it's still my fault."

"Brattle will do what he wants," Sophia says. She sits down with her back against the point of his chin. "He is also a hero. He is not a victim. We will find him."

"Where do you get your certainty?" Alan asks.

Sophia answers resolutely. "From the Framer," she says. "Do you think Brattle is dead? Do you feel responsible?"

Alan looks up at the belly of the bird. Hanegal's talons click against the golden bars as he flexes his toes. His wings pump, sending feathers whirling down through the cage. The sound is enormous. In his head, Alan can hear Hanegal's heartbeat. It flutters, but it is steady. If he hadn't been able to heal Hanegal, death would have had all of them. He's certain of that at least.

"No," Alan says. "If he thought he was going to die, he'd have left Stags the pack of food."

"I suspect we shall find him in the city," Sophia says. "And he will mock you for doubting your own strength."

"Magic isn't about strength, is it?" Alan says, crossing his hands over his chest. "I've been thinking of it as a muscle I can flex with focus, but it's not exactly that. It's more about not focusing, and that's hard. You live your whole life trying to manage things, but magic won't be managed – not like that, anyway. It can only work in the moment, when you're not distracted by yourself. It's here and now."

"Now you are learning," Sophia says. There's a smile in her voice. Her happiness is beautiful. It rises like a sun, burning away the clouds of Alan's doubt. He wishes he had even a fraction of that power.

They wait out the rest of the flight in restive silence. A storm roars out of the cloud sea as they approach Welkinbright. Alan lies on his stomach for a while, watching lightning bloom beneath the cage. The city grows like a crystal on the horizon. Bevel-topped towers appear in clusters, angling out from shared bases, shimmering with windows. White streets stretch out from black arches, flanked by homes and gardens on either side. Small birds flit in flocks from roof to roof, searching the empty neighborhoods for the last of the population. Sylph statues watch their approach from gray docks, the crowns on their heads crumbling. Hanegal sets the cage down between them and then flaps upon it for a moment, wheezing his exhaustion, before hopping down and squatting to pull broken feathers from his breast.

Kelen slips through the bars of the cage and helps the others out. Stag's Blood refuses his hand and leaps down on his own, his tail swishing. Worry dims his eyes beneath his plumed brows.

"This is as close to the Shrine as he is allowed to land," Kelen explains as he turns to offer Alan his open palm. "It is a short walk from here. There is the tower."

Once Alan is safely on solid ground again, Kelen approaches Hanegal. The bird croaks and flutters.

"You are a good bird," he says, stroking Hanegal's breast with the back of his hand. "A pretty bird. Aren't you? Thank you for carrying us. I'm sorry, Honnie. Rest here and watch for us. We will be back. I promise."

Hanegal shifts his shoulders and fans his tail out flat against the marble pier-stones. He closes his eyes, and Kelen pats him on the throat.

"It should only have been an hour's flight," Kelen continues, "but Honnie's injury hindered him. Still, it could have been much worse. Your power is impressive, Alan. I wasn't aware humans had such magic."

"Neither was I," Alan replies. "If I didn't know differently for sure, I'd have said they don't."

Stag's Blood paces through the group, his back arched and his shoulders pumping. He tosses his mane and grumbles from deep in his chest, and his eyes burn. Even with shadows falling across his face, his eyes are ember-bright.

"That won't be the last ambush," he rumbles. "Our enemies are here. We came all this way trying to avoid them."

"Someone in the detachment sent word," Faro says. "I felt in my heart that they were traitors – or that there were traitors among them. I have been swallowing suspicion too long. You drew them out, master human. They hunger for you. Can you feel them?"

Alan shakes his head even as he realizes that he can. Far away, at the bottom of the city, the shadow of Toven is growing.

"The hour is late. How long have we been on the road to ruin?" Kelen says. "How pleasant the walk – how easy the way has been to our undoing! But now it ends.

"They will need Welkinbright's heart. If they have not taken the Shrine, then they are on their way, and we might beat them there to kill them when they arrive. If they have, then we will kill

44

them where we find them. Either way, the deceivers die. Brattle will be with them."

"Assuming he didn't kill the bird before they made land," Stag's Blood says.

"I don't want to play any hunches," Alan says. "I want to know for sure where he is. We have to look for him."

"The Flame is our only priority, wizard," Kelen snaps back. "Your friend may be dead on the ground. If he is, my city will not join him."

Sophia slips from Alan's sleeve to pace in the air. She rings in the wind, fighting bravely to steer herself against the gusts that whip around the statues from the cloud sea.

"This is no time to divide," she says. "We should go where we're needed most."

"Think of fate," Stag's Blood adds, "and the dark seas that carried you here."

Alan remembers waiting in the hospital after the crash and Allison telling him to try to hear their mother's voice.

She'd say to relax, Allison told him that night. *Don't kill yourself with worry. Whatever will be will be.*

He nods and says no more. He might snap inside if he tries to speak. The enormity if what's ahead is too much for him to contemplate.

"East then," Faro says. "We will go through the garden. The gate will be locked, but I think we can risk breaking it now."

With this, they start up the road toward a high lane of houses. Beyond them is a hedge wall around three vine-hung tiers of stucco facades. The Shrine of the Flame rises from the garden's green center like a ruby, its facets bright in the last light of noon. The houses on either side of the road are boarded up, and their windows are painted black. Notes attached to many of their doors declare the properties condemned by official order.

"Where are all the people who used to live here?" Alan asks.

"Fairies," Kelen replies. "Some were sent north to live in shelters . Others had more private retreats awaiting disaster. Most are in the underworld."

"And some are dead," Faro adds, his eyes straight ahead. "Who knows how many now?"

Kelen sighs heavily. "If only you had seen her in the full flower of her youth – in the spring of her faith – my invincible country."

Faro starts to sing as they mount a low hill. His voice rolls from airy heights to depths as soft as Marmorean mud. Then it splits, and he produces two tones at once in harmony with each other. Alan doesn't understand the language he's singing, but he doesn't need to know the words to feel Faro's deep, patriotic sorrow. After a while, Kelen begins to hum along with them, and the sound of their four voices lifted together is rich and moving.

They come to the garden's trellised gate to find it standing open. Kelen stops for a moment to inspect it.

"Who has been through here?" he asks.

No one can answer.

"Perhaps we'll see," Stag's Blood says.

Through the gates, the garden spreads out modestly, its tumults trimmed back from little gray paths under gaslights. Bushes bloom at waist height, their flowers huge and dark purple on forking panicles. Shagbark trees reach from behind them to hang little curtains of green fronds over the path. The even sod is dotted here and there with flowers of every color. Deeper in, as the path expands and the trees grow thinner, moths appear in great profusion. They land on Alan's shoulders and flutter, sprinkling his robe with pollen.

"Can you smell it here, Alan?" Stag's Blood asks.

"No," Alan replies. "But I can see certain smells." He can also see the dead shining over the trees like halos, but he keeps this to himself.

"There's a sharp, clean scent on the air," says the cat. "It's like the moment just before lightning strikes."

"Pallblossoms," Sophia says. She's flitting through the group in careful circles. Moths follow her, and she bats them away. "They don't grow on the ground anymore. It's said that they sing on stormy nights."

The group falls silent then, as if listening for the songs of the flowers despite the weather. All Alan can hear is the trickling murmur of dead voices. There is a shadow on the garden. It spreads through the mulch and the carpets of leaves on the grass. It watches from beneath the benches, and it grows in his mind, making him uneasy.

"You have come a long way, master human," Kelen says into the tension. "Tell us what your sphere is like, if you will. Are there lights in the living skies as bright as ours?"

Alan comes hesitantly to the memory, but he finds it well and waiting for him. "There are lights," he says, "but they're always falling. They burn for the space of a wish and then are gone. If they leave anything behind, it's a pit and a rock."

"We know those lights," Faro chuckles. "What makes that world yours and this one ours? What did you leave on the other side of the veil that you will never find in Midion?"

"Nothing," Alan says, his heart sinking. "Everything is here now."

"Indeed," says Faro. "But you keep your living world's weapon. There must be something of yourself as you were there that you wish to preserve."

"I want to be what I am," Alan says, "not what I have or where I come from." He laughs at himself. "That sounds like something Brattle would say."

"He has taught you well," Faro replies. "You will be able to thank him when we see him again."

Around a bend, the garden opens out around a wide pavilion. In its center, Gamely's body is draped over a crushed fountain. A sylph woman lies nearby, her neck open, bleeding into the bunched mess of her gown beneath her.

"Brattle!" Alan cries.

He runs to the crow, Sophia on his shoulder. Kelen goes to the woman, while Faro embraces Gamley's broken beak and begins to weep.

"Go in peace, Old One," Faro whispers, "to the endless fields of corn and bright days on shining coasts you have earned, to serve no more."

"There's no sign of him," Alan says. "But here's his knife."

He makes his way around to the other side of the corpse, where Stag's Blood is waiting at the foot of the continuing path.

"He was here," Stag's Blood growls. "But he is not anymore."

"Thanoturge," Kelen cries. "Come here. I need you."

Alan scoops up Brattle's haversack and throws it awkwardly over his shoulder. He leaves Stag's Blood waiting, color brooding in waves above his head, his mouth tilted down into a toothy frown. Kelen is kneeling with the dead woman's head in his lap, pushing loose strands of her hair back under her head covering. Her eyes are closed under faint, bloody thumbprints.

"Can you help her?" Kelen asks as Alan squats beside him. "Her blood is not yet dry. Can you reach her where she is?"

Alan extends his hand, fingers splayed over her face. He is racing inside, but he tries to relax and let the magic come. After an achingly empty moment, he begins to feel her under his palm. She is deep and in pain, and she won't reach back for him.

"She's over the brink," he says. "She's just within the draug. I can't bring her back like this. I'm pretty sure it would be ugly."

Kelen's eyes are like pools of fire. "Can you make her speak?" he asks.

Alan hesitates. "I'm not sure I know how. That feels like a different thing."

Kelen puts his hand on Alan's wrist. The strength of his grip is incredible. It's all Alan can do to avoid crying out and pulling his hand away.

"You're new at this," Kelen says, recalling their first meeting. "But please. I need to know that you are at least willing to try."

Alan settles back over his heels, his arches straining to support him, and tries to meditate on the discomfort. He tries to relax into the sounds around him, to let the war of his thoughts rage as an observer, passing no judgment on anything. When he finds his place in that inner chaos, his focus begins to fray and the sylph woman's dying shadow reacts to him. He is just able to stop it on its fall toward oblivion, but it won't tolerate his interference for long.

The body writhes. Her kerudung comes undone. Her fingers dance and clench, and her heels bang the paving stones. Kelen claps his hands over her eyes as they fly open.

"Ask!" Alan says. "Whatever you want, you've got to ask now. This is getting dangerous."

"Who sent Gamley?" Kelen shouts.

The dead woman works her mouth, cords straining in her neck. Her cheeks go taut as she tries to remember how to speak.

"My power's in the flesh," Alan says. "Her spirit is almost gone."

The draug falls away into death from the black edge of the woman's failing mind. Alan has never felt anything so final. The chasm is immense, and the woman's spirit is like a bolt of lightning within it. What's one flash in the infinite? It would hardly be anything if Alan wasn't gripping it by the tail, trying to make it work a corpse for a few more minutes.

"We're only hurting her," he tells Kelen. "I have to let her go.

"Who?" Kelen continues. "One word! A name!"

The woman's spirit finally breaks away. It descends into the draug and death swallows it up, grinning. It leaves its answer in the woman's mouth to slip out in a wet groan as her body goes limp.

"Greenlea."

Kelen sets the body down, folds her arms over her chest, and brushes her eyelids closed again. Then he cups her cheek as if trying to feel the heat of her last blush as it drains away. Alan returns to himself slowly. All the voices in his head have fallen quiet. He can't even feel the Kingwatcher's bloom for the moment.

"Now we know," he says.

Kelen starts to remove the dead sylph's belt and sword. He stands and buckles the belt around his waist and loops it over itself in front, leaving the silver-tipped end dangling like a tongue. Then he slips the sword into the scabbard at his hip.

"Who is Greenlea?" Sophia asks. She flits around the corpse's face, her light casting shadows in the hollows of the lank cheeks.

"She is," says Faro from just behind Alan. "She sent Gamley herself. She is one of the conspirators."

"I knew little of her," Kelen says, "but enough to say that she was always loyal. I wonder when she began to stray."

"Brattle killed her," Alan says.

"I imagine he did. If he hadn't, we wouldn't know what we know. But now he is gone."

Alan pushes himself to his feet and puts his hand out for Sophia. She swings around it, too excited to land.

"Where does that leave us?" he asks.

"We walked into a trap coming here," Kelen replies, a smile creeping across his face. "Now we know who will spring it: Greenlea's husband, Plover. He held her enthralled to him. That was how he liked her. Only he could have turned her against us. We will meet him in the Shrine prepared. This may be fate after all, master cat."

Stag's Blood isn't listening. He's far up the path, pacing and shaking his head, eager to get going. Alan can hear his claws clicking on the paving stones.

"This was the second ambush," Sophia says as she rises from the corpse. "Will the next be in the Shrine?"

"The next will be ours to spring," says Faro. He bends down to pick up one of Gamley's feathers. It is one of only a few huge primaries that aren't crumpled and broken. The tip of its quill is gleaming sharp and stained with crow's blood. "We shall spread through the garden toward the Shrine until we see them. Then we will win Brattle back his life, as he bought us time and ours."

Alan reaches back with some effort and pulls his trash masher from the strapping on his knapsack. It thrums in his hand, bright with its own light, exhilarated to feel his touch again. Alan lets it fill his head with its peculiar fervor.

"You should know that I don't kill," he says.

"Oh no?" laughs the sylph captain. "Then you shall have to stand back."

Twenty-Nine

The garden ends in a great white sprawl through black arches. On the north side of the street, a line of homes and shops curves sharply east and down a hill. The Shrine of the Flame rears up in the west, the centerpiece in an integrated complex of pools and long gardens. Statues watch the Shrine from an amphitheater at the end of the street, their shoulders wet with fountain spray.

Alan and company stop in a dry channel under the hedge wall and push the leaves apart to look across the road. Stag's Blood puts his neck straight out and sniffs when the wind turns into his face.

"Where's your army?" he asks.

"Precisely where it needs to be to facilitate this treachery," Faro says. "Disbanded."

Kelen pulls his knees up to his chest, puts his back against the curve of the channel and asks Stag's Blood, "What do you smell?"

"They are waiting inside for us," Stag's Blood replies, "and they've posted no guards."

"How many?"

Stag's Blood sniffs again, and his whiskers dance against his cheeks. His ears pivot in unison.

"Twenty," he says.

Kelen rolls his eyes closed and puffs a breath between pursed lips.

"All right," he says. "Teams of two with eight for each. I think I can handle four. Faro?"

Faro nods. He has put the valravn feather through the belt of his robe, and it bobs ridiculously behind his head whenever he moves.

"Eight if I need to," he says. "All of them if you three fail. I will not tire today."

"Let's hope it doesn't come to that," Kelen says, frowning. "Master cat?"

"I've never had time to count before I'm finished," Stag's Blood says. He's still sniffing. "But these are not all your kind. There is a masking smell – most of them are from Gimcrack."

"Toven's golems?" asks Sophia, perched on the bulbous stigma of a violet blossom.

Stag's Blood growls. "Let's hope so.

"What about you, Alan?" Kelen asks. "What can you do?"

Alan leans back against the south edge of the channel and lets his awareness slip down into his inner darkness. The dead voices are roaring there. They surround him like a warm wave, surging as if to swallow him. His fear is there with them, and he tries to avoid it, but it's bound to him with a golden tether. He drags it around for a minute before his strength is gone. Then he returns to the late day's light and looks up at the red spires of the Shrine clawing up into the cold, cobalt sky.

"Four, yeah," he says. "Don't worry about me."

"Are you sure?" Kelen asks, putting his hand on Alan's shoulder.

Alan only nods in reply and holds up his trash masher.

Kelen leans forward, wearing the shadow of the hedge wall over his head like a hood. "We need to steer this. I will draw them out."

Sophia rises from the bloom with her arms crossed. "Wait a minute! You didn't ask me. I won't hide here while the rest of you fight. Cowering in safety is not in my nature."

"Very well, little Fetchlight," Kelen sighs. "What do you have to give?"

"Just watch," Sophia says, and her heartlight begins to fade. It bleeds through her, tinting the air with a brittle shimmer that vanishes into the flood of the sun. When it is completely gone, she is nearly invisible. There is only the single, thin outline of her body to give her away. "See? They will never even see me."

"That's a neat trick," Alan says, trying to focus on her as she moves.

Kelen nods. "It's a plan," he says. "You go in, and we'll move up to the wall. Give us twenty minutes, then lead them through the side door, and we'll trap them on the stoop."

"Take no unnecessary risks," Stag's Blood says. "We only need one to follow you out."

Sophia lands on Stag's Blood's back. With the sunlight pouring through her, Alan can barely see her hugging his neck and stroking his mane. Stag's Blood shakes his head, trying in vain to resist the urge to purr.

"Relax," she coos. "Worry is poison. We are here, we are right, and the sun is shining."

With this, she lifts away, a wisp on a beam of light, and vanishes over the hedge wall. The others wait while the day fades, drawing long shadows down the street. At Kelen's signal, they rush from the garden and cross the street to press up against the Shrine's south wall. The light seems too bright around them. The wall is open to the road, and they are in full view of anyone looking north or crossing in front of them. Alan waits to be caught, or to hear some kind of alarm, but the silence continues unbroken. Eventually, the tightness in his neck eases away and he can relax a little against the wall. Stag's Blood even sits down and starts to lick his paw.

"I'll go for the first to appear," Kelen whispers. "Whoever comes to look next is anyone's." He levels a burning look at Alan. "Steel yourself, child."

At end of the south wall is a pointed arch under a spandrel framed in stained glass. There is a door under the arch and a small set of alabaster steps leading up to it. Between the top step and door is a slab of red marble with symbols carved in it. Nothing happens in the Shrine for a long time, and Kelen starts to whisper anxiously to himself, but then the side door opens and a sylph steps out onto the red stoop. His eyes are glassy, and he is staggering like a drunk. He looks down, confused, and lingers as if reading the symbols carved on the slab. Kelen mounts the stoop in one bound and cuts the oblivious sylph's throat from behind.

Alan looks away too late. His stomach rolls when the dead sylph drops.

"Your wife died the same way," Kelen whispers through his teeth. "May you find her again, traitor. And, wherever you go, may she rule over you as you have ruled over her."

"Plover?" Stag's Blood asks.

Kelen nods and he leans back to the left of the door. Faro takes up a position on the opposite side, feather in hand. A chorus of shouts comes from the behind the door, and then the door crashes open.

The things that come piling out are not golems. They are small and sallow, and they flap their jaws mindlessly. They drag their knuckles like ghouls, their limbs moving with aid from mechanical fittings. Their eyes are windows into utter blankness. They are Toven's fairy monsters.

Faro and Kelen wait until the first few pass them, their eyes wide with shock. Then they charge into the column together, spreading the stoop with blood. Alan pushes against his leaden fear, and, in a herculean effort, rushes from the wall with his open hand out and his trash masher held high.

Alan worries that he isn't ready to connect with his magic again, but it responds to him more readily than ever. He allows himself a moment to feel strong and to be proud of his progress. Then he reaches with his mind to drag a whole group of the swarming terrors into the draug, but he can't even touch them. There's nothing in them anymore that isn't already on the dead side.

Alan can't be left reeling for long. The fairy monsters are clambering toward him, their mouths hanging open, their black-clawed fingers wriggling for his throat. He swings his masher, batting them aside, breaking their bones. Their dead flesh is like plastic wrap. They paw at his robe, hanging like petulant children, unable to penetrate the fabric. Alan beats them back with the dead screaming insanity in his head, and their blood runs off his coat like water. Their wounded howls are terrifying. The shocks that run up the shaft of his masher as he crushes the monsters' skulls leave Alan feeling sick. His limbs grow heavy, and he longs to retreat into his inner darkness, but they will drag him to the ground and pull him apart if he stops fighting. He tries to tell himself that they can't be any more dead than they already are – that the most mercy these monsters can hope for is utter destruction.

The fight starts to spill off the stoop and into the road, but Kelen and Faro drive it back toward the door. Pinned on the red stoop, the dead things have no recourse but to fall back into the building, but they barely have the sense to retreat. Kelen carves through the dead fae with obscene grace. Alan has never seen anyone with such command of his body. Every movement is calculated, and every turn of his blade draws blood. Faro struggles to keep up, but he is not nearly so nimble. His improvised weapon isn't helping his maneuverability any, either. It flops behind him, huge and awkward, its point dripping. He swings the feather wide to clear a circle around him, pushing his enemies toward Kelen to be dispatched. When one gets through, he lets it get within biting range before driving the point of his quill into it. These gambits are risky, but Kelen is at his back to make sure that they always pay off. Within minutes, the crowd is thinning.

Stag's Blood wades into the group to squeeze the last of them through the door. He empties all his fury on the fairy monsters, laying them low with huge swipes of his ruby claws and tossing them from his mouth in shreds. He is barely-bottled calamity, and even Kelen and Faro step back from him. When the door is clear and bodies are heaped at his feet, he leads the way out of the foyer with a roar that shakes the stained glass over the archway.

Alan leans on his trash masher for a second. His arms ache, and his fingers are twitching.

"Filth," Faro says, disgust contorting his face. His gums are bleeding. He spits a red wad at one of the corpses on the floor.

"We know these things," Stag's Blood says, pawing his face where a few of his whiskers have been ripped out. "Alan saw them at Gimcrack. Toven is breeding them."

56

"I know them, too," Kelen sighs. "Dregs. They have been made before. This is all Toven is king of now. He can have them."

"We must establish ourselves in the sanctuary," Faro says. "We have been very lucky. Come whatever horrors may, we might actually have a chance at ending this."

Faro drops his feather just beyond the door. He and Kelen tear off down the corridor as if driven by the whips of Hell. Stag's Blood matches their speed easily, but Alan is weak in the knees. Against every impulse pounding through him, he wills himself forward. Seeing him lagging far behind, Stag's Blood goes back for Alan.

"Are you well?" he asks. "The seal on your head is blazing. Conserve your strength: let me carry you."

"No," Alan says. "You don't have to. I promised. Just tell them to slow up for a second."

"I know how important promises are to you, Alan," Stag's Blood says, "but you can't swear your heart and soul into everything. Sometimes, you have to break a promise to grow. Just let me do this. It's my choice to make."

"This is my second life," Alan replies. "I want to do it right this time. I want to do it perfectly."

Stag's Blood chuckles. "Climb up, human. There is no place in this world for perfect things."

There's no time to hem and haw. Alan obliges, and he is instantly glad that he did. Stag's Blood's back is as strong as an iron rod. When he runs, it becomes an unbreakable spring. Alan holds onto Stag's Blood's flowing mane as they wind through the halls, following Kelen and Faro. They cross mirrored floors under vaulted ceilings, and they pass long rooms filled with reliquaries and display cases. Some of the corridors are filled with thick smoke. The quiet is alarming, and it makes everything seem small and close. Even the widest chambers seem to shrink in the silence.

At the back of a small throne room, Kelen leads them through a doorway behind a row of hanging quilts. Through here, the carven doors to the Sanctuary of the Flame stand dark and locked. He swings his feet to the floor and takes his trash masher in hand.

"Bash the door?" he asks Kelen.

Kelen nods, his hand over his nose and his eyes watering. Alan pulls back, but Sophia appears before him, filling with color, her hands up to stop him.

"Wait!" she cries. "There's something else there. Don't go in!"

"No more waiting," Kelen growls.

He steps forward and wrenches the trash masher from Alan's hands. Then he swings for the space between the two doors, striking them both just above their faceplates. Sophia spins out of his way, and the doors splinter inward with the force of a blow that would have crushed her to powder. One of the doors twists off its hinges. The way open, Kelen leaps down five stairs into the sanctuary, followed closely by Faro.

The Sanctuary of the Flame is huge. The walls and floor are flawless alabaster, and the ceiling is gem-pricked gold. A burgundy carpet runs from the entrance stairway to a dais flanked by monolithic pillars. At the center of the dais is a rough stone fountain with a face carved into its high wall. Black liquid trickles into the basin from the face's open mouth. A little circlet of fire flickers just above the surface of the liquid, sick and radiating pain. Its sorrow is cold and terrible. Alan can feel it in the pit of his stomach even from the top of the stairs.

Voices cry out to Alan from beneath the floor. Even in death, they are exultant.

See the Flame Empyrean! Welkinbright's life will burn forever!

"So low!" Kelen exclaims, falling to his knees at the foot of the dais. "We are almost too late."

Alan runs to Kelen's side and puts a hand on his shoulder. Stag's Blood prowls around the dais, head down as he pushes his nose through the dust on the floor.

"We are in danger here," Sophia says, circling Alan's head. "They had something big with them. I don't know where it is now, but it is looking for you."

"No," Faro says. "I will not leave. Black-clad death itself could not lead me away with my throat in the curve of its scythe. Pay your part, thanoturge. Prove your worth or fall with us."

Alan stares up at the Flame. He knows the sorrow burning in it. He has seen it at the edge of autumn, a handful of firefly nights left before him, and in Hannes's shadow growing long in the woods too early. It is the fall of every summer empire, but he isn't powerless to stop it anymore. Centered, he ascends the dais. He puts his hands on the bowl of the fountain and reaches out through magic to search the Flame. He finds the poison easily – it is the largest thing there now, but he is empowered to drive it out. He has never been so certain.

"It's death magic," he says. "It's working in two ways – I can feel it. A spell of dying on the Flame, and poison in the font to keep the Flame from healing itself. How have you been purifying it?"

"With white drops," Faro replies as he and Kelen ascend the dais to join Alan, "but our store is depleted. Someone has been buying it up in the underworld, hoarding it away from us."

Alan reaches his arm into his robe for his pants pocket. He is amazed to find the little vial still there, after all that's happened since he met Shimmer. He pulls it out and shows it to the fairies. The black stopper is still in it, and not a single drop of the white liquid inside has spilled.

"This might buy us some time while we work out how to heal the Flame for good," he says.

Kelen and Faro lean in to look at the vial, and the white flames on their heads dance together for a moment.

"This is not white drops," Kelen says, his eyes widening. "Where did you get this?"

"From a hedge spirit in Marmorea," Alan replies. "It slipped this into my pocket while Brattle and I were sleeping, I think. That vial must have been the last of its supply. Someone had bought it out – Winter White, I suspect."

59

Kelen and Faro look at each other, but say nothing for a moment. Then Kelen takes the vial. He pulls the stopper and puts his nose to the top.

"Watchers' Tears," he says. "Their blood, that is. Impossible to come by! Master Alan, you had a strong friend in that spirit. I hope you repaid it handsomely."

"Fortune favors you," Faro says. "This will drive the poison from the font for months."

Kelen tips the Watcher's Tears into the fountain. There is no visible change in the liquid, but the Flame roars up to a new brilliance. Alan's heart leaps with it. Then there is a groan from deep in the city. The floor rocks once, and gold flakes down from the ceiling.

"She is waking," Kelen says, tears in his eyes. "Do you feel her, Alan? Welkinbright is remembering her life again. My heart can't take it."

"The Flame still gutters," Faro frowns. "What comes next?"

"Black-clad death," Alan replies. "I have to break the death magic."

He tries a deep breath but can only manage a sigh. His confidence is faltering. He has to raise a whole city from the draug. He sees a black gulf death open beyond the dancing Flame. The draug is a white line across it with life on one side and death on the other. Like Greenlea, Welkinbright is clinging at the living brink, barely conscious anymore. Its energy is enormous. He is small before it, but he is not powerless.

"Can you do it?" Kelen asks, his lips trembling.

Alan leans forward over the fountain and looks down into his inner darkness. He finds his center again – another stroke of luck.

"Yes," he says. Then a portion of the east wall explodes.

Thirty

Smoke comes pouring into the chamber. It races over the floor, curls up the pillars, and crashes against the far wall like seawater. A large shape comes bounding through it toward the dais, and Alan races down to snatch his trash masher from the floor. The smoke is too thick to see through and it's only growing thicker, but there are dead eyes beneath the floor of this sanctuary. Alan looks through them to find his masher at the foot of the steps. They grasp at his mind, lonely and starving to be remembered.

Jewel of the sky, arisen from the underworld, cry the jubilant dead, *long live Welkinbright!*

Alan scoops up his masher and turns around just as the charging shape is bearing down upon him. It hits him head on, lifting him off the ground and sending him skidding across the marble on his back. His arms and legs burn as he tries to push himself to his knees.

"Spearback!" Alan hears Kelen say.

Through the eyes of the dead, he sees the sylph captain draw his sword. Faro leaps from the dais into an awkward crouch. As he finds his feet again, he waves his hand and the wall of smoke splits wide apart in front of him. Alan sees magic swell through Faro: a blue light branching through the twists of his veins, so bright that his skin seems transparent for a moment. With a few more quick motions, Faro pushes the rest of the smoke back toward the far wall, where it breaks like a wave and withers away.

All turn to see the beast revealed. It is poised above the dais, huffing in a vain attempt to muster more smoke, one broad paw on the lip of the fountain. Its eyes are as white as stars. Two of its upper teeth protrude through the top of its snout to curve back toward its face. Its lower teeth are tusks bristling around its cheeks, their black ends rubbed blunt to stem their growth. A mane of quills runs down its back and into a thick mat of spines past its shoulders. There is a gaunt, gangly body impaled there upside down. It swings and bounces as the spearback advances over the dais, and Alan swallows a knot into his stomach as he recognizes it.

"No," Stag's Blood growls.

"Conservator," Sophia says. She lands on Alan's shoulder, her heartlight blazing sunset red. "Framer help us."

The spearback stalks down from the dais, its head wreathed in smoke. It looks from the tip of Kelen's sword to Alan's trash masher quaking in his hands. It watches Stag's Blood circle toward it, a chuckle burbling up from deep in its throat. Brattle's corpse flops on its back as it snickers. His pearly eyes are open, and Alan can't bear to look at them. Death is there, staring back, the victor after all: everyone's destiny.

"Draw it right," Kelen says.

Stag's Blood nods. Then, with a roar of rage, he charges the spearback's left flank. He rises up onto his hind legs, his ruby claws flashing, and the spearback responds with a lunge of its own. They push and pound each other for a hot moment, teeth bared, Stag's Blood refusing to give an inch. He lands a number of heavy blows to the spearback's head, but he is unable to injure it. It laughs at him in its fury – a stony, hollow sound like stones falling into a well. Finally, it throws him down, drawing blood with its tusks, and rears up as if to crush Stag's Blood beneath its front feet. Before it can, Stag's Blood howls and a flash of gold light explodes in front of it. The spearback staggers, and Kelen ducks in quickly to slash at its underside.

The sylph captain's sword leaves no mark on the beast. Stag's Blood springs to his feet and falls back with Kelen while it gathers itself into snarling crouch.

"It's protected," Stag's Blood says, panting a little. He turns to protect his bleeding side.

"Dark magic," Kelen says. "Can you dispel it Alan?"

Alan has no time to respond. The spearback pounces into their midst, flailing its paws, and he scrambles away. Brattle bounces on the beast's back. His jaw flaps open as his head lolls from side to side. His gums are bloody, and he is missing one peg tooth. Unable to stop himself, Alan reaches out to him. He searches Brattle's body for any sign of his spirit, but he finds nothing. The corpse isn't Brattle anymore. It's cold as marble, having not even the memory of life inside it anymore. Alan staggers back, reeling with sick fury. When the spearback charges again, he meets it screaming with his trash masher white hot above his head.

The spearback pummels Alan. It cannot pierce his robe, but its strikes hit him like speeding cars, knocking him to his knees. His magic shrinks away. Alan tries to follow the pain deep – to ride every massive shock far away to a quiet place where he can be like steel. When it clamps its jaws around him, he is only dimly aware of tilting up and being shaken. When it throws him to the floor he is a million miles away, watching his thoughts sail by like clouds. His magic returns to him in his stillness, and he finds a stronger control over it than he thought possible.

Alan searches the spearback's mind as it turns, disinterested in him now, and leaps at Faro. He feels its dauntless, animal certainty: self-doubt is beneath it, as it has always been invincible. Toven's shadow burns its skin, but the pain makes it even stronger. Nothing will stop it until everything is dead and the sky is raining cinders. That is its task, and it will not turn away. This is all it believes about itself. This is all it has ever needed to believe.

The spearback is simple, but Toven's spell is not. Alan pulls away frustrated. He is still a novice, and Toven is too strong for him.

Alan stands and takes four long steps back, his hands down and the trash masher drooping. Stag's Blood has dropped back to Alan's position, his uninjured flank turned outward. The spearback advances on Faro, who holds up his hands as if pleading. The flame on his head whips into a towering frenzy, vaporizing his eyebrows as it expands.

"Alan," Faro says.

Alan continues to strain against the darkness. His trash masher grows so hot in his hands that he can barely hold it. His head begins to ache beneath the blazing Seal of Aiwass.

63

"I can't break it," he says, surprised to find himself on the edge of tears. "It's too strong."

Sophia appears before him in a gentle flash of silver. She lights on his shoulder and presses herself bodily against his neck to whisper to him, warm as the memory of a kiss against his erstwhile cheek.

"Do not give up," she murmurs. Her voice is rain running through her. Her heartlight swells incredibly, streaming clear and blinding rays. "Kill the shadow! Burn it away!"

Sophia gathers her heatlight's rays into a single beam and pushes it out along the line of her outstretched arms. Alan watches the beam spark from her fingertips and tries to imagine his magic moving across it – a beam of his own, working in concert with Sophia's. Merging with her is easy: she is a perfect mind, empty of lies, without any vanity to distract her. Their beam strikes the spearback, which howls and wheels around to face Alan, its shield of shadow finally disintegrating. Darkness falls from the spearback's face in scales, leaving it looking haggard and starved. Rage squirms in its mind, out of control. The beast blows a jet of smoke and roars again before ducking its head and charging.

Stag's Blood wiggles back over his haunches and then uncoils to intercept the spearback midstride. He slashes its face, leaving its lips hanging red and ragged. It rears up, shrieking in abject shock, and stumbles backward just long enough to allow Kelen an opening to slip his sword between its ribs. Alan feels its pain, and it breaks his heart. Blood spreads through the fur on its underbelly as it paws at the sword's hilt. Blind with fear, it lashes, tossing its head, and catches Kelen on one of its curving tusks. The sylph captain falls on the steps of the dais, and Faro howls miserably as he rushes to Kelen's side.

"Come," Alan cries. He backs away, trying to lure the spearback toward the door. "Come here, you! You're not done yet!"

The beast limps toward him, moaning. He waves his trash masher, inviting it to its death, though he doesn't trust himself to

64

withstand its fury again. The beast is hurt, but its mind is burning with fury. Its every fiber is taut, and it gnashes its teeth in anticipation as it draws nearer. Smoke streams from its nose, so pungent that even Alan can smell it.

"Come and sleep," Alan whispers. "Let go of your rage and fall."

The draug is waiting, but the spearback is still strong. Alan works in its mind, trying to push its spirit to the paralyzing edge of death, but he panics as it continues to resist him.

A new light of life appears in the gulf: a streak burning across the draug from death's frontier. Alan steps back, staggered by the rising power. There is a loud crack, and one of the spearback's spines lifts away, broken from its back in a pair of heavy-knuckled hands.

Brattle climbs up to balance on the spearback's shoulders. White light pours from his back like a cape. His eyes afire, he pulls the broken spine from the wound in his chest and raises it above his head. For a moment, his skin looks as thin as paper. He stands transformed, taller and straighter than he has ever been, his shoulders broad and his forehead crossed with a crown of gold. Bands of color swirl around him, following the new lines of his form to bunch around his upraised fist. Then Brattle drives the spine deep into the spearback's neck, and the beast crumples without as much as a whimper. As it falls, Brattle leaps to the ground behind it. When he emerges again to spit into its dead face, he is his whole, hunched self again.

Alan runs to Brattle's side. Brattle wards him off with open palms. Lights continue to swarm over him for a moment, and then they disappear.

"Greetings and explanations later," Stag's Blood says. "We have another miracle to perform."

Kelen is standing as Brattle, Alan, and Stag's Blood return to the dais. Faro is fidgeting nearby, trying to keep himself from helping his captain. He greets Alan with a tight-lipped expression, as if he's unsure whether to be relieved.

"Are you OK?" Alan asks Kelen.

Kelen scowls at him. "The Flame," he says, wheezing. "Forget about me!"

Alan hovers for a moment, his hand on Kelen's shoulder. The sylph's side is dripping red. His perfect white robes are stained and shredded. Faro nods, and Alan finally ascends the dais to kneel before the Flame.

Stag's Blood stands erect with his forepaws on the lip of the fountain. Sophia clings to Alan's shoulder, the light of the Flame dancing beautifully inside her. She glows with it, and her heartlight turns white. Brattle bobs his head and watches in silence. There is a new aspect to his face, a light of knowing and purpose that Alan finds stirring. His eyes go glassy as he stares into the Flame.

Alan tries to find a calming place in his inner darkness. It is cold and empty, as it has been since he discovered it, but it doesn't need to be that way. It dawns on him that this is his space, so he builds something in it. It's easy – like breathing used to be. He puts himself back in the summer fields of Ohio, his face turned up into a light breeze. Fear is there, but he allows it. Doubt comes down like a cloud shadow, and he doesn't resist. Hannes will be out soon, flashlight in hand; nothing can spoil that memory. In the splendor of a ruddy sunset and the first cool touch of night across Hannes's yard, Alan finds his center again and, finally, a way to see deep into the Welkinbright's heart.

Death rules the Empyrean City. It walks the streets in dwindling crowds, long as a shadow; stands still in the alleys at night, watching fairy children through their burning windows; and looks down from the hills of power wearing Toven's smile. It is ready to move, but it recoils in fear from Alan's power.

"Can you see it?" Brattle whispers, his big hand on Alan's arm. "Can you reach?"

Alan doesn't know how to explain what he's experiencing. Welkinbright fills his mind with gold. He goes giddy with the feeling for a moment and has to keep himself from laughing with joy. The dead in the ground praise the city's everlasting glory, but the other voices whisper warnings. Welkinbright's life is huge, but it is almost gone. Caught in the draug with death's black jaws closing around it, the city is one more fall away from lost.

"Yes," Alan says. "It's bad. I don't know what I can do, but I'm going to give her everything."

"We can feel it," Stag's Blood says. "Keep going, Alan."

Alan can't worry about the sanctuary shaking. He ignores the cries of the timbers and the dust raining from the ceiling as he reaches out to pull Welkinbright from the brink. A seizure grips him, and he falls forward over the lip of the pool. His stomach rolls as he pours his power out. The seal on his forehead burns, and his head begins to pound. There is a long, hard tug deep in his chest and he almost blacks out, but Welkinbright finally begins to respond. She rises from the draug, wounded, and death gnashes after her. Terrified of Alan's strength, it turns away. The Eternal Flame begins to roar as it grows. Alan gives of himself until he feels shrunken, and then he falls away from the Flame like a ragdoll. Brattle helps him to his feet again.

"Look," says the ghoul, pointing at the Flame.

Alan doesn't need to look to know that the Flame is tall and bright again. He doubles over, his hands on his knees.

"It's not over," he says.

Death isn't slinking away. It is rushing up again, heaving cold laughs across the draug. Alan recedes from it, unable to fight any more. He looks at Faro.

Sophia gasps, "Kelen!"

The sylph captain sags in Faro's arms, his legs stretched out in front of him with blood pooling under his heels. His jaw hangs open, and his eyes stare blankly into the middle distance. Sophia lands on his palm and puts her ear to his wrist, listening for a heartbeat. Alan knows what Kelen sees, but he doesn't have the power to stop it. He crosses the dais to kneel and take his hand.

"The Flame is restored," Alan explains. "Listen to me and look at it. We'll find someone."

Kelen tilts his head. An empty smile spreads across his face.

"Can't you heal him?" Faro asks, his voice ragged.

Kelen works his mouth. His throat quivers as he tries to make a sound. All the color is draining from his face, and the white flame on his head is gone.

"Don't," Kelen says. Then he is still, and the sanctuary shakes again.

The roof gives way over the fountain. The Flame swells, filling the chamber with light as huge chunks of gold and powdered stone rain down around it. Brattle and Stag's Blood scramble down from the dais to crouch near the smoking corpse of the spearback. Alan tries to help Faro away, but Faro is reluctant to leave Kelen. He clings to Kelen's body, tears streaming down his face, and screams to be left alone. Only Sophia's gentle whispering in his ear calms him. A column falls across the dais just as Faro and Alan reach the spearback. The fountain breaks apart, spilling black fluid across the alabaster floor. The Flame remains where it is, blazing huge and loud, as the sanctuary cracks like an egg.

When the last of the beams and the stones have fallen, Alan and the others approach the pile. Only a few threads of Kelen's blood give any indication as to where his body is beneath the rubble. White light streams into the sanctuary, and they can see the minarets of far off towers through the gaping hole above them. Life and color are sweeping across the Empyrean City: shadows peel away from the towers, revealing silvers and reds and greens on their roofs. Bells begin to ring far away. Suddenly bursting with joy, Faro leads them out of the Shrine to see gold blooming across the streets and flags brightening through the gardens.

"Jewel of the sky, arisen from the underworld," Faro shouts, "long live Welkinbright!"

Stag's Blood pads out into the middle of the street to look east toward the amphitheater. The statues there are resplendent in gold and sapphire.

"The gray city awakens," he says to Alan. "You've done a great thing. Pwysh was right."

"I brought life to the Flame, but it was spiritless," Alan says. "You can't bring a spirit back from death after so long — I already knew that. But, apparently, you can add a new one."

"Under the right circumstances," Brattle adds. "If the spirit is pure — and fresh — enough. I never seen it, but I heard stories. I thought that's all they were."

Sophia lights on Brattle's shoulder. "This is Kelen," she says, wonder rising in her tiny voice. The light of the Eternal Flame still dances in her. She's caught some of it in her heartlight. "He died for her — his invincible country. He gave his spirit to bring her back to life."

"Then he'll live forever," Faro says, "and so will you, Heroes of the Flame."

Faro puts Alan and the others up in a shuttered bell tower east of the Shrine. Night is coming on as they settle in, and Faro paces the dusty floor with dead Greenlea's sword slapping his thigh. There are valravn approaching the city from far away. Alan watches them moving across the sky in a spacious flock, their wings lit green from below.

"War torches," Faro says. "The first of our soldiers returning — may they still be ours. Battles remain before us, and I do not know what we will face now that the Shadow is lifted."

"Some devils are better stayin' hid," Brattle says. "Will you need us?"

Faro turns. The light of the setting suns is on his face. It draws shadows in the hollows of his cheeks and the furrows on his brow, making him look old and emaciated. His eyes are like fairy fire.

"More than the unfortunate fae at your next destination?" he says. "I can't say, but I doubt it. It's never safe to assume that time is on your side. The war for the sky is ours to fight. You've given us that. We will send you on, with our gratitude, when we have birds to spare. Where will you go from Welkinbright?"

"He and Winter White will be waiting for us wherever we go, won't they?" Alan says. "We thought we were outsmarting him coming here."

Stag's Blood growls a laugh and sits down with his front paws folded over each other. "We were wrong."

"You arrived in time to turn the tide," Faro says. "Your coming was incredibly fortuitous. Toven deceived us all but now his enemies are waking up. You cannot stop now; you must rouse them all – as many as you can muster. Clearly, fortune favors you. Where will you start next?"

Alan can't think of anything to say. Proud as he is of what he's achieved, he doesn't feel lucky or favored. He's tired and his whole body aches. The road ahead is long, and he doesn't see anything good at the end of it.

"Cheel Gar," says Sophia, perched on the handle of Alan's trash masher, "or Sepulchra."

Faro's eyes widen. His hand goes to his chin, and his neck stiffens. Alan remembers how interested Toven had been in who he was and what he knew, and he wonders how much they should really be telling Faro right now.

"To wake the Dead in Disgrace?" Faro asks. "It must be. You take no easy roads at Pwysh's behest. Their curse is the Flame's twin and just as strong."

"Tell us," Stag's Blood says.

Faro shakes his head and says, "I'd regale you all night, but I can't. I have to meet the coming birds and assemble our allies. Rest here, my friends, if you can. I will return in the morning."

When Faro is gone, Stag's Blood sits up and stretches.

"What do you think?" he asks.

"I pity him," Sophia replies. "He has turned so cold. There is a shadow on him now. He will always feel it. It will live like a pain in the furthest cloisters of his heart. When he sleeps. When he loves. It will darken him forever. I am sad to see him so changed. Death does not have to take you to claim you."

"His ordeal ain't over," Brattle says. "Death could take him yet."

Stag's Blood smiles. "But not you," he says, thumping his tail. He has licked the dried blood from his fur and left a sleek patch. He scratches at it with his hind leg, his red claws winking. "Why?"

Brattle sucks his lower lip, his gaze fixed straight ahead, as if he can see the answer on the horizon.

"I don't know," he says. "I rode that bird to a crash in the garden – busted up an armed party come looking for you and the ambush they was leavin' behind 'em. I hit the ground fighting, and I killed one of them, but they got their chains around me. There's a room in the Shrine they've turned into a beast pit. They took me there, hood on my head, and then they magicked me out – probably so I couldn't fight back. I'm glad I don't remember bein' speared.

"I was in the draug for a long time. It was just black at first, and then I saw lights far off. Bright lights, big explosions going on forever, like souls bein' born. Like the almighty storm, you know? Life arising, invincible. I reached the bottom. Then I saw Da, and Nettle was with him. I saw 'em both plain, whole and well, forgiving me. Nettle was trying to say something, and it was taking forever. Then the pain kicked up, the lights dimmed out, and I was awake all at once. I felt this power. I can't describe it, but it's gone now. I used it all up.

"Nettle brought me back, I'm sure of it. He pulled me out, but I don't know why. I have no idea. Best I can think is that I got something left to do yet. I sure don't feel done. I feel back. I feel like my old meat again." Brattle looks around the room at the others and smiles. "I seen a part of what I got waitin' for me on the other side, and, if what Faro's got is half as good, he ain't got nothing to fear. Death has claim on us all."

"Conservator," Sophia says in a reverent whisper. "Do you still doubt me? We all saw you transformed."

Brattle shrugs. "Call it what you will," he says. "I ain't naming it."

Stag's Blood pads over to Brattle and nuzzles him. He sniffs him hard and paws at his chest, his whiskers twitching. Brattle takes the attention in stride.

"You definitely smell like your old meat again," Stag's Blood says. Satisfied, he sits back down and rests his cheek on Brattle's shoulder.

"You ain't said much, Al," Brattle says, reaching back to scratch behind Stag's Blood's ear. "I can see your wheels turnin'."

The last light fades, pulling shadows down the wall. A wild wind wraps itself around the bell tower to howl at the one unblocked window. The dead in Alan's mind howl with it.

Be still, he whispers to them, and they obey.

"I'm just listening," Alan says, pulling his hood up. "You know me."

Brattle nods. In the glow of Sophia's heartlight, his spreading smile looks sinister.

"I think he'll do well," Stag's Blood says. "He is brave and good, and I saw him kill eight dregs with a plucked feather. I don't know whose hands Welkinbright belongs in, but she would not be bad off to fall into his."

Brattle cocks his head and asks, "Dregs?"

"Monstrous things," Sophia replies. "You saw them piled on the red stoop, no doubt. They are dead fae made to move by terrible devices. Toven employs them, apparently. He has fallen far."

"I gotta hear that story."

Alan tells it slowly, with help from Stag's Blood. Brattle listens without looking at them, his head bobbing between his knees. His eyes cast circles of light across his bare feet. When Alan and Stag's Blood finish, he waits this way for a long time. Then he looks up and nods, his gaze fixed on a point in space.

"Hard to top that," he says.

After this, the four sit in the growing darkness, enjoying one another's company. Stag's Blood and Brattle break open the pack of meat and eat a little while Alan reads a bit from Pwysh's *Grimoire of Plastromancy*. Sophia sits stone still on the bare floor, her legs folded under her, apparently praying. It feels like home for a moment, and Alan actually finds himself relaxing.

When he has eaten his fill, Stag's Blood stands and shakes his heavy head. He speaks around a cheek full of meat.

"I am tired," he says, "and I know we would all like to rest a bit longer, but I think we should proceed with the second part of Pwysh's plan."

"With all the excitement, I had almost forgotten," Sophia replies. "But Faro's decision to put us up here should have reminded me from the beginning. Do you think he knows?"

Brattle stands and stretches hugely. His skin shifts over his straining muscles as if it has a mind of its own.

"I ain't concerned whether he does or doesn't," Brattle says, dropping back into his crouch. "The task's ours."

Alan closes the Grimoire and slips it back into his old knapsack. Then he stands and leans on his trash masher.

"I was thinking of staying a little longer," he says. "I thought they might have some mages here who might help me, but Welkinbright has its own problems. I guess now is as good a time as any to get on our way." He looks around the room slowly. There is a fresco on the northeast wall that hasn't been touched up in a long time. He wonders where the sylph who made it is now. "It's pretty lucky that Faro brought us here. What's going to happen when we start to see the strings? What will we do when the puppetmaster appears? I've been worried about that. It makes me feel a lot less lucky."

"Bell, star, and spirit," Brattle says. "Only thing to do is march on, Al. Fortune's favor's got us this far."

Thirty-One

"Where are we going?" Sophia asks.

She is lighting the way down the tower stairs. The stairwell is cramped, and the block walls are wet with leaks. Alan and Stag's Blood follow her in single file. Brattle lags behind, trying unsuccessfully to hide a new limp.

"I don't quite know," Alan says. "To the bottom of the stairs, at the moment."

"There is a large community of bell collectors below," Sophia says. "I imagine a Welkinbright bell would fetch a nice price among them – assuming the sylves would deign to sell to underworlders. Perhaps it was melted down for swords or armor."

"I smell oil," Stag's Blood says, his voice low. "There's someone below us. We might do better to keep quiet."

They go the rest of the way without saying anything. At the bottom of the stairs is a cramped room filled with discarded furniture. The windows are covered with sheets of crumbling chipboard, and there is no door. Sophia dims her heartlight and they sit for a moment in the dark, looking across the room at the empty arch of the entrance. Soon, they hear raised voices and a light appears on the street outside. Torches wave into view, carried high by a mob of sylves. An army is marching west.

"Don't move," Stag's Blood says.

Brattle crouches behind him, his hand in front of his face to cover his eyeshine. He watches through spread fingers as two faces look through the doorless arch. Alan tries to sink into his hood.

"There is a back way," Sophia whispers. She has lighted on his shoulder, underneath his hood. Her cool lips move against his skin like falling petals. "Come slowly."

Someone shouts into the darkness, and then two torches land on a pile of chairs in the middle of the room. Another one bounces off the doorjamb. The two faces vanish as flames begin to rise. The chipboard roars alight, and then the mob moves on. Alan and the others flee quickly and quietly and are standing in a courtyard behind the tower when the bell tower begins to burn.

Alan sits down on a little stone bench. Stag's Blood stands beside him, looking up at the bell tower as flames lick up its sides.

"Are they going for the Shrine?" Alan asks.

Sophia comes to rest on the open palm of a statue.

"I do not know," she says. "I hope not."

"Up the street and away," Brattle says, craning his neck carefully to watch the mob's torches bobbing out of sight. "To spread their fire and spill their blood."

Alan throws his hood back and sags in his robe. "We haven't saved Welkinbright," he says.

"That isn't our job," Stag's Blood says. He stands on the grass, moonlight falling pale across his face. Fire dances in his eyes for a moment, and Alan can't look at him. Then he turns a circle through the courtyard with his nose to the stone flags. Finally, he puts his paw down on a carven tile. "Here. We have our own task. This points the way."

Alan gets up to look. On the stone is a carving of a round face wearing a bell-shaped hat. Its right eye is open and its left one is just a drooping curve. Alan recognizes it from the fresco on the wall at the top of the bell tower. Wondering who will remember that painting when the tower falls, he feels a deep twist of sadness.

"Left, then," Brattle says. "We follow the eyes. Look! There's another one here."

At the other end of the courtyard, to the left of the first carving, is a second carving with both its eyes open.

"Stop here?" Alan wonders.

"Straight, I think," says Stag's Blood. "If not, we'll double back."

"Where do they lead?"

"Not across any large roads, I hope," Sophia says. "Clearly, there are eyes out tonight that are best avoided."

They follow the carven stones through back streets and hidden alleys. There is a different Welkinbright here in the lonely spaces. Windows stare blindly across dirt lots and heaps of refuse, their shutters long gone. Yellowed clothes beat the wind from lengths of shining wire stretched between hovels. Shadows whisper under covered porches. Kelen died for this Welkinbright, too, and Alan can feel him powerfully in every standpipe and falling chimney. In the sagging roofs and the yawning cellar mouths, Kelen's spirit candle burns.

Alan and company never come very close to the main streets, but they see several more fires along their way. The carvings lead them into a cramped district dominated by dilapidated apartment buildings. There is a cemetery nestled on its western edge. Alan and the others enter it through a colonnaded gate and pause to rest at the highest point of the street. Cages arrive in different parts of the city all night, and not all of them are carried by birds. After dropping off their cargo, great featherless things circle the industrial quarters, swinging their crested heads like rudders. Alan watches them with cold fear knotting in his chest.

"Scours," Brattle coughs. "They can't be bringin' nothin' good."

"The Clockwork King is in the open," Stag's Blood says. "The battle for Welkinbright has begun."

Alan shakes his head. A chill runs through him. "What have we gotten ourselves into?" he asks.

"Nothing we can't get out of one step at a time," Stag's Blood replies. He places a comforting paw and Alan's shoulder. "Let's get on and find this bell. The sooner the better, I'd say."

Smoke begins to curl up from deep in the city. Alan looks past the rising ribbons to the vast spray of stars across the bluing sky. He has never seen so many so clearly. He feels helpless and small beneath them. The night swells with their light, pressing close around him, and he worries for a moment that it might burst and crush him.

The last tiles lead to a black stone tomb in a marble courtyard. A bare-limbed Barrowvale tree droops in front of it, its trunk bent as if by powerful winds and its bark shagging slowly away. Above the stele that blocks the tomb's entrance is a larger carving of the face they've been following all night. Both its eyes are closed.

"Suppose this's the place," Brattle says. His left foot drags as he hauls himself over to the stele. He heaves a shaking breath and presses his shoulder against the stone, testing it. It looms over him, motionless.

Stag's Blood goes to stand at the threshold. The starlight is alive around him. Little motes of it get caught in his mane and twinkle there until he shakes his head, scattering them before the door of the tomb.

"The bell's grave," he says, his voice a peal of distant thunder. "No gates. No guards."

Sophia lands on the mirror-smooth marble. Her reflection rises to meet her feet. The ground beneath the tomb begins to quake as she approaches.

"What do you expect to find, Alan?" she asks.

"Anything and everything," Alan replies, shaking his head. He approaches the tomb with difficulty, suddenly exhausted. "Help I hope, and maybe more danger. Or maybe nothing. We'll see."

Alan goes to the stele and puts his hands against it. It is covered in elaborate carvings, many of which still have traces of paint or gold leaf clinging to them. Alan leans beside Brattle, putting all his weight against the stele. It doesn't give an inch. After a minute of pushing, he steps back and puts his hands on his knees. Panting, Brattle sits down with his back against the wall of the tomb and his long legs stretched out. His heels bounce lightly as the ground continues to tremble.

"We're missing something," Alan says. "Sister Sophia, can you come a little closer?"

Sophia takes flight and approaches the door. As she nears it, the gold-laced slab slides back in a curtain of falling stone dust. With a groan, Brattle pushes himself to his feet.

"I'll be skinned," he laughs, slapping the ground.

"The light of the Flame," Alan says. "You caught some of it."

"I did not intend to," Sophia says, dimming a bit. "I do hope Faro did not notice." She pats herself down, as if feeling for the alien light inside her.

"It's the secret we need," Alan replies, "and probably Toven, too. And it's a secret we'll just keep for ourselves for now. Faro has enough to worry about."

When great, grinding gears lift it from the floor, Alan sees the door emerge through the tomb's roof. The symbols on its top complete a similar set of symbols at the base of the roof spire.

"That did it," Stag's Blood says, smiling and poking his head into the tomb's short, dust-blown throat.

"Look up there," Alan says, pointing at the door where it fits into the spire. "It's a word. 'Enlil.' Can you read it?"

Brattle curves down into his squat and tilts his head, squinting. "Magic letters," he says. "Can't make 'em out, but I know that word. It's a name. I heard it before." He presses himself against the wall halfway into the mouth of the tomb. "Da used to say that name in his sleep."

The four wait on the threshold for a moment, staring into the dark. Alan motions for Sophia to lead the way into the tomb, but she hesitates.

"The dark watches us," she says. "Now that it comes to it, Alan, I am not sure I can continue."

"But you have a light," Alan replies, "and I'll be behind you all the way. Don't worry."

"Even I can't see in," Brattle says.

Stag's Blood lowers his head and peers into the chamber. "Black as wrath and storm-hot," he growls, "but we must go in."

The ground is still moving slightly, but it isn't trembling anymore. Now it is rising and falling. Warm air moves back and forth through the entrance, pulsing in time with a rushing sound resonating in the back of the chamber. It's as if the tomb is breathing.

Sophia crosses her arms and continues to refuse, so Alan takes the first steps over the threshold. A knot cinches tight around his heart. The dark envelops him, its weight huge on his shoulders. He puts his arms out to feel for the walls as the chamber widens around him. His right hand finds a soft mass of warm, quivering flesh, and he stifles a scream of surprise.

"See?" he says. "It's nothing. Now come on in. I really can't see. And try not to touch anything."

Alan tries to reach out through his magic, but he can't touch the shadow here. It isn't really shadow. It's a life spread out and black with age - a trapped thing that has been alone in oblivion so long that it has almost become the walls of its own prison. He reaches for it and it tries to hide, but it can't conceal its enormous power. Alan's hands go clammy, and a frisson of fear ascends to his spine.

"Sophie?" Alan calls, and he is relieved to hear the tinkle of Sophia's wings and see her heartlight growing around him.

Brattle follows her, his eyes like dim moons in the dark. Stag's Blood lags behind. Alan can hear him purring, trying to calm himself.

"Seems bigger inside," Brattle says.

"There it is," Sophia chimes. She swings a bright circle around a bell-shaped mass near the center of the room. "What has grown over it?"

She boosts her heartlight a bit, and the savage blaze of the Eternal Flame illuminates the whole tomb. Alan realizes that the wall, the bell, and the entire ceiling are covered with quivering flesh. Bones protrude from beneath it in every corner. Blood pours across the floor as the mass begins to move, and Sophia screams.

A skeleton reels to its knees in the center of the room. It is chipped, crushed, and white as chalk. Its bones pull themselves together with a rhythmic clacking sound. The skeleton puts its hand on the bell as it finishes articulating itself. Then liquid skin begins to crawl over it, filling it out. Blood runs up its legs, and a light blush starts to color its tightening flesh. Its heart pumps to

79

life, and lungs emerge pulsing around it. Its guts coil into its abdominal cavity, and Brattle makes a retching sound.

"By the stone, Al," Brattle shouts. "It's coming for the light! Sophie, stifle yourself!"

The thing taking shape by the bell starts to scoop the last of its skin and muscles into place. The walls are dripping with blood, and the floor is piled with gore. Stag's Blood backs away toward the door, shaking blood from his paws. Alan looks on in horror, rooted in place. The dead mutter in his mind. They cry in his heart, leaving terrible echoes. The whole cemetery has awakened. The thing by the bell puts nothing on its bare skull. No eyes form in the gaping sockets, and no hair creeps up the cranium.

"Wait," Sophia says.

Brattle twists his face into an indignant scowl and draws his dagger anyway.

"Thanoturge," the thing whispers. Three of its bottom teeth are blue-black gems. Its voice slips out of the non-space like a fog, filling the tomb. The bell shakes and thrums out a low tone. Before it speaks again, the floor heaves and cracks. Brattle falls against the wall, and Stag's Blood rocks on his feet to keep his balance. The skull-headed thing hisses and moans, "Finish me."

Alan is tired. His every sinew smarts, and the Seal of Aiwass burning on his brow is giving him a lancing headache. He doesn't want to dip into the well of his power again - to feel the Bleeding cold at his edges - but the dead in his mind are screaming pity and he can't fight them. He remembers what it's like to be a shadow. His heart breaks for the naked, wilting thing, and he reaches out to take its hand.

The skull-headed thing's grip is pitifully weak, but it strengthens quickly in the flow of Alan's magic. The thing stands, finds its balance, and straightens. In Alan's mind, through the filter of his facility, the thing is like one huge wound. It is far beyond the draug and the black reach of death. Its spirit is like glass, clear and cold and lonely. As its skin firms up over its shifting muscles, the thing lets go of Alan's hand. In the light of the Eternal Flame

80

burning through Sophia's heart, the thing's flesh is a dry gray and hairless. It fits just well enough to hold everything behind it without bagging out, but there is no definition. It has neither nipples, nails, nor genitalia, and its feet are flat as flippers. It does one last check of all its parts, and, when it is satisfied that it has pulled itself together completely, the thing bends and starts to lift the bell.

"What did you feel?" Stag's Blood asks Alan from the far side of the room. "Is it friend or foe?"

"Nothing like that," Alan replies. His magic curls up to sleep. He tries to relax with it, but his head is still pounding. "I didn't get much of anything."

"Enlil was a light," Brattle says. "An ember left from the fire of the first dawn. King of the rising sky. That's what Da used to say."

"Enlil, yes," says the sky-king. "Sigh-born."

Enlil strains and the bell rises slowly from the floor of the tomb, dust and black beetles swirling out from under it. Newly firmed skin rippling, Enlil tilts the bell back against the wall. As the sky-king steps back, the ground heaves again, and the bell cracks in half with a huge sound. The whole tomb shakes, and the ceiling groans apart. Through the split above, Alan can see the white disc of the moon and columns of crest-headed scours circling the graveyard.

"Everyone in Welkinbright will know where we are," Stag's Blood says.

"We never had time," Alan replies, stepping forward to see what the bell was covering. "But we can work with what we do have."

On an ash-black altar in the center of the room, is a jagged fragment of eyestone. Little rays of violet light dance over the curve of its intact side. Sophia buzzes across the room to circle it, her heartlight pumping bright. The ringing of her wings is huge, and it draws a sonorous tone from the broken halves of the bell

"This is the prize!" she says. Her heartlight dances wickedly. "Feel the life inside it. It is terrifying."

"Nergal," Enlil whispers. The sky-king has stepped back against the wall and is clinging there like a gray line of shade. "The Servant."

Alan scoops up the fragment and starts to slip it into his bag. He pauses when it warms under his hand and something moves in its glossy surface. Looking into it, Alan sees a march of round, yellow lights. Streaks move across them like rain, scattering their reflections through Nergal's surface. There is a rhythm to their procession that reminds Alan of home, and he fights a powerful wave of sorrow as he tucks Nergal into his knapsack.

"And now we go," Alan says.

"Quick," Brattle adds, uncoiling himself at last. He stretches and sheaths his knife, and then he spends a good ten seconds coughing and spitting. He bats away Alan's comforting hand and clears his throat with a rumbling growl. "Quick now," he continues. "But where?"

"Secret ways," Enlil answers. "Follow."

With this, the faceless spirit detaches itself from the wall and crosses the tomb in three gliding strides. Brattle wraps his pall around his chin and pushes Alan away again as he knuckles out into the moonlit cemetery. The others follow at a trot, and Enlil leads them through heart of the graveyard toward a row of red stone buildings on its western edge. Just at the gate, where the grass ends in cobbles and slab lots under tall gem lanterns, a hill protrudes from the cemetery sod like the green tip of a giant thumb. A statue weeps above a door in its eastern face. Enlil opens it with a touch no stronger than a stern look, and light comes pouring out of it.

"To Kur," Enlil hisses, standing at the door with a hand outstretched. Draped in moonlight, the sky-king is terrible. Shadows play across its body, deepening every strange hollow. "Hurry."

Brattle stops to take a few big breaths. Stag's Blood approaches him, shows his flank, and tosses his head. Light blows down like dust from his mane.

"Are you fooling yourself, rustic?" Stag's Blood says. "You certainly aren't fooling anyone else. Come on."

After another moment's hesitation, Brattle clambers onto Stag's Blood's back and the two of them go through the door in the hill together. Alan glances up at the gathering flocks of scours and valravn. Firelight is bleeding up into the sky from somewhere. Where has all the distance gone? Where is the loneliness with which he has defined himself all his life? It's not in the ocean of starlight. It is gone from his heart, and he feels its absence as a pain.

Kelen's spirit is on the wind, moaning in anger. Alan thinks of Faro on the red stoop wielding Gamley's feather like a weapon. Then he ducks through the door, and Enlil pulls it shut behind him.

"The battle has just begun," he says. He pulls up his hood, and Sophia curls up beneath it in the crook of his neck. She is warm as a naked nestling against his skin. "Be safe, Faro."

Thirty-Two

The passage goes down along a gentle incline. It is spacious and warm, with clean ecru tiles on the walls. Lighting gems burn softly in the beveled ceiling, their sconces surrounded by colored glass. Enlil drifts over the slate floor like smoke, leading no shadow. Stag's Blood follows with Brattle fast asleep over his shoulders. His footsteps are slow and heavy, and his head is drooping. Alan feels burned down and blown away. His limbs ache, and he has to hold Stag's Blood's tail to keep from falling behind.

"Where are we going," Stag's Blood asks, "and how far?"

"Some way," Enlil replies, its voice straining like wind in a well.

"It must've been a long time since he's said anything," Alan offers. "Every syllable is an effort. And I get the sense that talking was never his strong point, anyway."

"It's a machine," Stag's Blood replies. "It doesn't have to live. It only has to work."

Sophia shifts against Alan's neck, stretching out to put her heels on his shoulder and her back against the point of his cheek bone. He tries to keep his head straight for her.

"I trust him," she says softly. "He is empty."

Enlil's shoulders move. A twitch runs up its sigmoid spine, but it says nothing. Alan tries to search its mind, but he is too weak. He can barely reach his magic now.

"Nergal the Servant," he says. "Toven would have thrown all of Welkinbright down for this shard of glass. What will he do when he finds out we have it?"

"He healed us before," Stag's Blood says. "He'll kill us next time."

"He knows where we're going," Alan says. "He told us where to go before knowing that his hand is everywhere - I have no doubt about that now. Look what he's done here. How can we stand against him? This is a war. It's a real war, and there are four of us."

"Five," Sophia replies, "if you count Pwysh. Do not forget his role in all this. Whatever he believed you could do, do you not think you have shown him right so far?"

Alan pretends to consider this, but he's really thinking about Nergal's weight on his back. He can feel the shard moving in his knapsack, cold as marble.

"I imagine there're fragments just like Nergal in Cheel Gar and Sepulchra. What will they make when we put them together?"

"A Framer Gem," Sophia say, "but it must be one like I have never seen." She goes quiet for a moment, and Alan can feel her gathering herself. Her heartlight beats a thin, watery blue.

"There is a story," Sophia continues. "May I tell it? I will try to keep it short."

"Please do tell," Alan says.

"Beginning to end," Stag's Blood adds. "Tell it as it goes. I have it on good authority that we still have 'some way' to walk."

"All right," Sophia says. "When the Framer made the old world, he had a plan. It was a story he told, and he was the center of it. When the old world's story ended, he decided to tell a new one. This one would have no center. In this new world, he would always be on the outside. This much is taught as truth, but the rest is heresy.

"At first, the Framer was happy with his decision, but he grew restless. He was accustomed to being omniscient, and not knowing how his new story was going to unfold upset him deeply. He made the Framer Gems so he could look all around the world, but they were not enough - he had been a god, and now he was just a watcher. So he made a mirror that could see through all the Framer Gems at once. The Framer's Mirror showed him everything he wanted to see, but it also showed him horrors. He became afraid of it, and he shattered it.

"Our Mothers would not accept it, but I am wondering now if this Nergal we found might be a fragment of the Framer's Mirror. If it is, I can see why Toven would think it worth Welkinbright's fall. If it is not, then it is some other great thing - one of many I know

85

nothing about. The Framer's story is vast and beautiful, and it constantly surprises me."

"It's a tale all right," Stag's Blood says after a pause to mull Sophia's story over. "In the absence of another one, we might as well believe it."

"I am afraid that is not a reason to believe anything," Sophia chides. She slips from Alan's shoulder to fly in a circle around his head, as if stretching her wings. "It is a possibility to consider, nothing more. Something worth looking at."

"I would thank the Framer Toven didn't find it," Alan says, "but I'm not sure if that's going to turn out to be a good thing for Welkinbright."

"Trust the Framer to ensure that it shall be," Sophia chimes. "The road to Cheel Gar lies ahead, whether you choose to do so or not."

They walk the rest of the way in weary silence. Alan thinks of his parents' wake and the empty sympathy of strangers. In hindsight, everything Toven did had seemed practiced. He was like a mourner playing the misery game, and Alan should have seen through it, but he didn't. He feels blind and stupid and small - every bit as distant from this world as he'd always been from his own. Then the dead begin to groan in his head, the bloom of Minos peels open, and magic kicks up within him like a storm. His heart swells, and he remembers that he isn't himself anymore.

I have power, he thinks. *And I have the first piece of whatever Toven wants. I'm not on the outside of the story. I'm smack in the center.*

The passage turns and levels out, and Alan can suddenly feel the wind. The ceiling drops and the walls close in until Alan and company have to follow Enlil in single-file. After another turn, the passage ends in a wide opening onto a broad shelf of rock. High overhead are the undersides of Welkinbright's alabaster streets. The cloud sea stretches out from the lip of the ledge into the dawning distance. Enlil stands at the brink and looks out across the dark.

"Wait," the sky-king says. Then it raises its head and lets out a long, ringing wail.

The ledge shakes. Brattle starts awake and slides to his feet from Stag's Blood's back.

"What's goin on?" he grumbles, his hand on the small of his back. "Are we out already? What are we doing now?"

"Quiet," Stag's Blood whispers. "We're waiting."

"How's your back?" Alan starts to ask, but Stag's Blood shushes him.

After a minute, there is an answering cry from very far away. Then all is silent. Alan stares into the sky as the dawn is growing, drawing huge shadows across the sea of clouds. Sophia sits in Stag's Blood's mane, her heartlight all but out. Finally, the clouds open and three white birds emerge. They heft themselves up on enormous wings, talons swinging under their robust bodies, and tails fanned out into the wind. A smaller shape appears behind them, and they part to let it pass.

"Gloombirds come," Enlil says. "Watch."

"That ain't all, Lily," Brattle says, squinting into the distance. "That's an old friend with 'em. What skin's the Venue got in this game?"

Enlil doesn't reply. Alan watches the four birds approach with a lump growing in his throat. The vulture flaps to a clumsy landing, and the other birds wing in quietly behind it. They are white owls with huge eyes as green as glass. Alan and Stag's Blood step back from the beating wings, but Brattle stands his ground. He frowns hard at them, his hand on the hilt of his knife.

"The man who lives," croaks the vulture, bobbing its wattled head. "I see you have lost your face again. Pity after all the work we did. The birds took you, did they? I suppose they take all in the end. Yes. The birds take everyone eventually. But we're well met again, whatever the circumstances."

"Atratus," Alan says. "You're a long way from home."

Atratus looks around at the others, lingering longest on Enlil. Then it clacks its beak and fans its wings.

"Speak for yourself," says the vulture. "All is my home. The Venue is everywhere."

"You haven't been," Stag's Blood says. "Have you seen what's happening in Welkinbright? Have you seen what Toven and Winter White are doing?"

Atratus bobs its head and hisses at Stag's Blood. The sound comes rattling out of its throat like a curse, accompanied by a small shower of yellow spit.

"What the Geier Venue does is greater, saddlecat," Atratus says. "What we answer to is more and older. What we see and what we do are not your things."

"And what are you here to do?" Brattle asks. "Drop us, maybe?"

At this, Atratus clucks a laugh and hops around in a circle beating its wings. The owls glower at it, still as statues. Alan continues to back away from them.

"Listen," Enlil says.

"Thank you, Your Serene Highness," Atratus coughs. "You have found it then? Valravn won't carry it, you know. Only Gloombirds, as they brought it. But only so far. Those are the rules. They won't bear it for long. It's too great a weight."

"I don't know what you're talking about." Alan says. "We don't have anything."

"Of course not," Atratus says, laughing again. "The owls will fly you to their roost. That is their job. The Venue keeps them to it, and I am the Venue."

"Absolutely not," Stag's Blood growls. "I don't know where these Gloombirds roost, but I'm certain that it isn't anywhere we want to go. We have things to do. We'd prefer to be returned to the Barrowvale, where we left our ship. We demand it, actually. I'm done being lead around."

Atratus looks at the group, searching their faces. Alan can't do much about his, but he tries to look resolute anyway. The vulture's ember eyes smolder. Finally, it turns to Enlil, but the sky-king says nothing. Alan wonders what passes between them.

"Give us something," Atratus says. It rocks on its heels, puffing its feathers out and opening its wings to make itself look huge. "The Venue does not overextend its authority for nothing."

"We have something," Alan says. "We have a special light I think you'll like. Show him, Sister."

Sophia doesn't ask for clarification. She rises from Stag's Blood's mane and shines her heartlight as bright as she can. The Eternal Flame flares up in her, brightening the whole sky. Atratus shields its eyes with its wings and squawks in disbelief.

"Thieves!" it shouts as Sophia lets the light die down. "We *should* drop you! But we need the Empyrean Fire in Kur right now - more than ever before. You are thieves, but you have stolen a treasure that the Venue wants. Yes, we will break our promises for that."

"I thought you might," Alan says. He allows himself a chuckle. "But you get nothing until we get where we need to go. Understood?"

Atratus bobs its head slowly. Its face remains still as stone. It blinks dim eyes and clucks.

"The Venue is proud of you, Alan," says the vulture. "You have grown into yourself, but there is still a whole world in front of you."

"You'll take us to the Barrowvale," Brattle says.

"Down to the graves, yes," Atratus replies. "All the way."

Sophia goes to stand at the brink, looking down into the roiling sky. The wind plucks at her, nearly lifting her off her feet.

"There are no cages this time," she says, hunkering down and flattening her wings around herself.

"No, but you needn't worry," Atratus clucks. "I've seen the owls carve out horses' hearts to swallow them intact. It's delicate work. They are quite careful and precise when they want to be."

With this, Atratus turns to Enlil. The vulture nods two bows and fluffs up its wings. Dawn has reached its clouded eyes early. There is a hungry, pink light moving across its narrow face. The wind whipping over the edge of the rock tugs feathers from its neck ruff to dance them over its bald head.

"You've emerged at last, like the worm you were," Atratus says. "Drawn maybe from the dying flesh of this sphere by the vague fear that it might wake up and come around. A survivor. I won't ask where you've been; there is much work now. Will the Venue see you in Charnea?"

Enlil stands as still as a column. Its face might be carved in white marble. Alan waits for it to reply with his shoulders tense. He searches its spirit and sees only his own reflection in it. Its life is not a life, and it is outside the scope of death's purpose. Enlil might have been a thanoturge once - Alan senses that Bleeding spark within it - but it has no such power anymore. It is actually beyond such power's simple trappings. In a way, Alan realizes, Enlil *is* thanoturgy.

"Very well," Atratus coughs. "We are on our way." The vulture hops toward the edge and turns to Alan and company. "Just relax. That's the best way."

The Gloombirds spread their wings. The plumes beneath them are black, as if flecked with bone char. Dust whirls up around them as they begin to flap, and they score the rock with their blood-dark claws. Waving sheets of red and green light blow up to circle them and spin off their backs in tatters. The first dives toward Alan and scoops him up, closing its huge toes around him. It's fast as fire, and Sophia barely has time to sneak into Alan's sleeve before it plunges away into the wind.

Alan watches Welkinbright rise into the dawning sky. Light worries over the city a like new widow. Morning peeks pink across the highest towers, tinting the last fading banners of smoke as they disappear.

"Do you remember your sphere?" Sophia asks as they fall into the sea of clouds. "The last sunrise you saw?"

"It was red," Alan replies. "And cold. And far away."

"Today's will be better," Sophia says, warm against his palm. "For all of us."

The journey down from Welkinbright is fast and rough. The Gloombirds alternate between stiff-winged spirals and meteoric plummets. Alan twists against his bird's ropy grip, but he can't turn to see the others. He can only look down at the dark, racing blur of the land beneath a film of clouds.

Morning warms in the east and the last cloud veils blow apart. The bird settles into a level cruise over rocky, treeless wastes. Bare hills rise up in the east like ghouls' knuckles, their tops scattered with cairns. Trees reappear around a strange, domed building topped with black flags. Looking at it makes Alan's stomach drop.

"What is that?" Alan asks Sophia, who risks a peek from the sleeve of his robe. She goes ice cold when she sees the dome.

"I do not know," she says. "Much of Midion is ruined. These lands were touched by a great darkness, and there are places in which one can still fill the chill of its caress."

A green lake shines at the tips of sandy fingers. Dunes rear beyond it, shedding streamers of sand over the curves of their shoulders. For a moment, Alan thinks he sees a troupe of red-robed beanies in the pit of a dune. He wonders if they could be the same ones he saw in the Depot. Then the bird turns west toward a wall of mountains and the desert disappears.

"Do you know the mourners?" Alan asks, "human spirits driven insane by the passage into Graveworld?"

"Do you wonder if you might be one?" Sophia replies.

The Tower of Alms appears on the horizon. The mountains begin their slow climb down toward blue-lit woods that Alan recognizes. He can see the Barrowvale in the distance with huge pieces of Welkinbright looming out of it.

"Sometimes," he says.

"Then you are not."

"I wonder if my parents might be. Or Allison."

Wrapped in claws and hurtling out of the sky, it's hard to concentrate on a conversation. Even were he not so distracted and uncomfortable, this admission would leave him in no less pain. He would wince from the ache in his chest if he could. There's a knot of air in his throat like he's swallowed a swollen cloud.

"When you come to that door, you shall open it," Sophia says. "Then, you may worry or be afraid, but not before."

"I don't open doors," Alan says. "I've spent my whole life closing them, putting ghosts at the thresholds, trying to keep the worst parts of the world on the other side. I've been consumed with the task of keeping things contained. That's who I am: the container. The door-locker."

Sophia balls herself up in his palm, clinging to his fingers. He cradles her like a precious fear. The dead voices in his head have become a meaningless din; he hardly listens to them closely anymore.

"Then you be surprised at yourself, if I may say so," Sophia says, her voice on the edge of a laugh. "You have coped. You have been the opener of the way."

The Gloombird turns into its final descent with the other birds hooting above it. Atratus circles nearby, tipping its wings with the rising wind. Alan tracks its fall toward the forest canopy until it vanishes. The owls follow slowly, complaining, and they set down one at a time on a bald knob of rock jutting up from the woods.

Alan stands looking west and stretches the ache from his arms and legs. A warm breeze mutters over the rock, tugging at his robe. Red is bursting out in bands across the trees. Crows move through the canopy in a large flock, cawing across the woods to each other. They circle past the towering ruins a few times, as if inspecting them. Alan can see the Tongue below, surrounded by little waving flames of russet. There is no one on it, and no sign remains of the sylph encampment there.

The owls rise away, and Alan turns to watch them. They shine in the light like ghosts, nearly translucent. As they ascend, the sky swallows them, leaving only sparkling green trails.

Sophia emerges from Alan's robe and shakes herself in the air. "Who are you that the Framer sends such things to your aid?" she says. "All his hope is on you, Alan. You must feel it."

"I'm just the guy who empties the garbage cans," Alan replies, a squeezing weight settling on his chest. "I hope that'll be enough."

Stag's Blood comes slinking up the hill, clearly stiff, and grumbling like the wind in the leaves. Brattle sprawls coughing where his bird left him. Alan goes to help him up, and Atratus hops over to laugh.

"Shall the birds fly you lower, dead-eater?" the vulture cackles, flapping to stir a little funnel of dust. "You've had a real taste of death, now. What do you think?"

"You are cruel," Sophia says, ringing with anger.

Stag's Blood coils down and crosses the rock in a bound. He gives Atratus a swat across the beak that sends the vulture flapping backward, a hiss rattling in its throat.

"If you aren't going to help," he growls, settling coolly over his haunches, "then shut up."

Brattle takes Alan's hand and hauls himself up laughing. He clutches his side as he finds his balance.

"Bitter as ever, Trattie," he croaks.

Atratus folds its wings and collects itself. In a moment, it is regal again. It walks a circle, bobbing its head, measuring every awkward step.

"What are you still doing with this swamp ghast?" it asks. "Did I not warn you?"

"You did," Alan says, "and we might all be dead if I hadn't ignored you."

"I'd like to know what you meant that Al shouldn't trust me," Brattle says. "Care to clear the air once and for all? It can only help.
"

Atratus clucks, seeming to ponder this. Alan wonders what it's really thinking about. Little motes of green and black move over its head and neck. Its eyes are unreadable. It squats over its feet and takes a deep breath.

"Do you think the Venue is petty?" it asks. "Do not take us for simple, bog-country bigots. You're a fool to think that the crude matter of my form is all that I am.

"Tell the rabbit why he must not eat the bull nettle. Tell him why he will die - how the poison moves in his blood. He will not understand. He can only know that the nettle is death - and then, perhaps, only by eating it. Perhaps not even then."

"I shalln't explain myself. I am prohibited from doing so. There are laws, you know. But I continue to urge caution."

"There's no one to hear you," Stag's Blood says. "Surely it won't shake the sky loose to give a plain answer."

The vulture clacks its beak. "It stays as it is. Keep your bad company."

"We cannot," Sophia says, "as you will soon be leaving."

Atratus nods and flaps its wings, amused. "Where now, then?" it asks, turning to Stag's Blood. "I see no ship. I see no one."

"We'll find our way," Alan says. He kneels and extends a hand to the vulture. "I'm sorry. I want you to know we mean no disrespect. I know you've been helping us."

"You don't," Aratus says, turning up its beak. "If you do, then we have failed. There are deeper things stirring than you can feel, Alan - forces that can only be challenged beyond the physical. What you do, we do ten times - maybe twenty. Make no enemy of the Venue. You have your share already."

"Trust me," Alan replies.

Atratus preens some fluff from beneath its wing. Alan thinks of Faro fighting with Gamley's feather.

"The Venue does not trust," says the vulture. It nods to Brattle. "But, for what it is worth in this dim sphere, you have our respect."

94

"Pardon my doubts, Trattie," Brattle says, "but I know what you think of ghouls. Your help without your scorn is worth more."

"Maybe one day," Atratus glowers. Its eyes flash like ball lightning. "But I doubt it. Now pay us our prize and I will return. There are dark deeds to do."

"How will you carry the Flame?" Sophia asks. She pumps her heartlight up until she is beaming. The day seems to dim before her.

"Inside," Atratus replies. "I will carry its spirit. Come here, Fetchlight."

Sophia flies in a circle, hesitant to approach. Brattle puts the blade of his broad palm against his forehead to shield his eyes from her light. Stag's Blood squints, fighting the desire to look away. The glow of the Flame dances across his face, aging him.

"Be not afraid," Atratus says. It cranes its neck and opens its beak an inch from Sophia, its purple tongue wriggling.

Three streams of sparks emerge from Sophia's heartlight. They twist around each other, forming a single strand of incredible brightness. Air sears to smoke around it. The strand flows out honey-slow, and Atratus sucks it into its mouth. The vulture gurgles as its throat swells with a squirming mass. Then it beats its wings, and the light is gone. Sophia dims and drifts back to land on Brattle's shoulder.

"Exquisite," Atratus tries to say. Its voice bubbles as if it is trying to hold water in its mouth. It swallows again and bobs its head. Relieved, it continues in its usual dusty squawk. "Rare as I imagined. The Venue thanks you."

The vulture turns to leave. It takes two short hops, spreads its wings, and flaps frantically. The wind scoops it up and sends it kiting over, wings in a V. It tilts into an unsteady circle, and Alan hears it calling down to them as it banks away.

"We are the children of the monstrous dark," Atratus cries. "We are storm winds on the edge of death. The light of the draug is failing."

They spend the rest of the day on the Tongue. The climb down leaves Brattle exhausted, and he sleeps on the bare rock until after midnight. In the meantime, and for hours, Alan sits over Brattle in deep concentration, searching through magic for wounds. To Alan's surprise, there is nothing in the flesh.

"It's spiritual," Alan tells Stag's Blood and Sophia as the suns are setting, "like there's a tether loose. His soul is rattling in his body. I'm not sure how to fix it. It's beyond me."

"Maybe it does not need fixing," Sophia suggests.

"Maybe," Alan replies. "I don't know what the long-term effects might be."

As night falls, Stag's Blood goes out to hunt. When he returns to the Tongue dragging a golden antelope, Alan is sitting on the round edge of the rock swinging his feet. Stag's Blood drops the carcass near Alan's bone fire and then steps out onto the ledge himself. There's another glow in the Barrowvale besides the fairy candles: sylves are leaving the forest in battalions under white lanterns. Watching them, Alan thinks of the mobs in Welkinbright and the fire in the bell tower.

"Lost in thought?" Stag's Blood asks, spreading himself out across the Tongue with his front paws crossed.

"Not lost," Alan says. "I needed a break. It's been a long day."

Stag's Blood blinks heavily and nods like a bloom in the wind. "You never speak of your home," he says. "You nevers say anything about the woods or the sky or the smell of the air. You never sing old human songs. Why? Do you not remember?"

Alan crosses his arms and leans forward, as if staving off a stomachache. "This is my home now," he says.

"I mean your former home," Stag's Blood says. Alan doesn't need to be looking at him to hear the exasperation in the cat's voice - he can practically hear Stag's Blood's eyes rolling. "It's as though you don't miss it."

"I never lived there," Alan replies after a moment's pained contemplation. "Do you ever get the feeling that you're only really yourself in dreams or memories - like the one special place where you belong doesn't actually exist?"

"Never," says Stag's Blood. "I have always been here, me, now. I make my dreams. They do not make me."

Alan searches himself for something to haul into the light, but his memories of his life before Graveworld are stuck fast in healing shadow. He looks down, but the trees don't know who he used to be. All he sees below are little moving lights.

"I didn't listen to what I heard. I didn't see what I watched," Alan says. "I remember how beautiful the sunsets were. I remember feeling the age of the sky, loving its immensity above us. It dwarfed all our little cares, stretching over the whole world, oblivious to us. The parts I loved most where the things that made me feel small. Human things always felt cold. They're nothing to reminisce about it. I didn't connect with my life there."

"That was mostly your choice," Stag's Blood says. "Investment means loss, and you didn't want to deal with loss, so you didn't invest."

"I was a coward," Alan says.

"No. You were a victim."

Alan isn't sure what to think about this description of himself. It feels just as wrong as it does right.

"Whatever I was, I'm not that now," he says. "I'm doing something. I'm investing. This is what I want to remember - nothing else."

Stag's Blood gestures toward Brattle with a swing of his head. "How is he?"

"Hurt, but it could have been much worse, all things considered. Sister Sophia is praying over him now." Alan looks up at the moon rising cold as lead in a veil of snow clouds. "He's not in the draug. He's not even close, which is good, but there's something else. I can feel it, but I can't approach it, and the books haven't been any help."

"At least you haven't lost them," Stag's Blood says.

Alan chuckles. "More weird luck."

Stag's Blood puts his heavy head on his paws and look straight down from the ledge. His ears swivel as if he's listening intently for something. He thumps the ground with pensive taps of his tail. Alan wonders what he can see there.

"Tell me about the draug," says the cat. "Atratus said that it's light is failing. What does that mean?"

"I don't know," Alan says. "When I see it, it's a ribbon of white light through this endless darkness. There's a dead side and a living side, and bad things happen to souls that get trapped at the borders. If the light were to go out, I imagine things would get pretty crazy."

"Can you see it now?" Stag's Blood asks, still looking straight down. Blue fire dances in his eyes. His whiskers shine like needles in the moonlight, erect and trembling. Back legs tight, he is a mangonel ready to fire.

"In a way," Alan says. "It's everywhere - under or behind almost every living thing. I can feel it like a wind in a flat place, always blowing, surrounding me, but I don't exactly see it the way I see you. The draug and the darkness are just symbols, I think. I thought that I was creating them to make sense of what I was experiencing, but it sounds like Atratus sees the same things I do."

"It creates itself in you. You're connected to it - a controller."

Alan feels his magic reaching out into the Barrowvale of its own accord. The dead answer softly.

"I don't know if I'd say that exactly," Alan says.

Stag's Blood finally looks up. "No?" he asks. "What then?"

"I'm as stuck in the web as anyone is," Alan replies. "I just might feel the individual strands a little more distinctly. I feel the plucking at them, but power over death is an illusion - another symbol we make to help us cope."

"Power in death but not over it," Stag's Blood says, nodding. "I'd say power is power."

As the sylves start to sing in the woods below, Stag's Blood retires. He curls himself around Brattle and the corpse of the golden antelope, and Sophia tries to cover them with Brattle's shroud. Alan reads until the fire dies to embers. Then he walks south into the woods, trying to catch the sylvan song more clearly. It is a high, quiet song, and the melody drifts through the trees like a streamer of smoke. Alan watches the gray processions through the eyes of the dead and wonders how the battle for Welkinbright is going. There are new flags flying triumphantly from several of the largest pieces of ruin in the forest, and this gives him some hope.

At the brink of dawn, as he is heading back to the Tongue with Pwysh's Grimoire in the crook of his arm, Alan feels a shiver in the forest. He stops for a moment, expecting a sylph to step out onto the path. The trees wave, whispering to one another like conspirators. Shadows shrink away from him, but nothing emerges.

"It's a rat in the bushes," he says aloud as he continues up the path. His deadsight shows him a pair of eyes like twin red stars glaring from beneath a cloak of unnatural darkness. "The dark is getting to me."

When he reaches the Tongue, morning is breaking gold and pink over the peaks to the east. Brattle is up and knuckling about, getting a feel for his returning strength. The golden antelope is carved open, and half of it hanging black from a spit above the remains of a new fire.

"I dreamed I was in my old bed," Brattle explains, "sleeping under a ton of hot, purring blankets."

"Nothing heals like a cat's weight," Stag's Blood says, smiling. "I remember my father purring me to sleep. The sound is a curing spell, you know. It is as close as you will ever come to hearing the world turning."

"I'm glad you're feeling better today," Alan says. "I'd like to get going as soon as we can."

"To find the Mercy Gale as we left her," Sophia says, "by the Framer's will." She settles on Alan's palm. The light of the Eternal Flame is still inside her, but she is trying to suppress it. "I do not like what this place has become. My new light is casting strange and dangerous shadows."

"I know just what you mean," Alan says.

"Let's light out then," Brattle says. He finishes stuffing the last of the cooked antelope into his haversack and swings it easily over his shoulder. He doesn't wince or pant, but there is something different about him. His shadow is fainter than it used to be. "Ain't gonna get more ready than now, given the circumstances. On to better tragedies."

Thirty-Three

They put dawn at their backs and descend into the Barrowvale as the woods are waking. Light floods the silver forest, leaving all in long, dreamy shadows. The warm air softens, and a weight settles into it. Alan feels draped in rich substance. He pushes through empty space like down. The canopy seems to press down on him, a new atmosphere, and he sinks into his work shoes beneath it.

"The Sky-King's welcome," Sophia whispers. The woods have become so still that any sound seems like sacrilege. Even the old kings are silent. "You can feel the life of the old world in this sunrise."

A watching presence follows them through the morning glory. It stays far away and it makes no sound, but Alan tracks it through his deadsight. The living darkness it wears cannot hide its rose-bright eyes. The watcher finally stops following when they reach a hooded glen, but it leaves a mark that persists until they step out of the woods into the banishing sun.

On the southwest edge of the forest, they find the Mercy Gale. She has new cladding on her hull. There are sylves standing all around her on her port side, and her legs are gone. Her truncated mast has been removed as well, and a new mast of silver wood stands toward her bow. A moon-white sail flaps huge against it, straining under gold battens. The ship is sitting upright above the scrub grass at the edge of the woods, just barely bobbing, her keel holding steady a foot or so over her shadow.

"What's this?" Brattle snarls.

As they approach, a sylph steps from the group to greet them. It's the tall one of the pair that took them to meet Kelen as prisoners. He wears harder lines on his face than before, and his robe is patched dark with dirt and sweat. There may even be a little blood on the hem. He presses his hands together in the same finger-gun gesture Faro made while praying in the Tower of Alms. How long ago did that happen? Alan feels like it must have been years.

"Captain Alan," says the sylph, his smile slipping, "and associates. Honored friends. I hadn't expected you back so soon. Our scouts were waiting for you at the tower, but you must have come a different way. We had hoped to have her painted before you returned." He turns to indicate the Mercy Gale. "No captain of Welkinbright should be made to crawl over the ground like a roach. We have improved your ship. May she bear you to new victories."

Alan wades into the shifting crowd of white-flamed heads. They stand well back as he passes them, their moon-eyes bright. They are tired, and their spirit is broken, but they have hope. It sits differently on each of them, dispersing its weight to spare the weakest. The tall sylph is one of them.

There are two pairs of discs astride the keel, fore and aft. They glow cornsilk blue behind cascading curtains of white. The air around them wavers as if distorted by heat, but they are freezing cold to the touch. Alan stands beneath the ship and reaches up to run his fingers along her keel. Her new fittings are clearly chunks of stone pulled from the Welkinbright rubble. They have Kelen's living energy in them - Alan can feel him shining, lifting the Mercy Gale above the grass. These stones must have started to come to life when Kelen gave up his spirit.

"You build fast," he says. "She yielded to you?"

The tall sylph shifts in his thin hide boots. "Hope is a powerful magic."

Bratle sneers. "You'd have killed us before. Now we're 'honored friends'. Allies of opportunity, I say - surrogates for the mercy of them you gave up or gave up on. Did you have someone inside? How'd word come down?"

The tall sylph looks pained for a moment. A shadow flashes across his face, the flame on his head gutters, and then he steadies himself. Alan wonders where the shorter sylph is. "In crows' beaks," he said. "We were listening closely."

Brattle narrows his eyes. Seeing that he is about to keep pressing, Alan says, "Your debts are paid down here. Welkinbright needs you now. Go with our best hopes."

102

"Your deeds are far beyond our gratitude," says the sylph. "The light of our thanks will not reach you for a million years."

"Thank Faro when the battle for your city is won," Stag's Blood says.

Brattle balls up his fists, but he doesn't say anything else. The sylphs depart in single file, bowing to Alan as they enter the woods. Crows leave with them, rattling from the trees one by one. When the raucous flock is gone and the sylvan torches' light is far away, Alan turns to Brattle.

"You were going to let him have it, huh?" he asks.

Brattle sniffs and spits. "They split from Kelen before. If they'd have trusted him like he trusted us, he might not be dead."

"Would you have given *your* soul for Welkinbright, then?" Alan says, crossing his arms. "You're not really mad at them after they did us a favor. You're a hero to them."

"They don't know nothin'," Brattle replies, "and they wouldn't believe it if I told. You don't see the black in their eyes when they look at me. I'm a bogworm - a lower animal. I can only be a hero in spite of my lowness, my crude make. No amount of fight or sacrifice will prove that I'm a real thing to them. Maybe it ain't right - cause they did try and make up for doubting - but I can only answer their lowerin' by getting' low."

Alan sinks to one knee to look Brattle in the eye. His joints scream in protest. Brattle looks at him as if he's never heard of embarrassment. A wolfish anger burns on his face, dark as the noonday sun behind a cloud of crows.

"Brattle," Alan says. "You're right. I'm sorry I didn't stick up for you when they were putting you down before. I didn't even think to. It's unconscionable, but I hope you'll forgive me. I shouldn't allow it."

Brattle's expression doesn't soften a bit. "Ain't your charge to change their minds. I don't blame you." He looks up at the Mercy Gale, and some of the light returns to his eyes. "It's a damn nice job they did on her, though. I'll give them that. Let's be done and go, right? Cheel Gar ain't waitin."

Alan looks to Stag's Blood and Sophia. The Fetchlight lands on Brattle's shoulder and whispers in his ear, bringing a smile to his face. Stag's Blood only nods.

"How far is it," he purrs, "and what shall we find there?"

"My Sisters," Sophia says, "and a warm welcome among allies."

Alan turns toward the Mercy Gale, and the others follow. The sylves have left her gangplank down. She is asleep, but he can feel her mind racing. His hands tremble at the thought of stirring her awake.

"That sounds all right to me," Alan says as he ascends toward the Gale's main deck. Brattle climbs onto Stag's Blood's back, and Sophia lights on the gunwale, waiting for them. "We deserve as much after all we've been through."

The deck of the Mercy Gale feels like home. Alan stands at the bow, wraiths shimmering around him, as she turns east under her own new power. A wind swings over the woods to fill the sail, and Alan holds fast to the gunwale as the ship rocks forward. She springs out across the fields, slipping easily over streams and cairns. The blue sky is frayed nearly to splitting, but it's clear and it goes on forever. Alan thinks of the skies over Paloma with their sentinel lights and drooping girdles of telephone wires. He isn't sure whether he misses them or not. They aren't too far away.

As the fields roll down into a rocky river basin, Alan returns to the orlop deck to sit in the warmth of the Gale's heart. He finds Brattle there alone, crouching in the shadow of a beam. If not for the lantern glow of his eyes, Alan wouldn't have seen him at all.

"Where's Stags and Sophie?" Alan asks, crossing the deck and putting his hands on the gem in the Mercy Gale's engine. They eyestone is almost too hot to touch for long. It's pushing strange new energy.

"In the captain's cabin," Brattle says. "You ain't even looked in it. Figured they'd stop and drag you along."

"It hadn't occurred to me," Alan says.

"Ain't you starting to feel like the captain yet?"

"I don't do much captaining," Alan replies. "I guess I feel more like a passenger."

"There's your problem right there," Brattle laughs. "Your whole life in eight words. You ain't the captain of your own ship. Who is?"

"The wraiths," Alan says.

Brattle corrects him. "Ghosts. But they answer to you. You gotta take the ship by the big wheel. Hop up to that cabin and have a look at what's yours."

Alan stands with his hands on the eyestone for another minute. He searches the glassy surface for an image of himself dressed as a Portuguese pirate captain, but all he can see is his fleshless face in murky darkness. His hands are thin. His nails have started to taper into points, the skin receding from his cuticles.

"I think I will," Alan says, stepping away. "Why don't you come with me? Do you feel up to it?"

Brattle closes his eyes and disappears for a moment. "I feel fine, bony," he says. "A little worse for wear, but that's hardly a surprise. I just need a bit of a rest before we get to Cheel Gar. Gimme a minute."

"I imagine the stoic thing must get tiring," Alan says. "I know it does for me."

Brattle sighs. His eyes creep open, dimmer than before.

"I'd have cuffed you for that once, I think," he says. "I guess I ain't got that in me now. That's likely part of the problem - a symptom of it. I never felt the weight of my own life. Now I do. I saw that black. There's no shaking free."

"You came out again," Alan offers.

"I suppose I did." Brattle emerges from the shadows. His face is pulled gaunt, and his skin is pale as ash in places. "What did *you* see?"

The Gale glides on in silence under the threadbare sky. Her heart pumps warmth, filling the orlop deck from floor to ceiling. Alan pushes his hands into the pockets of his sleeves.

"Light," he says. "Bright lights bearing down on me. Headlights."

"The draug," Brattle says. "You remember going through it."

Alan stumbles over this for a moment before replying. He remembers the chief of the dradtails saying: *Always something to bring back from the brink of death.*

"I didn't die," he finally says. "I woke up here, alive."

"But you changed and you kept changin'."

"How do you feel yourself changing?"

Brattle folds himself onto the floor like a blossom. Closing his eyes again, he seems to be meditating.

"Slowly," he says. "If at all."

"Are you going to come up," Alan asks, "or do you want to sit down here for a while?"

He searches Brattle quietly, reaching out through his magic, but he can't find anything. Brattle's spirit is tired, but it's not injured. It's still his. Alan tries to feel comforted.

Brattle takes a few long breaths. Color comes over him like a flame, and he pushes himself to his feet.

"No," he says. "Let's go. I'm fine."

With Brattle following, Alan slips back up the companionway to the main deck. He finds Sophia sitting at the richly decorated edge of the quarterdeck while Stag's Blood is standing on his hind legs, trying to push the door to the captain's cabin closed.

"Brother Alan," Sophia says. "There are clouds piling ahead. The sky-king is moving. We will soon pass through the wall of his rain."

"Your quarters are drab," Stag's Blood adds leaving the door ajar as he steps away. "You've missed nothing forgetting them. We were about to head down, as the storm is coming faster than we're heading toward it."

"We want to see," Alan says. "Do you mind? It's clear for now. We should enjoy it as long as we can."

"Conservator?" Sophia begins. She flits down from her perch, and Brattle waves her away.

"Time yet to settle in for a storm," he says.

With Brattle's help, Alan pulls the heavy door open again. It is solid brass pressed with gold leaf, and Pwysh's triskelion seal is hammered into the center of it. Dog-headed figures dance around it, some holding spears. Beyond it, the captain's cabin is cold and sparse. Faded squares mark the bare, black boards where shelves and chests of drawers must have stood. There are more dogmen on the huge oak desk, hunting across the filigree. The one chair is turned to face the bank of large, angled windows. Alan traces a line with his finger through the dust on top of the desk.

"Cleaned out," he says. "Toven said she went missing."

"You don't believe *him*," Stag's Blood says.

"No, but I wonder what the real story is."

A brief search of the desk reveals a hidden compartment full of dust. Alan turns and looks out the windows. There are no storms visible from the stern of the ship - the sky is clear and perfect. The Gale's shadow races along behind her. The Barrowvale is just a blue-green line on the horizon.

"It ain't a bad view," Brattle says, standing up to his full height and pressing his forehead against the glass. "What could Toven've seen out these windows when he scuttled her? Was it dark? Were there storms or fires?"

"I don't suppose we'll ever know," Sophia says. She walks across the desk, taking long steps like a ballerina, leaving little swirls in the dust. "May we put better sights behind us than he did, if the Framer is willing."

Stag's Blood noses around the corners, tail twitching behind him. In a long, starboard shadow, he finds something small and bright. He taps it across the floor in Alan's direction.

"A gem?" he says.

Alan stoops to pick up the object. A dart of pain shoots through his lower back, and he has to brace himself on the table to stand up again.

"A bead," Alan replies. "Turquoise - like we saw the dradtails wearing."

"Wasps," Sophia says, circling over to land on Alan's palm and inspect the bead. "They do not like us. I have never met one."

"They don't like Winter White too much either," Brattle says. "I can't imagine they think too much of Toven."

"They were closing all their walls," Alan says. "They said that something was happening in the west didn't they? Something was drawing their attention. What's west of the Colonies?"

"Everywhere we gotta go," Brattle replies. "Cheel Gar and Sepulchra. Northwest, anyways."

"And further on?" Stag's Blood asks. "Beyond Sepulchra?"

"Ossua and the Green Sea," Brattle replies. He tilts his head and puts his hand to his chin. His dim reflection in the window seems to hesitate to imitate him. Alan stares at the glass, not seeing the gem-bright day beyond it. Brattle's reflection looks back emptily, meeting Brattle's contemplative gaze.

"Meadowshore," Brattle continues. "Lichlock."

"What's that?" Alan asks. He pats his sides pointlessly. His map is in his knapsack on the quarterdeck.

Brattle's reply rolls out of his chest like a wave blown up from the open sea. He breathes fog onto the window, leaving his mischievous reflection blind. "The ruin of a fortress, small and with red towers, and surrounded by marigolds. A place that casts strange shadows. Ghouls lived there for a long time, but not anymore. Somethin' happened there, and now we don't go near it. "

"A good hiding place," Stag's Blood says. "Winter White could be attacking the Colonies from Lichlock. If so, we're heading straight toward her."

"The Necropolis will be there," Sophia gasp. Her wings thrum, and her heartlight swells a starry white. "And all my Sisters who disappeared with it.

"You phone-thing with Nudd's numbers in it," Brattle adds. "And maybe even Nettle's body - we still don't know what she did with him."

"We don't know that yet," Alan says, "but it's a good hunch, and it's worth investigating."

He closes his hand around the bead and Sophia takes flight to circle his head. Thunder snarls nearby, wild and huge, and the light in the windows goes dim. Rain begins to fall, tapping a careful rhythm on the main deck. Alan listens to the sound they way he would listen to language. The air in the cabin shrinks, and darkness deepens in the corners.

"Let's keep that idea in this cabin for now," Alan says. He takes a long look at the warped boards and the ceiling sagging over the rafters. "We'll put it right on this table. That'll be what this room is for. We'll cross the Lichlock bridge if, and when, we get there."

Rain sheets down all day, and at dusk it turns to snow under a buttermilk sky. Cold worms in through gaps in the Gale's hull, but the gem on the orlop deck is warm. Alan sits with the others in its glow, remembering how the grills at Ray's bled heat. When the suns' light fades from behind the screen of clouds, he slips back up to the weather decks with his trash masher in hand, leaving Brattle and Stag's Blood asleep.

In the captain's cabin, he walks the boards from the door to the bank of windows as slowly as he can. The dark there watches him intently. He reaches out to it, and it recoils. It blows away like heat distortion, tattered and formless, but it clings around him. Nothing he tries can dispel it completely. He stands with his back to the darkling glass and asserts himself, his trash masher glowing blue-white and stirring whorls in the dust around him.

"I'm not afraid," Alan says, but the dark doesn't care. Fear isn't what it wants.

Alan spends the rest of the night in his cabin, swinging his trash masher. It feels a little silly at first. He runs through old forms and combinations he devised when fighting with the masher was just a fantasy born from boredom. Somewhere, two boys are locked in combat with monsters in a summer hayfield. The sun is setting rose-pink, casting the bales in shadow, drawing the war ever closer to its end at dinnertime. Alan wonders who Hannes played with when he moved away. What monsters did he grow up to fight? What sticks or splintering broom handles has he turned to swords? Grief swells in him like a black-scaled storm cloud, and he uses it. When morning comes, he is sore and his hands are calloused, but he has mastered his weapon. He clings to it as he lies beneath the windows, dawn streaming over him, feeling its power.

I'm not afraid, he tells himself, and the watching dark believes him.

The snow continues into the afternoon. Dark flakes blow down on nervous winds, big as moths, and melt on the deck of the Mercy Gale in a wet film. Standing at the prow with his shroud over his mouth, Brattle catches a palmful of snow and swirls the meltwater around with his finger.

"It's mixed with ash," he says.

Stag's Blood is sitting up on his haunches, his front paws over the gunwale. His mane is covered with slick, gray flakes. "Welkinbright will rise," he says "but it must burn first."

The day warms, and the wind dies down. When the clouds thin away and the snow ebbs to flurries, Sophia calls the others to the quarterdeck. At the eyestone, she conducts a small ritual, singing and flying circles around it to wake a light at its core. Alan watches her, admiring her assiduous attention to detail. As the gem warms, he feels himself warming, too. Stray flakes falling on his cloak melt instantly.

"The abbey is mute," Sophia says, settling at last on the curve of the gem. Her heartlight glows glum-pink. "The Framer Gem in Cheel Gar is amaurotic."

110

The eyestone dims blood-red. The Gale groans deep in her guts. There is a faint note of despair in that sound.

"Slim hope for a welcome, then?" Brattle asks wiping snow and ash from his brow.

"We always hope," Sophia replies. Her voice is hollow - like a hot breath into the cup of a candle douter. "But it isn't always easy."

"Toven and Winter White are waiting for us," Stag's Blood says.

Sophia takes flight to land on his shoulder, and he turns his cheek to her.

"Don't worry, Sister," Alan says. "We're ready."

After a long day's journey through wasting sloughs, they reach the shallow border lakes of Kidhia. Here, gray pines slump up a wet hill toward a field of balding hummocks. Snow floats on black saline ponds surrounded by rushes. Curve-billed birds that Brattle calls judgies peck through the mud, flapping idly as they walk to keep from sinking. The Mercy Gale glides easily over the sucking mire, her sail full and her lifting stones casting blue circles beneath her. As night falls, the judgies return to their tree-top roosts and croak out a few short evening songs.

The swamp is dotted with graves. Alone on the poop deck, Alan looks down at the colors dancing through the reeds. The dead here are mostly silent. They are lost in a dark sleep, caged in nightmares, and full of mud. The few he can reach to find awake are broken and mindless. As the moon rises, small groups of spirits appear above the mindless ones' graves. They sway in loose circles, sparks dancing dim above their heads, and then they vanish. Their lights wink out in a line following the Mercy Gale across the moor. Finally, the moon retires and the lakes fall utterly still. Alan returns to the orlop deck to read with Sophia, and, in the morning, the Gale comes to a stop. They have reached the Pfahlwald.

The wraith crewmen bring the Gale as close to the forest wall as they can, and then they stand quivering on the deck while Alan and the others disembark. Black rock hills arise on either side of the forest. Clusters of pointed hoodoos stand sentinel at their feet, cones flecked with silver dust. The wood sprawls through the valley like a dead lover, bone-gray in the dawnlight, with judgies sleeping in its tangled canopy. Alan stands at the verge, staring up at the rows of bony heels swinging above him. Brattle bites his thumb and spits.

"Wow," he croaks in his best judgie voice.

"How many are there?" Stag's Blood asks.

Sophia replies from the crown of his head, her heartlight trembling. "One," she says. "One for each."

The Pfahlwald is a forest of towering, arm-thick stakes. Some are blunt, and some are dark with thick layers of grease. Many have grown broad, leafless branches and white roots that peek out from the dirt at their bases like kneecaps. All are topped with nude, disintegrating bodies of sylves and fairies. There are a few hobs and ghouls swaying in the branches as well, and some of the bodies are kinds of fae that Alan has never seen. He looks at them in cold shock, rooted in place, waiting for a wave of horror to hit.

"That's where we're headed," Brattle says, pointing to the great trees of Cheel Gar rising from the forest in the northeast. They are mercifully close. "Heads down and one foot in front of the other - that's the way to do this. And think of something nice: home by the firepit, coneys slow-roasting, spring coming in and flowers waking in my garden." He nods to himself, his hands trembling. "Don't stop, and don't look up."

Thirty-Four

There is no path through the forest. Thick brambles carpet the ground, their berries rotting. Threadleaf bushes tower together in great clumps, winding into each other, creating cascading walls of foliage. Dawn-red roses grow in great profusion at the bases of the stakes, weeping their petals constantly. Brattle plucks some of their blossoms and eats them as Alan and company struggle north.

"It ain't natural," he says, holding a cough behind a mouthful of rose blooms. "This quiet. It's curse work."

Alan fights the urge to look up. The dead above him are mute as stars. Their silence is maddening. It goes on forever, cold and clouded - an abyss that won't look back.

"I'm surprised you'd bat an eye," Alan replies. "I've seen how you fight."

Brattle chuckles. "Just cause I fight to win under mortal duress don't mean I wanna walk through fields of torture, pasty."

"This is how every death feels to me," Alan says. "One life lost is as great a waste as this."

"Who could live in this?" Stag's Blood wonders. He pads along low to the ground, his ears swiveling constantly, growling at every small sound. "The smell alone is appalling."

"I don't miss that," Alan says. "Not now."

Sophia takes flight from the thick of Stag's Blood's mane. Her heartlight is burning a dim, translucent blue. The color reminds Alan of the ocean, and he feels a sudden pain in his heart watching her flit in and out of the branches ahead of them.

"We stay where we are put," Sophia says. "Cast from Paradise, we build even on the shores of destruction."

"My Da once saw a place like this burned down," Brattle says. "Said it took three months, and the cinders blew in the wind for years afterward. Nothing grows even now where the ash fell. I always took it for a lie."

They continue toward the towering trees as the suns crawl across the sky. Huge shapes move through the forest nearby, calling to answering voices in the hills. The stake-trees creak in a hot wind and the bodies impaled upon them sway. Alan watches his shoes as he kicks through the thorns, but something is pulling on the back of his neck. Questions intrude upon him, divorced from his disgust.

Where are the poles inserted? Where do they come out? Is there blood in the corpses' mouths? Are their dying expressions frozen on their faces?

When he can no longer tolerate the ache growing in his head and shoulders, he looks up at the bodies in the canopy and stops dead in his tracks. The corpse above him is that of a fairy child. Straw-red hair rolls down her shoulders in loose kinks. The soles of her white feet are still rosy. Her eyes are closed, but her mouth is open and her tongue is gone. She blushes beneath a spray of freckles, the tilt of her head almost coy, as if she is playing embarrassed to be so exposed. The rest of her body has been tracked with scars by judgie beaks. Alan reaches out to her, but she's only a dishabited shell. The living color and the firmness of her intact flesh are a cruel trick. Her head cannot be turning - her eyes cannot be opening blue as gems in the firmament. There is no keening wail rising in her dead throat. The only thing alive in her is the curse that keeps her body so ghastly beautiful.

Alan can neither move nor look away. Some gem-blue thing is holding him in place, boring through him like a gimlet. The high, howling cry of the wind shatters his thoughts, confusing him. He feels Brattle pulling on him and Stag's Blood biting his arm, but the sensations mean nothing - they are happening somewhere else. With the last of his strength, Alan tells the curse and the dead girl, *I am not afraid.*

The shriek stops suddenly. The gem-blue lights burn out, leaving little curls of smoke rising from beneath the girl's dusky eyelids. Reality returns with a long, loud sucking sound, and Alan staggers back into Brattle's arms.

114

"Al!" Brattle shouts. "What're you - a moron? What'd you look up there for?"

Alan shakes his head and regains his balance. The wind has stopped. The world shrinks around him, and he returns to himself. There are strangers present. Four jackal-headed hunters stand nearby with bows and sickle-swords. A large basteta wearing a red-winged helmet is with them.

Alan pulls up his hood. "Nothing," he says, but this isn't entirely true. There's a new light in his mind. It is still and small, and it gutters when he reaches for it, but it wants to be noticed. It's the fairy girl's gift, and he will nurture it. "What's going on?"

"Are you right now?" asks the cat with the helmet. Her eyes are striking. They look exactly like Stag's Blood's.

"Better than right," Alan replies. "Are you from Cheel Gar? Are you stopping us?"

The cat makes a face and mulls this over. "I am Mackerel Sky," she says, "the Protectress of Cheel Gar, but I am from Mastaba." She stares at Stag's Blood for a moment, and then goes on. "These Cynopolitan dogs are Cheel Gar bred and will kill you to keep you out, though we hope you'll turn and leave in peace. Cheel Gar is falling. It is unsafe. Whatever you're looking for, it will soon be in the hands of the Coma."

Alan shakes his head. "I'm afraid we can't' do that. What we're doing is very important, and we won't be turned away."

The helmeted cat continues to eye Stag's Blood. A strange rumbling begins deep in her breast, and she starts toward him. Her movements are milk-smooth and sensual. Every twist of her hips is power.

"What are your names," Mackerel Sky asks, "and what is your important business?"

Stag's Blood steps forward, wild as the wind and the fields. He is larger than Mackerel Sky, and he walks taller, but she doesn't cower from him. Alan watches with worry building up in his blood. He reaches back to put a hand on the shaft of his trash masher. The dogmen raise their swords to the ready, and their ears go flat against their low heads.

"My name is Stag's Blood," Stag's Blood says. "Do we know each other? You don't smell familiar."

"Stag's Blood," says Mackerel Sky. The name is like a bleeding heart in her mouth. "You have hardly smelled me. Perhaps if I smelled of the pine trapwoods in Winter White's hunting hills, or of rank kennels and saddle leather, you would know. You're the scion of Fearsome, aren't you? Born into servitude?"

"You won't succeed in picking a fight with me, Protectress," Stag's Blood replies, stiffening and puffing out his chest. "We're your allies. Speak your mind."

Mackerel Sky narrows her eyes and sinks back on her haunches. Dawn slants through the grisly canopy just for her. The suns look down on her, gloating. Green spots shimmer in her plum-black pelt where the light falls across her shoulders. She slouches as if she's afraid she might split her skin up the back.

"For our allies' sakes, we have none anymore," she growls. "White presses us now, certain that we are hiding something of hers. Every day her searchers come, and, when they don't find it, they put up more stakes. What must you do so urgently in Cheel Gar? Will you drive the searchers away? Maybe you have what Winter White is looking for. Shall we have you spill your bags?"

"We don't know anything about that," Alan says, shifting the bag on his shoulder. Nergal is warm against his back. He worries that Mackerel Sky will be able to feel it. "Winter White is none of our concern. We're here to kill Rawbones."

The dogmen look at each other with wide eyes. Mackerel Sky licks her lips and thumps her tail into the leaf litter.

"Suicide, then," she says, shaking her head. A look of deep sadness comes over her. Alan can't meet her gaze for fear that he may disappear into it. "You don't need to come to Cheel Gar for that. Head west until you reach the caves. Wake him where he sleeps - that is the fastest way. Or you may wait here, and he will

116

find you. Die as you like, but stay away from Cheel Gar. There is a war on, you know."

With this, she turns to leave, and a scrim of clouds follows her to blind the suns. Alan feels a presence in the forest watching her, but it winks away as soon as he notices it. The Cynopolitans sniff through the trees, their hackles up and their tails curled tight against their legs. Have they grown accustomed to the constant stench of cursed rot, or are their senses of smell so sharp that they can smell beneath it?

Something cracks nearby. Alan calls after the dogmen, but they pay him no notice as they vanish into the maw of the underbrush.

"The strange remains strange," Sophia says. "Who was that cat? I do believe she knew you, Stag's Blood."

Stag's Blood shakes his head.

"Do you believe her?" Brattle asks.

"I don't know her," Stag's Blood replies, "and I haven't seen nearly enough to believe anything, but I suspect she's mad."

With this, they leave the south gate. In the west, the Pfahlwald grows lean, and snow blows hard in the open spaces. It lays high on frost-faced fairy chimneys and drifts up against the banks of a naked hill where the stake trees thin to groves of gallows. Alan doesn't look long at the bodies hanging there with hooks through their ribs - they are just as horribly empty as the impaled.

"The strange remains strange," Brattle says, pulling his pall tight around him as they cross the groves. "It hurts more to be here with every step."

"Most forests feel like maybe they're sleeping," Alan says. "You walk through them and you feel the quiet, secret life there, breathed out by the trees in their dreams. Not this place. You don't miss that secret life until it's gone. There are no dreams here. There's nothing secret."

"Mind what you wish for," Stag's Blood growls.

The hook groves go on until well past noon. Alan and company finally emerge on the rim of a rocky dell pocked with tent rocks and sinkholes. A sick little stream drains into it, its bed littered with bones and glittering silver. On the opposite bank, the hills rise up in a mud-red wall dotted with cave mouths. Alan watches blue and silver light moving across the cliff face and streaming from the cavern openings. Gold particles blow through it, stirred by an imperceptible wind.

"No recent sign of any well-pisser," Brattle says.

"We'll watch for it," Alan says, "and try and decide what to do when we see it."

"I imagine that killing it isn't what you have in mind," Stag's Blood purrs. "I'm starting to feel unprepared."

Sophia lights on Alan's shoulder. "There is a place for all things," she says. "The Framer's plan will become clear."

"I guess we might as well hope for that," Alan replies. "At the moment, I'm making things up as I go along."

"Why d'ya think they didn't want us in?" Brattle asks. He presses himself very low to the ground and scans the scene, his head on a swivel. "Who do you think White's searchers are?"

Stag's Blood shakes the snow from his face. "Whomever they are, Mackerel Sky thinks sending us away will get them to come after us," he says. "She saw right through us. I could read every twitch of her face. She was open to me in that respect, and we were open to her."

"A second bird," Brattle says, "and we only have the one stone. What do you think, bony?"

Alan lays down on his stomach. There are dead voices here, but they are afraid to speak. He seeks them out, opening himself to them, offering comfort. "It'd be nice to have something come to us for once," he says.

The wind dies down and the snow tapers off. Silence creeps into the forest. Nothing moves for a long time - even the stream seems to stop. In the hush, Alan finds himself capable of prolonged motionlessness. Sinking away from the frail cage of his flesh, he studies the fairy girl's gift in formless thought. It is incomplete - a relic of her spirit's power before she was ripped from the physical and cursed. Inside it, there is no trace of who she was. That part must have gone with her when she left the prison of her mortal pain behind. What remains is a disjointed system of power. Alan is surprised to discover that can read it like a diagram in a grimoire, but he can't make much sense of it in its current form. It's a cipher, and its key is with the dead girl's spirit. Still, it isn't useless. As the first sun starts its long crawl toward the horizon, he feels the gift expanding him. His magic wrinkles around it like clay, taking a new shape.

Deep purple appears above the domes of the hills. Shadows crawl across the dell, thin as veils. There is a loud crack from above, and Alan and company turn to see a dark swirl developing in the clouds above the Pfahlwald. In a flash of pink, three gaunt figures emerge from the distortion. Their skin is bronze beneath flapping strips of black and white gauze. Bright helmets cover their eyes, black plumes blowing from their crests. Each holds high above its head a jeweled polearm with a half-moon blade. A song accompanies them, and the hills tremble to hear it. The sick stream jumps its banks and spills across the snow until its bed is nearly dry. The hooked bodies cry out horribly, straining rotted vocal folds to produce a sound like metal grinding metal through great heaps of meat. Alan starts to his feet, his trash masher in his hand.

"More Coma," says Brattle. "White's searchers. Stags was right."

The figures descend to the ridge, moving in perfect unison. The ground goes black beneath their bare, toeless feet. Each is marked on its bare chest with a unique series of three deep, red brands: moon-cross-key, sun-ankh-eye, and scarab-wing-star. Alan thinks about the brand on his forehead.

His knees wobbling, Alan wakes his magic. He slips into his focus, drawing himself up into a perfect point at the back of his mind. It comes so easily to him now that he worries he'll grow lax and slip, breaking his balance, and fall into the powerlessness he knows so well. Settling into his center, he lets his magic flow from him through the glowing shaft of his trash masher. He searches the approaching figures for their spirits, but he finds only one. The soulless bodies are its puppets, but they are also its trap. Enraged and swollen with frightening power, it snaps at them like a wolf caught in a silver snare. Alan can't help but pity its pain.

"One mind in three bodies," Alan says over his shoulder.

"A marshal," Sophia whispers. "Another legend."

Stag's Blood coils himself down into a crouch. "It seems we're the legend finders," he says. "Our quest is the fulcrum of all this sphere's strangeness."

"And its evil," Brattle adds. "And its grief."

The marshal stops before them, and moon-star-key turns its weapon blades-down to lean lightly on the butt of its handle. When it speaks, the marshal's voice comes from all three mouths.

"Alan Shade," it says. The words hiss out like fire, and Alan takes a step back. "I am an officer of power. It is in my authority to execute you, as has been ordered, but I am prepared to lobby on your behalf if you give Nergal to me now."

Alan wrings his masher's handle, and the marshal advances. Its bodies quiver, wracked with pain. Cords stand out on their necks and arms. Fear takes up its mutinous roar in Alan's head, and he almost turns to run. He can feel himself doing it - pushing past Brattle and Stag's Blood as he bolts into the hook-trees. The dead in the ground are waking at last as the marshal walks over their graves.

"No," Alan says, standing his ground with a titan effort. He looks from body to body, unsure which of them to address. The marshal is rooted firmly in all three of them. "It isn't yours, and no one needs to die."

"There is a war on," says moon-cross-key, raising its right hand.

"Don't perpetuate it," Alan says. "Walk away. We're not your enemies."

The three bodies tilt their heads. Alan feels them seeing him, searching him, their master groping out from inside them to size him up.

"You are a criminal," the marshal says. "Murderer."

"You know what he did before, in Elrafa," Brattle spits. He bounces on the balls of his feet, pounding the dirt with his fists. "You ain't scared?"

"There is no fear where I am god," scarab-wing-star replies. Sun-ankh-eye adds, "There is only me."

Stag's Blood stands bristling, his haunches up and his ears pressed tight into his mane. He kneads the ground with his front paws, digging little runnels with his wine-dark claws.

"You aren't god here," he snarls.

At this, the air seems to swell with heat. The ground begins to shake and groan, and the marshal surges forward. Alan's magic thunders to life, booming huge inside him, and the Seal of Aiwass explodes with light. He pushes his masher out in front of him and channels all his power through it, loving the rush and the burst of tingles down his spine.

"Stop!" Alan shouts, but his voice vanishes beneath the monstrous cracking of the hills' foundations.

Shadows rise from the woods in a whirlwind. They slither from the caves, hot with rage and hissing like cobras. Darkness tightens around Alan in fat coils, pressing its fangs into him. The Bleeding screams through his veins, but he knows it now, and he can beat it back. He can use it. In an instant, sun-ankh-eye and scarab-wing-star are crushed into darkness, and their dying cries pour from the remaining body's mouth.

Moon-cross-key tightens itself against Alan's power, pushing the shadows back. Alan strains against the marshal's monstrous force, drawing shadow from as far as he can reach, but the marshal is too strong. It finally breaks Alan's shadow spell, and Alan falls to one knee. He has poured everything out, but it's swarming back quickly. He will be ready to deliver a killing blow soon, but it won't be soon enough: moon-cross-key is already raising its weapon.

Stag's Blood pounces. His wine-dark claws open moon-cross-key from its right shoulder to its left hip, and it staggers back. Its dark blood burns the ground and gives off a thick, perse smoke. Stag's Blood starts to cough, and the marshal bats him aside to confront Brattle as he leaps in with his dagger flashing.

Brattle lays into the marshal like a mad animal. He opens the gash in its chest further with his clawing toes, hacking hard against the smoke, and drives his blade again and again into its back and sagging shoulders. The marshal tips back onto its heels for a second, but it manages to catch Brattle by the wrist and fling him into the hook-trees. As Alan finds his feet, moon-cross-key lifts its crescent scythe again.

"I kill you in the name of power," it cries. "Into the Bleeding, spirit!"

Alan is still gathering his magic. The dead wail inside him, but he isn't whole yet. The Kingwatcher's bloom is closed - a dark bulb bobbing on its stem, waiting quietly to pour out the nectar of its wrath again. Brand beaming to beat the suns, Alan swings his trash masher into moon-cross-key's bleeding side. The body groans, but the marshal is hardly in it now. In a dim flash, Alan sees the marshal's spirit trying to pull itself free of moon-cross-key's damaged flesh. He swings at the body again, trying to break it down and trap the marshal there, but he doesn't have time. Its weapon is coming down, fast as lightning, in spite of Alan's fury.

A bellow rises from the Hookwood. Something crashes from the darkling east, big as fear and blowing wrath like a freight train. It collides with Moon-Cross-Key, and the two go tumbling into the dell with snow flying up around them. Alan feels the marshal's terror as the draug opens beneath it. It is still tethered to its body, and it can't free itself without the strength of its other two physical components. In a burst of panic, it is gone, a flash in the dark, and

Rawbones sits at the bottom of the hill in a heap of torn flesh and a growing plash of violet blood.

Thirty-Five

Alan stands. Brattle emerges from the hook-trees at a deep limp, his face covered with blood. A red cataract flows from a gash on his head, and Alan kneels before him to begin healing it.

Knit, he thinks, and his magic responds immediately.

"Back to full again?" Brattle asks, fussing and pawing at his wound while Alan presses the damaged flesh together. Sophia emerges from hiding and perches on his shoulder. She stands on her tiptoes to inspect the cut, and ghoul's blood spills over her. Her heartlight shining through it makes the blood look flecked with green and silver.

"I thought I was going to be the conquering hero," Alan says. "I wasn't ready. I'm not strong enough yet."

Stag's Blood stands at the lip of the ridge and looks down at Rawbones. He is unfazed despite a few scratches. Licking his paw and sliding it three times through his mane returns him quickly to glimmering luster.

"It wants us to follow," he says. "I suggest we do so quickly."

Brattle pulls himself away before Alan is done. Scooping up two palmfuls of frost gray dirt to daub on his significantly smaller cut, he turns to look east into the sky. Alan follows his gaze to see a black mass of shapes swirling over Cheel Gar. Some of the shapes detach from the mass and move toward the Hookwood.

Sophia shivers and sighs. "Framer, strengthen us," she says. "More of those black things. Mackerel Sky has earned her pound of flesh."

Rawbones stands at the bottom of the dell waving its long arms and hooting. The sound is moving and awful. Its face contorts as it gestures, twisting along strange angles independent of its head movements. Its lips curl ohs around uneven teeth that are hung with gore. Alan reaches gently into it to find the sad tangle of its spirit sick and damaged. He is struck by just how many living things are profoundly sad in their depths. Life has a weight, and nothing can escape it. Even monsters suffer.

"Let's go," Alan says. He feels the wheel of the ship his hands. The sea moves, but it can't shake him. Confidence is an alien feeling, and he doesn't trust it. "We're not done yet."

Rawbones clears the creek in a long bound and races for the caves, head low and knuckles thumping the ground. It doesn't look much like the brunnmigi Alan saw in Debtors' Orchard. That one had been dark and sleek, but Rawbones is crooked and ungainly, and its fur is the color of soap foam rolling over blue water. A bony frill rides high on the back of its hyenine head, black twists of hair bouncing long beneath it. Two yellow tusks twist from its lower jaw toward is scarred, balding neck.

Alan slides down the embankment and tries to leap the creek, but he ends up on his chest with one leg in the freezing water. With Sophia in his mane, Stag's Blood makes the jump easily. Brattle wades across the stream with his arms up, rocking into each step like a gibbon. He helps Alan up while Stag's Blood paces.

"It certainly doesn't seem too concerned with waiting," he says, turning to watch Rawbones disappear into one of the caves. "Are you sure it wants us to follow?"

"Scared of the death from the sky," Brattle says. "But it'll wait for us to bring death from below."

"I don't think so," says Alan as he hauls himself to his feet, one shoe filled with water. He can't see Rawbones, but he can feel it nearby. Its spirit is small and bright as dawn through a gem filled with fire and smoke. "It's not hunting. It killed that marshal to protect us."

"I shall entertain both possibilities," Sophia says. "Just to be safe."

Sophia leads the way across the snow-strewn dell. The caves watch from the hill wall, blind and breathing dust across their thresholds. At the wide mouth of the den Rawbones disappeared into, Alan pauses to look over his shoulder. The sky above Cheel Gar is like black glass. The whole Pfahlwald is waving as tall shapes push through the trees heading west toward the hills. A high, terrible grinding sound comes from the cloud curtain.

Finally, Alan steps into the cave. Sophia shines as bright as she can, burning the dark back before the light of the Eternal Flame. The tight throat of the entrance twists a long into the ground, but it isn't dank or rough. The walls and floor are clean and even, and a strange warmth sighs up around them from further below. Now and again, they see Rawbones waiting at certain bends, showing them where to go as the path diverges, but it leaps away whenever they draw close. For such a large thing, it is surprisingly quick, and it hardly makes any sound as it moves through the intestinal twists of the entrance passage.

Near the tall arch of a round chamber, recesses appear in the walls. These are carefully carved and evenly spaced, and most stone sarcophagi lying in them. Alan touches intricate inscriptions in shallow relief, feeling the old life still in the work. The dead whisper from the rock in sophisticated tones, and he greets them gently with his power.

"Tombs," he says. "I felt these dead above. They aren't from Cheel Gar."

"Then where?" Brattle asks.

Alan looks into his inner darkness and opens himself. The dead speak through him, moving his disembodied voice for their own purposes.

"Alabastion," says something that is not Alan. "May her glory never fade."

Brattle crosses his arms. "That ain't what I hear," he says. "And it looks like her glory's long gone from this sphere."

"Some respect," Sophia whispers. "This is a sacred place."

"It's no killing jar," Stag's Blood says, "that's for certain. I smell no blood. This is a sanctuary."

They enter the round chamber to find Rawbones crouched at its center. Its six eyes burn in the ancient dark, red as forges. Its bellows-breaths fill the room, and its long teeth flash like

126

hammered steel. Alan's heart pumps once to fill his veins with ice. The brunnmigi slouches forward, long claws dragging, until Sophia's light is on its face. Then it begins to shake and moan horridly, falling to the floor as the mass of its flesh and corded muscle overwhelm its skeleton.

Alan rushes to the monster's aid. White light floods the chamber as he stirs his magic to life, pressing hard through it all at once, leaving the Seal of Aiwass on his forehead blaring. Brattle and Stag's Blood follow as Alan tries to scoop the writhing Rawbones into his arms. Sophia circles him, ringing like a little alarm, her heartlight cycling through strained shades of red.

"What's happening?" Stag's Blood asks.

"Careful Al!" Brattle cries, grabbing for Alan's wrist. "Didn't you learn nothing at the Orchard?"

"She's not a well-pisser, Brattle," Alan says, stretching himself across the vast, new gulf of spirit between himself and Rawbones. The crystal is still turning there, far away, but the dark is changing around it.

"She?" Stag's Blood says.

Alan doesn't explain how he can tell that Rawbones is female. He's not sure how to explain the femininity of her light - the softer, subtler way her energy burns inside her. He wraps himself around the gem of her soul, letting her strength pour over him. Even as she shrinks, she is nearly infinite.

Finally, Alan lays Rawbones on her back and steps away. She doesn't need his help. A wail trilling from her failing throat, Rawbones sheds her fur. Her flesh slips, bleeding away from her, and the forge-fires of her eyes curl to smoke. In a long, gruesome convulsion, she unburdens herself of her brunnmigi's skin. The floor drinks her blood where it falls, and the chamber trembles. When her paroxysms subside, she is left naked on the floor, a fairy girl of igneous beauty.

Alan stares, entranced. Eels twist in his guts for a moment, at war with each other. The girl reaches up and he helps her to her knees, folding her thin fingers between his hands. Her nails are dull as tin and split with worry. Her hair shags in her face, blood-wet and coarse as coir. She slumps against him for a moment, and he brushes her hair away from her sand-dark cheek to reveal a cluster of freckles beneath her right eye like a constellation. Her breasts swing softly against him when she wobbles to her feet.

"You're a strange group," the girl says. "Is this all of you?"

Alan looks around the chamber. The dead hum through the ground, remembering old victories. Nothing living is watching them from the remaining shadows.

"It's just us here," Alan says. "This is Brattle, Stag's Blood, and Sister Sophia. And I'm Alan. We're here to help Cheel Gar - and you, if we can. Pwysh sent us."

"I don't know him, but I do know what you're carrying," she says. Her voice is snarled raw and husky. She looks from Alan to Brattle in the dying light of Alan's brand. Sophia's circling draws odd shadows across her face. Turning to Stag's Blood, she narrows her honey-brown eyes. "Show me."

"Hang on," Alan says, glad that he has neither a clumsy tongue to trip his words nor a tightening throat to strangle his voice. "What's your name? Why did you lead us here?"

The fairy makes a tight-lipped face. "You brought the shard here of your own volition," she says, still a little winded. "Show it to me now, and we can continue. I won't steal it. I could have done that already."

"It's a little difficult to know who to trust in this situation," Stag's Blood says. "You must understand that."

"Wait," Alan says. "Take this." He starts to remove his robe, but the girl stops him before he can pull it over his head.

"Are you ashamed for me?" she asks, hands angled on her hips, one foot up on its ball with its fawn toes pushed delicately flat. "Afraid of my form? Would you have offered to cover me when I was a beast?"

"No," Alan says, eyes determinedly not on the points of her nipples. "I just thought you might be cold."

128

"My blood is hot, Alan. Keep your robe to warm yourself."

"All right," Alan says, slipping the pack from his back. His trash masher clangs on the stone floor. A rumbling begins outside, followed by a liquid hiss that sounds like rain. "We've got it. Can the marshals get in here?"

Alan slips Nergal from the pack and sets it on the floor. It is hot beneath his hands, and shapes swirl across its surface. Voices rise out of it, pressing heavily on Alan's mind. It's frustrating being unable to make out what they're saying. The fairy girl's beryl eyes widen.

"The servant," she says, leaning down to press her cheek against the stone. Nergal lights up in response to her touch. It glows like a broken moon, lighting the whole chamber. Intricate carvings appear on the walls in luminous silver. Alan is reminded of the sylves' elevator in the Tower of Alms. "You found the bell - and Enlil. The Sky-King is whole again?"

"I imagine he's as whole as he gets," Brattle says.

"I saw the ashfall and feared for Welkinbright. Is she still strong?"

"Stronger than she was before we arrived, if I may say so," Sophia replies. She ignites again, pushing the light of the Flame Empyrean as hard as she can through her tiny body. The chamber is as bright now as if the suns were looking directly into it. "Strong and strengthening. The Flame is restored. The city has a chance against Toven now."

"Toven?" says the girl. "Another name for White?"

"Her general," Brattle explains. "Probably. Just as bad as her by all accounts. You don't know him?"

"She threshes her servants like wheat," the girls says. "I never learn their names."

Alan draws Nergal away slowly. Back in the pack, the shard goes quiet again. Darkness returns to the chamber, trickling in like meltwater. The carvings dim out and vanish.

"What's yours?" Alan asks. "And what's going on? Are we safe here?"

The fairy girl levels a dawn-bright smile at Alan. The knowing in her eyes is terrifying. She is at once as broad as the sky and as small as a pinprick star. There is still a ghost of the brunnmigi's forge-fire in her face. It could wake at any moment, roaring hungry.

"The malakeen avoid the caves," says the fairy girl, crossing her legs settling back on her hands. "They won't get in unless they beat down the hills, and there are secret ways out that they don't know. They can only make noise." She sighs and puts her hands flat on the floor, fingers splayed. "Moving on," she says, transcribing a slow circle on the stone with her index fingers, "My name is Nora, and these are the ruins of Alabastion. This is the Eye of Nudd - an arbitrarium. Great judges and protectors are buried beneath it, at the roots of the hills. Can you feel them, Alan? You're a death wizard, aren't you? I know the Seal of Aiwass."

Alan listens to the dead in the floor. They have stopped humming. Now they are mumbling over each other, their voices rolling like thunder deep in the soil.

"I'm more like an apprentice," Alan says, "but I hear them. There are older whispers further down. This chamber is like an amplifier."

"It is a throat," Nora says. "It will test you, and it will speak your lies if you're false. That's why I've lead you here. Many want the Chodash Gem. You're clearly collecting shards, and you claim to be enemies of Winter White, but, as Stag's Blood said, it's difficult to know who to trust."

"This must be what Pwysh wanted," Stag's Blood says.

Brattle crosses his arms. "It's like as much so," he says, "but I'd feel better if I knew what was in this for us."

"And what penalties we face if we decline," Sophia says, "or if we're found false."

Nora lifts a feathered eyebrow. "You have the right to refuse," she says. "Is that what you want?"

"We have nothing to hide," Alan says. "What do we have to do?"

"The same thing I do here, night after night, to keep myself honest," Nora says, a long smile dancing across her face. "Blood won't lie."

Alan volunteers to be first. At Nora's request, he removes his shoes and robe and stands in the center of the room. The chamber breathes cold air across his chest. His work shirt and pants are long gone, torn from his grasp by the giggling ghosts of children in Toven's château. Emerging from the legs of his plus-fours, Alan's calves are lath-slim. Below his jutting collarbone, his ribcage spreads like a pair of wings, every bone visible. His skin is as thin as pearly paper, but it is stronger than it looks. It takes five excruciating minutes to make a cut with Brattle's knife, and then he can only squeeze out three drops of blood.

The droplets fall from the palm of his hand, red as a flaming heath in Sophia's light. They pat on the stone, which, after a moment of suffocating silence, soaks them up into hairline cracks as it had Nora's blood before. There is a heavy groan from far away - a loving sigh from rocky lungs - and the floor shudders. Alan looks into his inner darkness, where the dead pitch their voices up into a roaring argument. He can feel them reaching into his veins, riding the soft pumps of his heart like steam to close his wound.

"You hardly bleed enough, but I'm glad you're cooperating," Nora says. Her voice swells huge, filling her mouth until she can hardly contain it. "We will continue. There is only one question. Think hard before you say anything, and find a dark place in yourself to answer from." She takes a deep breath, and the chamber breathes with her. "*Who are you?*"

Alan sinks into the mire of his mind. Memories twist together in thorns, making dams against bottle-green swells of pain and nightmares. In glens of golden trees, he finds little winds singing youthful oblivion through carpets of pine needles. He sees himself in faded photograph colors, his blue eyes shining, sitting barefoot on an open tailgate. There is no order, but there is power in his

131

mind. Sadness runs deep beneath everything, like veins of black ore. The pits are sealed with careful lies. He draws his reply from these depths, clutching it tight like an accident victim.

"Alan Shade," he says. "Thanoturge."

The floor of the arbitrarium heaves beneath Alan's feet. Nora scowls at him as she regains her balance, her eyes leaping like blown fire.

"No," she hisses through her small, even teeth. "Answer again."

"The question's a little vague," Alan says. "Can you give me an idea of what you're expecting?"

"Find your dark place and answer," Nora replies.

"I don't see how this helps you," Stag's Blood says. "What are you trying to assess, exactly?"

Nora closes her eyes and takes another breath. The chamber moans like a desirous lover.

"This is judgment," she explains, "the Opening of the Mouth and the Weighing of the Heart. Answer again, Alan. Don't hurry."

Alan steadies himself. He tries to feel roots shooting out from his feet to hold him to the ground. Returning to his inner darkness, he puts himself before the Kingwatcher's bloom. The flower bobs, its petals open, dripping honey over mounds of the moaning dead. He searches their gaping mouths, pressing their tongues up and probing their throats for secrets. At the base of the flower, caught in the tangle of its roots, he finds his father. A secret beams like a petal between his teeth. When Alan speaks again, his chest feels terribly empty. He holds out his hand as if to offer the secret blossom.

"Brother," he says, hearing a quaver in his voice. "Son."

The arbitrarium shakes again, and dust falls around Alan from the invisible ceiling.

"No," Nora says, "but better."

132

"How are you judging?" Sophia asks her. She lands on Alan's shoulder in a swirl of stone powder. Her heartlight breaks the tension in his back. "Why don't you ask what you want to know?"

"There's only one question," Nora replies calmly. "It's not meant to be specific. You're doing well, Alan. Don't stop now. *Who are you*?"

This time, Alan stays in the chamber. He quiets the voices of the dead in his mind and lets his magic slip back to sleep. He stops his body entirely and allows ultimate cold creep over him. Death dives in on owl's wings, white and silent with claws outstretched to claim its prize. In the stillness just before it strikes, Alan finds his answer.

"Angry," he says, and death slides past. "Bitterly angry. Allison got to be weak. She got to fall apart and give in, but I had to be strong. I carried her across an ocean of grief, keeping myself afloat by sheer dint of will, but she wasted my effort. It should have been me to get her rest. I'm hurt and I'm angry because she committed suicide before I could."

Alan braces himself, half expecting the cavern to collapse, but nothing happens. The dark stays dark, and the strange remains strange.

"Yes," she says, her smile sinister. "Acceptance."

Brattle puts his hand on Alan's arm. The pads of his fingers are like ridged rubber. "That's heavy, boss," he says. "What'd I tell you about keeping secrets in Graveworld? Even the one you don't wanna tell it'll drag outta you."

"Did you know?" Alan asks.

Brattle nods once, and Alan hates seeing sorrow in his eyes. He wants the gruff old ghoul back. All at once, he realizes how much he has needed Brattle inelegant genius.

"That is a terrible thing to envy," Stag's Blood says. "I'm sorry. Those are depths none should have to see, but you had a light. The darkness didn't destroy you. Take comfort in that."

"What light?" Alan asks, sagging. Misery falls over him like a shroud. He wants to take it in his fists and bunch it hard around himself, but it's not as attractive as it used to be. Now, it feels like a petty indulgence, so he casts it away. It is bittersweet to be free of it.

"Your heartlight," Sophia tells him, touching his cheek with her hot palm. "It never goes out, Alan. That's your strength."

"Are you finished, Alan?" Nora asks. "Do you need a moment before we proceed? The test can be draining."

Alan straightens himself. Something is growing in the mire of his mind, shrinking the thorns and clearing the water. Death slinks away hungry. Under the subtle influence of the arbitrarium's magic, the dead fairy girl's power is finally unfurling. It is like the bloom of Minos in a way. It will be a new bulwark.

"I'm fine," Alan says. "Who's next."

Brattle steps into the center of the room, takes his knife from Alan, and stands up to his full height. He is awkward, and he has to sway like kelp to stay upright. When he cuts his hand, the blood that comes streaming out is dark as sloe. The stone accepts it slowly, as if disgusted by it, as Alan heals Brattle's hand.

"*Aptrganga*," Nora says. "You're divided. That is dangerous."

"You shoulda seen the beast that killed me," Brattle says, coughing a laugh. "So how does this work now? I say some uncomfortable secret about myself and then maybe the roof falls down?"

"You answer the one question," Nora says, crossing her arms under her breasts. "You know how it works. Your impudence is inappropriate."

"But not entirely surprising," Stag's Blood offers. Nora isn't amused. She doesn't even look in his direction.

Brattle licks his palm where his wound has closed. "I still want to know what's in this for us. What's the test telling you, and what if we fail?"

"What it tells me is not at issue," Nora explains. "I can make my own decisions. The test is for Nudd. What you want is easy to know, but seeing why you want it requires deeper senses than I am capable of. Are you here for Nudd? Do you want to protect it?"

"It's on our list," Brattle replies, "among other things."

"Don't get this wrong," Alan says. "We've sworn no allegiances. We're not defined by our opposition to Toven and Winter White. We're just walking a path, flying no flags."

"Your path leads to allegiance," Nora says, "and to conflict. White's marshals don't care what flags you aren't flying. As far as they're concerned, you're the enemy - that's what your opposition to White will bring you.

"If you want to stop White, as must be your aim, then you can only wish to protect Nudd. But you cannot choose yourselves to be protectors of the Gardens Arcane - Nudd has been betrayed before. Nudd must choose you."

Brattle looks up, seeming to weigh this in his head. Sophia paces at his feet, casting his face in deep and moving shadow.

"You are some kind of gatekeeper, then," says the Fetchlight. "But why terrorize Cheel Gar? Stories describe you as a monster. You live in this wood of gore, seeking no help. Why?"

"Who I am is not the question, Sister," Nora replies, "and Brattle is the one who must answer. Think now, Conservator. This is the Eye of Nudd. Let it look in." She takes a little breath. Her lips purse, dark as cinnamon. She closes her eyes and speaks, and her voice fills the chamber again. "*Who are you*?"

At this, the chamber resounds with a series of booms and cracks. The marshals are hammering the hills with magic so black and ferocious that Alan can feel it in the very foundations of his psyche. He has to draw all of his new strength to keep from being shaken apart.

"They'll beat the hills down after all," Stag's Blood says. "You've underestimated them."

135

Nora shakes her head, apparently unmoved by the shriek of tearing stone beneath her. Brattle pays no mind either. He is lost somewhere, gathering black and natty wool. When the bombardment stops, the chamber falls into an awesome silence. The dark goes taut, as if its holding its breath.

"Protector of the Gardens Arcane," Brattle finally replies. "Conservator of Nudd." With a gap-toothed smile, he adds, "And Toven's murderer."

Suffocating stillness continues. There are no more grinding peals of thunder from outside. The marshals' magic pulls away, leaving Alan feeling exposed. He knows the water is drawing back, running away from the shore to feed a gathering tsunami.

"Not a lie in you," Nora says. She isn't smiling this time. "You did well. Nudd accepts your pledge, but there is still a danger. You're split, and you need to be careful. Don't bring Nudd the curse of your resurrection."

Brattle falls back into his frog-squat and swings himself backward on his knuckles, avoiding Sophia's light.

"I am proud of you," Sophia says as she takes to the air after him. "You have stepped in the direction of your destiny."

"Don't name that baby till its eyes stay open," Brattle replies, finding a shadowy place to sit on his heels. "Destiny's full of surprises."

"You don't seem too pleased," Alan says.

"Little to be pleased with yet, and I don't trust relief. I'll reserve my *own* judgment for my rest in fields of laurel. Ain't no test can tell me I'm not who I say I am."

"Again, that isn't the point," Nora says.

After another crash outside, she finally seems to notice what's been happening. She crouches and waves her hands at Sophia, who dims her heartlight until shadow lies thick over everything.

"We should lie low and quiet for a moment," Nora says, measuring her words very carefully, surveying them, as if they might support some new construction. "In the meantime, I'll tell you a story about who I am. You may know some of it. Sit and listen, even if you do. The story is like a ritual. It's important to say everything just right and in the right order.

"It's in Nudd's nature to be desired, so it has always had guardians. When a force of pixies stood up to defend it, Alabastion was given to them. They protected the Gardens Arcane for generations, and they were honored as heroes.

"At the height of its glory, a half pixie was born in Alabastion to a sylvan mother. He rose to prominence as a powerful thanoturge, calling himself Anastasis Nex. During a long peace, Nex used growing doubt about the necessity of Alabastion's armies to stir up anti-pictish sentiments. This lead to violence and a pogrom. Alabastion was seized by force and the remnants of its population scattered. With Alabastion crippled, Nex launched an attack on Nudd which killed him and led to the ruin of his influence. Betrayed, the Gardens Arcane vanished to where they are today. Nudd can be harmed, but it cannot be controlled. All who desire it are crushed."

"Nex cursed us, his race, to make us into the monsters he believed us to be. At first, the transformation is uncontrollable, but it can be controlled with practice. I am the first and last one to learn to do this. All the other cursed ones are dead, hunted down as brunnmigi. I am the last pixie, and I still serve Nudd. I'm cast out, hated, blamed for my forebears' murders, but nothing matters more than my service in the Gardens. This is why I watch the arbitrarium and oversee the test."

As Nora stops, the marshals outside pull away. Silence returns, growing in the darkness like a spider's web. It blows softly across Alan's bare chest, a real physical thing, much more than the absence of any sound. This is a living, sentient silence with the rudiments of a spirit inside it.

"The stories," Stag's Blood says.

"True until they aren't. Hate made real. I wasn't innocent at first. Like my father, I was a slave to my curse. Learning to control it hasn't made Cheel Gar hate me any less. Learning to love it has been my life. I ran at first, and Elrafa took me in, but they paid horribly for harboring me. "

Alan nods, remembering the grim, sandblown ruin where he fell ill from magic sickness. He can still hear the howl of the Elrafa wind far back in his head.

"How many have you tested?" Sophia asks. "Do many come? I have never heard this story."

"Your order has an image to maintain," Nora replies. "You walked the Pfahlwald. Did you look up? Did you watch the corpses watching you? They might have come off their stakes if you had. After Nex's deception, the Sisters of M arrested all of his coconspirators and executed them. For this, they called on witch-men, exsecrators from the crystal mines high east of Fetchwood. They were overzealous and killed many innocents. These poor souls languish in Stele Gorge now, in Sepulchra's Prisons, damned with the Dead in Disgrace. Their bodies rot eternally here. The Sisterhood was mortally ashamed at their executioners' brutality – it's no wonder they've softened the truth a bit. But now you know, Sister Sophia. I'm sorry."

"I shall not believe it," Sophia insists, but her color says otherwise.

"That's well with me," Nora says. She nearly laughs but appears to think better of it. "If I could remake the world in lies, it would be a better place, but I couldn't love it. And I've tested many here over the years. Accepted or not, most wandered away and did nothing. One I had hopes for, but he disappeared. His name was Arajtetatl, and he was Lashaseph."

"What do you hope for us?" Stag's Blood asks.

"I rarely have hopes," Nora replies. "I think it's safe to finish the test now. Stand and draw blood."

Stag's Blood uncurls himself from the floor. It's so dark, that Alan can't quite see where the stone ends and Stag's Blood begins.

"Who am I?" Stag's Blood asks, shaking his head so that his mane swirls in his face. He draws a red line across his wrist with one claw, mewling once as his blood begins to flow. He has to

138

stamp his paw hard to spatter the stone. "I am the scion of Fearsome, and I am afraid -"

Before Stag's Blood can finish, a blaring howl begins outside. More howls join it, and the walls of the arbitrarium begin to tremble. A crack appears high in the curved wall, and daylight pours in as it widens. The sounds continue, echoing under the hills as if to pull them apart, and Alan realizes they are trumpet blasts.

"They're coming!" Nora cries. "We're not safe! Follow me!"

The wind weeps through the wall. Stones begin to drop from the ceiling, each one larger than the other, until the blue sky appears far above. Nora falls to her knees, her mouth as wide as a church door. Claws pierce her back from inside, tearing her open. Rawbones emerges in blood, rage rolling from her lips in a roar, and tosses Nora's skin away wrapped in the tatters of Brattle's mortcloth.

"Follow," Rawbones shrieks.

Stones falls around her, banging to dust on the floor. She crosses the room in two great leaps and disappears into the east wall, her snuffling growls the only trace of her left in the Eye of Nudd. The dead scream terror, and the pain is so intense that Alan nearly collapses. Stag's Blood follows Rawbones, and Alan barely manages to catch his tail to keep from being left behind. Rawbones is waiting just inside the tunnel's hidden mouth to lead them deep.

"What's happening?" Brattle asks, swinging along in the rear and spitting rock dust. He is carrying Alan's robe with Sophia burning in its sleeve pocket.

"The malakeen have made Nora a liar," Stag's Blood replies. "Their prize is within reach, and they are singularly determined."

"I feel that sound still in my bones," Brattle said. "It's like my joints are floating. I might fly apart if not for my skin, and even that aches."

Sophia emerges to fly wildly around Alan's head. He has to catch her before she crashes into the wall.

"I might have shattered," Sophia says from Alan's palm. There is a faint ringing coming from her, though her wings are still. "I have never been so shaken hard in all my life. It was awful."

Alan searches into Sophia and finds her poised at the edge of the draug, dimming like and ember. Cracks spread out across the darkness toward her. He closes his hand around her and tries to heal her. It takes many long minutes' descent toward the hill's foundations before he can make her crystalline flesh respond. When it does, it moves like gel on paper.

Knit, Alan thinks. *Stick together.*

"Just relax," Alan tells Sophia. "The damage isn't too great."

"*Hud gwaed* will not avail you, Alan. I'm sorry," Sophia says. "We are unaffected by blood-bound magic."

Even as she speaks, Sophia's heartlight begins to swell. The small ringing of the horns in her crystal stops. Alan cannot meet her gaze. He can't smile down at her. What passes between them as he proves her wrong is deeper than skin and muscle. It is admiration of spirit, bare and honest without the superficial raiment of form. Though they are far underground now and the air is chilly, Alan feels flushed.

"I guess my magic isn't bound to blood," he says.

"You never finished, Stags," Brattle calls from close behind the others. "Does that mean you didn't get judged?"

Rawbones stops at a short drop. Her nose is tiny, and she must gasp through her mouth with her tongue out to catch her breath. Stag's Blood drops back to Brattle's side while Alan goes to the edge to look down at the path ahead of them. It is rough and wet with moss. Insects chirp on the walls. Alan can see them clinging huge far down the passage.

"I don't know," Stag's Blood replies, "but I imagine so."

"What were you ready to say?" Brattle asks. "There's something you're afraid of?"

"I am afraid of disappearing like my father," Stag's Blood says. "We all fade, and I shouldn't worry, but I don't know what's beyond it. I worry that it will be nothing. If we return to emptiness, perhaps I am empty."

"Nothin' ain't worth nothin'," Brattle says. "Not if it's all you got."

"Your Da?"

"That's all me," Brattle laughs. "A B-rattle o-riginal."

Rawbones slips down the ledge and starts off down the tunnel at a trot. Brattle helps Alan down while Sophia drifts over the ledge with her heartlight glowing white - a ringing snowflake making sentient turns into the dark. Stag's Blood springs into the tunnel, his grace untouched by any fatigue, and pads along at the back with his tail lashing absently behind him.

"There is air coming in from the other side," Stag's Blood says. "It smells like smoke."

"I hope we ain't walkin' into more bad trouble," Brattle says, rubbing his neck deep with the tips of his fingers. He hands Alan his robe, and Alan tugs it over his head. The dead are all but silent. Their voices arise weak, buried under the ruin of the arbitrarium.

"Framer, deliver us to safety," Sophia chimes, slipping into Alan's sleeve, "or prepare us for danger."

Thirty-Six

The tunnel winds down into the hill's dark heart. Calf-deep water babbles through it at its lowest depths. Alan wades across barefoot, his socks and shoes in his hand. Blind, black fish dart around him, long as oars, brushing his ankles with sensory spines. Brattle snatches them wriggling from the water and eats them noisily as the path finally begins to climb.

Near its exit, the tunnel opens out like a bell. Alan thinks about Enlil and the bell's grave in Welkinbright. Where was it Atratus asked if Enlil would meet the Venue? He can't remember now. He tries to think back to his last day at Ray's – to Iscela's clay-brown face and chestnut eyes and the beeping songs of grills and fryers – but that part of his past doesn't feel real. As distant and faded as it is, it might as well have been a dream he had in the womb. Only death stands out in his memory, a galvanic figure, its white wings open to cast everything in shadow.

Rawbones surges up the widening passage far ahead of them. When it ends in sand under the sun-blanched sky, she crouches at its mouth and waits. Alan stops in the light to rest with his hands on his knees. His calves are in aching knots, and the arches of his feet are burning.

"Where've we come out?" Brattle asks, falling from the mouth of the tunnel to pant on his back. "I ain't made for treks like this. I need a good long liedown in a nice patch of shadow. How far are we from that, d'ya think?"

"Getting further every day," Alan replies, standing to take stock of their surroundings. Peach trees stand in thin clumps not far away, where the sand turns to May-green grass. They sway to greet the wind, their blossoms falling around their feet. Not far away, a banner of smoke mars the sky above Cheel Gar. "But, once we get there," Alan continues, his heart sinking. "It'll be the best liedown you've ever had."

Brattle coughs. "Don't throw promises farther than you can run."

Stag's Blood emerges wet and stretches his toes in the sand. Sophia is a blue star in the tangle of his mane. With everyone gathered, Rawbones prowls the peach grove for threats. The marshals' trumpets ring across the hills, harmless at this distance. At the hills' feet, the forests are full of fairy graves. Many are empty, and a few are the traps of deathlike things lying in wait to capture unwary thanoturges' minds, but there are enough good eyes for Alan to see a long way. Through his deadsight, Alan watches the hill over the Eye of Nudd falling inward. Plumes of dirt and rock billow up into a wild wind and blow away. The marshals are thinning out, but the sky still looks wounded trying to contain them.

The dead won't look the other way. Alan can't see into Cheel Gar from where he is. All the graves running east toward the city have been desecrated.

Satisfied that they are out of immediate trouble, Rawbones returns and kneels to change again. Alan remains in his deadsight, not wanting to watch Nora peel herself out of her monstrous form in full daylight. When she is free of the brunnmigi's flesh and strong enough to stand again, Nora addresses the group.

"They will not stay," she says, out of breath. As Rawbones, she had seemed tireless. Now, all the fatigue of her run through the tunnel seems to be crashing down on her at once. "They always return to their masters." She looks into the sky as if she might see the malakeen retreating. Alan watches them through the eyes of the dead. Only he can see them pulling away to vanish through tears in the sky.

"These are the Hanging Peaches," Nora continues. "Something bad happened here a long time ago, but no one remembers what it was. There's a secret way into Cheel Gar through these woods, and I think we should hurry there. I would suggest we wait until nightfall, but you can see the smoke. Are you all rested?"

"What has happened in Cheel Gar?" Sophia asks. "I hope we haven't brought the Coma's wrath upon them."

"It was always coming," Nora says. "Blame only the wicked for wickedness. Come. Suck your biggest breaths and follow."

Nora leads them among the peaches, her hair bouncing over her shoulders with each worried step. Peach petals blow across her brow, crowning her. She picks pink flowers from between her breasts and flicks them down to crush them under her calloused heels. Sophia follows through the trees, stopping when she can to run her hands over the flossy curves of low-hanging fruit.

Light takes on an oneiric quality in the grove. It falls over the branches like rain, heavy and hissing with sparks. On the ground, it swirls in a mist, and the shadows thrown through it move independently of the objects that cast them. Alan can feel the watchful sadness here, the blood flowing just under the ground. The grove is more beautiful because of it.

Brattle droops on Stag's Blood's back with his eyes half closed. The color is just starting to drain from his face, and there is a strange halo clinging to the back of his head. It brightens as they near Cheel Gar, and shadows appear in it, moving like blind cave fish.

The wood of the Hanging Peaches ends in a gentle hill with a ruined building on top. The structure slumps on its columns, the tin sheets of its roof rusting and slipping from its corbels. The spire in its center is topped with an iron star.

"There it is," Alan say, standing on the slope of the hill with his hands in the straps of his knapsack. "The next symbol. What is this place?"

"It was a house for owls," Nora replies, her voice low. "There are nesting holes inside, and they still come here, but no one uses this building for anything anymore. There's a passage beneath it that leads to the Sisters' monastery." She looks at Sophia, who has come to rest on Alan's shoulder. "Your Sisters, Sophia. They've been quiet since the malakeen started coming here."

"That's why they would not answer," Sophia says. "Are the Mothers there well? Do the Sisters come and go?"

"I rarely go over the walls," Nora frowns. There are some who know me here."

"The smell is bad," Stag's Blood says, wrinkling his nose. Brattle is squinting from his back, his halo like a sylvan fire. "I'm afraid to hope, but perhaps the Mothers and Sisters escaped through the secret passage. They could be hiding in the Hanging Peaches even now."

Nora's frown deepens. Darkness touches her face with its loving hand.

"We'll enter through the side," she says. "Alan, what symbol did you mean?"

"The star," Alan explains. "The first was the bell – the one in Welkinbright where we found Enlil."

"Third's the spirit," Brattle says, sounding far away. "Pwysh marked 'em out for us."

Nora tilts her head and cups her chin. "He knows some of what I do, then," she says, "and more than Winter White."

"He did know," Brattle says, "till he crossed Winter."

"Like wheat," says Nora.

Brattle continues. "We gotta you're different. We intend to take this Chode Stone of yours. That's our mission. If you ain't on the same page, we should have it out right now before we go rushing into trouble."

Nora considers this for a long time. A howl rises from the peach grove, and others join it as she thinks in silence. The wind carries the hungry sounds like gifts to her.

"I'll do what's right for the Gardens," she says. "You'll need me."

They enter the building through a crack where the ground has shifted. Inside, the floor is strewn with peach blossoms. Multicolored orbs of petals hang from the ceiling, dingy with the dust that sifts down from the rafters. Light leans in through the slats over a round window. There are no birds here, but there are ruined nests spilling from shelves and cubbies in the walls. A large stone slab covered with carven circles is set flat into the center of the floor. Alan kneels to inspect it and recognizes the symbols on its face.

"These are like the glyphs on my phone," he says, trying to whisper. Subtle attenuations of his disembodied voice are still somewhat difficult. "What is this stone?"

"A gravestone," Nora replies. With the others gathering behind her, she kneels at the edge of the slab and runs her hands over it. Her nails are long with bruise-purple lunulae. "I don't know where it came from. It's been here longer than even the Pfahlwald. The words are the key. It says: 'Skuld the Bloodless, Princess of Charnea. The light of the draug is failing.'"

At this, the slab grinds aside, the symbols upon it burning blue as moonlight. Beyond it is the mouth of a clean, well-kept tunnel. Its floor is sandy, and the walls are lined with little sarcohpagi.

"You can read it?" Alan asks.

"Pictish is not read," Nora replies. "It is felt."

"Toven wants you alive," says Alan. "You're the only one left who can read that language. He may have been trying to kill you before, but now he needs you to read what's on my phone."

"We're walking into a trap," Stag's Blood says.

Brattle laughs. "We always were," he says, making his way past Alan to climb down into the tunnel.

"There's no trap big enough for what's coming," Nora says. "Whomever Toven is, if he is wise and if he is listening, let him hear the wings of death around him."

The gravestone slab slides back into place to shut them in as they make their way down the tunnel. It is roomy and warm, and Sophia's light fills it nicely. The sarcophagi standing against the walls are carved in the shapes of owls. Alan searches them, but the dead inside are silent. He feels them awake, the little white spirits of birds, but he cannot connect with them. They watch him emptily, and he withdraws.

"I can feel the owls," Alan says. "They lived above and, when they died, they were buried here. So many spirits are trapped with their bodies, but some flee. The marshal we fought tried to pull its soul away from its body. Why stay trapped in dead flesh when there's - maybe - some better place to go?"

"Spirits latch deep to bodies," Brattle explains. "It's the way of things. Spirits don't know they got options. Deep in that formless 'me' we all got, there's a fear that maybe there ain't nothing but flesh to this world. Makes sense to hold tight, build yourself around the illusion of now. Even when the flesh dies, a lotta spirits can't tear away."

"If I may," Sophia says, "we were taught that life began with crystal. The body is the gem, and the spirit within it is the fire. Without the fire, the gem is dark. Without the gem to amplify its light, the fire is dim. Unprotected, it goes out. The bond between spirit and flesh is not just powerful, but sacred. Who would sever it deliberately except under extreme circumstances, as Kelen did?"

Sinking back into his inner darkness for a moment, Alan sees his sister's ghost bleeding in the bathtub. Her mouth is open, and she is staring at him. Did she long to return to her flesh? Was she lying with her body now, awake and empty as these owls, or would she whisper to him if he could reach out to her?

"The Grave of the Owls," Stag's Blood says. "Noctua, I believe. I've heard of it, but I don't remember where. It must have been when I was a kitten."

"Ain't no tracks in the sand," Brattle says, "but somebody keeps this place." He shakes his head, holding his temples and wincing in pain. His halo has dropped, thinned, and spread into a faint aura clinging close to his skin.

There are two thin sheets of linen hanging on either side of the ladder. On one, owls in red armor winging into battle against pearl-white doves. The other shows a funeral procession carrying a beaked coffin over a green sea of trees. Both feature night skies spread thick with stars. Nora pulls down the one depicting the battle and cinches it around her body, pressing her breasts up toward her collarbone.

"May this shield you from the terror of my flesh," she says, "until the beast returns. And may the owls forgive me."

At the top of the ladder is double trap-door. Nora climbs the ladder and pulls the small loop of a silver chain to open it. It swings inward on singing hinges, and Alan makes his way up first, pulling himself out over the trap-door with some difficulty. Sophia rises alongside him, and she chimes in dismay when she realizes where they are.

The trap-door is under the crossbeam of a gallows platform. The old noose is coiled on a peg nearby, covered with dust. An iron maiden stands open in one corner, its spikes bone-white. There is a false head in the basket of the guillotine at the front of the room, and a limp dummy is strapped nude to the nearby breaking wheel. Mallets, awls, and corkscrew knives festoon the walls, arrayed in fanciful patterns and ordered according to the weights of their heads and the lengths of their piercing parts. Impaling stakes are stacked against the wall like cordwood. Beyond the guillotine, little glints like scattered glass wink in the light from an open door.

"Violence enshrined," Sophia says. "This is a mockery of sacredness, despite what my Sisters may have intended. The sanctuary is tainted."

Alan doesn't reply. The dead are howling in his mind like never before, and he is fascinated by their desperate power. These are not buried corpses - these are memories of pain and horror so intense that they have come to life. New knowledge emerges through the gift of the fairy girl, and Alan embraces it. Each voice is a kind of truth. Every shriek contains a whisper: something he can learn from. He takes them all in, enthralled, and, in a strange, subtle process that he doesn't understand, Alan feels his magic maturing.

Thank you, he thinks. The ghosts of pain scream back from far beyond any sentiment he understands.

Brattle scrambles onto the scaffold. Stag's Blood has only to leap from the ground to reach the red chamber above the tunnel. There, he walks to the edge of the platform and sits down with the skin around his neck and shoulders twitching.

"This is a gruesome place," Stag's Blood says, "but the collection is impressive. It must have taken a long time to gather all of these instruments."

Nora takes the rope and stretches it in her hands. Color falls from it with the dust. The noose gapes as if starving.

"This isn't a museum," she says, laying the rope across the scaffold rail.

As they cross the room, Alan reaches back to slide his trash masher from its straps. It is light and eager for strife. Near the door, a clamor from outside the building becomes audible. The masher quakes in anticipation. It starts to glow as it draws Alan's power into its shaft. Brattle stops in the doorway to inspect the little piles of shards there. Sophia cries out in despair before he can say what they are, and her heartlight beams into a rage.

Alan kneels to see the little wings and broken heads in the glittering shards. Even in shards, these Fetchlights are beautiful. They defy death's paling touch - the caress that makes everything ugly. There is no way to know what they felt as they died - what splinters of their faces remain are blank and featureless, as he expected. He can't even tell how many have fallen together.

Nora steps through the door and waits in the hall. Sophia falls to the floor, white-hot, and leaves a black ring seared into the tile.

"In fury, mercy," she chants. From a distance, Alan admires her control over her voice. Her light belies her calm. "In wrathfulness, grace. In death, peace."

"We will avenge them," Stag's Blood says, "but we must continue. Their killers are outside."

"They would not have wanted vengeance," Sophia wails. "We are peaceful!"

"What *would* they've wanted?" Brattle asks. "What's to give them that's fitting for their lives?"

Sophia kneels trembling for a moment. She leans forward and put her hands in the mess of slivers that was once a Fetchlight. There's a trail of crushed crystal going out the door and all the way down the hall. Her heartlight pours into the shards from her hands, and every pile Alan can see from the door of the chamber onward starts to rattle and glow.

"We need to keep going," Sophia says. "Is the shard of the stone in this abbey? Where is the Framer Gem?"

"Across the street in the cloister," Nora replies. "Now I see the significance of the star sign you were looking for, Alan. The Star of Henrietta: there's an altar there. The shard is well hidden, but let's hurry. Can you go on, Sister?"

"Whether I can or not," Sophia says, "I must. No more stopping now."

From the narrow back rooms, draped in dark reds and eggplant blacks, the abbey opens out like a lotus blossom. It is wide and bright at its heart, with walls that soar up to points and banks of impressive glasswork. At every arch and altar, there is a perfect sphere of iridescent crystal. If these are Framer Gems, they are stone blind now. Nothing moves but the wind in curtains, blowing new snow through open windows. The atrium ceiling has collapsed, leaving broken basalt blocks heaped on the seal in the center of the floor. Not even Sophia can find a way through the rubble, so Nora leads the group in the search for another exit. After minutes of fruitless wandering, a trail of smoke appears down a windowless, gabbro hallway.

"Danger and death," Brattle whispers. "Don't follow."

"We followed it into the Debtors' Orchard," Alan points out.

Brattle's eyes narrow to blazing slits. "Into an ambush," he says.

"You must see, Brattle, that things are changing," Nora says. "A way out is a way out."

"There ain't no way out," Brattle grumbles. "Only deeper in."

Nora ignores him. She follows the smoke and the clinking of a swinging chain to the calefactory door, Alan and Stag's Blood close behind her. Brattle creeps after them, chest to the ground, until the smoke blows away at the end of the corridor.

The calefactory door looks northwest down a lane flowering bushes. Beyond them is a wide, green garden with enormous trees rising around it. Much of Cheel Gar is built across their crowns. The roads below follow the walkways above haphazardly, branching away in places to end in peach-planted courts of cottages. In the distance, the dark stakes of the Pfahlwald are barely visible.

Nora stops on the abbey's statued porch and catches her breath. Alan steps past her onto the walk, Sophia hiding against his arm. Fire is dancing in the streets. The great trees groan in the grip of a beamless flame, casting down the structures between them. Forked tongues of fire cross bridges and scale rope ladders to reach tree house platforms, moving with impossible care and consideration. On the ground, larger structures burn from the inside out.

Alan reaches into the flames. He finds little souls there, but they won't respond to him. Like the owls, they only stare.

"It's magic," Alan says. "Is it Winter White?"

"She's never done anything like this," Stag's Blood replies. "At least not that I ever saw. Her magic was quiet. No one was ever really sure what kind of magic it was."

"I smelled this flame before," Brattle says, tears beading in the corners of his eyes. Color dances across his face like a storm. His halo has returned so bright that Alan can hardly look at it.

"Follow close," Nora says, springing from the porch.

The Star of Henrietta waits across a wide lane paved with setts and flanked by market stands. Many of these are burning. Their tarps belly in the hot breeze, caught high on char-scaled timbers, before they blow away. On the strip of grass before the abbey's portico, a carriage leans over its flywheel, its front axels shattered. A curtain of flame ripples across the abbey's roof, peeling its tiles

151

away and melting the copper cladding from its stepped embrasures. Dead dogmen lie head to foot along the curb before the cloister, wrapped conscientiously in white, blue, or paisley sheets. Alan reaches out to them almost without thinking, and he finds them easily in the draug-light. Their spirits are like little flames of pain. Horror burns white at their hearts, but they have been laid to rest with ritual dignity. He watches as they slip away in peace, dying through the band of light at last toward whatever waits.

"This is chaos," Stag's Blood says as they reach the cloister's horsehoe arches. "No one did this in search of anything."

Sophia emerges from Alan's sleeve. The firelight moves across her like cloud shadows. "The marshals beat down a whole hill to find us," she says. "Is this really beyond them?"

Just inside the cloister is a reflecting pool with three burned bodies lying in it. They are on their backs like sated lovers, arms draped over each other. Their faces are hidden under eyeless helmets. One has a bare spot on its chest where part of its three-sigil brand is visible.

"Not in the least," Nora says.

Sophia lights on the edge of the pool. Fire climbs the topiary walls and sends its red fingers over the cloister roof. Heat hits Alan in waves. The wind roars through the flames, and Stag's Blood fur bristles down his back.

There is a small brick chapel in the center of the cloister. It is surrounded by peach trees and draped in golden fabric. Two more marshals lie dead around it - six bodies charred black and scattered with peach blossoms. Dogmen are piled at the door, torn and bleeding but untouched by flame. These are not at peace. They scream in the dark as they fall toward the draug, hurt and angry. Alan draws on his new strength to calm them as they fade.

Stag's Blood paws idly at one of the malakeen corpses. "They moved at last," he says, "but their timing was terrible."

As they near the chapel, something moves inside it. A shadow steps out from under the doorframe, reed-thin and small.

152

"There," Brattle snarls. "The daemon that did this. Come out! I know you!"

The thing steps into the dying light as if it owns it, a smile on its face befitting a queen. It holds fire in its hands, and its flesh is ash-black with burns. Alan knows it, too. Even under the vast mask of her new scars, he recognizes the fairy girl he saw impaled in the Pfahlwald. He can feel her gift in his mind like a spring watering the garden of his magic. In those depths, and just for an instant, Alan hears the Lashaseph shaman saying, "*Always something to bring back from the brink of death.*"

"Depart, little spirit," Sophia commands, her voice like a grave bell ringing.

She gathers her rays into a bright lance and hurls it at the dead girl. It strikes her in the chest, and her mouth falls open. She twitches and moans, and a change comes over her. A veil is torn aside, and Alan sees the red-eyed watcher that followed him through the Barrowvale. The burning of Cheel Gar has made it strong. It has grown in the girl's body, taking its own gift from her to feed its hunger. Alan has seen that same hunger in Brattle's eyes.

"Oh," says the thing inside the fairy girl. "Yer going to pay for that. I ain't a daemon like you seen before, Sister. Tell her, Brattie. Tell her about my fire before I melt her down."

Alan turns to see Brattle shaking and gnashing his teeth, his fists balled in front of him. Rage rolls off of him like smoke. Anger is so heavy on him and he is drawn so taut with fear that he can barely draw his knife.

"I mourned you," he croaks. "I prayed through nights you'd transcend. I *forgave* you, but you were bad from the egg. I should've known."

"Name me," says the daemon. "What're you skirtin' it for, brother? Tell yer friends the price you paid for death to let you free."

"You ain't my brother," Brattle replies. "And you ain't got a name anymore. Not to me."

Dusk runs blue across the sky. Cheel Gar howls with fire and the death cries of dogmen far away. The great trees groan around the Star of Henrietta, wearing flaming judges' wigs. One of them cracks through and falls to flatten the north side of the cloister, but the daemon Nettle doesn't turn. He takes a straining step forward, fighting to maintain control of the fairy girl's rotting tendons. Removed from her stake, the curse that has kept her body in decay has weakened. She is disintegrating, and the daemon's will cannot keep her together for long.

Alan looks into Nettle, who opens himself willingly. He is proud of his fury, but there is a small sorry in him that he does not suspect. Alan finds it cowering in fire and tries to heal it, but it's beyond his power. It has been somewhere that is outside the sphere of thanoturgy, and it has returned a hunched mutant.

The price of Brattle's resurrection, Alan thinks. *His murdered brother is back from the traitors' darkness as a monster.*

Alan puts his trash masher on its head and approaches Nettle. "Stop," he says. "Why does everything have to be a fight? This is your second chance, isn't it? What do you want if not to make things right?"

Nettle tilts the fairy girl's head and her mouth falls open. "Ain't about wills and wanting," he says. "Those're small forces in this world - barely amount to anything. You oughtta know that. There's so much more. I couldn't stop this if I tried."

The fairy girl lurches forward under Nettle's control. He raises her arms and pushes his fire through her hands in a wide arc. Alan whirls around, taking the blast on his back, and pushes Brattle to the dirt. Stag's Blood ducks away and rushes back in from the side, his claws flashing. Nora shrieks as the fire rolls over her, and Rawbones tears from her flesh with white fur curling black from its shoulders. Then she lunges, meeting Stag's Blood in the middle as he rips into the fairy girl's flank, and the two of them shred Nettle's stolen flesh to strips in a matter of seconds.

No sooner is the fairy girl scattered through the peach blossoms than one of the dead dog soldiers jerks up from the ground, limbs stiffening. This one still has life enough in it to whine as Nettle forces hot air into its lungs.

"I seen what you saw, brother," Nettle says, the dogman's voice grumbling from its lacerated throat. "It ain't what's in store. I been beyond it into echoing chaos. You ever belonged so much to one place that the place becomes you? It's better than this, Brattie. It's better to be in the pain you deserve than to wander your life away here, tryin' to rise to planes of worth that're beyond you."

Brattle springs to his feet and charges past Alan. Nettle pushes a gout of flame through the dogman's paws, but Brattle barrels straight into it. He drives his blade into the dog's dead heart, knocking it down to kneel over it. In the rising fountain of fire and blood, he pulls his knife from the dogman's breast and drags it across its throat, severing its head. The corpse convulses, starts to smoke, and then a dawn-gold sheet of flame spreads across it. Brattle leaps away as it bursts into wild flame, his chest and arms covered in burns.

"Al," Brattle says, coughing black curls of ash and smoke.

Alan tries to heal Brattle's wounds, and he is mostly successful, but there is something in them that he can't touch. Nettle has left part of his fragmented spirit there, smoldering with rage. The best he can do is will Brattle's flesh to knit and cover him with a shroud of cooling shadow.

Nettle's fire starts to die away. Dusk stars shine though the veil of smoke as it clears, and Alan watches them, wondering where his world is in their clusters.

Planes of worth that're beyond you. Alan hears Nettle's voice in his head, uncolored by the thrumming of the dogman's vocal folds. It's an echo in formless chaos, belonging nowhere anymore. It means nothing, but it weighs heavy on him. *You ever belong so much to one place that the place becomes you?*

"See to the corpses," Alan says.

Sophia circles down to light on the tip of a peach branch. Light as a blossom herself, she barely bends it at all. "Framer forgive us defiling the dead," she says.

Rawbones stalks forward, lips curling back from her star-bright fangs. Limned in Sophia's heartlight, she leans under the peach boughs and starts to disassemble one of the marshals' corpses. It's an act she undertakes almost lovingly. Stag's Blood and Brattle work together to sever the other bodies' arms and legs. When he can, Brattle stops to swallow a hunk of flesh with ritual solemnity. They aren't nearly done when a trumpet starts wailing over the walls of the city from the west, where the last of the suns' light is bleeding dark.

"We're outta time," Brattle says, tearing a fistful of meat to shreds in his teeth. "I'm surprised they didn't get here sooner."

"Now they unleash all their wrath," Sophia adds. "A daemon has shed malakeen blood here. This is the start of a war."

"Another war might be just what we need," Stag's Blood says. He turns to follow Sophia into the chapel. Brattle joins him, and Rawbones stays hunkered under the trees, sniffing the air.

Alan takes up his trash masher, straps it to his pack, and approaches the brunnmigi with his heart in his throat. He can see Nora inside her, but it doesn't salve his fear.

"We brought death here," he says. "There was a delicate balance, and we tipped it into this conflagration. Everywhere I go, I bring destruction."

Rawbones stares at him. The moon is in her six eyes. She heaves her huge breaths and pulls at her burned skin with gleaming claws.

"All follow death," she labors to say, "not just you."

In the chapel, a vivid and elaborate mural covers all four walls. Alan could stare into this painting forever. The small space of the chapel expands in its depths, stretching out toward a dawning horizon through fields of goldenrod and purple willows. The clouds seem to move, the blue advancing up the sky from the pinking east, where a city stands dark against a line of white mountains.

156

Tall figures march through the grass toward the horned altar at the back of the chapel. They are dark like Nora and bare as earth, and their hair blows behind them in thick, black ringlets. Their eyes shine with tears so real that Alan has to touch them.

Nora enters the chapel wrapped in the tatters of the sheet she took from the Grave of the Owls. Still slick with brunnmigi's blood. She kneels beside the altar.

"I haven't seen this since I was two piles high," she says. "These paintings are new. The Sisters must have done them."

"Penance," Sophia says from Brattle's shoulder. "But not enough."

"Show us the shard, Nora," Alan says. "I know the malakeen didn't take it."

"Can you feel it?" Nora replies. "It's waking up. It knows its brother is here. Marshals spilled their blood for it, but it wasn't meant for them. It was meant for me."

Without another word, Nora slides her bloody hand across the altar. The stone drinks the stain before it can set. Then it quivers and splits down the middle. They work together to widen the split until they can see the shard through it, glowing lightly under a starry sheet. Nora's smiles.

"The moon," she says, reaching in to push away the blanket and run her fingers up the shard's glassy curve. "It's smaller than I expected. Its name is Shudur."

"Snatch it up and let's burn," Brattle says at the blast of another trumpet. "Time ain't on our side. And pray to whoever that the Coma ain't found the Gale and scuttled her."

Thirty-Seven

Nora leads the way east from the Star of Henrietta toward the ring of great trees in the city square. Alan searches the dying flames for traces of Nettle, and he isn't comforted when he finds nothing. The fire recedes from the wrecks of homes to sink into the ground. It blows from the arches of the canopy in red veils, falling harmlessly on the ruin. There is only an emptiness where Nettle was, but emptiness is not necessarily absence.

Near the square, there are more dead marshals. They lie in the piles of fallen walkways, broken or half burned to ash, side by side with the wrapped bodies of dogmen. The occasional pup lies in its mother's crossed arms, face covered with whatever pieces of paper, bark, or fabric were handy. Alan feels sick looking at them. Death is in the gardens, peering out from behind waving sunflower stalks. It crawls the streets, the King in the Rubble, strong as any flame. Alan pushes it away when it approaches him, disinterested in its gloating. Unperturbed, it follows him all the way to Cheel Gar's south gate.

It has won here, as it will always win, Alan thinks, *and now the Coma is coming to sweeten its victory.*

The south gate is shattered, and there are dogmen lying uncovered around its base and on top of the wall. Beyond it, the Pfahlwald rocks like a field of reeds. Alan and the others push through the forest as quickly as they can, their heads down and their eyes on the ground in front of them. The marshals arrive in long, rattling blasts of their trumpets, and the whole wood of stakes bends away from their approach. The ground shakes as Cheel Gar begins to fall, and the last light of Nettle's fire winks out.

Moonlight spreads silver down the lawn beyond the forest's edge. The wraiths have moved the Mercy Gale out into the marshes. Alan stops at the edge of the wet grass and turns to watch the end of Cheel Gar. Brattle knuckles up to sit by Alan's side, Sophia dimming blue on his shoulder. Stag's Blood paces before them. Nora stands by herself, straight as a pillar holding the sky above the ground. The marshals circle in the air, shouting chants and blowing thunder from their trumpets. The sky roils as if there is something huge thrashing on the other side of it. Cheel Gar's great trees collapse. Her walls roar down, tearing stakes from the ground with them. The whole forest begins to lean, then the marshals blow their trumpets and the Pfahlwald bursts open. Judgies start to croaking flight in huge numbers. Stakes shatter, flinging wood and bodies east across the bog hills and out toward the lights of the Gale where she stands waiting.

"Why?" Alan asks. The dead writhe in his head, howling something that isn't quite pain or anger. Something is dawning inside him, and the gift of the fairy girl springs at the root of it. "It's such a waste."

"A display," Sophia replies. "But they could have done it any time. Why do they ever wait?"

Nora sighs. The blasts continue toward the Hookwood to blow it apart as well. "Things are changing," she says.

"Daemons an' Coma," Brattle coughs, "that ain't changed. If not Nettle, someone else woulda started it up again. It don't take much."

"Is he gone?" Stag's Blood asks.

Brattle bites his bottom lip and shakes his head.

Alan turns to see a light approaching. A Cynopolitan dogman is coming up from the moor carrying a lantern, and Mackerel Sky is following him. Her red-winged helmet is gone, and she is limping. They cross the swamp and turn north, heading up the hill toward Alan and company with grave lights swirling around them in a sea-green cloud. As they draw near, Stag's Blood steps forward to greet them. Nora stands far back from the others, tight as a bowstring.

"I expected fewer of you - or none," Mackerel Sky says, easing back over her haunches. There is blood caked in her fur. "Instead, you've added another to your number. Your quest to die is a failure."

"You knew what was coming," Stag's Blood says. "You sent us away to stall the attack, but I think you also wanted to save us."

"You served my purpose," Mackerel Sky replies. "I don't care what you believe now."

"Who *are* you?" Stag's Blood asks. "How do you know me? No more games."

Sadness moves over Mackerel Sky's face. "I ran with Fearsome. He was my mate. I am your mother."

"My mother was Gatebreaker."

"Why lie? Everyone had stories about sweet, young Pearly. You were the death of her, you know, but I hope Fearsome remembered her fondly to you. You're owed that at least, if I couldn't save you."

A smile starts across Stag's Blood's face. His whiskers bounce as it wrinkles his cheeks. He chuckles and shakes his head.

"All right," he says. "What did you name me, then? I must be owed my birth name, too."

"Name you?" Mackerel Sky says. "When you were born, I wanted to kill you. You were so small and beautiful. You were weak, and the evil in this sphere is invincible. It was cruel to let you live to face it, but Fearsome was always cruel to me. He abandoned me and raised you in a lie, and here you are in the teeth of the beast. I wanted you to leave this sphere a pure thing, blind to horror, never knowing the dauntless crush of wickedness. You should have been allowed some hope. Now you are going to meet death alone and tainted. Your life is my greatest failure, because I loved you."

The last blast of the marshals' trumpets knocks the Pfahlwald flat. Its remaining stakes explode on the ground, and then the marshals circle in silence. Cheel Gar is a pit of dirt and wood. Stag's Blood watches over his shoulder as the marshals descend upon it before he turns back to Mackerel Sky and nods.

"I don't know who you're sorry for," he says. "It isn't me, but I don't much care. I'd advise you to learn to love being sorry. Living is a gift. I wouldn't give a moment of pain or fear for any measure of nepenthe. I cast my shadow wherever I go, and I believe that the

160

world is a better place for having me in it. May that comfort you - whatever you really believe."

"And if I'm telling the truth?" Mackerel Sky asks.

"I am who I am either way," Stag's Blood replies.

He sits down before the Cynopolitan. The dogman tilts his head to look down at him over his long, straight muzzle. His pointed ears swivel back, and he narrows his eyes.

"What is your name?" Stag's Blood asks.

"Badrun," the dogman replies. His voice is high and clear as a howl in the woods.

"How many died, Badrun?"

"Less than we thought, but still too many."

"I want you to know that we will avenge them."

Badrun cocks his head. The lantern swings on the pole he carries, showing the faint glint of a bared fang.

"You didn't know them," Badrun says. "You came to rob us."

"Your understanding is not required, Badrun," Stag's Blood says, his smile still intact and in full effect. "All that is necessary now is for you to take your Protectress and find a safe place to stay."

"Where will you go?" Alan asks, but Badrun and Mackerel Sky ignore him. They turn west toward the ruined hills, and the dogman puts his lantern out.

"That's enough of that," Brattle says. "This ain't the best place to tarry."

"The Gale's waiting," Alan says, looking after the shapes of Badrun and Mackerel Sky as they disappear. "Will you come, Nora? That's our ship in the marsh. Our next stop is Sepulchra."

Nora hugs herself. A hot wind blows her hair over her shoulders and tosses the embroidered sheet around her body. Owls look out from it, red-winged helmets on their heads.

"Thank you," Nora says. "I've nowhere safe to stay."

"Then you are lucky we do," Sophia says. "Luck follows us, you know."

"I've seen."

"Onward then," Stag's Blood says, "to luck and dawn. The noose is closing."

The Mercy Gale sails east into the moors on a wild breeze. The moon burns down over the wreck of the Pfahlwald, half-lidded in shadow and lit from beneath by dancing, golden light. Moaners flap far away, howling to her. The hills shrink to hummocks across stunted flatlands strewn with extruded clasts like giants' teeth.

Brattle and Stag's Blood retreat to the orlop deck, exhausted, and curl up together at the foot of the Gale's pursling engine. Nora finds a place of her own below and falls asleep wrapped in the half-shadow of an intermediate form. Sophia shines beside her for a while before making her way to the quarterdeck to commune with the eyestone there.

Alone in the captain's cabin, Alan guts his knapsack. Pwysh's two books slip out on top of each other along with Brattle's store of flints. Nergal and Shudur are wrapped in the dark blanket Brattle was carrying in a roll on his back when he and Alan first met. It is threadbare and stained with rats' blood. Alan runs his hands over it briefly and remembers his Coward List. It has been so long since he felt the need to torture himself, he's not even sure he remembers how.

I'm not a coward anymore, Alan says to himself. *At least not the way I was. There are real fears to face now.*

At the bottom of the sack, Brattle's odd goggles have been reduced to scattered gears and tiny shards of glass. Alan counts each piece onto the floor, arranging them by size and shape. The parts make him think of the Clockwork King and his golems: crushed to their springs and complications, they will never be whole again. Sifting through the piles, he finds a four-sided reciprocating arm made of glass and copper. In the strange light of the moon through the windows, it appears to contain a loop of some filmy fabric. He spends a long moment staring at, entranced, watching it awaken in his hand. A dreamlike beauty emerges from

162

within the fabric, and his heart flutters. The dead voices fall into reverent silence.

Some kind of reliquary, Alan thinks. He slips it into his pocket, resolving to ask the others about it later.

The last thing in the pack is a palm-sized obsidian mirror. Alan slides it out of its pocket and tilts it to look at his dim reflection. Mud and char stain the dome of his skull. The Seal of Aiwass is dark and quiet beneath long, ashy smears. Alan moves his hands over his face, trying to remember the width of his nose and the curves of his mouth with his fingers. The bone is cold and rough to touch, but it doesn't feel like someone else anymore. He is the skull - he has accepted this without thinking, and his memories of his face have all but faded away.

Slipping the mirror back into the knapsack, Alan picks up Pwysh's magic books and sets them on the desk in the middle of the room. From there, they whisper to him, and he feels their power in the depths of his mind. He looks inward, shrinking himself into a point of intense focus, and searches his new gift for the source of its power. He remembers being unable to see himself in his mind. There was only fog there once, but now he is vividly within himself. He walks through the new gardens of his magic and listens to the secrets of the dead. Flowers open at his feet, and vine-hung trees bend bows as he passes beneath them. Sciomancy is a wind in the grass. Osteomancy pushes bone-white rocks up from the banks of hematomancy's warm, red river. Flesh magic is rich black soil. The Kingwatcher's bobbing flower is bright as the sun in the center. The fairy girl's gift is cold and strong under everything. He wades into it, and he hears Toven's words in its depths.

The Bleeding is where thanoturgy was born.

Alan feels the Bleeding all around him, even in the cabin where he is standing in meditation. He looks into it, and the fairy girl is there. She isn't burned, torn, or pushed over a stake. Her smile is bright, and her cheeks are rosy. At first, he thinks she resembles Allison, but that similarity vanishes. She looks more like

Winter White, but she seems more alive. She is his guide through the ruined world. This is the nature of her gift to him - how it strengthens him.

Peril opens around him, but Alan isn't afraid. He walks the Bleeding holding the fairy girl's hand. She laughs and tells him her name.

"Theia," she says.

"Aren't you afraid to be here?" he asks.

Theia says nothing more. She leads him in no direction in particular, and he doubts that direction is relevant in the Bleeding. Her purpose is to show him that the Bleeding can't touch her and that her, as long as she is with him, he is safe from it as well.

"The Darkle isn't evil," Theia says. "It's been abandoned for a long time. Just because it's dead doesn't mean it's not lonely."

"I know how that feels," Alan says. The Bleeding wraps its many wings around him. Its loneliness is huge and terrible. Rage burns at its heart like a dying star.

Back in the garden of his mind, Theia sinks away with a watery giggle. Alan stands in power for a long time, putting down roots, until he is part of the garden himself. He stretches his branches, tasting Theia through the skin of the ground, and he opens blue blooms with golden centers.

They need the truth, says the old voice from the Whisperwood graves, *or they take you into leaves and bark.*

Returning to himself feels like waking. When he emerges from his inner darkness, Alan is as refreshed as if he has slept well for a long time. He turns from the desk, intent on finding a way to wash his skull, and is surprised to see Mackerel Sky standing in the doorway.

"Spirit," she whispers, "I need to speak with you alone about my son. I need to warn you."

Alan feels his magic springing awake. The few hairs still left on his arms rise as if he's about to be struck by lightning. Death is hungry. He wants to lash out with all his power, but he stifles himself.

"How did you get past the wraiths?" he asks.

Mackerel Sky takes a step further into the cabin. "My time is short," she says. "Don't go all the way to Sepulchra yet. Winter White is ready for you."

Alan looks deep into Mackerel Sky. She is barely there at all. Her spirit and substance are wasting away to vapor. She circles him, and he can see the windows through her.

"You're dead," Alan says.

"Not dead," says Mackerel Sky. "I've been granted leave. I'm fading at last, going back to hunting lands we're promised, and this is my last act. There is an army waiting at Sepulchra. Go first to the Lake of Escar and find the exorcist, Rapalion. He will give you the power to break Winter White's forces."

"What power?" Alan asks.

"Say that you will do this - for him, if not for me. For my son. Don't lead him into Winter White's trap. Promise me! I cannot take fear to the hunt."

Alan considers the pleading look on her face and thinks of his sister. It won't hurt to send Mackerel Sky to her promised land with certainty. Maybe that was what Allison's ghost had been looking for in the blood-red tub where she died.

"Yes," Alan says. "I'll go to Escar and find the exorcist. You have my word."

Mackerel Sky sobs with relief. It's a rattling, chaotic sound - like a drain opening suddenly to suck down too many years of water. She leaps up as if to put grateful paws on Alan's shoulders, and the first sounds of "Thank you" are in her mouth as she fades away.

The air in the captain's cabin grows thin and chills to a mist. Alan sits on his desk in the cold for a while, testing Mackerel Sky's last secret like a scab. He slips Pwysh's notes from between the two magic books and looks them over, moving his fingers over the words as if he might find another meaning hidden in the ink.

Bell, star, and spirit.

Danger is growing in the world. Alan thinks of the first night he spent in the hospital after the accident. He'd heard footsteps outside his door all night. He'd felt the air move around his bed as if stirred by someone he couldn't see. The TV had been a dark eye watching him.

Can you hear me, Theia? he asks. The fairy girl burbles in his head, content to feed the garden of his mind and having nothing important to say.

Alan steps out onto the main deck. The sky is spectacularly open. Darkness lies for miles above the mast, rich with stars and bleeding silver. The chief mate shifts back from the bow, where a cluster of wraiths are working to clean the ship's cannon. They move around it like a knot of living moonlight.

"All's well, Captain," the chief mate whispers. Gooseflesh runs up Alan's arms. "Sepulchra is a good way away, and it'll get cold before we see the tombs."

"Do you know Escar?" Alan asks.

The chief mate shimmers. Its starry eyes reposition themselves in the part of it that Alan thinks of as its head. "Yes," it says. "It's on the way. Shall we change course?"

"What's there?"

"A flat, white waste before the tables of Sepulchra," says the wraith. "And Columba - the Tomb of the Doves."

"Take us that way," Alan says. "I mean, set course for Columba. How's that strike you?"

The chief mate bows like a candle flame. "Aye," it says. "As you order."

On the orlop, Alan finds Brattle curled asleep like a coyote. His halo is gone and he seems healed. Stag's Blood is stretched out near the stairs, chin on his reaching forelegs, his paws clenching as he dreams.

Sleep well, he thinks. *You deserve it.*

He works a small spell of healing over them before he turns and slips back up the stairs.

Nora is on the quarterdeck, nude as the full moon, talking with Sophia. They pause as Alan climbs up from the main deck, leaving him feeling like a waiter intruding upon their conversation.

"More to drink?" Alan tries. "Diet here. And was it peach tea, miss?"

Nora fixes him with a burning stare.

"Restaurant humor," Alan says, embarrassed. "Doesn't really work, I guess. Do you two mind a third?"

"Not at all," Sophia replies. She is glowing like a fallen star. The pinpoints above could be her Sisters. "I was telling Nora about Welkinbright. The fires haunt me. I hope the sylves were able to reclaim the city." She looks over her shoulder. They are entering high country, and the ruins of Cheel Gar are hidden. She must feel them, even from here, seething like a wound. "It's like we failed in Cheel Gar. We came too late."

"And I was telling her not to count her defeats just yet," Nora says. "What do you believe?"

Alan leans back against the gunwale. The westward wind pulls his robe tight around him. "I think we're due a clean win," he says, "but I don't foresee that happening any time soon. Nobody gets out clean -that's what I'm learning. Not even if they have a mother like Mackerel Sky who's actually able to follow through on her delusions and rub them out the day they're born. She couldn't have spared Stags if she'd tried."

"I don't believe her," Nora says, frowning.

"Should we not?" Alan asks. "Do you know her that well?"

"I know that no mother could honestly wish death on her child."

Pain shoots through Alan's chest. He sags for a moment, skewered on it. Would his mother have taken his life to spare him pain?

"Tell me about Cheel Gar," Alan says. "How did Mackerel Sky became its Protectress?"

Nora straightens. Stiff as a flag in a gale, she crosses the quarterdeck to incline against the gunwale beside Alan. Her naked feet barely touch the boards. She looks out across the rising ground, and pushes her hair behind her ear.

"The Sisterhood built Cheel Gar as a living monument after Nex's War," she says, far away. "It was a graveyard for innocence built in the simplest imitations of Pictish style. In mockery of their own guilt, they put it right in the Pfahlwald's teeth. I was one of the few pixies who lived there. I thought it was beautiful, but it was wearing a mask. Now the mask is broken, and all that's left is the city as it really was: dead.

"Mackerel Sky arrived only recently. The Coma were pressing the city, looking for Shudur. When Mackerel Sky appeared, the Cynopolitans called her the Star of Mastaba because the marshals were afraid of her. She created the office of Protectress and then slipped away into the halls of power like bad water. She let the marshals closer even as she turned them away. I don't know her, but I suspect she was a Coma spy."

"It's interesting that you say that," Alan says. "I just saw her. She came to me while I was alone and made me promise that we wouldn't go to Sepulchra right away. She wants us to go to Escar. Supposedly, there's someone there who can help us. What do you think of that?"

"Anything could be a trap now," Nora replies.

Sophia flies up from the eyestone to walk the gunwale between Nora's elbows and Alan's. "What kind of help are we going to find in Escar?" she asks. "

Alan follows Nora's gaze over the side. There is a light burning nearby at the pinnacle of a sprawling ziggurat. He feels the breaths of the Mercy Gale beneath him, heaving the decks up and filling the sail with veering wind. The canvas creaks, and tension sings down the ropes as the ship scuds along.

"I don't know," Alan says. "She didn't say. That's part of what worries me."

"Mackerel Sky is dangerous," Nora says, turning to face Alan. Her eyes are star-bright beneath her knitted brows. "You didn't see what she did in Cheel Gar. You never will, now. The legacy of her wickedness is crushed. She'll crush you, too, if you trust her."

"I don't," Alan replies, "but I know White and Toven are expecting us, and I trust them less."

Thirty-Eight

The next day, Alan tells Brattle and Stag's Blood about Mackerel Sky's last request and the change in plan.

"Sounds like the right call, bones," Brattle says, leaning over the gunwale on his tiptoes. They are at the prow in a dead calm, the Gale's engines humming through her decks. "We're gettin' in deep, now. Everyone's out to get us.

"We've seen little real fighting," Stag's Blood says. "I have a feeling that's about to change." He licks the side of his paw and slicks his mane back. It pokes up into a rebellious spike at the top.

"You say she faded right in front of you?" Stag's Blood continues. "What did it look like?"

"She was happy," Alan replies. "She talked about the hunt. Then she was just gone, and it was cold afterward. It made me a little sad."

"Matilda's Ride," Stag's Blood says. "I've been dreaming about it lately. Fearsome told of lush green woods full of shadow and fields of long grass as far as you can see. The ground is as quiet as sand, and the elk all have bulging jugulars and spines of cork. It's paradise, but he was afraid of it."

"Mackerel Sky said she'd been granted leave," Alan says. "What do you think she meant by that?"

"I don't know," Stag's Blood says. "The will to fade can be revoked. Someone may have been keeping her here. That must have been torture."

"Have you felt Nettle any more?" Alan asks Brattle.

"Ain't felt nothin', but I know he ain't gone."

"How do you know that?" Stag's Blood asks.

Brattle pushes an exaggerated sigh through his lips. It comes out like a raspberry, and then he spends a moment spitting over the side.

"How'd you know there's nothin' in the dark watching you sleep?" he asks. "How can you say with any sureness you're alone? I'm certain in that way."

170

"I'm sorry about Welkinbright," Alan says.

"Don't be," Brattle says. "Dyin' woke me."

Alan spends the next few days in meditation. He can improve his spell-casting skill with practice, but there is an aspect of his facility that can only expand in quiet contemplation. So much of magic, he is learning, is theory, and no amount of physical drilling will benefit him for long if his power can't grow in his mind. To this end, he sits before the eyestone on the orlop deck and stares into the Bleeding for long stretches, its purifying energy pouring over him, searching for phantoms.

What is the heart of death magic? he wonders. *Where do I intersect with it?*

The Mercy Gale skips across high white fields in whirls of snow. When the wind dies, the wraiths roll her sail and she cruises on sylvan power. Stag's Blood takes to prowling the ship looking for larders, storage hatches, and dark corners for Sophia to light. The two map the Mercy Gale by night, and Stag's Blood spends a good part of most days sleeping.

Whenever the Gale has to stop to let Alan recharge, Stag's Blood and Brattle hunt the frozen badlands for rabbits and large, six-legged elk with silver antlers. Brattle cooks the meat over an open flame in the galley, and their dinners are long and loud. Alan sits in on them despite having no interest in food anymore.

Nora prefers to eat alone in the cuddy - a cold, cramped hole beneath the poop deck. Alan finds her here the night the Gale arrives in Escar, sitting with her feet crossed on the stave of a cask and sipping loose meat soup from a tankard of dichroic glass.

"May I come in?" he asks her, knocking softly on the doorframe.

"Certainly," Nora replies. Owls troop across her midriff in red-winged helmets. Doves cower before them, small and outnumbered. The sheet she took from Noctua is torn and straining over her curves. She stares over her cup like a spy watching the door for her mark. "It's your ship."

"It's our ship," Alan says. "Is that the snow fox sausage Brattle ground?"

Nora puts her cup down and looks into it. "Yes. It's terrible. Cold, for one, and I think the stock was just boiled blood."

"What are you accustomed to?"

Nora chuckles. "Did you come to ask me what I like to eat?"

Alan bows into the room. Beams cross the low ceiling, and he can feel the bare, gnawed wood floor sagging. He takes a seat beside a pair of cabinets stacked on top of each other.

"I want to make you feel welcome," Alan says. "You've been distant, and I totally get it. Maybe you need some reassurance."

Nora hugs herself for a moment. "I don't like this ship. It's haunted. How can you tolerate it?"

Alan thinks about this while he listens to the songs of the wraiths on the weather decks.

"It's my magic powering her," he finally says. "Maybe that's why it doesn't bother me."

Nora flares her nostrils like she's catching a sour smell. "Toven," she says. "Another thanoturge, I gather. Why put your faith in death magic? Does it love you? Does it serve you? I think it's disgusting."

"I'm not sure about love," Alan replies. "I've never thought about it that way. I trust it because it works."

"And how does it work for you?"

"Well," Alan begins, unsure how to distill the complex actions of his magic into a concise answer, "it's a little bit like sleep. It's something you can do, but you don't know how. You lie down, you close your eyes, and it happens. It's gradual like that, but not as automatic."

Nora remains uncomfortably still throughout this explanation. Alan wonders if she's even listening.

"My experience has been quite different," she says with a laugh, still staring into the middle distance. "Not like sleep at all. *You* close your eyes?"

"So to speak," Alan replies. He turns to follow Nora's gaze over his shoulder, and he sees what's gotten her attention.

There is a wraith shivering in the hallway. Motes dance through it, caught in the thick of its strangely knife-shaped body. When it finally vanishes, Nora is able to focus on Alan again.

"You're like Enlil," she says, "but not for the same reasons, I suspect. Will you tell me what happened?"

"Can we talk above? It's a little close in here, and I don't the floor is entirely safe."

"No. This is the only place the wraiths won't go. I prefer to stay here."

"All right," Alan says, nodding and trying to fold himself into a comfortable position. Finally, he resorts to sitting on the floor, which groans beneath him. "I tried to go through a portal in Marmorea soon after I arrived. It didn't work. The portal spit me out like this, and the Geier Venue had to save me. They said that magic is the only thing keeping me alive now."

Nora sits up and plants her feet in front of her. Her hands on her knees, Alan likes the way her toes curl to take her weight. Her calves are hard and tight with sinew.

"The weirs between spheres are not like doors," Nora explains, "nor like gates into gardens. They're parasites on Midion's will - physical emanations of guardian spirits. They feed on this sphere, and it uses them as trials, like the Eye of Nudd. What happened to you was judgment. The vultures know this, and they did as the gate commanded. It's all they can ever do. Where did you intend to go?"

"Back where I came from," Alan says. "The living world. Animus."

"Another living human," Nora says, a smile pushing up her freckled cheeks. "No wonder the weir spit you out."

"You think I'm supposed to be here."

"You're here aren't you? Magic is keeping you alive. Midion's magic. Midion's will." She lifts her hand to the point of her chin and taps her fingers at her jawline, as if measuring the thickness of her skin. Her eyes gleam like vitreous gems.

"Perhaps you've come for me," Nora continues. "We may find your destiny together - or we may make one."

"How do you mean?" Alan asks.

"Close the door," Nora says. "This is thorny country."

Alan does as she asks. The door to the cuddy is three uneven planks of ash held together by battens. In its proper place, it sits loosely in the doorframe, unattached to any hinges. With passage to the rest of the deck more or less blocked off, the cuddy feels tiny. Alan turns back to Nora as she rises from her chair, graceful as a heron with her neck bent and her head bowed. When she looks up into the empty depths of his sockets, he wonders what she sees. There is nothing to read there. For her part, Nora is glowing with nervous fear.

"I am the last pixie," she says, approaching to shrink the cuddy even further. "I don't know what's ahead of me. There is so much of my future I can't design, but I can try. I can take steps to foster the continuity of my race. I want a child, man of destiny. Will you give me one?"

Alan buckles backward, slipping with his shoulder against the plank door. His knees wobble, but he catches himself on the jamb. He hears his heart start hammering in his chest and worries for a second that Brattle is beating on the floor from below, trying to get them to quiet down.

"No," Alan says. "I mean wait."

"I *am* waiting."

Alan takes as deep a breath as he can manage. His lungs don't seem to care to draw much anymore. "You may not know exactly what's ahead of you, but surely you can see that it's not likely to be big stretches of relaxing free time. Are you sure you want to get pregnant right now?"

"I appreciate your concern," Nora says. "You're a lot like a father already, you know. I would carry the baby, but the beast would not. We are separate in that way, among others."

"And if the beast dies?"

Nora squares her jaw. The wraiths' song has picked up. It's ringing across the weather decks, leaking like rain through the ceiling, but she isn't hearing it now. "There are risks," she replies. "Do you not *want* to?"

"To be a father?" Alan says. "I don't know. Besides, I'm not even sure I can. I don't eat, I don't sleep, I barely breathe. A lot of things are different."

"You aren't sure if you're virile," Nora says. "That is a case for experimentation. Regarding the physical processes, I have this."

Nora puts her hand low on Alan's back. Her fingers tap the wide curve of his waist along his iliac crest the same measuring way they tapped her jaw line before. Alan can feel her hand through his impenetrable robe almost as if she is really touching him. Heat flows from her fingertips.

"You should have heard what they used to call us," Nora says, leaning in to whisper under Alan's chin. "All the old hate is dead. It spilled with the blood of my kind on the ground, wasted, but you should know well that dead things can rise. It only takes a look, a touch on the street, a whisper overheard to disinter that hate: a look to make you follow, a touch to make you stand, and a whisper to finish you."

"You're talking about sex magic," Alan says, his hands shaking. Lead sits in his gut, and his spine is lightning.

"*Life*," Nora replies, taking her hand away at last. She steps just beyond his reach and stares at him, sizing him up like prey. "Sex, yes, but pixie magic makes life. Life above all things. Our child would have the best of both life and death. Will you put life inside me Alan?"

Alan looks into his inner darkness. His mind is aflame. Desire is raking the garden of his magic like a fire, burning bright but

175

consuming nothing. Squelching it requires so much of him that the Seal of Aiwass begins to glow on his forehead.

"OK," Alan says. "We know it can work, but I still want to wait. I'm sorry." Nora crosses her arms and squeezes her mouth into a hard frown. "Does it have to be right here and right now?"

Nora's eyes are livid as coals. "You could die in Sepulchra."

"I know," Alan says, "but this is the way it has to be."

"Very well," Nora says. She sinks back into her chair again, feet wide apart. "I won't press you. Fear is outrunning me, Alan. It will overtake me. So much could die with me. I don't know how to be what I am anymore."

"Come down and eat with us," Alan says. His heart is the cold, quiet lump once more. The fire remains in his brain, a little candle waiting in a part of his mind he hasn't visited in a very long time. He will be back to fan it, he's sure. It will leap again through his garden before long. "It'll get you thinking about something else. I know it always helps me."

Nora looks into her flagon of soup again. A light appears behind her, small and beautiful – a single orb glinting in place just over her right shoulder. When she lifts her head to favor Alan with a smile, the light disappears, leaving a purple streamer curling through her hair.

"Thank you, Alan," Nora says. "I think I will."

Morning brings a hesitant storm. The suns are veiled as they climb the sky, and noon breaks too cold to part the clouds. Alan meets Brattle and Nora on the quarterdeck when the storm makes up its mind. Snow blows down over the Mercy Gale to heap in wet drifts along her prow, where the heat pouring up from her engines is less intense. Fat flakes melt on the eyestone's glass, where Sophia sits with her wings pressed flat on account of the wind. Stag's Blood leaps up onto the quarterdeck after Alan, soft as a feather falling on new banks of powder.

"Thank you again for agreeing to come," Alan says. He is wearing a new knapsack that he found in one of the holds that Sophia and Stag's Blood discovered. It is small and comfortable, and it ties at the top with bright red tassels. He has only Brattle's blanket and flints inside it. The reliquary he found in the mess of Brattle's broken goggles is in the pocket of his robe, where he can feel its dreaming warmth against his skin. It reminds him of Nora's probing fingers.

"The next ward is done," Alan continues. How is yours coming along?"

Nora is sitting cross-legged before a large, black chest with silver handles. She is wearing a triangular poncho with red-violet flowers blooming across the back and high boots that Stag's Blood found in the hold. Snowflakes dance around her head, caught in the concentrated surge of her glamour. She sings, and the words of her song fall from her mouth like fire. Orbs blow through her hair and down her shoulders in great shimmering profusion.

Alan watches, entranced. He knows nothing of warding. Watching Stag's Blood and Sophia place guarding spells throughout the ship has been a humbling experience. Nora's spell seems to be the most complex of the all the wards they've placed - though, like all but one of the others, it shall make a dummy ward. Watching her weave, feeling the magic looping through her, Alan feels incomplete. His magical knowledge is crude and perforated by gaps.

"What's she doing now?" Alan asks Stag's Blood.

Stag's Blood closes his eyes for a moment. "She's twisting it back on itself," he says, head bowed. "Doubling it over. She's almost finished. Her style is strange - older than mine. It's beautiful."

"What does it feel like?"

Stag's Blood looks up. "What does it feel like to see the draug?"

"Like I'm looking through a secret window. I'm always afraid someone's going to catch me peeping."

"Well," Stag's Blood chuckles, "it doesn't feel like that."

Minutes pass, and the wraiths stow the sail before Nora stands to reply. "It's done," she says. The light of her spell collapses around her. The captive snowflakes drop at her feet to melt. She turns, and the lines on her face looked as though they were carved with arrowheads. "It will fool any seekward, but it hasn't bolstered my confidence much."

"No rest for the hunted," Stag's Blood says. "Confidence is a luxury. We can only trust now in the best precautions."

"This is better than hauling them with us through the open," Sophia adds.

Nora's frown is a storm of its own. Behind it, she is old and beaten. "I know," she says, shrugging, "but I feel like I'm abandoning my post."

"You're not alone anymore, that's all," Alan says. "Your burden's not gone. It's just shifted. Now, if you're ready, we should get out there. I don't want to dick around here anymore than we have to."

Alan looks out across the blinding fields. There is just enough midday shine on the snow to tell the horizon from the sky. A huge range of long plateaus marches off into the east. Columba watches from the foothills like a widow waiting to see her husband's ghost.

Brattle appears on the main deck clutching his walking stick. He is swimming in a poncho just like Nora's. "Ice from here to the place," he says, "but it's thick as rock for most of the way. Do we got the goods stashed and locked down?"

Nora sighs and pushes her snow-flecked hair back behind her ear. Her auricles are tall and petal-soft. She ties a strip of cloth around her head to keep them warm.

"I hate leaving the shards behind," she says to Alan.

"The wraiths will protect them," Alan replies. He thinks twice about putting a comforting hand on Nora's shoulder. Instead, he takes a step forward and clenches his fists at his sides. "And even if someone manages to get by them, the dummy wards will keep them guessing. I promise that you don't need to worry."

"Whether or not I need to leave them isn't the issue. The issue is that I am."

"Then why go?" Stag's Blood asks. "You have the option to stay."

"Stay on this ghost ship alone?" Nora replies, making her way toward the steps to the main deck. "I'd sooner hand the shards to our enemies."

On the main deck, Alan helps Brattle lower the gangplank. He stands aside, trying to lift it with magic. The hand of his mind is clumsy, and its strength exceeds his ability to control it. Frustrated and with his head aching, he gives up.

"That bit ain't coming easy?" Brattle asks as they heave the gangplank over the side.

"I can move flesh and bone well enough," Alan replies. "Telekinesis is a utility. I just don't have much of a handle on it beyond the sphere of my power."

"A rustic can learn to sign," Brattle says, "but he ain't ever gonna stand up and give a talk about sign language. Everybody's got their heights, boss."

"Is that what I am? A rustic thanoturge?"

"Glibbers and meeps," Brattle replies.

The gangplank reaches the snow with little left over on the main deck, but it will serve. Stag's Blood and Nora start down it at Alan's behest. Brattle lingers for a minute longer, while Alan helps Sophia down from the quarterdeck, cupping her in his hand as the wind picks up.

Alan passes Sophia to Brattle, who slips her glowing into the pocket of his flowery coat. She smokes as snow melts against her, making Brattle look like an ember thief. Before Alan follows Brattle and his trail of Fetchlight smoke down onto the ice, the chief mate approaches him with one of its helpers.

"How are things on your end?" Alan asks.

"Checking in before you go," hisses the chief mate, thin as film and streaming in the breeze. The wraith behind it wavers, unconcerned by the fragments of its superior officer blowing through its body. "Five wards are in place. Precious stones are in the cuddy."

"Stand guard until we get back," Alan says, nodding. "Let no one aboard. All right?"

"Captain," the chief mate groans. A tense ripple moves through it. For a moment, it is as real and present as the ship herself, and Alan can barely stand to look at it. It is like a scar on the world. "We hope for your pardon, but this is a bad place. The ice is thick over a waking threat. The crew are uneasy. Mind your time away."

"What scares wraiths?" Alan asks.

"Splintering timbers," says the chief mate's helper. "Bulkheads breaking. Splitting bow to stern. Mind your time away."

With this, the wraiths sink into the depths of the ship. Alan imagines them shimmering into shadows, hiding in the crooks of beams with their stellar eyes dimming. The Mercy Gale goes quiet save for the creak of her mast and the thrum of her sylvan engines.

"We won't be gone long," Alan says to the empty air before he turns to mount the gangplank. "Don't worry. Just wait."

The others are standing in a semicircle at the bottom of the plank. Brattle brushes snow from the ice to look into it, but the surface is clouded with frozen haze. Alan tries to reach into it as they set out for Columba, and he can feel a still, small life beneath it. It reminds him of the draugs.

"Hunker down," he tells the others as he pulls his hood up. "Let's get this over with."

The snow beats down in wet, white lashes. Unstoppable, it drips through everything, and it isn't long into the walk before Alan is soaked from neck to feet. He thinks of the freezer at Ray's and its roaring cold. For a moment, he is there again, coughing through deep breaths of massless air. He can hear Iscela's duranguense bouncing softly through the north wall. The sound is odd and lonely here, but Alan holds onto it. He hums a few comforting notes of *Sentimientos Encontrados* as the ice moans beneath him.

"This was a plain long time ago," Brattle says, swaying upright through the snow with his hands above his head, "and there was a war on the plain - the last battle of a war. After was a day so rich for Death that he froze the ground to frost in his delight. The cold creeps east while the memory remains, and Sepulchra's near all covered now. But the story's finally fading away. It might start warmin'. Here was the worst of it in Escar though. It'll always be cold here - Death's cold."

"Stories are like ice on our memories," Nora says. Alan can barely hear her. She is wrapped in her coat, her collar pulled up over her mouth. "In the cold of truth's absence, we send tales' tendrils out to make something that meets and knits together."

"This ain't a fabrication," Brattle grumbles. "Can't you hear the war horns still ringin'?"

"All I hear is the wind," Stag's Blood says, "and that is scarcely more comforting."

They push on across the ice with a tempest wailing up around them. Stag's Blood strides ahead of the rest on his wide paws, leaving only faint clover-shaped tracks behind him. Alan and Nora slip along, clinging to each other, Sophia pressed flat in the hollow of Alan's shoulder. At the foot of Columba's splintering, white dome, they huddle for a moment on the covered porch of the open south door.

"Catafalque pine," Nora says, running her hand up the wall. Her knuckles are chapped red. "These trees don't grow anymore."

"Why not?" Asks Alan.

"The live ones left the sphere," Brattle replies. "Their seeds sleep in the ground, waitin' for 'em. In fields where they lay thick, you can feel their dreams sometimes."

"It looks strong," Alan says. "I thought it was stone."

"It has to be," Brattle says. "You'd be, too."

The wind abates to a thready roar. Snow blows out of the tomb on drum-beat breaths, caught in collapsing spirals. Two statues stand on either side of the entrance, their features so worn that Alan can't tell what they used to represent. He peers into the dark beyond the threshold, humming a bit more of the song stuck in his head.

"What are we supposed to be looking for?" Nora asks. "It sounds like there's something alive inside."

"I don't know," Alan replies. "Something to help us at the prisons. What could do that?"

"A key," Brattle chuckles.

"I'm ready for anything at this point," Alan says, taking his trash masher into his hand. It glows faintly, and its warmth soothes his hands.

Alan leading, they duck into the tomb. Sarcophagi sit in the high walls like drawers. The marble ceiling is braced across black pine beams and covered in elaborate carvings. Snow blows in through the remains of an oculus in its north side to lie thick on the wide floor. The light falling through rupture in the top of the dome might have been focused into a thin beam when the oculus was intact. Now it is just a white spray with motes and snowflakes swimming through it — a bright lance of dawn light that should be hidden behind the solid sheet of clouds outside. Near the center of the snow-blown chamber is a sarcophagus decorated with birds cut in flying angles.

"There sits a good place to start," Sophia says.

She works her way out of Alan's robe and, upon checking the strength of the wind, she flits over to land on the sarcophagus. Her wings ring as she moves her hands over the face carved into its top.

"He must have been some kind of dove king," Stag's Blood says, padding across the snow to circle the coffin with his nose at its base.

"I don't feel anything dead inside it," Alan says.

182

They gather around the sarcophagus and try to pry off its lid, but it is stuck fast. Alan can feel little spells working over it, keeping it in place. Their age has not affected their strength - no amount of effort on anyone's behalf can break them loose. Finally, Brattle looks up at the shattered skylight.

"OK," he says. "Square one. You think that light's got something to do with this?"

"Perhaps there was a lens there when this tomb was built," Sophia says.

"We don't have a lens," Alan says, feeling defeated. "Can we dig this thing up and drag it to the Gale?"

"I can help," Stag's Blood says. He steps into the brightest part of the light and stares up at the sky with his eyes shining funeral fires. "I can make a ray. Let me try." With this, he spreads a fanged smile. "Working light is good for the hunt, and my kind are mostly light anyway."

"Show me, Stags," Alan says. "Do the thing. Let's see what happens."

Stag's Blood sits down and closes his eyes. He fills his chest with long breaths, and his jowls quiver as he growls them out again. The wind calms, and the air goes still. Alan sees Stag's Bloods breath flowing from his mouth in blue-white waves. The Tomb of the Doves seems to shrink, and Alan tenses up, afraid for a moment that it will close like a night bloom and crush them. Shadows splinter on its walls, crawling over the ancient fretwork to gather around the wound in the roof. There, the curtain of light starts to waver, and sparks appear in it. Stag's Blood takes one more deep breath and heaves it out, and the light twists into a crackling shaft as it strikes the sarcophagus. The lid pops loose, and Stag's Blood opens his eyes. As he relaxes, the wind resumes its wailing, and the light expands until it is just a frigid spill again.

"Remarkable," Nora says as she leans in with Brattle to push the lid of the sarcophagus further open. It slides easily, and little green globes come swirling out from beneath it. "What a gift to have. Fae train for decades to master photomancy."

"I've not mastered anything," Stag's Blood replies, his shoulders low and his breath puffing out in simple steam. "Fearsome was an unparagoned lightweaver. I was a disappointment, though he never showed it."

"Why don't you come see what you've opened, then?" Brattle says. "It wasn't your Da here to do this. It was you."

Stag's Blood pushes himself up off his haunches with a weary sigh. Looking into him, Alan sees Stag's Blood's deep fatigue spreading into the steady fire of his spirit - forking apart and burning black like lightning scars. He gives a bit of himself to slow the spread of weakness through Stag's Blood's muscles before he turns to join the others.

"It's too dark to see in," Nora says. "There's an umbra guarding the bottom."

Beneath the carven lid, the sarcophagus is deep. The darkness there is as thick as a mist of ice crystals. It only parts when Sophia pushes her heartlight until the Eternal Flame shines through it, and then it hisses and squirms while it dissipates.

"The last defense," Nora says. "Primitive, but it still works. What was it hiding?"

Inside the sarcophagus, lying on a bed of wings with riveted feathers, is a robot's skeleton. Two copper arms lie beside its silver spine, the balls of their joints roughly aligned with the sockets of its steel-plated shoulders. Its legs are similarly disjointed, and they end in three-toed feet with talons of black iron. The head is a horned skull tilted back, barely holding together, and the lower half of its jaw has fallen into its open chest cavity. There, in the spread of the iron ribs, the lost mandible beside it, is a large organic heart.

"Looks like Toven's work," Brattle says.

Sophia lands on the tip of a rib. "Older than that," she says. "King Toven's work was never his own."

"There," Nora says, pointing to a placard that is just visible beneath the lolling head. "It's Pictish: 'Rapalion, Owlsbane, Exorcist.'"

"The owls and the doves," Alan says, reaching down to stroke the heart with the tips of his fingers. The black, satin flesh quivers in response. "Tell me the story."

Brattle shakes his head. "I ain't got one," he says. "I'm sorry, Al. I don't know."

"The bones of the last aeon," Nora replies. "Or the one before that."

Alan to Brattle. "Death is everyone's destiny."

Rapalion's heart continues to tremble against Alan's fingers. He tries to enter it through his mind, and it blocks him. He teases it open with a series of new spells so abstract that he barely understands how they work. In the Bleeding emptiness, the heart is huge, and it beats like thunder. Its valves spasm, squirting color across the gulf of the draug. Just beyond the dead side of that dividing light, Alan finds a still small life that he recognizes. It is sleeping just as he felt it sleeping beneath the ice - asleep in something like death, and dreaming. The dead awake in Alan's mind to assail him in unison. There are more within him now than ever before. Has he been collecting them?

Alan prods the spark of life, but it doesn't react. It is enslaved in its dreams, and it can't feel him. It hasn't felt anything for a long time. Coaxing the spark into a leaping flame requires a subtlety that Alan was unaware that he was capable of. He has to dig new wells into the reservoir to get new power flowing. When it finally wakes, the still, small life burns the draug dim. It roars into the Bleeding, and the heart begins to beat hard under Alan's palm.

"What are you doing to it?" Nora asks.

Brattle adds, "Careful, Al. Remember what happened before."

"This is different," Alan says, briefly terrified by visions of Brattle's Da surging up in the rain with the Bleeding in his eyes.

If I had known more, Alan thinks, *I might have been able to save Pick.*

He can't dwell on this thought. He centers himself again and continues. "It's in a different state - not dead, but sleeping. Frozen, kind of. Or paralyzed. *Preserved*. I just have to wake it."

Rapalion's heart pumps feverishly until it ruptures. Blood spills out of it, cold and char-black, and Alan steps away. The still, small life is free on the living side of the draug. It soars for a moment on wings of dove-white light, radiating such joy and gratitude that Alan feels that his own heart might burst as well. Then it flickers out, leaving peace in the Bleeding and new power blooming in the garden of Alan's magic. Alan reels; giddy, propping himself up on his trash masher. He starts to tell the others how full he feels before the ice beneath them starts to quake and whine. A dove-white light appears in the frozen deep, bright as morning even through the snow and the milky haze on the surface of the ice.

"Another last defense," Brattle says, looking up at the shattered dome with his stained-glass eyes wide as the walls begin to shake.

"Yeah," Alan says. "Let's go."

Alan leads the others out of the south door and onto the frozen lake. Brattle sits astride Stag's Blood, fists balled in his mane. Sophia hides in Alan's hood. The Mercy Gale stands waiting where they left her, all her lights on - the warm heart of storm-cold Escar. The ice heaves and bulges, twisting the Tomb of the Doves apart as it splits open. Alan breaks into a run, trying to use his slipping momentum to propel himself forward faster. Cracks trace his stride, and he stumbles to avoid them. He fights through a hard, hot twist in his knee to reach the gangplank last as Stag's Blood and Nora are mounting it. The ice roars apart behind him, hurling him forward on a rising block, wrapped in frigid spray. He hits water clinging to the splintered end of the gangplank, and the first longing strains of *Sentimientos Encontrados* rise in his mind as he begins to sink.

Thirty-Nine

The Lake of Escar wraps around Alan like velvet. Its grip is loose, almost loving, and he hardly feels wet at all. Cold presses in on him, but it can't fill him. It stays just against his skin, soft as a kiss, until he is all but paralyzed. He feels death moving around him in the dark, stalking him, but he keeps it at bay. He can still do that at least.

"Move your arms," Sophia says, warming against him. He tries to comply, but the water isn't thick enough to push.

"I'm going right through it," Alan says. "How can I get up? The water's thick where I'm from."

Panic sets in as Alan beats his arms. He kicks against nothing, his feet aching. The end of the Mercy Gale's gangplank drifts away from him. His robe binds under his arms, the only thing here that feels heavy. As he thrashes, Alan feels hard lumps near his hands. The water starts to move, and the lumps swirl against him. He claws at them, trying to use them to climb out of the water, but they sink into the black when he touches them. One of the lumps comes close enough to his face for a moment that he can see that it's a dead bird.

You have wings, Alan thinks beneath the melody he's still humming. *Why can't you lift me out of here?*

The bird says nothing in return. He reaches for it, and it sinks to join its brothers at the unseen bottom. The lake is full of dead owls.

"It's working," Sophia cheers. "Keep fighting!"

"It's not working," Alan replies even as something closes around him and he feels himself rising toward the surface. "I can't move my arms anymore. "This isn't me."

Alan's spine becomes a bolt of lightning. Something closes on him, squeezing him hard, and hauls him out of the water at dizzying speed. High in the air, the storm battering him, Alan has a moment to look down at the giant fist that is holding him and the towering thing it belongs to.

It is Rapalion on an enormous scale - the real Dove King pulled from its dreams of the last world by Alan's magic. Wings of riveted feathers hang from its shoulders, broken and useless. Its skull head smokes, crowned in black orbs. The ichor dripping from inside it catches fire as it falls. Its life is neither still nor small any longer. Standing up to its hips in the lake, the Dove King swings itself around with its gears shrieking. It tightens its fist, and Alan catches a glimpse of the Gale's lights before he slams into her deck. Wood collapses around him. He can hear Brattle shouting as Rapalion lifts him again.

"I am still here," Sophia says. "Alan, are you with me? Are you all right?"

Alan reaches out in desperation, but he can't touch the Dove King now. Its life is too deep in the machine. All he can feel is burning oil and the incredible strain on his ribs and shoulders as the Dove King prepares to swing him again.

"Get out," Alan says. It seems ridiculous for his voice to sound so calm. "Get away."

"I shall not be going anywhere," Sophia says. "I am with you to the end. Brace yourself. We are going to hit the ship again."

The Dove King pulls its arm back. Its joints creak, half-frozen. Water pours from it in shimmering tassels. Still clutching Alan, it drives its fist into the forecastle, crushing the Gale's gun into a knot of metal. The impact leaves Alan blind and addled for a moment, but, to his dismay, it doesn't knock him out. He wonders if that's even possible anymore.

"Sophie," Alan says. Sophia says nothing. He can't feel her anymore, but then he can't be sure how aware of her curled up on his shoulder he has been of late. "I hope you went somewhere safe like I said."

The Dove King puts its fist in its other hand and starts to squeeze Alan as hard as it can. Something bursts against Alan's leg, and there is a long flash of gold light. The robot staggers, screaming behind its blank face. Its arms go stiff, and its grip starts to weaken. Wet warmth spreads down Alan's thigh as the Dove King struggles to regain control of itself.

Let go, Alan thinks, trying to reach out to the Dove King again. *You aren't Owlsbane anymore. All your enemies are gone.*

Rapalion stops its mad twirling and looks at Alan. Its eyes are as empty as his. There is a flicker inside it - a signal fire burning far in the distance. It tilts its head, looking for all the world as if it's about to reply. Then its chest screams open, a white light comes blaring through it, and it flings Alan away in its death throes.

The blizzard cools into a silver thaw. The Mercy Gale is broken and listing, and Columba is strewn across the last of Escar's rooted ice. Rapalion dies in the water. Its still, small life reaches out to Alan, but it is unable to make a meaningful connection before it disappears.

There are so many ways to be alive. Some are loud and demanding, but most are subtle. They flash by like static arcs, made and broken in an instant. Alan lies half buried in a snowdrift and watches the clouds change. Light appears behind them, turning them to pearly glass. He tries to sit up when Brattle comes to find him, but he can't move. There is a disconnect somewhere. He feels dragged apart and distant from himself, but at least he doesn't hurt anymore.

"Here you are," Brattle says, his thinning hair trailing behind him in the wind. Alan can't look down far enough to see anything more than the top of his head. "I'm so sorry, boss. Maid's grace on us - and on me. I was supposed to be guiding you. Come on back to the Gale. We'll get you fixed up like you deserve."

"Shut up with that," Alan replies. "Is everyone OK?"

Brattle gasps. His wide-eyed face appears, and Alan feels himself rising into the air. It is a strange, weightless feeling.

"Al!" Brattle cries, his voice breaking into a giddy laugh. "Holy crap! Say somethin' else!"

"Is everyone all right?" Alan asks again. "Is anyone hurt?"

Brattle's face is uncomfortably close. He looks Alan over intently, his brow furrowed.

"Can you feel your arms and legs, Al?" he asks.

"I can't," Alan says. "I'm too cold. I can't even move."

"Al," Brattle says, "your head's off. I found your body an hour ago and drug it up to the Gale. We wrapped it up like for a funeral."

Alan is shocked dumb. He slips into his inner darkness and his whole body is there. He can see it blazing like lightning in a bottle - or a map of his meridans flowing with qi. When he returns to the ice storm, he is bouncing across the snow in the crook of Brattle's arm.

"Brattle, wait," Alan says. "This is nuts."

"Just clam 'til we get back," Brattle replies, panting. "I reckon it might be best to save your strength. You'll see soon enough."

Brattle pushes through the snow at speed. The Dove King watches them in dead silence, a bent hulk lying half out of the lake with a hole smoking in its back.

"What happened to Rapalion?" Alan asks. He is dismayed to find his previously invincible voice has weakened considerably in the last few minutes.

"Quiet," Brattle snaps. He goes on, but Alan can't follow. His senses are drying up.

Reaching the Gale, Brattle swings himself up the rope ladder on her undamaged starboard side with his fingers hooked into Alan's eye sockets. He presents Alan's skull to the others on the quarterdeck, but Alan can't make sense of their responses. Their voices run together into a single rainy hiss. Their faces are clouds with the noon suns burning behind them, turning them to glass. Death coils into the world so subtly it is almost beautiful, and Alan is helpless to stop himself from falling into it.

Theia is waiting at the bottom. She is a little pressure in the depths - a filling feeling like water in Alan's lungs. This, at last, is unconsciousness.

"Where are you going?" Theia asks.

Alan takes hold of her. Through her, he sees the Bleeding all around him and death quivering inside it like heartflesh. He remembers the image of his body as energy and conjures it as clarity returns.

"Is that you?" Theia laughs.

"Yeah," Alan says. "It's what's left of me. I have to reassemble it."

The image before him pulses in time with *Sentimientos Encontrados*. Looking deep, he can see his whole life in it.

Everything is pasted onto everything else - triumph inextricable from tragedy. He struggles to understand it.

"What's that song?" says Theia. Her voice is a tug on his energy.

"It's a way back to my life before Graveworld." Alan replies. "It's the rope I'm handing myself to tie who I was to who I am."

Theia laughs again. "Use it, then. Put yourself back together."

"Who are you really?" Alan asks.

"Theia. That's all. Just your Theia."

Alan tries to focus, but he loses himself in abstraction. He remembers hearing Univision Radio through the freezer and seeing Allison's ghost bleeding naked in her steaming bathtub. He thinks of the dry fields and fog-masked ponds of Paloma, Illinois and how his parents called it Pickleville. There is no change in the vision he's created as he leafs through himself, blowing the dust from pages he closed in pain a long time ago. The dark does not respond as he stirs new power from his magic to wind himself back into the last sparks of his life before they disappear.

Knit, knit, he thinks, and he feels himself reintegrating. He returns to the garden of his magic to find new lamps shining there. One is the heart of the Dove King, which burst in his hands at Columba. Its light is pink as the flare of a conch shell, and little beaks of coral push up around its base. The other lamp is strange, but its red-gold glow reminds him of sunset and Hannes.

"You did it," Theia says. She appears beneath the sunset lamp, her face bright with a smile and her eyes twinkling. The freckles framing her mouth ride high as her cheeks dimple toward her ears. "Make sure you remember how."

"Thank you," Alan says, tousling Theia's titian curls.

"Don't," Theia giggles. "Go back and be whole again."

Alan will wait to do that. He wants to walk his garden first, putting everything in order. He moves the trees around, setting them in stands like the ones he saw across the border in Missouri, where he was not allowed to go unsupervised. He fluffs the grass and strings a chill through the stream, remembering Allison's hilltop funeral. Long after he starts feeling whole again, he stays in his garden counting flowers. There is one for every sun that has set since he was born, and each has a memory burning at its core. Finally, he sees what powers his magic: it is his life and his active presence in it that makes his gift. He is only as strong as he is true to himself. This revelation is cleansing, and, when he finally sits up on the quarterdeck of the Mercy Gale, he feels not just revived but reborn.

Alan stands, shifting off the bolt of hunter green burlap meant to serve as his cerements. He feels light and stretched like spider silk, and it takes him a moment to remember how to stand against his own weight. When he can balance again, he looks down at himself.

"Where are my clothes?" he asks. He can hardly feel the cold. There is new gravel at the bottom of his voice, but he's relieved to hear it strong again.

Sophia crosses to him from the eyestone, and he catches her on his palm. "We were prepared to bury you, Alan," she says. "We had your funeral. I officiated. You were all but in the ground."

"Well I'm back," Alan replies. Sophia hugs his thumb, her heartlight pulsing pink and petalsoft. "Thanks for sticking with me, Sister."

"I thought I had failed you. I had the proof in front of me."

"There's always another reason to doubt."

Stag's Blood steps forward and bows clumsily. His right front leg is splinted beneath him. His mane is pinched back tight in a brass ring. "You're a hard flame to smother. I want some of what you're burning. What happened?"

"I'm not quite sure," Alan says, pulling the burlap around himself again. "You go first while I try to think of something."

With the blizzard blowing up again, the five of them retreat to the captain's cabin. The wraiths on the damaged decks take up a shriek to beat the storm. Their pain courses through the ship, warping the boards and popping closed doors from their frames. The windows in the captain's cabin roar and rattle.

"That monster thing came up outta the ice, and we saw you go under," Brattle explains as he hands Alan his shoes and folded clothes. "The rest fell out real quick: the wraiths fired on the thing, but they couldn't bust it. It just kind of shrugged, you know. Then it reached and grabbed you - maid knows why - and started beating you against the ship. "

"I was knocked from your hood," Sophia interjects. "I might have shattered if not for Nora. She had changed, as she does, in preparation to leap upon the titan when its back was turned. I landed in her discarded skin, which, as it happens, is soft as linen underneath. I owe her thanks despite the coincidence, and you do, too."

"Sister Sophie set her light on the giant," Brattle continues, "and Stags pulled his trick to make it strong. That's what did it in. We punched a hole right through that mother, but then it hucked you. We didn't find your body for an hour, but your head was nearer. The rest you know - and only you."

"Good luck and quick thinking," Alan says. He steps into his pants and finds the left leg soaked with gelatinous fluid.

"There was something in your pocket," Nora says. "It burst in the machine's grip."

Alan scoops some of the goo onto his hands. It is warm and alive. It spreads itself over his palm and between his fingers like a second skin.

"I almost forgot," Alan says. "Your goggles broke in our backpack, Brattle, and I found something mixed in with the parts. I thought it was a reliquary. I was going to ask about it, but I got a little distracted." He looks at Nora, who meets his gaze with a wintry stare. "It was a glass tube with some kind of fabric rolled up inside. I guess this stuff was in it, too. It's bizarre."

"Of course!" Sophia chimes. Her heartlight strives up through purple into glittering green, and she rings her wings together so quickly that they disappear. "You must have found a dradtail's anacle. Rare luck indeed! There are few left. I have never even seen one."

Nora takes Alan's wet hand. She is hot despite the cold and as bare as the suns on a clear day. Her flesh is pricked with goosebumps. Snowflakes melt in her hair to run down her round cheeks like tears. Lifting a finger to her lips, she tastes the thick stuff that is now crawling down Alan's wrist.

"Like rose syrup," she says. "The dogs used to make it. I remember sneaking into their gardens to steal it."

"Anacles are said to contain fragments of the dawn spiders' webs left over from the weaving of the new world," Sophia says, "suspended in liquid from their yolk sacs. The Sisters of M consider the wasp-fae's creation stories heretical, but I suppose there is no doubt now of their anacles' healing power: the stuff in that anacle saved you."

"I can't say for sure what it was," Alan says. His hand growing hot, he flicks the goo onto the ground before him. It slips off easily and disappears between the floorboards. "After the Dove King threw me, I sat in the snow for a while. There was no pain. I thought I was whole. Then I started to slip, and that got worrying quickly. The heart we found in the tomb gave me something that helped me maintain. I've been getting stronger and stronger this whole way. I feel ready now. For the first time, I feel ready, but it hasn't been easy."

He looks at each of his friends in turn and is astonished at the power of their familiar faces. Even Nora's face is comforting, - cool and hungry as it is as she eyes him.

"You've helped me more than charms or any special kind of luck," Alan continues. "Thanks for sticking it out - for guiding me."

Brattle rolls his eyes. "All right. This is over," he groans. "Al's well and all's well - 'cept for Mercy's busted and we got our work cut out for us still to get out of here."

"The quest goes on," Stag's Blood says, smiling at Alan. "Good to have you back."

With this, he shakes the silver barrette from his mane and turns to leave. Sophia hugs Alan's thumb for a long time, her heartlight pushing heat up his forearm to his elbow. She towers in his mind, as large as the Dove King, and she fills his heart with the last warmth and power it needs to heal itself. Brattle follows as Stag's Blood carries Sophia away in his mane. He dips a nod to Alan as he knuckles out into the storm.

"Need a bit of a sleep," Brattle says. "The cold wears me out. I ain't meant for it. Find me below if you need me, but gimme a bit. And you might need some rest, too, if you can get it. Don't stretch yourself too thin, boss. Be careful."

When he is gone, Nora pads over to the door and pushes it closed. The storm starts to moan outside, lashing tendrils of snow into the captain's cabin through the space beneath the door jamb. Nora kicks up little snow snakes as she approaches Alan, and Alan remembers similar swirls racing away from his parents' car in the winter.

"Well," Nora smiles. Her eyes are arc furnaces rendering iron, all but smoking. "You certainly do get into some trouble, Alan. I can see why Winter White wants you dead, but I suspect she'll have a hard time getting satisfaction."

"I'm not invulnerable," Alan says, "though I'm a lot less vulnerable than I used to be."

Nora gives Alan a long look, surveying him. "You're going bone thin," she says. "Soft, but strong and intact. Won't you cover up?"

Alan pulls on his basteta robe. It is still warm and satiny. The individual hairs stand proud, untouched by any wear. Nora grins, her tongue between her teeth, as Alan arranges the collar on his shoulders. Her gaze is oppressive.

"That must feel better," Nora says. "I don't think this spiders' egg yolk is going to be easy to get out, but I may have found some proper trousers for you below. Come to my cuddy tonight and get them?"

Alan searches Nora. She is on high alert, every sense locked down. Her lust is plain, and it feels obscene at first, but it is a shell

196

closed tight around a radiant pearl of fear. He tries to pry her open, but she won't allow it. She stares him in the face as he fails, her lips parted, showing him that this isn't the way to penetrate her.

"I will," Alan says. He tries to nod, but his neck feels stripped of muscle. "It'll be late, but we should talk."

Nora says nothing more before she turns to leave. The blizzard wind wraps itself around her, pouring snow over her ophidian curves. She disappears down the companionway, and Alan waits alone in his cabin until the roar in his head dies down.

"Are you there, Theia?" he asks.

His inner darkness is silent. He thinks about doves, owls, and anacles, and he picks up the threads of *Sentimientos Encontrados* to hum them again as he pulls on his socks and shoes.

"The quest goes on," he says to the books on his table.

They whisper in reply, full of power and spells he hasn't seen yet. Then, Alan wraps the burlap into a train around his legs and steps out into the rising storm.

Thirty-Nine

Alan ascends to the quarterdeck pulling the dark bolt of burlap that was to be his funeral shroud. It slows him like a dragging anchor, and he thinks of all the years he spent moored in the port of grief.

With a little concentration, Alan finds that he can make the burlap lighter. His magic has grown. He lifts the trailing fabric off the stairs, pleased with the new strength of his focus. Every petal of his power responds to him. He is more connected than he has ever been.

Death is not who I am, Alan tells himself. *It is part of me – an eleventh finger. I've taken the bad forces that made me and used them to grow stronger. I've used the wreckage of my life to build a scaffold, and I can see all around me from atop it.*

The chief mate is on the quarterdeck with the boatswain. They greet Alan as he mounts the deck, their eyes burning bright with pain and worry. The boatswain is a towering cauliflower cloud of shifting greens.

"Captain," says the chief mate. "We have not been down to meet with you. Forgive us."

"You've got a lot to deal with," Alan replies. The main deck is teeming with wraiths. They seem to be pullulating from the boards. Alan has never seen this many at once. "What's the damage?"

"Bad," the boatswain says, its voice almost indistinguishable from the screeching of the storm wind, "but we were lucky. She still runs."

"Show me," Alan says, and the wraiths lead him down into the thick of the repairs.

The whole main deck is writhing. The phantom crew members move together in one thick mist, knotted into each other. Everything is shared. Star-eyes shift from head to head, amassing into galaxies. The strange, starving energies of their individual lives wind into one immense hunger. The wraithmass parts only for the chief mate and Alan.

The first fist-hole is at the base of the mast. Three decks are smashed, the storm blowing into them. The wraithmass covers the hole like a scab, pulling wood together as it can and spitting scrap and splinters out onto the ice. A web of cerulean light is growing where the hull is caved in.

"What's that?" Alan asks.

"Fuel lines," says the boatswain, emerging from a tense silence. "The Gale's veins – connected to the eyestones above and below."

Alan extends himself into the web. He stretches out, trying to fill every strand, and finds it as deep as it is distressingly cold. There is very little energy moving through it.

"Almost dry," he says. Returning, he has taken some of the Gale's weakness into himself. It sits like a chunk of ice in the pit of his stomach.

"She is dead," says the chief mate, "but she needs a substantial infusion. Are you prepared for a long and difficult drain?"

Alan pats himself down as if feeling for imperfections. There aren't any. He feels strong as fire, and he finds this troubling.

"After a rest," Alan replies, "I'll be ready for anything."

At the prow of the ship, the bowsprit and port boomkin are both shattered. The winged figurehead is gone, lost beneath the hardening ice. A crack forks astern across the forecastle, opening the galley ceiling around the leaning stove cowl. Alan peers through the bulging swarm of the wraithmass at the wreck of the Mercy Gale's cannon.

"I went through that," Alan says. "I don't remember what it felt like. I'm going to call that striking it rich."

"We can repair her with time and material," says the boatswain, "but her gun will never function again."

"That's to bad," Alan says. He looks across the lake. Columba is a dark mound in the distance, as far from solid ground as it is from Sepulchra's storm-swept tables.

"Catafalque pine," Alan says. "We'll take Columba with us when we leave. It seems fitting."

The chief mate confers with the boatswain silently. Alan can feel their exchange in his mind where the dead voices remain unsettlingly silent. The wraiths' thoughts dance up from them in swirls of color.

"We will start there, then" the chief mate finally says. "It will be a long operation."

"And there's your time," Alan says. "See? It made itself. It usually does – all you have to do is wait. What about the other materials?"

The boatswain shivers. "Mechanical. We thought we would strip the giant."

"Fine. We'll take him, too," Alan says. "I'm ready to be out of this place. DO as much as you can with what you have, then come to me and we'll get our exit cooking."

His tour of the Gale's damage over, Alan makes his way below, the bulk of his burlap train wrapped around him like a toga. In his cabin, he throws the makeshift shroud in a heap and sits down to read. The air is heavy with wraithsong. Despite surging distraction, he pores through a new section of Pwysh's *Grimoire of Plastromancy*. Then he sits for a long time listening to the buzzing in his head and feeling the power of the words coursing through him. The dead voices finally return, pulled as if from sleep as Alan contemplates his new strength.

When he can sit still no longer, Alan descends to the galley and tries to wake the bones of an antelope in the fire pit. The charred remains respond, moving at his every whim, even trying to gallop. Then he reaches deeper, finding the animal's spirit deep in the teeth of its old death. The little dwindling fire would have been beyond him before, but now, with modest effort, he can tease it up toward life again. He brings it close to the draug, leading it as lovingly as he would have when it was a living animal. Death has warped it – made it strange – but it retains some aspect of its original beasthood. Alan wonders how a fairy spirit would react to such coaxing. Death seems more like sleep with every minute he spends studying it.

This exercise leaves Alan feeling stimulated. The dead voices build in his head, and the Seal of Aiwass starts to glow on his forehead. Finally, he heads up to the cuddy to find its door closed. While he is pacing the short hall, distraction finally overwhelms him. Pressures move through his body, leaving him feeling swollen and tense as a soap bubble. The wraithsong roars on, drowning out the snarl of the storm. Alan thinks of the ship's veins cerulean veins glowing cold in the blizzard. Then, as he is about to knock, Nora eases the door open to peek out from behind it.

"Did you rush here?" she asks. "It feels like just talked."

"I feel like I'm carrying around at least a week," Alan chuckles. "Did you want me to come back?"

"No," Nora smiles. "Come in and rest your week. Your night's just beginning."

Alan enters, his chest tight and a war of wings beating low in the heat of his stomach. He closes the door behind him and leans back against it. Nora stares at him, a smile bright in her cheeks, watching for the right time to spring into effect.

"You're covered," Alan says, trying to remember how to prop himself up. He flops a nervous hand, indicating the odd, shapeless garment she's frocked herself in. It is heavy and bright as an awning, and she has cinched it too high with a braid of jute rope.

Nora's smile uncoils. It hits Alan like a crow's quill spear, pinning him in place with softness and sinister beauty.

"I know my natural state makes some uneasy," Nora says. "I don't much care, but I know that you're unsure. I wanted you to be comfortable. Do you like this?" She sweeps her hand in a line down her body. Her curves are barely visible under her wrapping. "When you were dead, we scoured the ship. The Sister wanted to give you a stately funeral, and we found this in the hold along with crates of candles, hammocks for the sleeping deck, and enough burlap to bury fifty headless thanoturges."

"I wonder if it belonged to Toven's wife," Alan says. "He called her the Lady Nightjar. I think he built this ship for her."

Nora shrugs and turns to take a bottle from the shelf behind her.

"We found this, too," she says. "It wouldn't be a ghost ship without spirits. I thought a swig might help you relax."

"It probably would," Alan says, looking at the triskelion seal on the bottle. He wonders who crewed the Mercy Gale before she was lost. For a moment, he lets his thoughts drift through the ship to feel the sorrow in her boards. The wraiths sing songs of pain through her decks, sobering him. "I don't drink though."

Nora nods. "I didn't think of that."

"Well, I can't really, but I never drank anyway. I don't like alcohol. Or I didn't." Alan pushes himself away from the door and takes the bottle in his hand to test its weight. Most of it is already gone. He can see it blooming across Nora's face. "I guess I'm still not feeling how permanent this is."

Nora places the cup of her palm against Alan's zygomatic process. He doesn't feel her fingers tapping toward his chin, tracing the faint lines of new bone scars.

"Back from the dead," she says, her eyes wide with fire. "Midion has a plan for you. If you doubted before, you're a fool to do so now. What do you think it is? Have you seen it opening before you — plumping like a peach?" She takes a step back and pushes her fingers into the fur of Alan's robe. There, she kneads for the lines of his chest — the jutting curves of his ribs beneath his thinning skin. "You're not the first skull-headed spirit I've seen. You know that. Where did you see the other?"

"In Welkinbright," Alan replies. "Enlil. And Rapalion, too — the Dove King."

"What do you think that means?" Nora asks.

"I don't know," Alan says. "Maybe nothing. I'm a little distracted; why don't you tell me."

"No more telling," Nora says, smiling spears again. "This is what you came for."

She finds something else on the shelf behind her and hands it to Alan. It is a pair of black hide trousers. He unfolds them, letting the legs roll out to swing at his ankles. They are fine and light, and they have a built-in belt with Toven's triskelion seal tamped in red on the buckle.

"Thanks," Alan laughs. "I didn't think you actually had a spare pair of pants."

"You assumed I had an ulterior motive."

"Didn't you?"

Nora crosses her arms, pushing her breasts up to strain the fabric wrapped around her. Out of habit, Alan tries not to stare. "But you came here anyway."

"Yeah."

"Then yours was the ulterior motive. I've made my motivation entirely clear."

Alan sets the trousers aside and paces away for a moment. He is racing inside, frightening himself. "I'm sorry I dismissed you before," he says. "It's been a long time. Thinking about this as a transaction - something utilitarian - is a little weird. It threw me, but I've reconsidered. I want to do this for you."

"For me," Nora says, "but not *to* me. I understand. You want love's frivolity - to pretend that our union will mean so much that I will allow you to waste yourself in my hand or in my mouth. I can give that. I am, by virtue of being the last of my kind, a genomancer without equal. You will come many times tonight, and yes: most will serve my singular purpose, but it will feel as empty and as lavish as any lovers' dalliance."

"If you still had to convince me," Alan laughs, "that'd have done it."

Nora's eyes wink like torches failing in a nightmare of shadow. She loosens the rope around her midsection and her rumpled shift falls open. Beneath it, she is smooth as cemetery marble.

"You must think me crude," she says, "and you wouldn't be the first. We have been hated, persecuted, massacred for our delight in ourselves. But we guarded Nudd faithfully. I promise to take you with gratitude and to remember your needs, human as you are – though I have my doubts about that."

She approaches Alan, and her arms vine around his waist. Pressed against him, she feels heavier than the Mercy Gale. Magic pours from her in dazzling waves of color. It blooms through the air, filling the cuddy with light and heat. There is even a scent to it: the smell of peaches and lavender, strong enough for Alan to detect. The wraiths above stop their work. Their songs die down and are replaced by the moaning wind. The Mercy Gale falls still as Nora weaves her spell, and Alan gives in to it without complaint. It stirs him, awakening humanity he had thought dead or sleeping.

"You are saving us, Alan," Nora says, looking up into Alan's empty eyes as she stoops to kneel. "I am beholden to you. Receive my praise."

Alan finds himself alone in the morning. He stands, hips aching, and dresses in the roaring quiet. Nothing is moving above, and the almost imperceptible hum of the Gale's engines is utterly gone. Its absence is like a space missing from the world - the shocking stump of bone beneath a suddenly missing finger. Alan tries to search the ship from where he is, but his magic won't wake up. Troubled, he opens the door and steps out into the hall to find out what's going on.

The hall is not the hall. It is a tall, narrow room with fans blowing cold from the ceiling. The walls are lined with shelves of condiments: spring mix, shredded cheese, habanero ranch. To his right are gray pallets of milk shake mix and flavored yogurt. He is in the cooler at Ray's. He's even wearing his uniform.

Alan turns around. The door to the cuddy has been replaced by the walk-in freezer's thick, steel-hinged slab of pressure-sealed aluminum. He jerks it open with clean, young hands, his nails trimmed and milky pink. The freezer yawns dark, one light out, boxes stacked against silvered ribs along the walls. In the center, fry boxes lean too high, every box marked "SALT THE FRIES" - as if this was something Ray himself used to say. The refrigeration unit thunders and shakes like a calving glacier. Ice bursts through its insulated hoses in big, gleaming fists. Alan closes the door and turns around, feeling the old dread of the cold creeping back. There is a place for it in his mind. He has missed it being filled.

Alan steps out of the cooler. Ray's is completely empty. The power soak is running in the sink, meat trays churning in it, throwing little tufts of soap onto the floor. Iscela's phone is playing samba nearby. Ray walks past the assembly table, where sandwiches wait on squares of paper. He wraps a double cheesburger and places it in the heated bin, ready for no one to enjoy. Arriving at the counter, he taps on the register and finds himself still clocked in. He prints his time slip and stuffs it in the pocket of his work pants, where he finds his keys. Then he stands for a while, looking out at the empty dining room. Grief rears up to crash over Alan, and he is overwhelmed. Tears start from his eyes, and he smears them away with the butts of his palms. Sobs hitch up his throat and get stuck there painfully until he laughs them out, amused by the depth of his pain.

"I miss you," he says. It feels stupid.

He checks the other pocket as he heads out the south door, finding only his earbuds. His phone isn't there. He steps outside with salt still stinging on his cheeks.

The sky is wet with stars. There is one white car in the parking lot, its headlights blaring, but all the other spaces are empty. Fireworks burst far away, launched from the water at Gateway Park. They fill the night with deep, stuttering claps like the last breaths of a man coughing himself to death. Alan turns left to walk past the drive-thru and makes his way down from Ray's toward the department store behind it. He closes his eyes and runs his hand over his face. He takes off his hat and feels the storm-calm wind tousle his hair. The night smells of gunpowder and of oil drawn from the grass by recent rain.

Alan has walked home before, and he remembers the way. He remembers it like his head remembers headaches - like his stomach remembers squeezing emesis. There is a path cut through a copse of virgin forest on the east side of the department store. He heads toward it past the little wet sink of sewer land where the store dumps its wastewater. He used to watch birds there. When they mowed it down, it broke his heart, but it grew back.

"It always grows back," he says into the darkness. "Into leaves and bark forever."

Pointing his keychain light at his shoes, he makes his way down the path with his head down. After all he's been through, he still feels haunted in this little finger of wilderness. It's good to feel the press of that old fear around him again. At the head of the path, where a moon-white sycamore stands guard, he catches the ghost of smoke on the breeze. The trees whisper above him, the fountain booms of aerial shells in the distance punctuating their hissing sentences. Alan approaches his sister's house across the trimmed lawn on the other side of the copse. It squats in the dark, broad on a too-small patch of mown bluegrass and gravel. The back porch light is on, and a small black shape is waiting for him beneath it.

Winter White, Alan says to himself, and the shape steps free of the other shadows and approaches.

The girl is small and thin and pale as gossamer. Alan stops at the fenceline and she meets him barefoot, a trapeze-shaped sun dress blowing in tatters around her. The garment clings to her boyish hips and flat stomach like a lecher's hands. Her breasts are but points beneath it, her nipples cat scratch welts. In the light of the moon, her dress may as well be invisible. She's nothing - a waif, barely heavier than gunsmoke.

"Welcome home," says Winter White, pushing a short, black lock behind her ear. Alan looks away from her. "Come in and take a rest. You deserve it."

"What is this?" Alan asks, grateful as a cloud scuds across the moon. "A dream?"

"Death and sleep are sisters," Winter smiles. "Dreams are the blood that makes them related."

"Why are you doing this?" Alan says. He finally looks directly at her. Her eyes are like waves' eyes. They hold him, batted behind spidery lashes, and he feels his heart start to labor in his chest. "What do you want?"

Winter White purses her cherry lips. "I thought you might like to see the life you left," she says, "before life - spells and all - leaves *you*. Was I wrong?"

"All this comes down to threats?" Alan laughs. "You can't psych me out with this. It's weak. I'm disappointed."

"Come inside," Winter says again, her fairy voice slipping down into a whisper like the wind in the trees. "Don't you at least want to look in the mirror?"

Alan looks at the house. The fireworks growl behind him.

"This isn't real," he says. "You've made this. Nothing in there can hurt me."

Winter White laughs and crosses her arms. "Illusion is no guarantee of safety."

Alan nods and heads for the back door. On the way, he stops in Allison's garden. Its lamps are dim, and its flowers are thin and shriveled. Heat has scalded the red poppies. He kneels to touch a curling blossom, and then he goes to the back door and unlocks it.

The lights are out in the den. Alan flips the switch, but not much changes. Shadow sits heavy in the corners, its tendrils meeting across the floor as diffuse lines. Darkness is on the basement door and in the smoke-stained maw of the fireplace. It has always been there - a gloom like scabs over light-scarred sores - impenetrable.

"What do you see?" asks Winter White.

"An umbra," Alan replies. The shadow squirms. The den seems to shrink a way into its depths. "Did you put it there?"

Winter pushes past Alan to stand on the first step of the stairwell leading toward the living room. "Up the stairs," she says, hopping out of view. Alan hears her naked footfalls on the tile floor above after she vanishes. "More to see."

The kitchen is across the hall from the living room. Both are dark and silent as tombs. Light trickles in through the dining room curtains, blue and cold, heavier that Graveworld water. Memories sleep in the walls, their warm forms bulging out through the wallpaper. They creak like old hearts beneath the floor, and they cover the furniture like an age of dust. Years of quiet mornings still live here. Nothing can repress them. The smell of cumin hangs around the stove, and Alan spends a long moment inhaling it.

"You're going to kill me," he says. Winter White watches from the arch of the living room with one hand on her hip. Her face is wreathed in light that illuminates only her. "Why? I've got you here, so I might as well ask. What's the point of any of this? Where do you see this leading if you get what you want?"

"I am too old for wrath anymore," Winter says. "This is about destiny. It is our ineluctable fate to fall before injustice. We rarely get any real chance to exact revenge, and, when we do, it is snuffed out as quickly as our labors were long building the fire. At some point, fury dies away inside us. We are revealed as meek and left with only resignation." She curls her fingers into a weighty O. "This is where we build. Bedrock. Failure is in every foundation. And at the top? Climb the stairs with me and see. You're almost there. Don't stop now. It'll all be clear."

"Is that a no?" Alan asks.

A savage smile stretches across Winter White's face.

"Yes," she says, and then she glides up the next set of stairs.

Alan hesitates. The dark beats around him like a womb. He has always hated this staircase. At the top is a cramped hall of wood paneling - a walk-in coffin full of moth-ball smells. The day room is first on the left, and the Blue Room is at the end. As a child, he was sure that there was a clawing ghost in that room.

"I heard it crawling," he says, just as he did to his parents so long ago, when the Blue Room had been Allison's. It leans against the door at night. I've seen its fingers sticking out under the door."

208

Alan answers himself in his father's voice. "There's no such thing as ghosts. There's nothing here in the dark that isn't here in the light."

"That didn't help much, did it?" Winter White says from the top of the stairs.

"No," Alan says, allowing himself a sigh of relief. "But he was right."

Alan mounts the stairs. He stops for a moment to look at the mirror on the wall in the stairwell. He can hardly see his face, but he remembers it. Just seeing the curves of his cheeks and the whites of his eyes brings it all back.

"That's isn't the mirror I had in mind," Winter White chides.

"I know what you want."

"Then come on. I worked hard to put this together."

Winter disappears down the hall, turning right to enter the bathroom. Alan follows, his heart pumping lead. He tries again to rouse his magic, hoping to be able to punch through this dream and wake up, but it's no use. He's exhausted. He steps into the bathroom enfeebled and in the grip of choking terror.

Winter White is sitting on the toilet lid and swinging her feet. She pushes her hair back again and nods a greeting, shadow sitting in the hollows of her cheekbones.

"There," she says, indicating the bathtub. "You've looked into Nudd's eye. Now look into mine."

The shower curtain sways aside, and the bathroom fills with swan-white light. Something is roaring far away, its voice cleverly disguised as fireworks exploding Alan's blood burns. Fear writhes in his flesh, as if trying to evict him from it. He bites his lip, closes his eyes, and turns toward the tub with all his strength.

"You look ridiculous," Winter White says. She goes to his side and runs her hand up his back. "Don't worry. Just open."

After a few quick breaths, Alan opens his eyes. There is nothing in the tub but water. He can see through it to the fish stickers on the bottom.

"Do you think I came here to scare you?" Winter smiles, her fingers tapping along the ridge of his spine, counting his vertebra. "You made the fear. Not me. Relax and watch."

"You picked the wrong place to put me if you expected me to relax," Alan says with a sigh. His shoulders are like knots of steel.

Winter White puts the tip of her finger to her pursed lips and blows a soft, "Shhh." Then, the water ripples, and luminous bubbles rise from the drain to burst silver across its surface. Images appear in the new shimmer, dim and colorless, moving into each other like dreams. Watching them feels like prying open something secret to be damned for it.

A child is born dead and then buried. Another child is born sick and is thrown alive into a ditch of corpses. Death and sorrow bloom in the water with little girls at their ripe centers, wrapped hopelessly in their twisted stamens. The children are many, but they all look the same - dark and light. One girl is born all over the world, time and again, to families of all kinds. She grows through the visions, sometimes reaching womanhood. She has many children of her own, but they vanish. Time rakes the pictures like rip current, pulling everyone away, but the girl remains.

"I don't know what happened," Winter White says. "Quitting spirits pay their minds to enter the exchange. I've seen them leaving like smoke, peeling away from dead meat, ready for glory. In Midion they are purified and made ready to wait on the Plutonian Shores for reincarnation. Midion is a gift to the formless, but I was born wrong. I am thin as air in this flesh and too bound in form. Because the exchange refuses me, death has forsaken me. I have been myself for far too long."

"How did you end up in Graveworld?" Alan asks, unable to turn away from the bubbling stream of images.

"There are paths over which death has less authority."

Finally, the water clears. The silver billows down to the bottom of the tub, taking with it the images of Winter's many births and deaths. When the bubbling stops, the silver sheen darkens, turning red, and Alan has to look away.

"I've seen death come," he says, meeting Winter White's unsettling gaze without fear this time. "It stalks us like something young, burning up with young hunger. Do you remember when you thought your youthful fire could do anything? I think it's new here. A child. I've seen things that are older. For all its certainty, death can't touch everything."

"It denies me rest I deserve. It's certainly cruel enough to be a child."

"I know why we're here," Alan says. "You want me to help you commit suicide."

"I am abandoned," Winter says, her full, pink mouth turning down into a dismal pout, "but I am not defeated. In all my years, I have found a great and terrible hope. I can make an end from which no one will be reborn. I'll collapse the exchange, and Nudd is the key."

"Collapse the exchange. That sounds a lot like 'break everything'." Alan puts his hand on Winter White's. She jumps and sucks in a squeaking gasp. Wrapped in his, her fingers are like bundles of matchsticks. "I'm sorry for what you've experienced. I'm sorry you've suffered so much. It isn't fair, but this doesn't have to be all or nothing. Your pain doesn't have to be a war, and your life doesn't have to be about death. Stop this, come to me, and we'll find another way."

Winter recovers quickly from her shock. Her eyes narrow, and her smile cuts back across her face like a dagger scar. Her eyes are suddenly very old. Alan can see every year she's lived pushing up from inside her as if to break through her skin and drown him.

"That isn't how this conversation goes," she hisses. "You aren't the first to try and save me, but you will be the last. Wake up now, Alan. You've made your choice. Hurry now to your death, that I may have mine."

With this, the illusion crumbles around them. The blasts of the fireworks rip it apart, and Alan screams as the shockwave obliterates him. Then he is thrashing on the floor of the cuddy and Nora is shaking his shoulders. Brattle and Stag's Blood are looking down at him, and his hands ache horribly. He lifts them up to see his knuckles beaten bloody.

"Alan!" Nora cries.

Alan lets himself go limp. The others back away, and he stares up at the ceiling for a moment. The wraiths are singing above him. He reaches out to touch them with his mind, and his magic snaps awake as if it had never been sleeping.

"We have to go," Alan says, sitting up. "We've got to get this ship moving. There's wood in the wreck of Columba to repair her."

Sophia lands on Alan's thigh. He looks down and is relieved to see that he has his new pants on.

"What happened?" Sophia demands. "You were seizing for hours!"

"We ain't goin' nowhere till we get some relief, Al," Brattle says. "We can't handle no more scares like this. What's goin' on with you? Are you all right?"

Alan stands. His legs are like rods of molten metal. He totters back against a shelf, and Brattle helps him find his balance again. Without knowing why, he reaches into his pocket. His time slip is there. He crumples it between his searching fingers.

"We're going the right way," he says. "Winter White's running scared. I think she just hit me with her best shot, but I'm OK. Let's get bundled up, and I'll fill you all in on the ice."

Forty

It takes the rest of the day to move all the scrap wood from Columba. Alan is tired, and his limbs feel like stretched taffy, but his magic has never been more active. With its help, he is able to carry large stacks of lumber by himself as if he has been doing it all his life. He supposes he has in a way: so much of grief's weight is at the cutting edge of sleep, suspended between exhaustion and indefatigability. Alan remembers this burden well.

He tells the others as much as he can remember about the dream Winter White gave him, but it fades quickly as she pulls it out from under him. No one asks what he was doing in the cuddy with Nora, and he considers this for the best. As White's strange spell recedes, Nora's is revealed in full effect. It isn't until the ruins of Columba are stripped to the stones and the wraiths are working the catafalque into new cladding that the tight heat in his loins begins to dissipate.

The storm breaks after sundown, and those few ghostly crew members who are strong enough go down to pull Rapalion for parts. Alan joins the others for a quiet dinner, and then he and Brattle go down into the belly of the Gale to talk in the heat from her struggling engines.

"Maybe we shouldn't go to the prisons," he says, supporting his unsteady back against a post with his arms crossed. "What would happen if we just smashed the shards or threw them into the ocean?"

"We ain't near the ocean," Brattle replies, "and smashing the shards is like as not bad, or someone woulda done it before. Maybe there's a better place for 'em than here, though. You wanna ditch now – leave the fight to someone else?"

Alan puts his hands on his face. His skull is warm to the touch where the Seal of Aiwass is glowing.

"I don't know what's ahead," he says. "I might be walking us into something we can't walk out of. I don't want that."

213

"You don't want what you'll get if you cut and run now, either," Brattle says. "Trust me."

"I have new power," Alan says, looking down at his shoes. One of them is starting to split above the sole. "I'm a little afraid of it, but I think that's good. It might help us. I'm just hesitant to rely on it. What if it's not what I think it is? I might screw up. What if I'm a bad leader?"

"Then you're bad," Brattle says, "but you didn't give up."

"Do you think trying justifies incompetence?"

Brattle shakes his head. He knuckles over to Alan and stands up to pat him on the shoulder. He is frightening at his full height, his lamp-eyes burning like signal lights through fog.

"I dunno," he croaks, "but you gotta keep trying. What d'you think was Winter White's was trying to do?"

"Psych me out," Alan says. "I don't think she was lying, though. I don't know why should would."

"She can see into you: that's what worries me. She can take you like that any time she wants? That ain't good."

"I wasn't myself," Alan says, suddenly tense. His shoulders were drooping, but now they are bundles of taut ropes. "I think there were mitigating circumstances. She won't be able to do it again."

Brattle stares into the eyestone and nods slowly. Bands of red dance around his head, circling it as if to form a crown.

"This place makes you weak," he says. "It leaves you vulnerable. I felt it, too." He looks at his hands for a moment, flexing his fingers as if unsure they can still stretch anymore. "Sometimes I feel Netty in *my* head still. Da, too, but not as much. It ain't a good feeling."

Alan searches Brattle. His magic responds so eagerly that, for a second, he isn't in control of it. It jumps in his grip like a bird, and he has to scrabble to get a good hold on it. When he's finally got it in hand, it takes all his focus to make it behave.

"I only see you in there," Alan says. "Don't worry.

Brattle considers this for a long time. Doubt whirls together with fear, leaving his spirit dark as lamp smoke. "That's good to hear," Brattle says. Alan isn't convinced. "Whatever's ahead a' this, I'll be glad to get out."

The wraiths move the Mercy Gale west from the ice at midnight. They leave Rapalion stripped to its rivets, having built its guts into a new power system. The Gale hums over the drifting gap into Sepulchra, her lightness returning and her sail filled with freezing wind. Alan watches from the prow as the land turns stony. He drops his hood to feel the breeze on his neck, missing the bite of cold in his bones. Stag's Blood comes up to join him, his mouth red with supper's blood.

"Stele Gorge," Stag's Blood says. "What do you think of Mackerel Sky's warning now that we have been to the Tomb of the Doves? Is Toven there with Winter's army?"

Alan wrings the handle of his trash masher. The wraiths recovered it from the ice – another stroke of unusual luck. It pulses in time with the hum of the Mercy Gale's engines.

"Best to expect them," Alan says.

"The dream she gave you – what was it like seeing your sphere and your home again? "

"She really thought it would scare me," Alan explains, "but I don't belong there anymore. It's like a shed skin now. I grew out of it."

Stag's Blood stares straight ahead, unblinking, through snow rakes his face. "I have a memory of the Hunters' Fields," he says, "though I've never been there. There is a longing for them in my heart like a little sickness. I feel it every day. I am lonely for a home I've never seen. I would give my mane for a sip of your nepenthe."

"Tell me about them," Alan says.

"It hurts to speak of them," Stag's Blood sighs. "I am holding on, but I should be going. I smell them everywhere. I hear the wind in the rushes. The Fields are calling me. It's hard to bear."

"I had no idea," Alan says, turning to face Stag's Blood and put a hand on his back. A purr is rising up from his throat to tremble in between his ribs. "I'm sorry. You know I won't keep you here."

Stag's Blood growls a laugh. "What White and Toven want will end the Hunters' Fields as surely as Animus and Midion. I can't leave while I can still do good."

"But that's what I'm telling you: you don't have to torture yourself for this fight."

"Don't I? Would you retreat to your forgotten place? Is suffering a choice?"

"That's different," Alan says. Stag's Blood smiles.

"You aren't at home, Alan Shade," he says. "Like me, you're in exile."

After three days' limping travel, the Mercy Gale emerges from beneath Escar's merciless cloud shelf. It is just after sunrise when she makes the edge of Stele Gorge, and gold is burning to dream-blue on the horizon. The wraiths drop anchor in a stunted forest to finish bending the Gale's new cladding, and Alan climbs to the ground with the others. The wood ends in a bone-white precipice with the root-wrapped corners of burial vaults peeking from the wall. Alan stands at the point of the cliff and looks down at the dark marks branching across the valley floor.

"Are those the prisons?" he asks. "They look like red coral growing from burn scars."

"Prisons're underground," Brattle replies. He squats in the thigh high grass well away from the brink. Dew clings to him, shining like glass. "The outer parts're passion wrack — tubes writhers make of blood and waste."

"Writhers?"

"Great algovorous graveworms," Sophia explains. "They feed on the pain of the damned. Few things exist that were not made by the Framer. Writhers are among them."

"It's not just prisons then," Alan says. "The Dead in Despair are being tortured."

Nora crosses her arms and scowls into the valley. "No matter how terrible, justice is justice."

"Not where I'm from," Alan says.

"There are camp smokes," Stag's Blood says. "Mackerel Sky was telling the truth about that at least: there is an army in the gorge. And look! A large force is coming up from the south. We're not alone."

Alan looks down the wall through his deadsight. From miles of soil-bound ash and the stacked graves of sylves, pixies, and child mages, he peers up at a large, eager army of fairies wearing Toven's triskelion.

"They mean business," Alan says, flattening his hands against his sides in an effort to stop their trembling. "That's a big host – assuming I'm any good at judging that kind of thing. The war is real and here. Frankly, I can't believe what I'm seeing."

"How much can you see from here?" Nora asks. She leans too far forward on the tips of her toes. Alan looks at her just long enough to see her breasts sway lightly behind the curtain of her hair, and then he looks away again down the corridor of the dead.

"Not much on my own," says Alan. "There are graves upon graves all over these mountains, and I can see through the dead in them. I call it deadsight."

"Are the dead not blind?" asks Sophia.

Alan shakes his head. "No," he says. "Not all of them."

"A proper gift for you," Stag's Blood says.

"And handy," Nora adds. "Tell us what you see, deadeyes."

"Hobs in large camps with dredges leashed to stakes nearby. Spearbacks in pens being fed by huge, muddy-looking keepers. I've never seen those before. They look like they're made of runny clay."

"Mire-ogs," Brattle says. "There ain't never been such unity before. Hard not to be impressed."

Alan continues. "There are a lot of tall catriders – dark skinned, wearing bright armor. They're beautiful, really. I remember seeing some at Debtors' Orchard. They were with Winter White when she first appeared. They look like the leaders."

"Knocks," Brattle says.

"Goblins," Stag's Blood adds. "White and Toven must have reached very deep. This isn't unity."

"Desperation," Sophia says, her voice falling. She lands in a tree and shines there, a sad lamp drawing clean shadows on the ground. "The power of lies. This is a misfit horde brought together by lies and fear. I pity them. What boon from Toven are their families awaiting? How many kingdoms of goblins are starving to pay for Winter's war? You may be impressed, Brattle. I am offended."

Alan continues to search, pushing his deadsight further than he ever has. The dead offer no resistance anymore. At the heart of the passion wrack, he can feel the Dead in Disgrace screaming underground. Their pain pumps out through miles of unclean stone, tainting the air. Above the deepest pit, knocks on armored scours circle in columns with Malakeen soldiers. Alan's heart starts to ache with terror.

At least there are no daemons, Alan tells himself. He clings to that, trying to be thankful in spite of his fear. *Any light is welcome*.

"What about the other group?" Nora asks.

Alan turns his gaze south toward the new force marching up the valley. His chest feels lighter immediately.

"dradtails," he says, returning to himself. He spins on his heels and starts off toward the Mercy Gale. "Thank god – or whoever. Thank the Framer. We're not alone in this. Let's go down to meet them."

"Never thought I'd be happy to meet hymies," Brattle clucks, knuckling along behind Alan, "but friends are friends."

"One moment," Stag's Blood says. "The Mercy Gale doesn't look ready to me. Should we wait until she is whole again at least?"

Alan stops to let Brattle up the rope ladder first. The hot wind from beneath the Gale swirls his robe around him.

"I'm not ready, either," he says, "but waiting's not going to help that. We'll anchor the Gale in as safe a place as we can find once we get down there."

"Are we likely to *find* a safe place down there?" Stag's Blood asks.

Nora leans in to interrupt Alan's response. "No," she says. "Gird yourselves up, guardians of Nudd. Your next test is a big one."

The Mercy Gale heads west with her sail full of morning's wet breath. The little wood thickens, and the trees tower up to scratch at her mast with their swaying fingers. Briar walls break upon her prow, and great sheet webs adorned with spiral stabilimenta blow across the deck from the leafless understory. The wraiths burn these webs wherever they land with coral pyromantic flames. When the Gale starts down a toppling path from the top of the cliff wall, she is wearing flame scars like war paint.

Alan and the others gather at the forescastle. A little ship of clouds has appeared in the sky and is slowly growing larger. Sunlight falls across its head, leaving it crowned it rich, rippling detail. The rest of it remains in flat shadow. Nora nudges up beside Alan, her elbow in his side, and looks at him.

"You've been avoiding me," she says.

"I'm sorry," Alan says. Something is racing inside him. It isn't his pulse. The dead twist in his mind like worms. "I've had a rough few days, but we should talk."

Stag's Blood and Brattle turn to look at him. He is embarrassed at their attention.

"Not here," Alan says. "You know?"

"Know what?" Brattle asks. He is wearing his knife and is leaning on the black horn he repurposed as a walking stick.

"Do you have something to hide, Shade?" Nora grins. "Now isn't the time."

Alan pushes his hands into his sleeve pockets and shifts from foot to foot for a moment.

"That magic you used on me," he says at last. "I think it might have left me open to Winter White's psychic attack. Is that possible?"

Nora puts her chin in her hand and presses her lips into a pout.

"What magic is that?" Stag's Blood asks.

Sophia lands on Alan's shoulder, her heartlight pulsing a deep and heavy red.

"Genomancy," she says, placing the flat of her palm against Alan's cheek. Her hand is unexpectedly cold. The judgment in her voice makes Alan feel sick to his stomach. "Is that it? I thought as much. I wondered what you had been doing in her sleeping cupboard before we found you seizing."

"Sex magic," Brattle laughs. "Good for you, boss, but that's a sight I'd rather not contemplate."

"The Sister chides and Brattle mocks," Stag's Blood says, "but you have nothing to be ashamed of, Alan. Sleep is denied you – you deserve at least some comfort."

Alan sags and shakes his head. "Just tell me about the spell," he says. "What does it do, exactly? How does it work?"

Nora beams with pride. The light in her eyes is like a ray of sunshine piercing a bank of cloud. She puts her hands on her hips and tosses her hair, a conqueror. Her nipples are tight points in the cool air. Alan remembers seeing Winter White's body through her dress.

"First is the Opening of the Mouth," Nora replies. "You remember that. That's my favorite part. Then is the weighing of the heart – and yours weighed surprisingly well. Both rituals are necessary for a proper rooting.

"If you were connected to White weakly before, my linking spell could have strengthened that connection. Still, I felt no connection beyond the deep one your root made in me. Do you have reason to suspect that one exists?"

Alan realizes he misses the feeling of blushing. He pulls his hood far up over his head, wishing he could fold himself up into it.

"Winter wanted me to believe that she was in complete control, but she wasn't," he says. "I felt myself in her delusion very strongly. I think the connection goes both ways."

"That's not an answer," Nora says, still smiling. "I don't know what doors I might have opened when I was pressing your pleasure apart. My magic works both flesh and mind to maximize sensation, but I understand the mental aspect the least. We shared each other but I brought only myself. You brought her in – *that* I *do* know." She sucks her lower lip between her teeth and wraps her hand around Alan, squeezing him crudely for a moment while the others watch.

"She must have come with you into the linking spell like a disease," she continues. "I wonder if you left any of her in me! What a terrible thought. Where did you pick her up, do you think? I've indulged you – now answer me plainly: what is the connection?"

Alan bats Nora's hand away and takes a step back from her. They are riding into battle. He is in no mood for her teasing.

"I don't know," he replies, "but it might be something we can exploit."

A giggle bubbles up from Nora's throat, and her eyes flash danger. "I certainly hope so," she says. "I've not had my fill of you."

"Mysteries within mysteries," Sophia says, sadly. "This could burn you, Alan. You are dancing with fire. Please be careful – for me."

Fear presses on Alan's chest, making him feel lead-heavy and tight as a spring. Every muscle aches, but he tells Sophia not to worry.

"Relax, Sister," he says. "It's me. I'm lucky. Remember?"

Sophie flits from his shoulder to do a blue-green lemniscate in the air. "Cheel Gar wasn't lucky," she says as she lights in Stag's Blood's rippling mane.

Two-thirds of the way down the valley wall, the Mercy Gale runs out of ground. Alan and the others leave the wraiths to their repairs and climb down to meet the dradtail swarm in the clear, blue light of midmorning. The wasps don't stop for them, but no one objects when they fall in with the heavily armed chiefs at the vanguard.

"I'm Alan Shade," Alan tries to say as he struggles to keep in step. "One of your shamans helped me before, when I was sick. His name was..."

"Tulabek,"Stag's Blood says.

"Right. We've come to fight beside you. It's the least we can do to repay Tulabek."

A few dradtails turn to scowl at him.

"Why not fly? Are there fliers behind you?" Alan tries. "Your armor's too heavy, right? Protection over mobility."

"Strange and little help you bring, separates," says one chief over his hound-bone pauldron. "Tulabek die. Not much honor you can do him now, and you owe us nothing."

"Help's help," Brattle says. The chief marches on, ignoring him.

Alan takes a moment to look back through the ranks. A grim sadness follows the column, shining pale and cold as choking lips. Ribbons of color flow through it, the pink sparks of thought piercing them. The hivemind feels bigger than the gorge – bigger even than Sepulchra itself. It is sobering, and Alan shrinks from it inside, knowing that he is unworthy to share the dradtails' perfect union.

Finally, a dradtail in light armor lands nearby and makes her way to them. Neshushuni embraces Alan, in the midst of the march, and her brothers-in-arms part around them like water.

"Gone-face," she says, squeezing Alan with surprising strength. "I hear tell of your works far away, then nothing. I was worry that you die. Haven't stop wonder since you leave. I'm happy to see you again – happy that you've come to fight with Lashaseph. You are good. I know you were."

"It's a pleasure, Shuni," Alan replies. "This is Nora and Sister Sophia. Nora, Sister Sophie, this is Shuni."

"The wall-builder," Sophia says, emerging from Stag's Blood's mane to wink in greeting. "Shines, Shuni. I heard how you helped Alan. I have never met a Lashaseph before. I am sad that we must meet in these circumstances."

"What's this force?" Nora asks. "There are so many of you."

"The Colony is near empty," Shuni says, picking up the march. "Winter White break our walls and sack the nectaries at last. She take all our stores and leave us to starve. Our spies find her here, and now we come. All hive give many soldiers. Big battle to fight. Biggest since before I was born."

"She's baiting you," Stag's Blood says.

Nora nods. "She knows you can't win. You're marching into her massacre."

"This is Lashaseph last stand," Shuni sighs. "We crush Winter White or we cease to be. Chiefs are scared bad. Me, too."

"No one else has come to help?" Stag's Blood asks. "Fae clans that have been killing each other for centuries are allied against you, but you stand alone."

"Lashaseph have no allies," Shuni buzzes. "Always alone. No outsiders. But you bring something to help? Have a plan?" She bends a difficult smile and seems tired afterward. "Maybe your spirit gift."

"I believe I do have a plan," Alan says. "Can you get the chiefs to wait and hear me out?"

"No need," Shuni says, smiling. "I know, everyone know. How do you think I know you here? Tell."

"All right," Alan says. His nerves start to buzz and spark like bursting capacitors. His blood is neon. He looks down at his arm for a second, wondering if his veins might luminesce. A stored charge of terror sits in his heart, waiting for the right catalyst to unload.

"I want to start with a shadowstorm," Alan continues when he's reclaimed his focus. "I'll need some space to do it. Hopefully, I can whip one up that will be big enough to trim their ranks significantly. Once I can't hold it anymore, I'll fall back and you can rush in. What do you think of that?"

Brattle replies as Shuni is mulling this over. "The enemy ain't gonna wait," he coughs. "They'll shoot you down if you're standin' out in the open by yourself. I assume they got bows and rock guns. Magic cloak or not, it ain't a good idea to bank on you bein' invincible."

"OK, so it's not perfect," Alan says. "Let's make it better. What do you suggest."

Shuni buzzes in thought. Her antennae wiggle in the waves of pheromones that pour over her.

"Drive you to the center and leave you," she says. "Give you time to make your magic, and then pull back, like put a bomb."

"That might be as close to better as we're going to get," says Alan. "We need a big hit or a lot of help, and this is the biggest hit I have to offer. I'll put everything into it."

Alan shivers. The power is growing in him already. He must be brilliant with it — a torch to rival the sun. His handles tremble around the haft of his trash masher.

"Risk is high," Shuni says. "Stupid risk, but necessary. War hurt to think about — hurt to face. Help my grubs wrap my coffin today. So brave, they are, but small. Grubs shouldn't have to be brave like that never. I am bad for put fear in front of them."

Nora makes a show of biting back a chuckle. Shuni doesn't even look at her. There are tears streaming down her painted face. They shine in the hollows of her cheeks like emeralds until she wipes them away.

"We'll burn that coffin when we get back to the Colonies," Alan says, taking the dradtail's slender hand. She has dipped her fingertips in white paint, and some of it comes off on his palm. "I promise. Even if I can't, I do. You'll see your grubs again."

"Can't burn Lashaseph coffin," Shuni says. "Made of wax and special resin. Fire won't stick. Have to break it apart." A better smile spreads across her face now. It lights her up, but it still hurts. Pain lives in the bight of that smile, and Alan can't look at it. "Maybe put enemy heads in. Or maybe burn *them*. Cruel flesh burn just fine."

"That's the spirit," says Nora. "No time for fear, no time for grief. Bring me the blood and the darkness."

Forty-One

Noon burns the sky as bare as bone. A dry wind rips the last of the campfire smoke into a rising haze and kicks grit and ash through the passion wrack. Shadows shrink across the floor of Stele Gorge with their faces in their hands and their hearts sinking to sleep. It is a bright and terrible day.

The rust-black tubes of the writhers are ten feet high and as big around as truck axles. They branch out in drunken spirals from anvil concretions, sagittate organs waving like sails from the highest spires. Alan can feel the worms in the ground as the dradtail swarm draws to a stop at the edge of the wrack. Their minds are old, and they have strange roots. They are as much a part of the Bleeding as they are of Graveworld. The draug is dim in their darkness.

A dradtail chief steps forward and holds up his glaive. Its blade emerges from the skull of a shrieker hound.

"Bad idea," Brattle says under his breath.

"I can take about sixty down right now," Alan tells Shuni. "They won't even feel it."

Shuni hisses. "No! Dishonorable. You fight for Lashaseph, you fight *as* Lashaseph."

"What honor?" Brattle asks. "Ain't you gonna start killing them anyway?"

"Defend," Shuni says, her voice flattening into a thin murmur. For three beats of her glassy wings, her voice is the voice of the swarm. "Always defend. Honor til death, or else just death."

The dradtail chief screws himself up into a painfully upright and confident stance. He bounces on the toes of his hide boots as he demands, "Send out Winter White!"

Then he rattles his wings, and the other dradtails follow suit. Soon, the gorge is loud with their buzzing.

The misfit horde jostles into lines. Hobs push and threaten each other at the front. Dredges snarl, barely contained by the chains hooked to their copper collars. A tall knock rides out on a

226

blue cat to meet the dradtail chief. Stag's Blood watches the cat intently through slitted eyes.

"A wild thing," he whispers. "I pity it."

"All cats were bastethai once," Nora says. "Most have lost their speech, but their minds remain, trapped in feral bodies that won't obey them. Your race is cursed."

Stag's Blood growls and drops his head. "You should say," he sneers, pressing his chin to his chest. When Nora only smiles at him, he goes on. "I shall break many curses today."

The knock dismounts and doffs his silver crown. He doesn't feel Alan in his spirit, coiling around him – or he doesn't care. The smile on his face is so corpse-rotten that Alan can almost smell it.

Sweeping his gold-piped short cape back from his shoulder, the knock draws a sword from a scabbard beneath it. He takes it in both hands, and it rings a clear song as he tugs it up into a lethal slash. Its white edge flashes for the dradtail's neck, but the knock crumples like a scarecrow before the strike lands. Alan strangles his spirit with a thought, sending him falling from his helpless body just into the dead side of the draug. It's hardly a chore. Alan could have done it in his sleep.

When the knock falls, the dradtail swarm surges forward. Alan sees their fury explode around him, and the suns go dim behind its crimson curtain. Green lights of vespine bloodlust burst through it like blooming peonies, and he finds himself rushing into the passion wrack surrounded by buzzing wings.

The dradtails bunch into knots to support each other. They strike from flawless caution while the misfit horde simply pours forward like a wave. Their frenzy is ugly and foolish, but it works. They cut through ranks of soldiers fighting in formation in the first charge, keeping the dradtails at bay. Rawbones roars through Nora's flesh. Hobs die in her maw or beneath her feet.

Brattle and Shuni carve a way for Alan toward what he hopes is the heart of Winter's force. Alan watches hobs and dredges drop like leaves to litter the ground around him. Their animal death howls are horrible. He wants to freeze, but he can't. Something moves in him that is neither fury, nor bloodlust, nor fear. It burst from him like Rawbones, crushing his hesitation, and swinging is easy. He stops blades on the haft of his trash masher, and he pushes his foes down into near death, all the while barely aware of his limbs moving.

Focus, he tells himself. *Know their faces. See each one of them before you them. Watch them reveal themselves and shoot in like an owl. The draug is hungry.*

Alan sinks into Atratus's warning as a mantra.

"The light of the draug is failing," he repeats, and it helps him find his center in the chaos of overstimulation. Once Alan regains control of his will to fight, the enemy splits away from him like clouds around a fork of lightning. He reaches out to push whole bands of hobs and knocks past the draug, stretching himself until his vision blurs and his head fills with white-hot pain. There is no time for fear, there is no time for grief, but he feels them anyway. He makes a point to. They bind him in the fight when the screams of the dying make overwhelm him. Fear makes it real. Grief keeps him sane.

Dredges surround them, gnawing-mad now that they've slipped their leashes. Stag's Blood bounds ahead with Sophia in his mane. She pushes rays of her heartlight from her tiny hands, augmented by the unmistakable red-gold blaze of Welkinbright's Eternal Flame. Stag's Blood's photomancy gives Sophia's beams enough mass and heat to perforate the rushing dredges, and Nora rips any lucky stragglers apart.

The swarm finds a foothold to advance and drives the misfit horde back into the passion wrack at the tips of their swords. Then they withdraw, pulling their wounded with them. Their chiefs gather at the vanguard to rally their troops with slogans and battle cries. Pipers emerge from the swarm, their wings ripped and their armor cracked. A drummer joins them to tap out a rushing rhythm on her djembe. The misfit horde falls back to regroup as well, leaving Alan and his company in the trough of their rising wave.

"Is everyone all right?" Stag's Blood calls.

"We missed the first chance," Brattle replies. He stands on the bowed back of a broken knock, his knife in his fist and blood smeared around his mouth. The world seems to swell in an effort to contain him. "Next one's comin' soon. We gotta stay closer together."

At this, a mire-og comes tromping from among the writhers' red towers. It is ten feet tall and neckless, with an oblate mass for a head stuffed low between its broad shoulders. Its flesh sags in great flaps and drips like creek mud. Alan can find nothing resembling a spirit inside it.

"Here we go," Alan says. He twists his aching hands around the shaft of his masher. Power gathers there as heat and subtle vibrations. The weapon whispers comfort as the mire-og breaks into a run and flails its arms downward in an attempt to crush him.

The light of the draug is failing, Alan thinks. He reels away from the mire-og's hammering blows, frustrated by his clumsiness. The rest of the misfit horde crashes in again, renewed and screaming with notched weapons raised. Stag's Blood rips a hob rider to the ground and and then stands to collide with his sun-yellow saddlecat. Rawbones leans into the mire-og with howling abandon, clawing hunks of its soft body away to reveal naught but more of the same underneath. Panic threatening, Alan rolls away and looks into his garden for succor.

Where Alan's inner darkness used to be, there is now a long, winter's sunset. The sky above his garden is pink and copper-bright. Fireworks burst far away above red hills crowned in the sun. He can see the draug in the fields and the woods. It shimmers white upon the rivers and falls down mountainsides in slides of snow. Alan's garden has grown beyond the bounds of his mind. Dead voices rise on the wind, and he understands them. Blended together, they sound like Theia.

"The draug hasn't dimmed at all," dead Theia says. "It's bright, alive, and perfect."

With this, the sun sets and the garden fades. Alan returns to himself and the madding battle with a healing sense of power and calm.

Rawbones tears into the mire-og even as it stands on her neck and pounds her. Shuni pushing her pike into its side is the only thing that keeps the mire-og from beating Rawbones to death. Brattle is on the mire-og's back, hanging on with one hand buried in the running muck of its body. Knocks have Stag's Blood hemmed, keeping him from running as a spearback circles him. Alan pushes himself to his feet and heaves his trash masher over his head, drawing his power forth like breath. The Seal of Aiwass shining from his forehead, he swings his masher wide and pushes the mire-og apart with magic. It staggers, its arm dangling, and Shuni lunges in to sever the limb completely. As it reaches to clutch the oozing stump, Rawbones surges up from beneath it to tear it open.

The mud-thing totters, spins on one broad heel, and topples as Rawbones rams it with her shoulder. Alan pushes again, feeling force flex out of him to warp the air, and the mire-og bursts into a cold, luteous mess.

Brattle squirms from the muck, his face drawn tight as if by cords of steel.

"Bless the sky," he spits, knuckling mud-flesh from his brow.

"Ahet," Shuni says, but Alan has turned away.

The spearback advances, laughing at Stag's Blood. Whenever Stag's Blood backs away, the knocks thrust with their pikes. He is bleeding from several punctures, and his magic has sapped his strength. Sophia sends her Flame-light out, and it keeps the knocks at bay, but it isn't hard or hot anymore. Alan reaches out to the spearback first. The beast in Welkinbright was beyond him, but he has grown so much. He is a different mage now. He seizes the spearback's radiant, smoking spirit and eases it into the draug. It looks up at him like a child, and he smiles down at it. It sinks to the dead side secure and comfortable.

When their spearback collapses, the knocks surrounding Stag's Blood leap back in horror. They are less of a challenge for Alan: each goes under after the other, wheeling through the draug into oblivion. There is no time for fear. They have no time to fight or to grieve for their wasted hopes — for the small work of their lives. The fall over each other as Alan paralyzes their spirits at the brink of death, and Stag's Blood leaps to his side to nuzzle him.

"You're owed more gratitude now than any one of us can ever repay," Stag's Blood purrs as Alan heals his wounds. "What have you found within yourself, my boy?"

"My own gardens," Alan says. He gives Stag's Blood's mane a long stroke, stopping to offer Sophia his palm.

"More remains to be done," the Fetchlight chimes. "I shall withhold my relief until we are out of this gorge with our prize. When shall we finish the plan?"

Shuni leans in panting. One of her antennae is bent and bleeding. She has left her stinger in some hob, and her thorax is torn open. Alan reaches into her strange, green light to heal her.

"What prize you look for?" she asks. "Ngashing Stone?"

"If that's a piece of the Chodash Stone, then yes," Alan says. "Do you know it?"

"Lashaseph want to take it to keep in the nectaries. Lashaseph guard Honeylands once, too," Shuni says. She points to the hulking Rawbones. "Like you. Lashaseph guard Nudd."

"Never," Rawbones growls. Nora blazes in her eyes, bright as sundown.

Shuni nods. "Once and always."

"You weren't exactly forthcoming with that information," Stag's Blood says.

"No reason to be and neither were you," Shuni says. "Nudd is secret – important secret – and we swear to keep it. But we not lie. *I* not lie. Defend. Remember? Always defend."

"Then we're all here for the same reason," Alan says. "Good. If there's any more to be talked about, we can do that later – when we all walk out of this. Now stand back. I'm going to do the thing while I've still got momentum, and it's going to be big."

Alan puts the head of his trash masher on the ground and leans over its handle to marshal his strength.

"This is good," he says. "It's a perfect spot. Now come on. Get back!"

"We gotta go farther in, boss," Brattle shouts, tugging on Alan's arm. "This ain't going to give us maximum damage."

Alan won't budge. His feet grow roots from the garden of his magic. The dead move beneath him as though they might burst from the ground to greet him personally. There is no better place.

"No. Now," Alan says. "I'm going to do it. Watch out!"

His muscles burning, Alan strains to direct his energy. It is greater than him now, and it knows. It doesn't want to obey, but it has no choice. Finally, he owns it. Magic is in the deaths of his parents and his sister. It is glass on the street and blood in the bathwater. It's easiest to find in funerals and pain, but it's in every triumph, too. Magic is total integration. The revelation is exhilarating.

Be the change you want to see in the world, Alan says to himself. *I never had any idea what that meant until now. Hold on tight, Sepulchra, because I'm about to become that change today.*

Brattle and Shuni fall back toward the dradtails. Stag's Blood and Rawbones circle Alan as close as they can, only dodging away as the storm starts to scream around him. Alan reaches deep. He touches every lost spirit in the mountains and on the valley floor. The Dead in Disgrace respond with wailing hunger in his head, but Alan isn't afraid of them. All his fear has melted away. He draws power into the handle of his trash masher and balls it up in his body. Raising his hand, he starts to pull the shadows from beneath the writhers' towering tubes. Darkness bunches around him from the hollows of hobs's cheeks and the foaming depths of spearback's mouths. He swirls it, shaping it like clay on a wheel, amazed at his new ability to be so delicate.

The storm touches down. Alan stretches it out from its eye into a huge, howling funnel. It expands across the battlefield, crushing passion wrack to powder and tearing Winter's misfits apart where it catches them. The ground sinks and cracks. The writhers scream around Alan, and he feels them like little fires in his mind. They are afraid, but he doesn't care – he is so wide in his power now that Stele Gorge feels far away. Graveworld looks small from the precipice of his strength. Then, as he turns to check again that the others have gotten to safety, the ground groans open and Alan falls deep into the prisons of Sepulchra through a wreck of dust, worm blood, and blocks of stone.

Alan drops through the dark in terrified silence. His fall is brief, but it takes forever. When he hits the ground, he is frozen bone-stiff. He doesn't cry out when he feels his fibula break beneath him. His knee slips, and the pain is incredible, but he makes no sound. Nothing moves for a long time while he lies in agony, staring up at the moon-shaped hole he fell through. The sounds of the battle above drift from the ceiling like snow and evaporate before he can make anything of them. Finally, he sits up out of the light and looks straight ahead into nothing.

"Why can't I see?" Alan says. His voice echoes deep into the colossal chamber. "I can see. Eyes need light, but I don't." He concentrates, trying to find the power and certainty he's just fallen from. "I can see. I can do it."

The darkness blows away, and the cavern opens before him. It is taller than his house in Lakewood Balmoral, and it goes on into invisible distance in two directions. The walls shine black and smooth, and streams of green liquid cut long rivets in them as they trickle to the floor.

Like dradtail blood, Alan thinks.

He sits still for a moment, watching the writhers' tubes. They descend from the ceiling in clusters like organ pipes, their huge mouths dark and open. Flakes of red, chalky matter sift down from them as things move inside. While Alan stares, waiting to see if any graveworms will emerge to taste his pain, he realizes that his pulse has stopped and his lungs have gone still. He is utterly quiet inside.

I didn't need them either. I was clinging, but not anymore.

Alan looks down. Even covered by the fabric of his pants, his broken leg is shockingly ugly. He stares for a while, trying to get a feel for its strange, new shape. Pain pumps through him from the break, growing in intensity with each freezing pulse. He resists the urge to hold his injury and reaches out to it through magic instead.

"The old me would have cried and shaken," he says, trying to distract himself. "I won't. I'm the new me. I'm new. Knit, knit. Come on."

Magic moves in Alan's leg. His skin crawls as it pumps into his marrow. The bones align, grinding over each other, and he screams. Something is wrong. The magic is angry. Alan tries to rein it in, the seal smoking bright on his forehead, but it bucks his control. It throbs hot in his muscles, asserting its will in bursts and shocks, and Alan is too weak now to subdue it.

"Oh, forgetful," dead Theia whispers. "There is no king in the garden."

The Bleeding opens in Alan's mind. The magic moves into his other leg, and Alan's pants split to shreds. A seizure tugs hard on Alan's spine, and it is all he can do to resist arching back into its grasp. He keeps himself upright on the shaking pillars of his arms and watches as the Bleeding reshapes his legs. He needs to see everything he feels, no matter how horrible.

Alans legs start to shrivel. Scales and black growths of horn erupt from them in asymmetrical patterns. Where the anacle burst against his thigh, the remnant gold stain burns red as passion wrack. His rebelling magic uses what's left of the anacle's contents on his skin to change him further. His feet spread to rip from his non-slip work shoes, and his toes fuse together around curving claws. The pain is enormous, and yet more comes into him from the Bleeding. The void fills him with ancient, alien suffering, torturing him, trying to make him pass out. Alan resists, though his spirit burns. With every fraying strand of his strength, he roots himself where he is and binds his spirit together.

Alan can't hear the rumbling in the ceiling over his own howls. He is so focused on staying conscious that he doesn't see the writhers emerging from their tubes. When the pain starts to ebb away, he can hardly believe it. Stymied, the Bleeding shrieks endless, terrible anger. Spirits thrash across it – nightmares of betrayal and ruin from the abyss of its heart – but it can't regain control. Its power in Alan has been severed. Alan looks up, hesitant to feel relieved, and finds himself surrounded by a waving wall of graveworms.

Forty-Two

The parts of the writhers that are in the sphere of form are red as hate and crowned with bone-ribbed fans. They swirl around Alan in a Gordian knot, eyeless and gulping through slit mouths lined with conical teeth. Alan finds his trash masher beside him and wraps his hand tight around it. He tries to stand, but his new legs defy him. The worms lean in, jostling each other to try and get a taste of his exquisite pain, but it is subsiding. Frustrated, one of them wraps itself around Alan and starts to heave him up. The others crowd in, their mouths working, and Alan begs his magic to push them away.

Like strays fighting for scraps, Alan thinks. *But I have nothing left. They're going to have to beat the pain back into me. They'll pull me apart if I can't stop them now.*

The worms haul him up and coil around his limbs. He screams as they tug him in opposite directions. Something pops in his shoulder. Finally, Alan's magic responds. Theia brings it back and reassures it with promises. Alan sees her in his garden, a little barefoot girl standing before a towering darkness. She quells it with just a touch and a smile, and it disappears.

Alan plunges into desperate focus. In place of his pulse, there is a new force banging inside him. Rapalion's heart throbs in the center of Alan's body, huge as the cavern itself, filling him with power. Alan casts his magic wide, reaching into every dead mind and spirit he can find, and the Dead in Disgrace respond.

There is a roar from the depths of the prisons. The writhers stop tugging to twitch and twitter amongst each other. A mist rises from the floor, and shapes appear in it.

"Wake up," Alan cries as the worms tighten around him. "Help me!"

A voice comes out of the mist. Alan remembers the wind in the little wood near Allison's house. Wracked with pain and fighting with all his strength to stir the dead, Alan finds himself thinking of the guardian sycamore at the head of his path home from Ray's.

"These dead are bound, thanoturge," says the mist voice. "They have a debt to pay."

"It's resolved!" Alan screams. He thrashes against the writhers, but that only makes them slither tighter around him. "Their sentence is finished! Please!"

"Forgive me," the voice replies. "I did not know. It has been so long."

With this, the guardian mist dissolves and the air goes cold. The writhers panic and drop Alan. The chamber fills with shimmering wraith-shapes that mount the walls like a wave, cresting downward to cream across the floor. There are so many spirits teeming together that Alan can't even begin to count them all. They are like one thing – or else the distinctions between them are time-rotted and meaningless.

Blade-bright flashes of opaline light cut the writhers down. The ones that aren't left steaming dead on the floor shoot back up into their tubes. Alan watches from his back, pain exploding through his body, as the wraith host clouds black over the great fist of dead writher flesh. He reaches out to them again, probing deeper this time, and he finds the mass writhing with scar tissue. Fury lives in it, dark and heavy around the white coal of pain. There is a monstrous sucking sound. Then the cloud luminesces to transparency again, and there is nothing left of the graveworms when it breaks.

Alan pushes himself to his feet, using his trash masher as a crutch. His new legs feel numb, but they are responding now. He hates to look at them.

Thank you, he says to Theia, but Theia doesn't reply. She is sleeping now, curled up like a mouse in some warm corner of his garden, and he can't find her.

The freed wraiths approach. But for their constant flickering, they are not too unlike the ghostly crew of the Mercy Gale. Alan straightens himself before them, fighting exhaustion. Fatigue is not a physical thing anymore. It is deeper than that, occurring at the level of his spirit. For a moment, he worries that he will always feel it.

Mist starts seeping into the room again. It stays close to the ground this time, swirling around Alan's feet like dry ice fog. It leaves a light tingle on his skin when it touches him.

"The Wraith King remade," says the mist in its gossamer voice. The throng of wraiths seems to shift to look at it, though it's difficult for Alan to tell which way they're facing. Few forms stand out from the others any more than one ripple of heat distortion does from the rest of its native mirage. "We expected to wait eons. The Dead in Disgrace are humbled by your magnanimity. "

"I'm not the king of anything," Alan says, remembering Theia's warning, "but we don't really have time to argue. Are you free? Will you follow me?"

The mist stirs. Alan peers into it and is surprised to see a full spirit – like his own or Brattle's – just on the living side of the draug. Unlike the Dead in Disgrace, this entity is still connected to some kind of life. Alan wonders if it could be the spirit he is looking for.

"I have always been free," the mist says. "Sadly, I cannot follow. That is the way of things. But you have freed the Dead in Disgrace, and they will."

"I need out of here, and there's a fight going on above," Alan explains, flexing his new legs to test them. They feel as weak as paper. "If they think I'm their king, then I command them to fight." He looks at the scintillating mass of spirits before him. "Fight with me. Let's go."

"These cursed spirits have grown together," the mist says. "They cannot sort out how to speak anymore – there are too many conjoined. You shall need a mouthpiece."

With this, a wraith steps out of the glimmer and curves herself together in front of Alan. He knows her even before she starts to fill herself with color. She takes on weight, but she never becomes fully real. Her white-blond hair floats around her head as if suspended in water. The green gem at her throat winks like a star, its light cold and distant. Her eyes are the only solid thing about her. More than anything, it is the sad light in her face that Alan recognizes. He wonders if Toven burned her picture in his catharsium.

"Winter has come," says the Lady Nightjar, touching her green jewel. "Stir the fires of your wrath at last, oh fairies. Revenge, revenge, revenge."

The Dead in Disgrace purl up around Alan. He searches into them as they lift him toward the moon-shaped hole in the ceiling. The mass of their conjoined minds is beautiful. Beneath the pain that has twisted them together, there is a new kind of spirit. It is beyond the draug, and the Bleeding can't touch it. In the rush of their grasp, Alan's magic feels as pure as the first dawn in a newborn world.

The world after this, Alan thinks. The wraithmass quivers around him. *I've seen the world that was destroyed and the world that was allowed to end. If there is to be a newer one yet, this is where it will start.*

Aboveground, it has started to rain. The dradtail swarm has pushed deep into the writhers' towers at a terrible cost of life. Winter White's misfit horde is advancing, pouring into the swarm's weakened ranks to finish the slaughter. Scour riders dive from the valley wall to rake the ranks of the wasps with halberds thrust forward. Brattle waits to pull them from the air when they swing close. Alan is relieved to see that Brattle still wears his fragment in his haversack. Mire-ogs batter the front line in great, cruel waves. Nora and Stag's Blood struggle to hold the last of the vanguard against them. Malakeen terrors plow the battlefield, swinging swords of fire and pulling whips of lightning through the air. None can stand before that withering onslaught. Where the Coma strikes, the draug swallows spirits in massive knots.

"Spare the wasps, the cat, the ghoul, and the well-pisser," Alan says as he washes to his feet from the wave of wraiths. "Crush the rest."

The Dead in Despair cascade across the battlefield, sweeping hobs and dredges up into their shining swirl. Passion wrack pillars topple and burst as mire-ogs fall against them. The horde can't flee. Death falls on them, breaking them apart, and the draug sucks their spirits down into gluttonous havoc. The dradtails stop where they are, unsure whether to cheer or try to fly away.

Alan races along the edge of the dead tide on his new legs, reveling in their strength. The garden of his magic is in prolific bloom, and he has control again. Rapalion's heart fills his chest with a wild pounding. The anacle's influence is subtler, but no less thrilling. Clear fluid fills his garden streams: the yolk from the Dawn Spiders' egg sacs. It feeds him with a constant, quiet abandon, eroding the boundaries of his strength until they seem to disappear entirely. Driving annihilation before him at the head of his trash masher, Alan can feel every boon he has received exploding inside him. It wouldn't surprise him to see Hannes following him through the massacre.

The King of Wraiths remade, Alan says. *My golden youth reborn in unreal beauty. I'm everything. My power is complete.*

Alan is careful to let the magic have its say. Cooperating with it, acknowledging its autonomy, he becomes that much stronger. Hobs and dredges blow away from him like browning leaves. Lessons he's read in magic books swirl over his inner garden like healing storms, clearer than they have ever been. Remembering what he read in the *Book of Horns*, he rips a mire-og apart with one thrust of his outstretched palm. *The mind moves flesh. Bone and blood respond to the Aethereal Hand.*

"And mud," Alan laughs.

Scours fall screaming from the sky, their spines splintered and wings wrenched apart in Alan's invisible grip. Those spearbacks he cannot reach to drown in darkness flee up the valley walls and disappear. The dradtails pull back from the wave of death, terror buzzing through their hivemind. By the time Alan reaches the dradtails' vanguard, the Battle of Stele Gorge is over.

Brattle meets Alan at the edge of the passion wrack. He comes swinging up on pulpy knuckles, his face a mess of blood from a livid gash across his nose. As he takes Alan's hand, Alan notices that one of his fingers is missing.

"There's my good luck charm," Brattle beams, blinking blood from his eye. "My dead-waker. Tide-turner!"

Alan holds out his masher. It is gem-white with power and pulsing like a flame. "Necromasher," he says, and Brattle laughs.

"That's right," Brattle says, knuckling in close under Alan's arm to whisper to him. "And a stone-cold killer now, I see. What happened to make ya break yer restraint, boss? How does it feel now bein' free of it?"

Alan looks inward for a moment. He can feel the new dead for the first time. They aren't angry. They have no broken hearts. Their hearts are gone – or changed. Alan is bitterly sad, but not for them. The dead are gone from the past. They have only the present anymore. Alan feels the past like a yoke around his neck. He is sad for himself.

"I'm not," Alan replies. He starts to close the slash across Brattle's face.

"Oh yeah," Brattle laughs, the lips of his wound blanching gray as they purse closed. "You ain't."

"Where's Shuni?" Alan asks. He searches the hivemind for her, but it is in a state of deep shock. So many nodes have been ripped away that it can't order itself, and it has given up trying. It retreats until Alan can't feel it anymore.

"I ain't really sure about that," Brattle replies, suddenly sheepish. "There was a couple good pushes, and a lotta hymies went down. Some of 'em carried the injured ones up the canyon, but I can't tell 'em apart so good. I dunno if she's one of the carriers or one of them that got carried. Let's go. I'll show you where."

Nora comes down from the wrack with Stag's Blood limping behind her. dradtails stop where they are to gawp at her nakedness. Stag's Blood's left side is soaked with blood. Alan searches into him to find sprays of small stones stopped in his thick hide. With a wave of his hand, Alan draws the stones from Stag's Blood's flesh and pushes them to the ground. They rattle around Stag's Blood's feet as his gait evens out. Death is small in his wounds, a shadow spreading from mere pain and damage, but it is finding a hold. Alan drives it out like snakes before a flame, and Stag's Blood smiles as his wounds start to close.

"The spirit," he says between deep, careful breaths. "It cannot be too great a leap to presume that you found it."

"Several of them," Sophia adds, emerging from Stag's Blood's mane. Her heartlight is bright and strong. She lands on Alan's hand, and he presses her gently to thegrooved and dirt-striped plane of his malar bone. Her warmth sets his spirit soaring.

"I don't know yet," Alan says, lowering his hand so that Sophia can fly a few quick circles before lighting on his shoulder. "There are wounded to help, and I want to find Shuni."

"Lead the way," Stag's Blood says.

Nora chuffs a brittle laugh. "And tell us what happened to your legs while you're at it," she says. "This is a day of stories."

They set out, following Brattle. The Dead in Disgrace race through the canyon. Alan calls out to them, trying to get them to return to his side, but they refuse, and he lets them run. They deserve their revelry. They howl their freedom, their wild, animal cries of echoing across the mountains. Far away, something answers them. Songs thread from the west, where the woods thicken. They are empty, pained, and beautiful – the hymns to oblivion. Alan remembers them from his first days in Graveworld.

The remaining dradtail chiefs gather their troops to follow Alan up the gorge. There are few wounded lying unattended in the eastern choke. The mouth of a cave set high in the north wall has been hastily covered with a funnel of raw, white pulp, and dradtail healers are buzzing around it. On the rubble field below the cave, a number of stung hobs are struggling for life. Wasp soldiers pick their way across the rocks, planting spears like flags in the dying. Alan walks out to stop them, but they warn him away.

"Mercy must be guard," the dradtails insist, "or the wicked will steal it. It mean nothing if it is give to everyone."

"But I don't hate my enemies," Alan says, kneeling over one hob as it fights for breath. "I don't want to kill them."

"Then your mercy is a lie," say the soldiers. "You waste it on the merciless."

Alan crosses his arms. The soldiers can't stop his healing magic. He reaches out to heal the hob, but it slips away of its own volition. He feels its terror as it goes, and he lets it pass with a whispered apology. Grief knots in his throat.

"I know it hurts, but you can't bring everyone back," Sophia says.

Nora offers him a hand up and guides him away from the bodies.

"Do they hurt?" she asks, nodding down at Alan's legs. Her hair swings perfect angles around her face. For a moment, she looks as safe as milk. "I've never seen anything like them."

"Something my magic gave me," Alan says. "It's so alive now – it's a thing of its own, and I made it angry. And no, they don't hurt. It's a little weird walking with them, though. I feel kind of like a guy in half a monster suit."

Nora gives Alan an absent nod. "A gift or a punishment?" she asks. "Maybe something of both – one for you and one for me."

"Magic is change," Stag's Blood says, saving Alan some embarrassment. "That is the lesson here, I think. I wouldn't call your changing done just yet, Alan." He looks down the tail of the gorge toward the red towers. The writhers are squirming from their tubes, abandoning the empty prisons in search of better pain. "I hope never to be done changing. I hope never to be *finished*. You have new legs, you have a new face, but you must also have a new heart – a new mind. Perhaps you're on your way to a profound change of spirit. Your own may be the spirit you're looking for."

"A little heavy, Stags," Brattle says. "But that's you. You're heavy."

Alan and the others make their way up the sliding hill. They stop at the mouth of the cave, unable to reach the opening in the pulp dome the dradtails have built over it. The two wasps guarding the dome lean their spears against the valley wall and expand the funnel so that Alan's party can climb in. Their faces are like stone. They aren't hurt, but death is looming over them, drawn to their anguish. As the dradtail hivemind returns from its withdrawal, death's winged darkness circles through it, riding thermals of grief.

The cave is wide and shallow, with smooth walls and dry floors. Gems burn from wet cells of pulp affixed everywhere, and a bit more light limps in through a pair of fist-sized holes worn in the outer wall. Bodies lay on the ground in no shadow, their wounds looking no less horrific for being clean. Too few healers walk the cave with skins of water or bowls of medicine paste. Alan searches the wounded and the stiffening corpses for Shuni, but he is distracted by the desperate cries of failing spirits. Bombarded by pain and fear, it takes all his focus to keep from collapsing.

One of the healers looks down at them from the ceiling. "What you want, one-mind?" she says, fighting to push her weary voice through the moans and buzzing. "Lots to do. You be long in the way of Lashaseph work if you're not help?"

"We're looking for Neshushuni," Stag's Blood replies. He barely fits in the cave. Some of the injured reach out to touch his flanks, his mane, or his swinging tail. "We want to be out of your way as soon as possible. Is she here?"

The healer points to a dimple pressed into the north wall beneath a blade of shale. Alan is relieved to see Shuni kneeling there, spooning medicine from a bowl to a throng of reaching hands. As he approaches her, she stands to cross the room. She greets Alan at a dead wasp's side.

"Again I think you were dead, gone-face," she says, grabbing her wrist behind her back and staring emptily into the corpse's glittering eyes. "Many are, and many more will be. Push your sleeves up. Chase death from this place with me. You get your prize at least?"

Alan looks down at the dead dradtail. Her face is marked with war paint. Her mouth is set into a hard, determined line. The dark and the draug are behind her – she is a match burning far away on the dead side. Alan can just feel her flickering.

"Not yet," Alan says. "Who was she?"

"Anacadeshisemta," says Shuni. "Cousin. Crush inside by mudthing."

Dying groans press in on Alan, shrinking the cave until the noise and the heat are like a bag around his head. He reaches deep into his garden, turning up the soil for power. He thinks of Pick, Brattle's father, lurching up from death with mad eyes.

"I can reach her," Alan says, searching down into the draug-split dark to find the little flame. She is further away than the sylph woman he woke in Welkinbright, but he was green then. Now he is strong – certain. "It might hurt, but I can bring her back."

"Others in need," Shuni says, turning to look at Alan through slitted eyes. "Anaca die. Come and help the living instead."

"Wait," Alan says. "She's not gone. I can do it."

In his garden, the cries from the cave disappear. The hum of wings bleeds into the murmur of wind in the willow branches, where magic hangs like fruit and anthers. The bonds that held Anaca in her body are hopelessly eroded. Alan draws on himself to create new ones. Her spirit is deep in the teeth of death, and her will is splintered. Alan balls his fists against his thighs, squeezing his magic for all it has. The forces that resist him feel elemental – like gravity. The *Book of Horns* said that the Desolate couldn't be returned to any good kind of life, but Alan won't be denied. He thinks of the fairies he pushed to death while the Dead in Disgrace were ravaging the battlefield. He slipped then, drunk on anger, and

245

he hates himself for it. Now he will push until he breaks to save Anaca.

Alan dives headlong into darkness. His magic explodes, and he feels as though he is threading apart. Far below the draug, deep in the great green swamp of death, trapped spirits shine like frogs' eyes. Alan spreads his magic like a net and pulls Anaca's little light into it. He hauls her up, whispering, "Knit, knit" and feeding her bits of himself to reconstitute her withered spirit. Anaca's body arches on the floor, and the dradtail healers gasp. Alan has caught many spirits in his net. The other dead wasps in the cave start to thrash and groan. Alan can rebuild them all. He has the fire to do it raging inside him.

The impossible twists apart. Darkness gathers behind Alan, spilling over his shoulders. The lights dim, and the cave goes black except for the Seal of Aiwass. Alan pours out more power than ever before, ignoring the monstrous strain on his psyche, and the Bleeding itself starts to howl in protest. Anaca heaves, rolls, rasps a choking scream, and then sits up. The other corpses follow suit, but they aren't corpses anymore. Alan has brought them all back at once.

Alan doubles over, spent and hurting. Nora wraps her arms around him to keep him from falling forward. His head feels ready to burst like a levy under the roiling, white force of a wave. The Bleeding fills him, burning his veins with poison, but the seal on his brow holds fast. He is amazed at its strength. The cave erupts into happy sobs of disbelief, and the two guards look in from outside with their stony faces pulled long in gapes of shock. When he can finally uncoil himself, Shuni wraps Alan in a hug.

"You great power, gone face," she says, her wings a deafening blur. "I not know. Should have welcome you better before! Should have let you in, let you help, tell you everything. I test you, waste your time. You great power! How you do that, huh?"

Alan puts his hands on Shuni's waist. She is thin as a tube, and he can feel her blood moving under her skin. When Shuni pulls away, her eyes are bright with tears.

"You great power, outlander," says the revived Anaca. Alan can hardly hear her over the joyous commotion.

"Thank you," Alan says, "but we're not done. You said so yourself Shuni: there are others in need."

"Alan, please," Sophia says. "You should rest. No one will fault you."

"I *will* rest," Alan replies, swaying like a reed on weak knees. The old dead voices rise in his head again, and he takes comfort in them. His garden is silver in the light of a rising moon. "But if there's more good to be done, I can't just walk out. I have to be a part of it. It's what I'm here for."

Forty-Three

The sky is thistle-pink when Alan and Brattle emerge from the healers' cave. The two stand together at the bottom of the hill, watching the stars come out. Stele Gorge is deep in heady quiet. The spitting rain has stopped, and the clouds are thinning banners. A moon rises that Alan has never seen before. It is caught in the red halo of a ring system, and its face is black as char.

"Ummo," Brattle says, sitting still as bog water. "They used to call that moon a sign of something, but not anymore. It's like the flag of a nation that don't exist. A portent without a prophecy. Where's the prophet, Al? White wasn't here. Toven wasn't here. What was this about?"

"I could say anything," Alan says, adjusting the knapsack strap across his shoulder. Shudur thrums there, warm and hard. "We won't know till it's over."

Brattle shifts and looks down at the ground between his long, ashy feet. "You ain't the kid I met in the swamp, but I bet I ain't that different. I don't feel like I changed at all."

"Of course you have."

"Not like you," Brattle sighs. "I want a change to hold in my hand – I wanna look in the mirror and see every line of pain on my face. I wanna see every step on every road an' the blood I've spilled riverin' out. You got it. You wear it." He stretches and yawns wide, spreading his toes in the red dirt and shale.

"I get the feeling that you did the impossible back there," Brattle continues. "I want strength like yours and a clear way ahead."

"You're too certain," Alan replies. "That's your clear way. It's what I like about you."

"That an' this," Brattle says, swinging his hand in a circle in front of his face to indicate his handsomeness. "An' my heart of gold. But gold's soft, boss, and it ain't worth nothin' on its own. It's worth what we give it."

"Do you feel worthless?"

Brattle scoops up a little pile of dirt and presses his thumb into it. "No," he says. "Just changeless – no more and no less than I ever was."

"You were expecting to improve on perfection?" Alan jokes. Brattle shakes loose a laugh.

Vultures land in the passion wrack. Rustic ghouls come down the walls in scared little threads and hang back at the brushline while the valley fills up with wraith shimmer. The Dead in Disgrace approach from the west to swell in the gorge like a train of peach tree sap, drawn behind a violet sphere. The great host of freed spirits pours into the tail of the gorge, and the sphere unfolds to greet Alan as the Lady Nightjar.

"My King," says the ghost of Annun, bowing as best she can in her vaporous form. "I am leaving soon to gather the Sylvan host. We must speak now and conclude our business. I doubt I'll see you again."

"I'm going west to heal more wasps," Alan says. "You can come with me, but I won't rush. I have things to do here yet."

Stag's Blood comes down from the cave with Sophia shining white on his brow. Nora lags behind, a beautifully embroidered dradtail sarong straining around her meretricious figure. The healers descend the hill with their resurrected dead on sedans above them, crowned in strings of battlefield scrap. Nightjar stares at every new face as if seeing her own reflection.

"The Queen of Gimcrack," Sophia says, suddenly going red. "Can it be you? What has happened?"

Annun extends a tendril of vaguely hand-shaped mist to touch Sophia, but Stag's Blood recoils.

"Little bell," says Lady Nightjar. Her voice is like the hiss of hot metal cooling under running water. "Beat, my dead heart, the sky is bright above me today! I'm sorry about what Toven did to you. I know you gave your prophecy willingly, but his greed for it twisted your righteous act. I have always thought that he raped you of your gift, my girl. But now Toven is dead – may it please you and comfort you. The dream is yours again."

249

"What do you mean Toven is dead?" Stag's Blood asks.

Nightjar turns from him to look at Alan. She seems enormous even with the whole roiling legion of the Dead in Disgrace behind her. He can barely see her face through the mist pouring over her form. When she addresses him, her violet cloud becomes tense and reactive. His every tiny movement elicits a swat from a protective protuberance.

"Don't go into the field," Nightjar says, "until you hear what I have to share. You need my knowledge, Alan Shade. I am Pwysh's spirit."

"There is much to tell, but I have to be brief," Annun begins. "You must have been wanting this for some time. I am pleased to educate you."

Alan sits below the healers' cave on the field of scree and dead hobs, twirling his trash masher. Brattle and Stag's Blood stand on either side of him, still and watchful as gargoyles. Nora paces in circles around the meeting. Now and again, she pinches small pebbles between her comely toes and tosses them into the wall of wraiths waiting nearby. They respond with no more concern than a wall of stone might.

The Lady Nightjar continues. "You are the King of Wraiths, the ninth reincarnation of Goithion, the last fairy born in Nudd. The eighth was Anastasis Nex."

"Nex?" Nora huffs. "He was a traitor. His betrayal of Nudd brought Midion closer to the brink of utter darkness than it's ever been. No power would remake his spirit."

"Most are unworthy of Goithion's legacy. Nex was one of many betrayers. Do you not know his face when you see it? His body? Look at Alan, and you will see him again – the Great Murderer. But you will also see Enlil, the truest protector of Nudd since Goithion himself."

Nora circles close to Alan and slips her hand up the dome of his skull. "It must be your goodness that masked the face of the Destroyer," she says. "Or perhaps it was because I have always

250

thought that Nex's face was a mask. I have seen only shapes of stories drawn in black ink on cave walls all my life."

"Pwysh brought you here to find Nudd," Lady Nightjar says, "to protect it. But how terrible, after years of fear and secret toil, not to get to see you."

"I did see him," Alan says. "He sent me looking for you. His ghost showed me where to go."

"Pwysh had no ghost," Annun explains. "If you think you saw him, then you have been uncommonly lucky. Pwysh had a sluagh – a vile thing he coaxed from a meteor pit. It mimicked him out of hate. It might have killed you."

"Uncommonly lucky," Brattle chuckles. "That's our boss."

Lady Nightjar shivers for a moment, and bolts of green light shoot through her. The wraiths behind her groan before she goes on.

"Here is the whole story. Winter White first came to us when we were newly married. Toven was certain then – capable – and he had the presence of mind to turn her away.

"Then his life advanced, and he made nothing of himself. He was wise and good, but a failure. His certainty eroded, and Toven became desperate. That is when he met you, little bell."

"I brought him my dream," Sophia says. "I had to do it. The Mothers sent me to him."

"To be deflowered," Nora smiles. "The virgin prophetess losing her innocence."

"Toven spread your vaticinal dream as his own," Lady Nightjar says. "He said that a living human would show him the way to the Gardens Arcane. He wanted fame, and he got it. When Winter White returned, Toven had become a professional liar.

"Winter wanted Nudd, and Toven promised it. She lured him close with sex, and his promises expanded. He saw in her the fulfillment of the prophecy he had stolen. Her persuasion is dark and wrong. I'm convinced that Toven couldn't have resisted even if he hadn't been blind with ambition. She must have pixie blood."

Nora laughs with her mouth lying dead on her face. Her eyes burn to smoking coals.

"Toven couldn't give her Nudd," Stag's Blood says. "She can't have been happy about that."

"No. She cut him off. He starved for her body. He bowed to her attention as if she were a god. In the worst of his fits of misery, he gave himself to the Bleeding. I was no one to him anymore, but I still loved him. Love is a grim thing. It is like a worm born in the corpse of hope. Once raised and fed, it becomes like death: it is irresistible. It never dies. Love is the Cuco, and I followed it here."

"What'd you do?" Brattle asks.

Annun says nothing. Night draws up above her, star-splashed and blue as a bruised orbit. The sky seems pinched tight behind the milky veil of light it wears. Ummo is gone; there is no moon now.

"This will be difficult, Alan," Annun says. "I don't have time to reassure you. I will be late already. Pwysh found a way to project his spirit across the exchange and into Animus. He gave up his ghost – the fragment of his spirit that could have survived his death – to be your father."

It's Alan's turn to laugh.

"My dad was a patent attorney," he says. "He was not a thanoturge."

"Pwysh inhabited your father at the moment of your conception," Lady Nightjar says. Her normally flat voice shifts slightly into something like pity. "You are his son by a human mother – part fairy, as Goithion was; and part human, unfortunately. Pwysh studied for years to achieve your creation. In the same years, he built Winter White an army of draug-caught souls. When she learned that he had deliberately made them imperfect, she ordered Toven to kill him. And when she learned that I had helped Pwysh prepare for your coming, she sent Toven to kill me, too.

"But love is a grim thing. Remember? It gouged through my husband great chasms of hate and despair. With his hands crushing my throat, he cursed my spirit. I remember his wedding ring winking on his hand, burning with the power of his terrible spell. He damned me to these prisons, but now I am free. The curse is gone. Toven is dead — at Winter White's behest, no doubt, and probably at the hands of whatever hapless soul she has newly twisted into her service."

Alan leaps to his feet, fists bunched at his sides, but he can't think of anything to do with his new energy. Nora settles onto the large rock he was sitting on as he circles off. She eases one leg over the other and bounces her foot above the ground, her tongue in her cheek.

"And what will our child be?" she asks. "What new era of light will our progeny see? Nudd green and whole again? Midion restored? This is good news, Alan. This is a boon. Don't sulk."

Alan watches the rustics picking across the valley floor. He thinks of the ghoul he was as a child: an outsider even at home, hopelessly different and disengaged. School slipped by like a mist, meaningless. Friends were boats rising and falling in their slips and then finally pulling away, pointed toward life and destinations. He had always felt, in his deepest eddies, that there was a bright treasure sunken inside him. He remembers feeling it in the woods at sunset — a richer love for the world than others knew. That was what had made him different. And love doesn't die. It's irresistible.

"Can you imagine sulking after all this?" Alan says, rolling his trash masher between his fingers. "I've always known — I'm just waiting now . No flash of light. No peal of thunder. Nothing. It's perfect. It's just what I expected."

"You face the truth with grace," Annun says. "Pwysh would have been proud."

"My dad would have been, too," Alan says.

"We all are, Alan," Stag's Blood says. "You've brought us this far. I can feel the brink beneath my feet. Even with the sea of our journey draining into a cataract at the world's edge, I trust you."

"Then we shoot the cascade," Alan says, turning to face Annun. She has faded considerably. Night pours through her, thick and honey-dark. "What's next?"

"Next you listen," says Annun. "Because of who you are, you were able to rob death of spirits. This puts you in a kind of debt — the worst kind. You may not feel it yet, but death is leaning on you now. It will not abide your interference in its business much longer. Pay the debt before you incur more. Appease it, perform a ritual — how you do it is important, but there is no secret way. I cannot instruct you. The matter is between you and the Highest Power — the Dread Illimitable. Meet with Death and make amends."

"Then mighty Death is an entity," Nora says, "a lender keeping track of arrearages? It has fallen pitiably far."

"I imagine it would seem so to one who describes it so crudely." Lady Nightjar's voice is a slow dagger. "Remember your debt where you are going. At the heart of the prison is a guardian watching over Misha — the last shard of the Chodash Gem. In the deep halls sinking toward his cell, you will find pleading spirits. Cursed time is cruel, and many of the Dead in Disgrace have gone mad with misery. Leave them as they are. Do not reach out to them. They are not yours to save."

"I won't," Alan says, "I promise. But who is the guardian? What do we do when we find him?"

"You will be alone. Say that you understand."

"He don't," Brattle says. "We don't do nothin' alone. This is our joint."

"Do as I tell you," Lady Nightjar says as she flickers away. "The damned are yours now — the spoils of war. Lead them into the last battle. Welkinbright will meet you there."

"Where's the last battle gonna be at?" Brattle asks. "Where're you supposed meet us? How are we supposed to do what you say if you ain't sayin' nothing?"

Annun is gone. The wind sucks around the space where she was burning, and then it claps in over the void, leaving no sign that the Lady Nightjar had ever been there.

"There's your peal of thunder, Al," Brattle says. "She left out the most important part! You see why I said you shouldn't trust ghosts?"

"Let's take the next step," Sophia says. "Then we'll get the following one mapped out. That's what we've done from the beginning."

"I'm tired of walkin' blind," Brattle gripes. "You can't tell me you ain't."

"I don't feel blind, Conservator," Sophia replies. She tries to land on Brattle's shoulder, but he shoos her away. Her heartlight flares yellow. "Honestly, I feel led. The way will open. I believe it."

"First thing's first," Alan says. "A lot of umans are dead. If we don't get what we came for, it'll be for nothing."

"You heard me before," Brattle says. "Show me into the prisons. The edge of the world ain't that far down."

Forty-Four

The Mercy Gale comes down from the mountain wall to anchor in the peat-soft swale at the valley's western neck. Night deepens around her masthead until even her brightest lights barely illuminate anything. As Dead in Disgrace gather in the bog, the Gale's wraiths call down to them through the gathering dark. The mutant mass of damned spirits can only shiver and groan in reply.

The last of the dradtail healers lead the injured out of the cave, and Shuni is with them. She goes to Alan's side, wearing freckles of blood across her face, and holds out her hand to present him with something.

"From Anacadeshisemta," she says. "Her death gift. Big thing to let you have it, but smaller than Lashaseph gratitude. You deserve more. You help Lashaseph without ask for anything. A good heart is special. Should be honor."

"Don't get ahead of yourselves," Alan says. "Just like you, I came here for something."

"Kind ones shrink kindness," Shuni replies. "You do a miracle for us today. Lashaseph so grateful, Alan. We follow you — not like queen, but we take your advice. We help. Lashaseph always help."

"It was an honor to fight beside you," Stag's Blood says. "Selfish as it may seem, I hope I proved my worth today. I'm sorry for every death. I'll wear them in my heart forever — marks of failure."

"No need for that, cat," Shuni says. "Funeral life is no life at all. You prove plenty. Lashaseph feel humble enough today. Sorry for mistreat you — sorry for lots of things. Outsiders won't know them all. But this was victory. Be victorious."

"Where will you go now?" Sophia asks.

"Our interests are align still," Shuni replies, squinting to see the Mercy Gale across the gorge. Alan watches the light of her mothermind playing over her face. Pheromone smells waft from Shuni in thick bands. "We wait and heal, and more come, and we follow you to Winter White."

"And what about *you*, Shuni?" Brattle says, pinching his nose. "Are you OK. You need anything?"

"Who is this ask about me?" Shuni laughs. "Not strong ghoul who say 'Help us or don't' when first I meet him!"

Brattle crosses his arms and gives Shuni a toothy scowl that is just visible in the light from his eyes.

"We need all the help we can get," he says. "If yer comin' with us, you ain't any going to be any use hurt or distracted. How much of that battle did you spend here in that papered-up hole? Maybe you got soft in the last few hours. Maybe you got scared."

"There he is," Shuni says behind the mask of a smile. "I go back to meet with Lashaseph chiefs. Indebted to you one-minds, yes, but to the Allmind first."

Alan zips the golden feather into his knapsack. "We understand, Shuni," he says. "Go and do what you have to do. We'll see you in the next fight. Stay safe. Short flights to sweet blossoms."

"And you, my friends," Shuni says. She puts one arm across her chest and bows, her wings swinging against her sides. "Death is sweetest. May we both find it if one does, Alan."

The dradtail swarm pulls itself back together. Colors braid across their hivemind, sick and hurt but ever-brightening. Alan watches them for a while and feels the weight on his chest starting to lift.

"It smells like sweat and heather," Stag's Blood says. "What does it look like, Alan? You can see it, right? Their collective consciousness is regenerating."

"It's beautiful," Alan replies. "I wish it didn't have to end."

Alan and the others follow the shivering wraithmass into the bog. The proper entrance to the prisons is a crimson door framed by a marble arch. Trees weep over the arch, their wide branches quivering with arrowhead leaves and pink blossoms. Alan stands before the door and runs his fingers over the vast spirals carved into it. It has no handle on the outside.

"I imagine it is pointless to ask, Brattle," Sophia says, "but are you really going in with him? The Lady Nightjar was quite clear that he should go alone."

"You really telling me you ain't?" Brattle says. He leans back against the door and digs his heels into the loam at its sill. For all it gives, the door might as well be a mountain. "After coming this far, you're gonna leave the work to us two?"

"We haven't been informed of the risk," Stag's Blood says. "Anything could be waiting down there. This is both a reason to stay and a reason to go in together. This could be a test like Nora's."

"I say we wait," Nora suggests. She is sitting on a stump with her back curled and her hands on her spread knees. The Dead in Disgrace wave around her like ocean wrack, their many twisted hands plucking at her hair and the wrap knotted just above her breasts. "Why not take a vote?"

"No need," Alan says. "You can vote with action. I'm going, and Brattle's obviously determined to come. That's his choice. If you want to come, you're definitely welcome to. If you don't I won't fault you." He presses his palms against the door and feels death's hunger twisting behind it. The dead in his mind start up a war of shrieks and groans from which none can emerge the victor. "I don't particularly relish the thought of going down there either."

Alan turns to the Dead in Disgrace. "And what about you?" he asks. "What are you going to do?"

A clamor shivers through the ranks of the damned. They raise their voices against each other, creating a cacophony that mirrors the one in Alan's head. The only sound that makes any sense is the word "King."

"Stay here and guard the Gale," Alan says. "You're not the Dead in Disgrace anymore. That title's over. Until we can solve this mess, you're the Forgiven. You're my army. Shade's Army. The Ghost Patrol."

The rattling sound that emerges from the wraithmass sounds like a laughing contest. Alan puts both hands on the crimson door again and pushes it open. It responds to his power, splitting into equilateral halves and swinging in with a bovine groan. The darkness behind it is an umbra. It thrashes, desperate to rush out into the swamp. Afraid of Alan's power, it turns away from him. Alan can feel its mind burning. Rapalion's heart pulsates in the center of his chest. Without another word, Alan steps into the living darkness, and Brattle is the only one that follows him.

For a while, there is some light behind Alan and Brattle. When it disappears, Alan takes Brattle's hand. He hums as they move through the low, smooth corridors.

"What's that you're singin?" Brattle asks.

"A song," Alan says. "*Sentimientos Encontrados.*"

"A human song?"

"You want it? It can be a ghoul song, too."

Brattle peers into the black, his lamp-eyes shining. His grip on Alan's hand tightens.

"I know one ghoul song," Brattle says. "It may be the only one there is to know. My Da sung it to me. You wanna hear it?"

"Lay it on me," Alan says.

After a moment's hesitation, Brattle purses his lips and sucks his voice down into a rattling hiss. A buzzing arises in his throat, and he catches it under the curl of his tongue. From this, he draws a broad and stunning melody that shakes the roof beams. He only sings for a moment, but when he stops, the walls and floor are thrumming. The living darkness rolls in fury, tumbling whispers around Alan and Brattle as they forge ahead.

"Wow," Alan says. "Where did you learn to sing like that?"

"Nettle taught me," Brattle replies, clearing his throat. "He could sing a lock open and a stone up from the bottom of a river. He could sing lamps to sudden fire. It used to scare me."

"But you learned how to do it?"

"I learned what you heard, but that ain't half of what Nettle is. You can't learn to be what Nettle is. You can only touch a piece of it. Be thankful. Chaos ain't made."

"Nettle was born evil?"

"Nah. Chaos ain't born either."

The halls descend in doglegs, their inclines almost imperceptible. At a certain point, they cross into standing water. Here, Alan starts to sing to shut out the din of dead voices in his head. Coldness clamps around him, and whispering lights emerge from it to tug at his clothes. They step from the umbra and into a darkness left paling in the glow of dense orb swarms of spirit candles on the ceiling.

"They aren't dead," Alan says. "They aren't spirits. What are they? I remember seeing blue ones in the Barrowvale. Do their colors mean something?"

"Balefires," Brattle replies. "They're old, and first-world ruins draw em. Nobody knows what the colors mean, but I'm guessin' white ain't good. This whole place ain't good. Quit gawkin' and start walkin'."

Beyond the room where the balefires burn, the corridor drops into a wide chamber lit with turquoise lighting gems. The pale walls are lined with hexagonal cells stacked on top of each other, and the floors are strewn with shard of nacreous crystal. Shadows lie dead in the glittering mess: umbras killed in the mass exodus when Alan's call broke the cells open. Alan searches into them to find the strange stuff of their spirits threading away into the Bleeding. He tries to peer deeper, but a pressing pain in his chest stops him. Death's hard gaze is upon him.

"I wonder who they kept here," Alan says, clutching his chest , his hand a quivering claw. "That spirit army we left above is all twisted together – there're barely any distinct individuals among them. They must have been held in one space, but these spirits were separated from the others, whoever they were. Why?"

"Listen to the deadspeak," Brattle says.

Alan nods. "I hear it."

"It's like nothin' I ever heard," Brattle continues, wiping a wet streak of tears from his cheek. "How d'you shut it out?"

"Torment. Madness," Alan replies. "I can't shut it out. It feels too important. I'm supposed to feel this. I'm the Wraith King."

"Yeah, you been the Wraith King for all of three breaths," Brattle growls. "Soph was right. I ain't never wanted to be anywhere less."

"Stay with me. Sing your song again."

Brattle shakes his head, his jaw like a jut of stone from the cliff of his face. The color in his eyes is far away. "I ain't goin anywhere but on from here. You sure you ain't sore about them others not wanting to come with us?"

"No," Alan says, trying to make himself laugh, "I *ain't*. No reason to be sore. It was their decision. I can't begrudge them that."

"But you don' think they chose wrong?"

"It doesn't matter if they did. They're all here of their own free will – you, too."

"Then you ain't no kind a leader," Brattle says with another of his giggle-coughs. "I'd've given them no option. We all go down, or nobody's goin' down."

They reach the end of the cell chamber where a rough hole in the far wall gives on a great pit with stalactites jutting into it from the rolling ceiling. Carvings like those Alan saw in the Eye of Nudd glow among the pointing stones.

"There were extenuating circumstances," Alan replies. "Plus, they're scared. I used to hate seeing people acting out of fear. It made me so angry to see the way it could paralyze. I was never allowed the luxury of fear – I had to face every challenge head on with no help – so why should anyone else get to retreat? Why should anyone's fear earn them pity when my fear was meaningless? I felt like people who were slaves to fear were wasting a precious gift that I would never have. I think I finally get it now, though – my envy. We're all afraid almost all the time. I may not be much of a leader, but I like to think of myself as a pretty good friend."

Brattle stops and looks over the rim of the pit. Lights twinkle on the distant floor – the blinking eyes of wraiths that lay prone and spread out like broken wrack victims. They look back as Alan leans forward to get a feel for them.

"Yeah, well," Brattle says. "You got me, and I ain't got no one. Not sure what that says about your friend game, bonesy. Or mine." He squints and then covers one eye with his paddler's hand. "Whatever the case, I'm thinkin' the only way to go from here's down."

Alan nods and takes his trash masher into his hand. He twirls it for a second, amazed how much lighter it feels now. It hums, light circling the shaft, feeding on him

"All right," Alan says. "Down it is. Let's burn."

The great pit is hundreds of yards wide. There are more umbras on the heat-smoothed walkway around the rim, most of which are deep in the process of fading into natural shadow. Seeing them shrinking to small, cold shapes on the stone makes Alan feel a little sad, but he knows that what they are experiencing isn't exactly death.

"Back to the Bleeding," Theia says. Her voice is low and choked in his mind. She is weakening. His gardensin blighted. "There, they will be remade – as all shadows are. "

Alan and Brattle walk in heavy silence for what seems like an hour. Mineral veins laid bare in the walls give off a pale and sickly light. Occasionally, huge, wet beards of mold appear on the wall. Luminous blooms bob out of them, bright as halogen bulbs, and fairies the size of Sophia flit around them with tiny buckets on their arms. These die back further on along the rim and the veins of light worm away into the rock and vanish. At the threshold of utter darkness, Brattle takes a lighting gem from his pack and rolls it between his palms until it burns to life. Then, in the dim glow of the crystal, he and Alan march on toward the curve of the pit and the slope of a ramp slanting down into it.

The dead moan over each other in Alan's head. They pull him like moons, moving things inside him, coaxing the tide of his power to a steady pulse. This tomb is bigger than he can see. Parts of it extend into formlessness. Heat rolls up from the pit's invisible reaches, blowing Alan's hood back as he starts down the incline. Brattle shields his face with his arm. Avernus is waking in the dark. Alan's body aches to feel it near.

Brattle asks as they descend into the pit. "I got a real bad shiver. I'm thinkin' things're about to get rowdy."

"I have to be careful," Alan says, taking his trash masher in hand and spinning it. "I don't want to take too many chances down here."

Brattle closes his fist tight around his gem and draws his dagger from its sheath against his breast. "Looks a bit too late for that," he says. "Sweet maid, guide us out."

Wings beat in the pit. A low din rises into a chorus of shrieks from its bottom. The spirits that were lying on their backs start to disappear, raked up in huge claws and shoveled into maws that burn iron-red beneath ingot eyes. When they are all gone, five howling shadows advance on Alan and Brattle, blowing billows of smoke from their nostrils as they climb the incline.

"Moaners," Alan says.

Brattle hitches his haversack high up onto his back, spits hard straight up into the air, and charges.

I was born November first in Paloma, Illinois. Leaves fell late that year. Flowers bloomed black. The doctors wouldn't cut me for a long time. When they finally did, they had to hide me away. I stayed hidden for the rest of my life, but now I'm here at the brink of something after – a sojourner home from exile in the land of the living.

Thunder rolls over the valley. Alan can hear it even here, in the depths of cold Sepulchra's heart. The chasm shakes, and stalactites break loose from the ceiling. A glittering stone drapery crushes one of the moaners to death as it falls. The others step over the corpse, moving like the tide, mindless and inexorable.

Who is your mother? Alan asks himself in James Lipton's voice. *Who is your father? If Heaven exists, what would you like to hear God say when you reach the pearly gates?*

"Heaven will be mowed fields in golden autumn," Alan says, wringing the handle of his trash masher as the remaining moaners bear down on him. "God will be Hannes, small as me, and I'd want him to say, 'Let's play'."

Brattle leaps into the pit, taking the small light with him. Alan is left in motile darkness as three moaners jostle against each other in a sudden rush to crush him. He searches into them instinctively, his magic now as much a part of him as fear. Deep pressure in his chest stops him as he pushes for their silvery, flame-ringed spirits, and the nearest moaner swats him into the wall while he is standing stymied. Death is in the pit with them – he should not have been surprised. He feels it leering at him as he scrambles to collect himself, every bone in his body aching.

"You won't take me before I settle our score," Alan says. "I'm strong without your power. Just watch me."

Alan twirls his trash masher as the moaners gather around him. They are black as hate and tall as thunderheads. Their mouths open into throats of brume and fire. Alan drives them back from his open hand, but they are strong even against his awakened skill. They circle him, lashing out with huge claws and tails as thick as logs. Alan's basteta-fur robe protects him from harm, but not from pain. His muscles cramp tight, and his hands go cold. When he drops to one knee beneath their jackhammer blows, the moaners start to laugh.

"Nothing avails you," one of them growls. "Beneath that shell, you are only flesh and bone."

Alan reels. Thunder is still booming through the walls – it will be his weapon. He reaches from the dark, sending his power up the deepest roots of marsh trees above them. The night sky is bright beneath the storm. Alan stretches himself like a skin across the feet of the clouds. He teases their breasts apart to borrow their thunder, thinking idly of Nora for a second. Then, his consciousness fraying, Alan lifts his trash masher above his head and brings it down with a ringing cry. He sends his strength through its haft into the stone, the whole wrath of the storm following it, rocking the pit chamber again. The ceiling cracks and another moaner dies in a roaring rockfall. Its blood spreads flaming, and the others back away.

Alan levers himself back to his feet and strides after them. He swings his trash masher, clearing a wide swath of stone before him. The moaners fall to the bare floor.

"Who made you?" Alan demands.

"No one made us," one of the moaners says. "We are the Uncreated."

"Fatherless. Motherless," Alan says, the storm pouring out through his voice. "Burn away, shadows. Depart from me, children of nothing. You have no power here."

The moaners start to laugh again as they pick themselves up. Alan allows it. They move to stand on either side of him, towering.

"We *are* the power here," the nearest moaner says. "Learn your place."

At this, Alan lifts his masher again and lets the storm's wrath explode from within him. The pit is bright for a second, and Alan can see a tall, white being dismembering a moaner near a tooth-shaped door in its deepest wall. Then the force of the storm bursts through him and darkness collapses into the pit with a train-whistle roar. The shockwave rips the moaners apart and flattens everything in the pit. The prison shakes like a wet dog, its skeleton groaning beneath it.

The dead scream in Alan's head. The last of the stalactites fall, and Alan crouches to take shelter in the long folds of his robe.

Pillars of stone pummel him until he blacks out. When he wakes, the pit is deathly still and he is pinned under a colossal heap of stone. The thunder has left him, and he feels as empty as a quill. His magic aches hotly in his head – as if the cognitive muscle that controls it is hyperextended. The three moaners lie dead around him, broken under piles of splintered stone. Their blood burns from their bodies, flames licking up from the streams like the last of their living fury, until they curl away into ribbons of smoke.

"You are no mere thanoturge now," Theia says. Looking inward, he can see her standing in the heart of his garden. Her hair is lank and black, and her skin is ivory-blue. A steely wind stirs the grass around Theia's ankles. The sky is dark, and clouds hide the stars. Death looks down from their shadows. "Welcome to power, Wraith-Lord. How does it feel?"

As his strength creeps back, Alan stretches out through magic to search the pit. The ground hums with spirits' voices. The last two moaners are dead at the door in the lowest part of the pit, and there is a great and powerful energy near them. It stands out from everything, Coma-white, bright as the draug and ever-brightening. The Bleeding quivers around it, terrified. Beneath the slab-floor, the dead mutter in awe of it. Alan tries to be afraid, but he can't. He knows this spirit. The rough little light at its heart is Brattle.

Alan tries to focus. His new legs are trapped flat beneath an edge of rock, but there is no pain. A larger stone is wedged into his back, propping up the slab that would otherwise be crushing him from the waist down. Reaching out with his mind for some of the smaller chunks of debris, he brushes them away until he can twist onto his side. From there, he kicks hard against the weight upon him, his claws squealing along the floor as he tries to lever the larger stone up on his magic. He imagines a great wedge tilting up between himself and the stone, and the stone groans as it starts to shift. Then the weight slips from him, and the stone rolls mightily away in a cloud of dust. A white hand emerges from the darkness above Alan. Its fingers are long and thin with even knuckles and pink lunulae on clean, healthy nails.

266

"Come on," says Brattle. "Reach, stupid."

Alan grabs Brattle's hand with both of his and heaves himself upright. His new knees bend without complaint, and his new feet are soft as springs. He brushes himself off, straightens his robe around his shoulders, and turns to find Brattle in the process of shrinking. As he watches, the shining thing before him falls into a frog-crouch. Its narrow face widens, soaring cheekbones sinking along graying cheeks that swell to minor jowls. The hay-gold locks recede to a bare, wrinkled pate, and the nose dwindles to a flattened peak. Only Brattle's eyes remain the same. The pupilless pools of pear nacre narrow as Brattle settles back into his ghoulish shape.

"What're you gawpin' at?" Brattle asks, running his thick-knuckled hands over the dome of his head.

"Sister Sophie's Conservator," Alan says. "You as you could be, I think. It's quite a sight. Beautiful, even. I think I saw it in Welkinbright, too."

Brattle gives a long, condescending laugh, his mouth comically wide. "Can't improve on this," he says. "You all in a piece, bony? I'm about ready to quit this place if we don't get where we're goin' soon. If you got all your parts, let's lump on."

Alan pats himself down. His trash masher is lost under some pile, and there's no time to start moving rocks to find it. As he turns to lead Brattle toward the bottom of the pit, Alan is surprised at how painful it is to leave his masher behind. Standing under the white arch at the deepest part of the pit wall, his palm flat against the carven door, he finds himself hung up thinking about it. He remembers the nights at Ray's when he would haul the trash out and take a few minutes for himself to practice twirling the trash masher in his hands. Letting it go makes him feel uselessly sad – it was the last piece of his old life he had left, but it's silly to grieve. Life isn't made of pieces. Alan knows that he isn't the sum total of his possessions – or even his experience. What the masher meant isn't in the masher – it's in him. Alan laughs at himself and pushes

267

the door into a steep, black passage. The tail of his laugh bounces down, and it never comes back. The darkness drinks its echo.

Brattle scoops his haversack up off the floor and ties its broken strap together across his chest. His lighting gem is burned out on the floor, so he produces another one. This one is cobalt blue, and it does little to dispel the dark. The way ahead is a smooth, tiered angle that must once have been the bed of a waterfall. Alan and Brattle climb down with great care in a shallow sphere of soft, sulky light. They slip and catch each other, too focused to talk. When they reach the bottom, the world feels huge above them and the ground feels thin. Alan wonders, if he hadn't lost it, if he'd be able to bash through the floor to the other side of the planet from this spot.

"I like holes," Brattle whispers, "but I don't like this."

"This isn't a hole," Alan says. "It's the grave of graves."

From the wet base of the hard climb down, a low corridor opens into a chamber full of fairy fire. Here, terrible spirits wander in whirls like black winds. They jar together, full of rage, until they see Alan and Brattle coming. Then they slow and fall from their howling funnels to approach with their hands out and their star-eyes shining.

"Wraith King," they moan over each other, "Is the door open? Are you here so soon? Restore me – restore us. We are here unfairly."

Alan pushes the first few spirits away. They moan at him and pull at his cloak. Their faces are clusters of light like those of the wraiths on the Mercy Gale. The half-formless stuff they are made of is wearing thin. Some are bleeding little streams of distortion into the air. A few sift away and vanish before they even reach him.

"Won't you speak to us?" they cry. "This punishment is cruel!"

"We ain't here for you," Brattle says. "Who's at the bottom of this hole? That's who we're here to see."

The last of the spirits' whirlwinds dies down. The throng thickens, and their cries grow louder. Now their hands pinch and scratch. They poke for Alan's eyes, apparently oblivious to the skeletal state of his face.

"We didn't deserve to die with Nex," says one particularly strong and vivid spirit. "We were murdered – victims of his like so many others. You will not turn us away. We deserve absolution. We deserve revenge."

"Your wrath is not my job," Alan says, temporarily caught in the absent grip of spirit with green fire burning inside it. "If you let me through, I will pardon you all.

"Lies." The word ripples across the chamber. "All the living lie. We must cut contrition from your chest and drink it red from your heart."

There is another door at the end of the chamber. It is black and wreathed in thorns. Stuck in the growing mob of spirits, Alan can't push toward it anymore. The lights inside them are as red and as hot as fanned coals. Their sorrow rolls out to fill the room, and it is more than he can stand. His magic awakens, and it's all he can to rein it in. Overwhelmed by the spirits' damage, it tries to lash out. It could heal them all, but it would sooner destroy them. Their grief is poisonous.

"Why did you die?" Alan shouts over the buzz of pining voices. "What put you here that I can repair?"

"The executioners' zeal," moans the crowd of pawing ghosts. "We died innocent, and now we must sin to justify our own torture."

"Abolish us," says the greater spirit. "We have earned oblivion. Send us down to the draug, or we will rip you apart."

Alan has never hurt so much for anyone. His head is pounding, and his guts are rolling into knots. The spirits rob his mind of dim, dead faces with which to mask themselves. They pull on his father, his mother, and Hannes's dad. Alan tries to center himself in the garden of his mind, but the spirits are there, too. They reach from the ground and the river, pushing up trees and flowers as they surge from the soil. The dead voices in his mind have turned against him. Even the Kingwatcher's bloom is wilting.

"Look what she did to you," say the spirits as Alan and Brattle push fruitlessly against them. Alan returns to himself to see that they have all taken Allison's face. "She did nothing for your life but blacken it. Don't you want to crush her? Don't you want to forgive her?"

"No," Alan says. He stomps a shockwave across the floor, and the spirits stop. A few of them start to back away. *"I am your King. Let me pass."*

The spirits stand for a moment, their clusters of eyes swimming in their heads. Alan sees into them darkly. Looking through their shimmering bodies, Alan can see that the blank, bone-white walls of the chamber are actually covered with otherwise invisible carvings.

"We have no King," says the strongest spirit.

At this, the spirits fall on Alan and Brattle. They move as one great thing, strong as a rushing sea. Alan braces himself as the break upon him. They howl, and their voices are like riptide currents dragging at his mind. Their sadness swirls into a vortex that threatens to suck him in. Again, as he gathers power, he thinks of Nora.

What will our child be? She wondered.

"Cursed," Theia says from somewhere. "And strong."

Alan puts his fist in his palm and squeezes his magic hard. A wave of force roars out from him, following the lines of his forearms and the tips of his elbows. The crazed crowd of spirits is split and scattered, and they don't fall in again. The chamber is still and hot with the spirits' stares as Alan leads Brattle to the door and pushes it open.

"Could be you're more dangerous when you're careful," Brattle chuckles. "Ain't this costing you?"

"Pushing isn't death magic," Alan says. "At least I don't think it is. Death is still heavy in me, like an anchor or something. It's awful to feel. If it weren't for my debt, I'd have done worse than push them."

"No doubt," Brattle says.

The door from the ghost room opens on a short, hot foyer and beyond this is a shaft of rock miles high. In the center of the shaft, its bell end half submerged in the shallow pit beneath it, is a teardrop-shaped crystal chamber full of luminous fog. The walls around it rise dark into blind distance, thin tiers of stone climbing them in jagged leaps like frozen lightning. The floors are lit from beneath by torrid green light, and yolk-yellow gems burn along the crystal's surface. A shape moves inside the crystal, pacing carefully, weaving to avoid the brighter areas. Coiled around the crystal's tapering end, its log-long head hanging to the floor is a great, serpentine dragon. It claws the floor as Alan and Brattle enter, heaving a huge breath that fills the shaft with terrible heat. Brattle puts his arm up to shield his face. His eyes go so wide that Alan can see a hint of white around their edges – a flash of telling sclera.

"I know you," says the dragon, smoke ribboning through its teeth. "You were the one making all the noise above. You are the Wraith King remade, but you cannot have Misha. It will stay here; that is my decision after all these years. Turn and leave, or I will burn you both black and suck your ash."

The dragon slips itself from the neck of the gem, white-gold scales sparking as they flex against each other. It stirs a growl up from its belly and opens its mouth to let a little rill of fire run out onto the floor. Alan and Brattle take a few long steps back.

"Calushar," says the shadow in the crystal prison. "Peace. Let them come."

"Peace is gone," snarls Calushar. "Only I remain now."

Calushar gathers its great length into a heap of spring-tight rings beneath its head. Alan looks into it to find its spirit blazing like a sun. It is magnificent, but there is a spot on its face. A black wound blocks its light, consuming it slowly, savoring it. Calushar's impressive power is feeding a crawling sickness in his heart.

"There's something wrong inside you," Alan says turning his palms toward the dragon. "Death is sitting in your chest – I can see it. Do you feel me touching the shadow that's going to take you?"

271

He reaches for the growing, angry wound, but he can't probe too deply without the dead in his garden starting to wail in fear. "We're trying to do the right thing here. I can help. Don't take a stand for the wrong side."

"Liar," says the dragon, "hisser of forlorn hopes. Your faith amounts to nothing. It is blasphemous."

"Then burn me alive," Alan says, crossing his arms. Calushar lifts its head. The frill of plum black spines on its cheeks rattle as it starts to inhale. The room suddenly seems tiny. Heat shrinks the stones, pulling them apart, and fairy moss appears in great shaggy patches along the walls. Brattle ducks behind Alan, and Alan puts up his hood up and spreads his arms, his hands thrust into his sleeve pockets. He braces himself for a flaming embrace, but the shadow in the crystal steps forward to stop Calushar.

"Please let me try to speak to them before you resign yourself to their incineration," says the shadow. Alan is stunned as he leans into the light. The shadow is like him – and like Enlil – bone-faced and thin as a lath. "Look at them, Calushar. They're more shadows than I am. Indulge me."

Calushar glowers at Alan and Brattle. Its black-glass eyes seem to squirm behind their nictitating membranes. It snorts smoke, and long whips of fire lash out of its mouth to encircle its head. Then it swallows and relaxes, a growl of frustration rattling in its fluttering chest.

The prisoner motions with his hand, and Alan and Brattle approach to press their faces against the multifaceted walls. The shadow's empty orbits stare. His bare jaw is fixed in place with a few teeth loose. He scores the floor of his chamber with clawed feet on the ends of scaled legs. The tattoos on his arms and sunken chest have been burned to scars by torturers' irons. They glow cold and bright, like the Seal of Aiwass. Alan knows him – not just from Nora's stories of the pixies' betrayal, but deeply and darkly, as he would know a picture of his father as a child. He knows in his stomach who this prisoner is.

"You can see into him?" asks Anastasis Nex. "What a marvel. Dragons are impenetrable. If you are trying to lie to buy your life, you are wasting your time. I don't want you dead. I have penance to pay to you."

"I'm not lying," Alan says. "I can see it clear as day. Calushar is sick."

"The Wraith King remade," says Nex. His voice is like the mourning song of the wind in the shaft of a single reed. "I know what grief's threat has brought you here, wanderer, so urgently and full of your own power. Now you will listen to me, because I am the only one alive who has walked your road."

"You're Rawbones's betrayer," Brattle says, shuffling away from Calushar where it lies grumbling in smoke. "He looks just like you, Al! Only a shade less human." He nudges Alan with his elbow. "You got the rock we're after? Why don't you just give it? Sure you got nothin' to gain anymore."

"You might've been where I am, but you're not me," Alan says. "We won't leave here without Misha no matter what you say."

"Then you have nothing to lose," Nex laughs. "Listen. You are trying to break a cycle of death and resurrection that has been unbroken since this new aeon awoke. The place that is Nudd, in itself, is nothing. I learned this with great pain. It's only the power of Nudd that has any value. That power is too great to exist for long without being poisoned, raped, or drowned in blood. It is a phoenix that must burn to ash to be renewed – it is a virgin born to be defiled and torn apart. Only when she is reconstituted can she be pure again, but we cannot wait. Her death grows as she does in the womb – her twin sister.

"Understand this, guardians: you are a garment to be torn away. The good you do now *will* be undone. The cycle cannot stop. Death is everyone's destiny."

"It can't stop until there's nothing left," Alan says. "Is that what you were trying to do – burn everything down to keep it from being thrust back into danger?"

Nex crosses his arms. His skin moves oddly over his bones. He swells for a moment, as if trying to contain a sky. Alan watches to see if a sunrise might tear him open. White-gold flame dances around his shoulders, casting long shadows across his bare skull.

"Nothing left to want," Nex says, "nothing left to steal or to kill for. Safety in the arms of ruin. You're wise. You know. That's your burden."

"*You're* my burden right now," Alan replies. "Give me what we came so far for. Your ruin will have to wait."

Nex bows and swings his hand toward Calushar. The dragon rolls over onto the bright loops of its body and slips its huge paw down the broad plate of shingle scales covering its breastbone.

"Oh, that it would end like this," Calushar sighs. "If I had been as strong as my mother, as wise as my father, I might have outlived them. I shall never see my mountain again – and may it long for me, for my claws in its shoulders and the beat of my wings in the woods at its feet. May all Sepulchra weep when I am gone. I die now for Nudd, but I would have you know me first, and I would know you, wanderer."

"The rock's in you?" Brattle says. "You gotta kill yourself to take it out?"

"The witch-men were cruel," Nex says, a smile in his voice. "There are pixies here who were no more than sprigs. There is no justice – see? Only rule. Only might. Divulge your secret, Calushar. Show them the cost of their valor."

"Don't," Alan says. He steps toward Calushar to put his hand in its claw. It growls, and smoke rises from its nostrils, but it allows him near. "I can take it out safely. Relax and let me help. Tell me who you are while I work."

Calushar looks at Nex, but Nex might as well be made of stone. He neither moves nor speaks. Even the loose garment he wears around his waist stops flapping.

"Don't cut yourself," Brattle says. "Trust Al. He's on a roll today."

Alan searches into Calushar's chest. He pushes his mind past the horny armor and into soft, swollen flesh. Misha is wrapped in a pocket of muscle and tissue just beneath the dragon's left lung. Alan wraps his magic around it carefully. It is warm as an organ and slick with blood and fluid.

"Who were your parents?" Alan asks as Calushar starts to go rigid and whine. "Where were you born?"

The dragon heaves a ragged breath and closes its eyes. Its bifurcated tongue slips out between its bottom front teeth, blue as a bruise and soft above a rough sublingua. It begins to speak, moving as little as it can.

"I was born at the peak of Mount Baur eighty miles west of here," Calushar hisses. "My father was Gadishar, and my mother was Callo the Wounder. It was red summer when I hatched – fire in the sky – a dawn of blood and promise. There were prophecies of my ascendance, but they were all wrong, and their proclaimers are long dead. I have fallen far, far from the heights of Baur now. Fallen to this."

Calushar starts to cough. Blood fills the space where Misha was sitting. Flesh tears, and Alan has to seal it as he goes, forcing the shard up toward Calushar's throat. Death glowers over him, crushing his strength, but he pushes on. His garden goes dark.

"Now you," Calushar struggles to say. "I cannot continue. The pain is terrible."

"What about Heaven?" Alan replies. The dragon's whole weight fights him. Death breathes hard against him, and his joints start to go loose. "What about God?"

"I don't know," Calushar gurgles. "No gods. No Heaven."

"After death?" Alan says. "What? Tell me."

Calushar tries to laugh and can only manage a bloody hack and a smile rimmed with red foam. "You do dive in! The Black Gates. Haron, the Lord of Serpents. Old stories. They cannot comfort anymore."

"You're not going to the Black Gates today, Cal," Alan says. He slits Calushar's esophagus gently and pushes Misha through the gush of blood. "If you did, what would you want to hear Haron say when you got there?"

Calushar gags fire. Amber-brown saliva runs from its mouth to smoke angrily on the ground beneath its head. His legs trembling and his spine barely supporting his weight, Alan seals Calushar's esophagus shut around the fragment. Then he runs through the scars in the dragon's throat and chest, staunching blood flow and closing wounds tight behind him. He can no longer see the garden of his magic. Theia is gone from his mind, as are the voices of the dead. As Calushar begins to cough again, Alan falls to a knee.

"Spit," Brattle shouts at Calushar. He points with both fingers at the bulge in the dragon's neck. "I see it! Cough it up, Callie!"

Calushar sucks in a long series of shallow breaths, its eyes squeezed shut and it body seizing. Once it's sucked all the air it can over the swell in its throat, it rears up and hauls a massive, choking exhalation. Misha bursts from Calushar's mouth on a plume of flame, and Brattle knuckles off into the foyer after it.

"'Go back,'" Calushar says, sagging on the floor like a thousand feet of discarded streamer. Its wings flutter against his sides, and it beats its finned tail on the floor far away at the other end of the cavern. "'Go back.' That's what I would want Haron to tell me. 'There will be a place for you at my side when your time comes.'"

Alan pushes himself to his feet with a huge effort. Darkness crowds into his vision – ink tendrils winding in to clot over the world before him as if he had eyes to blind. He shakes his head and sways to keep his balance. His muscles are hard with hot and urgent pain. Death roars into him from everywhere, bigger than everything. He feels tugged in half between form and formlessness. Brattle brings him Misha, and he holds the stone hard to his chest, as if it might anchor him in Graveworld.

"I want to free you, Calushar," Alan manages to say. He looks down at the shard in his hand, and it meets his gaze with hollow eyes. One side of it is carved into a skull face.

Of course, he thinks.

"I don't need you for that," the dragon says, propping itself up on its forelegs. "You want more from me. What? Ask carefully – my strength is returning."

"You're a guardian of Nudd," Alan says. "Come to war with me. We're going to need you."

"Al, you need to sit down," Brattle says. He wraps his ropy arms around Alan and tries to help him to the floor.

"You've overreached," Nex says from the back of his crystal prison. He wears fog and shadow like garments that were cut for him. "Are you at that brink? Do you know what is staring up at you? You won't know whether my dragon will accept your offer or not."

"Nora said he was dead," Brattle growls to Alan. "If he don't shut up, he's gonna wish he was."

"Nora?" Nex says. "My sister? She is a liar."

Alan doesn't hear what comes next. Burning hands push him into darkness. A vile, smoldering power forces its way into him, and he slips from himself in a blaze of pain. His last thought as the draug swallows him is that he knows the spirit that has usurped him. He saw it last in poor Theia's tortured body, dancing in the pinpoints of her eyes like a failing flame.

Forty-Five

Alan opens his eyes. He is standing barefoot in a field of amber grass. Evening is dying in the sky, bleeding pink into black behind far-off mountain walls. To his right is a high, round hill with a marble porch and a door sealed behind a lattice of leafy branches. A bird croaks down at him from a low, red arch.

"Don't make things easy, do you?" asks Atratus, spreading its wings and bobbing its bare, knobby head. "Nettle took you. Do you know that? I told you not to trust the ghoul."

"A land of liars," Alan says. "I remember. It was Nettle that was dangerous, not Brattle. He possessed me? He was in that pit with us?"

"Struck in your weakness, Wraith Lord," Atratus says. "You left the door wide open. Now he's pushing you as hard as you can go. Do you feel it? I suppose you don't. You're almost to Suttea in Midion – legs giving out, back broken. You're just his puppet now. And you're stuck here."

"Where's Nettle taking my body? I guess that's a stupid question. He has all three shards of the Chodash stone. He'll take me – and them – to Winter White. Won't he?"

"Not my business," Atratus replies. "This is where your business is. Come on. Follow me."

Atratus leaps into the air, flapping madly, and soars into a wide circle. As it evens out, heading west, Alan walks after it.

"Where are we going?" Alan asks.

"To see what you've made," cries the vulture. It banks into a little wind, wavering to correct its course. "This is the edge of the exchange – this is the draug. Don't you feel it? You must. Like a storm or an earthquake coming. Like ice groaning to crack underneath you. This is eventuality."

"Death is waiting here," Alan says.

Atratus coughs a rattling laugh. "Just said that, didn't I? Eventuality! Anyway, welcome. Welcome to the dimming, Alan. Not far now. Keep up!"

Alan takes up a sprint as Atratus tips his wings in for speed. Running in the failing light, springing over the soft ground with grass rising to brush his thighs, Alan feels young again. A little wood comes up on his right, and there is a rail fence running through it. He imagines tracing its gray paths with Hannes, and he sees himself there. His father calls, not far away, telling him to come in for dinner. Lightning bugs appear before him in lazy clouds that swirl apart as he runs through them. A warm breeze brings the smells of smoke and cedar, and the draug is everywhere. Alan feels it tugging at the world around him, a silver filament stuck in the core of the reality on a hook. As it pulls, he palms tears from his eyes.

"It's coming now," Atratus says, flapping down to land on the reaching branch of a sycamore. "Stop here a little. Just for a spell. Ha! Stop and rest, though there's no time."

Alan jogs to a stop and doubles over, his hands on his knees. He takes a few big breaths, his pulse racing in his neck. He tilts his chin up and closes his eyes to let the world wash over him. The draug creams across his chest, pulled by otherwise imperceptible gravity. The ground rises and falls beneath his feet. The grass paws up at him, leaving small cuts on his skin like love bites. The wind kisses his ears with sycamore whispers.

"I want you to be ready when you meet your maker," Atratus continues. "You've put quite a problem to us, you know that? But you've done a lot of good, so you deserve this rest."

Alan opens his eyes again to see the last crown of the sun slip below the horizon. Stars awaken in a long tendril across the sky. Somewhere behind that shine, deep in the arch of the fundament, something is changing.

"Thanks," Alan pants. "You said the light of the draug is failing. What did you mean by that? Is it because of Winter White?"

"White is a symptom," Atratus clucks. "There are many others. Just rest. Be here for now. All that is yet to come. Not my job to explain."

"I don't understand," Alan sighs. "Am I dead?"

"Dead or not dead is a difference that doesn't apply to you," Atratus says, shaking his head. "Like real or not real doesn't apply to a dream when you're awake. You aren't part of the draug anymore – that's why my obligation ends here."

"Because you're an agent of the draug."

"Right," Atratus says. "This is a satellite task – a little bit of extra credit. I'm done now, though. You rested up? Ready to go on?"

"What's next?" Alan asks.

Atratus laughs. "Everything."

With this, the vulture beats its wings, lifts itself into a tight spiral, and disappears into the night sky. Alan walks toward the edge of the little wood. There is a gate in the rail fence, and he recognizes the garden of his magic beyond it. The sun is out above it, and it is in prolific bloom. For a moment, he stands with his hand on the gate and listens, letting night breathe against his back. Then he pushes the gate open and steps into the garden.

A girl meets Alan at the foot of the Kingblossom's hill. She is tall and sickly thin. She parts the curtain of her lank black hair with one hand and Alan sees the red grid of deep lines on her wrist. As Alan approaches, she dives into hug against him, wrapping her vine-weak arms around his neck.

"Laney," Alan squeaks, choking on tear-wet surprise. "Allison. Holy shit."

Alan squeezes his sister as hard as he can. He expects her to burst like a cloud, leaving him soaked and lightning-burned, but she remains s she is. Allison sobs for a moment before pulling away to look into Alan's face. There are fat, purple bruises beneath her red-brown eyes. Tears shine in her bat-wing lashes.

"You haven't changed," Allison says, putting her hand on Alan's cheek. "You're just like the last time I saw you."

"You have no idea," Alan says. "I have so many questions. What are you doing here?"

"Oh, Allie, I have to go," Allison says. Alan's heart aches at the sound of her voice. "I'm sorry. It's good to see you. It's great, but I'm not on my own time here."

Alan stares had into his sister's eyes. He extends himself into her mind to find her spirit. It is weak and wounded, and there is another behind it that is terrifying to look at.

"I understand," Alan says. "Just one question then – give me one: why? I have to know. What were you thinking? You'd looked into that dark before and you knew it wasn't going to last. It would have burned itself out – it always does. You could have gone to the store, or you could have called me. Any small act of reaching out into the light of the world and other people could have brought you back from that brink. What happened? Why did you give up? Please tell me. If this is all I get, you can't refuse me."

"That's more than one question," Allison says, smiling. Blue lights dance above her head. The wind tosses her hair around her shoulders. "This isn't about me. This is about your debt."
"Screw that," Alan says. "I deserve this."

"This is business, Alan. You brought things out of the dark that should never have seen the light again. Your spirit should be forfeit, your debt is so great, but there are mitigating circumstances. Do you know what I mean?"

"I do," Alan says, "but I want my answer. You're here, Laney. Say a few words for yourself. That's all I want."

"You created a life, Alan," Allison says, tears quivering in the corners of her eyes. "And then there's Winter White. An agreement must be reached – then I'll tell you. Don't keep me here any longer than I need to be. It hurts. I don't belong."

Alan runs frustrated fingers through his hair. He pulls at the crown of his head, and he brings his hand away with some russet strands in his palm. He thinks of Nora asking, *Will you put life inside me, Alan?*

"OK," Alan says. "What do you want? How do we fix this?"

"A spirit took your body and peeled you away from it," Allison replies. "Now it's dead like mine, and you should fall into the draug, but the draug won't absorb you. Maddeningly, you've put yourself beyond its reach. Because you can't pay your debt, it should pass to your daughter. That is the righteous way, but there is another. Death wants Winter White. Your debt can roll over into power – enough power to force White back into the cycle that failed her. You can have flesh again, you can be remade, but only as a servant of the Inexorable. Do you understand? It's you or her. Return to Midion as a servant of Death, or pass impossible spiritual debt to your unborn child. That's your choice."

"A daughter," Alan says after a deep breath and a long silence. "It's not even a choice is it? Take me back to Graveworld."

"Don't leap into this lightly," Allison says. "It's important that you know exactly what you have to fear. Worse things than you serve the Dread Illimitable. Will you obey until the end of the world, Allie? Do you have it in you to look into that dark and know that it will never burn out?"

"Take me back to Graveworld, Laney," Alan says again. "Answer me why, and I'll serve. I'm not going to run no matter how bad it gets. I will not give up. I'll be the shadow my daughter fears if it spares her oblivion."

Allison smiles again. Light spreads across her face, driving the shadows from the hollows of her cheeks. She pinches one skull earring between her fingers.

"You've always been the strong one," she says.

"I had to be strong for you," Alan says, "but it didn't help you in the end. I failed you – or something did. I couldn't stop you from failing yourself."

"'Why?' has an answer, Allie, but it won't help anything. There is no good answer that will put me to rest inside you. If I say it was a cry for help that went too far, or if I say I was too sick to see how I was hurting people doing what I did, you'll still be broken. I know it's in your nature to be a beast of burden, but I'm not your responsibility anymore. I took that responsibility from you forever. Your only responsibility now is to bury me and go on living."

"You don't think I should do it," Alan says. "You think I should let my child take the debt. What happens if I do?"

"You made your choice," Allison says. "Not that it matters, but I think you made the right one. I think it's the only one you could have made. Give me another hug. I can't take this anymore."

Alan embraces his sister. Tears won't come, despite his sorrow. He remains dry-eyed, a knot in his throat taunting him. Allison's scars leave tracks of blood along his arms.

"I'm going to find you," he says. "I promise. I can bring you back. Wait for me."

"Go to the one flag," Allison says. She pulls away too soon, and the garden evaporates around her. The terrible spirit inside her rises from her mouth to pull everything into swallowing darkness.

"Goodbye," Alan says, but nothing is left.

He fades, too, falling back into a frigid quiet. Dead voices rise around him one at a time, laughing, cheering. He is one of them, now. He is their master. Power fills him until he feels as big as the Bleeding, and young Theia's voice cuts through the cacophony.

"Welcome back," she says, "Wraith King."

Alan wakes in a hot pit under a putrid weight of rotting bodies. He tries to move, but he is not fully in flesh. A strange kind of panic steals over him, is stripped from the physical, an essential terror of hopeless disembodiment. Alan buzzes with it, lost for all focus as it swells across him and desperate to anchor himself in something. The dead groan around him, pleading. They reach out with rain-thin minds, begging to be allowed to give their husks to accommodate him. Alan is too scattered to choose a vessel, so his magic chooses for him. It alone is calm. At last, Alan finds himself sinking into the rigid tissue of a corpse near the top of the heap, and, oddly, his terror subsides.

Alan's new body is broken and cold. He shivers up its bowing spine to fill its empty synapses, stretching himself into bloodless fibers until he is able to move again. There is no rushing this process. The spiritless husk resists, despite its former inhabitant's eagerness to serve the Wraith King. The eyes move slowly, the neck is tight as a hangman's collar, and the arms and legs flail as Alan storms across the body's nervous system. The blood creeps, sucked for salt and nearly drained, but the heart responds to his squeezing. When he has finally taken full control, he lies where he is to let his magic make him whole again.

Knit, knit, he thinks. *Heal this shell. Make it mine.*

Alan's magic crackles through his new body, pulling wounds to scars across his back and face. It stirs his organs back into place, pushing clots of blood and bile into his mouth. He turns on the fly-loud mound and coughs for a long time, spitting rosey pleural fluid. As he grew scales and claws on his legs before, now he stretches new pink skin over bare knobs of bone. Pain blinds him in flashes, fisting up through his gut to stretch beneath his ribcage. He straightens, every joint popping, and he cries out as function returns to his vocal chords. His voice is so weak and frayed that the wind won't take it. It dies against his lips, insubstantial. The suns roll toward a blistering noon, and vultures appear in the sky. Alan watches them descend as his magic reshapes him. They stack into a kettle, their bald heads red as pricked thumbs. White light dusts down from beneath their wings, leaving them in deathly shadow. By the time the first birds land, Alan is able to roll out of the pit and get to his feet.

"Get out," he says, finding more weight in his voice this time.

The vultures on the ground fan their wings and croak at him. Crows cough from a nearby stand of trees. Alan scoops up a hunk of glass-black chalk and throws it at them, drawing a chorus of cawing laughs from the flock.

Alan slouches away. The birds fall in to feed in the pit, unconcerned with him anymore. He's no longer dead, and he's getting stronger all the time. In spite of his growing strength, Alan had never been more exhausted. He takes a knee at the side of a white-paved road and starts coughing again. His new hands are coffee-light, and his nails are well trimmed. There is no hair on his arms, but there are heavy locks on his head shagging to his shoulders. They swing before him, a black curtain, and he brushes hem back behind his leaf-shaped ears.

I'm a knock, he thinks, *or I was something like one once. Now I'm something else.*

A sob rises in Alan's throat, and he chokes trying to contain it. It bursts from him, and he sniffs into his hand as tears bead in his eyes. He cries bitterly, hurt under the weight of loss. Tremors thunder through him, rooting him in place, a quivering, miserable mass of pain. His body is gone, and he has no idea where it is. It was never him, and now it's nothing. When his seizure finally subsides, Alan looks up toward the road ahead, and he has never felt so small or so far away from anything.

Before Alan is a golden field between the horns of a great forest. It is cut deep with grids of wagon tracks from grave mounds in the east to its western border with high, stony country. Toven's three-story château sits askew in the field, its spires broken and smoke rolling through a hole in its roof. Beyond it, stretching out like a hand toward the horizon, is a city of towers behind walls of pearl. A small army of hobs and daemons is assembled at the south gate, ragged black banners caught high in a new breeze. Only one of the towers in the city is flying the same banner. The rest have only bare poles with flowing halyards.

Alan speaks just to be saying something, hoping the effort will get his sobbing under control.

"Suttea," he says. The word sits in his mouth like a dead second tongue. "The Necropolis. Winter White. She's here – not in Lichlock."

The clearing he's in is littered with clothes, refuse, and wood ash. Alan finds a short, moth-eaten coat and pulls its furred hood over his head. He doesn't bother with the sleeves as he sets off down the road.

"It all comes down to this," he says, but he can't believe it. His life has not come down to anything yet. He feels born again from the dead. The light of his renaissance is harsh, and his new shell is still squirming with rot. There is yet more pain than spirit in his body – with every step, he tugs at anchor, and it's all he can do to remain corporeal – but he is strong. His power is huge inside him, and the garden of his magic flourishes. To cope with the pain, he stays inside his strength, studying it, and it sees him down the empty road to the broken ruin of Gimcrack Castle.

Gimcrack leans over its east corner. Its floors are falling in on each other, and most of the windows are crushed to slits. The remains of Toven's tunnels are scattered across the field, the great dredge tanks leaning out of the grass like hideous tombstones. The front doors are missing, and the darkness beyond the threshold spins with ghosts and sluaghs. There is no cathartic sigil there anymore. It has been burned out like sick flesh, and Toven's trapped spirits are escaping through the wound, one howling shimmer at a time. Alan runs his hand over his forehead and feels only tightening skin and lank strands of hair. The Seal of Aiwass is gone – lost somewhere with his skull – and so, he presumes, is his protection from corruption. He becomes aware of its gaping absence all at once, and he shudders remembering his magic sickness. Stopped with new fear in his path, Alan stands watching the storm of spirits for a moment.

A figure emerges from the doorway – a ghost unlike any of the others swarming in the blind foyer. It is black and twisted, like a living jellyfish scar or a blasphemous letter carved into the air by some cackling evil. The other ghosts stop to watch it float by, and a few of them follow it. It howls from two shapeless mouths and beats at the air with tendrils like gouts of blood. As it nears Alan, it takes the shape of an uman, and he recognizes both its faces. It is Mawn and Toven fused together – a mutant spirit like the damned in the Ghost Patrol.

"We thought him dead," says Toven in an eel-slick, shimmering voice. The star-clusters of his eyes wink, uneven. "We thought him dead but, lo, he lives – as we live. Low. Has the grave spit you out, Hogar? She is cruel. What do you want from us now? What can we still do for her?"

"I'm not Hogar," Alan replies. "You know me, King Toven. I'm Alan Shade, the thanoturge – your enemy."

The double spirit flickers. Mawn's face moves like an illusion, dancing away whenever Alan tries to look directly at it.

"Alan," says the spirit. "You are nothing, and nothing we know. My mind is not what it was. It's busy with something now, and I can't interrupt it." Toven's ghost quivers and breaks. Alan looks into it to see the furnace of rage at its heart. Mawn is rooted in that cinder, choking Toven's madness. He stands against the Bleeding, the only thing keeping Toven from exploding into a maelstrom.

"What are you?" Alan asks. He feels sick with terror at his strength returning. "I need a shield against corruption. You branded me once. Do you remember? Right here." Alan points to his forehead. "The Seal of Aiwass."

"Do you like what I've done?" Toven asks. "My home is new. It befits us, I think. You can't go inside anymore; I've seen to that. I went down every hall and I locked every last door. It took nights and nights, but I stitched the wound of Gimcrack closed, Hogar. If you want to taste the blood inside it now, you'll have to eat the scab."

Alan watches the spirit as it wavers before him. Pain explodes from Toven's part of it, but Mawn keeps it constrained to a wheeling corona. Tongues of anger and lightning-bright shame swirl together inside it, twisting sorrow into red knots between them. It could be a gash on the world for the Bleeding to writhe through, but Mawn keeps it closed. There is no battering down his special mercy – Alan is amazed that Mawn can be so loyal to Toven even now.

"I suppose you've always tried to hold him back," Alan says to Mawn. "Live in me, now. Be my seal."

Mawn says all he needs to say in silence. In the garden of Alan's magic, the trees begin to sway.

"Yes," Alan says. "I am your king now."

Mawn's head swims apart like a bottled cloud. The spirit quavers, and then a wind takes it. It blows to shreds, and Toven screams from the threading mess. Alan holds out his hand and pulls the last of Mawn and the Clockwork King into the cup of his palm. The ghost shines like a sunrise against his skin, sending monstrous heat roaring up his arm. Alan claps his hand over his brow and presses the heat there as hard as he can. Smoke rises from between his fingers. He smells his flesh burning and he pushes deeper. This body may not be permanent, but his shield against the Bleeding must be. He opens himself and lets the new brand burn into his spirit.

Alan's knees weaken, but he takes the pain. He lets it wash over him, and he finds bright and complex patterns of beauty inside it. A new lamp appears in his garden, burning pink and black, and Theia comes to stand beneath it with moths swinging a crown around her head.

"It befits us, I think," she says, her voice bursting red clouds in Alan's internal sky. "No one can come in. We've closed every door. Let the Bleeding scream for nothing."

When Alan takes his hand from his forehead, there is blood in the creases of his fingers. He traces his new scar, feeling the power there. It is stronger than Aiwass ever was. Mawn and Toven move in it, two opposing forces, the Bleeding stopped utterly between them.

"That's that," Alan says.

As he starts off down the road again, Gimcrack Castle begins to crumble. It groans and cracks in half, and severed spirits tumble out through the split. The ground sucks the leaning dredge tanks down one by one to crush them where the dead lie laughing.

Alan takes a moment to feel Toven's evil die. It is a sad, pulling feeling — like the last light of a bad day slipping west. He remembers standing at the bus station the night after Allison's funeral and watching cars whisper toward the highway. What grief was before their drivers? Where would they be when he was nowhere? He can still smell the rain on the street and see the wet halos clinging around the streetlights. That hurt and that fear can go down, too – into the pits where the dredge pits burst or the halls of Gimcrack as they shattered apart.

His steps rising as the weight of death and pain quits his shoulders, Alan puts the fall of Gimcrack far behind him. He leaves the road when it veers east away from the Necropolis and the wilted army milling at its gate. The one tower still flying a flag is built into the center of a keep on the west side of the city. Clouds band across the sky, their tails fraying to wisps like cats-o-nine. Their shadows fall over the walls.

Toven brought the city here in shadows, Alan thinks. *Now I'll wear the shadows in.* He chuckles, imagining Sophia saying, "The Framer provides."

Alan heads for the wall, swimming in and out of darkness, and spreads himself into the cloud shadows to slide over. He crawls over stone and gables, cold and stretched, weighing nothing. He moves down streets and past stoops haunted with a knowing silence and the graying stains of some recent horror. All the city's uncomfortable beauty is darkling now, marred by something more terrible than the ghosts it contained already. Alan wishes he could have walked the Necropolis before Winter White arrived in it.

I still may, he tells himself. *I will. Absolutely I will.*

The city is mazelike, but darkness carries Alan easily across it. Reaching the keep, he slips from the shadow and gathers himself into flesh again. Dead Hogar's body is stronger for having Alan wearing it. He stitches it tight, pushing healing power through its blood. It remembers strength, and it is still hungry. The sun is high in his garden, and its streams are running swift and white. He is at the apex of his power, balanced so that nothing can shake him. Alan builds himself better out of the darkness, and approaches the guards outside the tower with perfect courage.

Before they can greet him, Alan pushes the small swarm of knock guards beyond the draug as he reaches the stairs, leaving them paralyzed and mindless atop each other. The steps to the pinnacle circle the shaft of the tower on the outside. He slips up the stairway like a dark breath, easily spreading his corpse-form again until he is thinner than mist. His magic is more open to him than it has ever been, and he lets it lead him up with loving praise. At the ivory balcony just below the top of the tower, Alan stops to settle himself and peers through an arrowslit at the field below. There are young dead in this neighborhood. Their anger pushes up through the ground like gnarled roots' knuckles, invisible to all but him.

"Nothing good has happened here for so long," Theia says from deep in the woods of Alan's mind. "The terrors we make – the blood we draw from each other. We are all vampires."

Alan casts his Deadsight under the wall toward the mouth of the great green sward that opens into Suttea. There is a new army on the march. The dragon Calushar leads it, followed by Alan's Ghost Patrol and Annun's sylves clad in balefire black. The sky fills with cage-bearing valravn as far as he can see, the Mercy Gale beneath them with her sail billowed. The dradtail swarm stands on the landship's main deck, and Brattle sits among them astride Stag's Blood. Alan's heart fills so full of joy to see his friends that he feels light enough to fly to them. In lieu of that, he stirs up his power and gives his voice to the dead. They carry it across leagues, clamoring to serve him.

"I'm with you," he says, and the dead kings of Suttea speak his message to his army.

With this done, Alan turns and makes his way to the copper-roofed room at the top of the tower. Two of the three guards there fall helplessly before him, and the third throws herself from the balcony wordlessly. Alan knocks the iron door in with a jerk of his hand and tosses it to the floor in an ugly twist. His magic is raging now, riled up into a white-hot fury. He tamps it down gently, promising it complete freedom when his task is done.

Alan is calm and straight when he enters the room at the top of the tower to find Winter White standing inside. She is leaning over a table surrounded by her generals, gaping in shock. The skull-faced Chodash gem shines pink before her. It casts rings of gold and sparks through curtains of bruise blue and purple, its orbits full of fire. Winter White hasn't used it yet. She doesn't know how. Alan isn't surprised. The gem isn't for her. It's his.

"I'm the end," Alan says. "I'm the finish. It's finally over. You can rest now, Winter. I am death."

Forty-Six

Winter White's eyes go as wide as twin lunatic moons. Alan feels her stare penetrating him, burning past his borrowed flesh to sear his spirit like the brand he made of mad Toven and Mawn. Though she knows him immediately, she says, "Hogar," and her goblin generals don't attack. They just stand and wait, expectation pinched high between their raised eyebrows. One of them starts to speak, but he never finishes. As he pushes them past the draug, Alan wonders if Winter White might have misidentified him on purpose.

The goblin generals fall into heaps atop each other. Alan moves them as they fall to ease their landings. They are gorgeous in their senseless paralysis. Their ash-gray eyes open into leagues of cavernous nothing — into blank years of uncreation straining backward endlessly, catching no reflections. It's a strange little horror to look at them.

"Alan," Winter White finally says.

Alan is still distracted by the bodies on the floor. One of them is too small and bent all wrong. There is no skull in the hood of the robe it is wrapped in. The skin is pulled so tight that veins bulge beneath it around long planes of fractured bone. Only the body's scaly legs look untouched.

"That's me," Alan says. He points to the twisted form in the robe. "And so's that. Where's Nettle?"

Winter White looks at Alan with her chin tipped to the right. Light falls across her face and glances off, as if repulsed by her angles. Even this is beautiful. Even the dauntless shadow of her ire is lovely. She comes around her table and leans against it, the Chodash skull beaming behind her, framing her in hopeless rays.

"Is that what's next?" she asks, crossing her arms. "Nothing more? You made such a big deal out of this at first. What a pity to have wasted your entrance after it was so long in coming."

"Tell me," Alan demands. A huge banging sound begins outside. Calushar's voice splits the air above the Necropolis, and the tower shakes. "Do you hear it falling down out there? I can give you what you want. Tell me with your last breath."

"What do you know from my power, thanoturge?" Winter snarls. Her face goes lupine for a moment. "I have seen many pinnacles. I have been born for centuries. At the height of my power here, this time, the fire-swarms of Avernus and the Coma-blind malakeen were eating from the same hand." She cups her palm, as if weighing grain. "Nettle came back into the world as a direct result of your actions at Welkinbright, whether you know it or not, and I know you don't. Then he went to Cheel Gar and burned it, and he killed some of my marshals. When word spread that a daemon had shed malakeen blood, my best allies turned on each other, and they abandoned me. Now my army is spread like a whore – waiting and tired. What do I care where Nettle is now? He paid his price, but you haven't."

"It didn't have to be Us versus You," Alan says. He moves forward a few paces, stepping over his own corpse. "Nettle didn't make this happen, and neither did I. You did."

Winter White's shoulders go loose, her arms swing free, and her face slips sweetly until it is as deep and as soft as a bucketful of congealing meat grease.

"Then take revenge," Winter says. "I'd have starved all my long, cursed life if not for this hope. I built my war piecemeal, and I've died in it a thousand times. I have been the mud under my own boots. I've seen storm-washed skies stretching on forever above my cenotaph. End me and taste real sustenance. You will never be so full again – I am rich with hate, Alan. Or come with me to the Gardens Arcane and see the famine of souls for yourself."

"No," says Alan, and he reaches into Winter White.

The Necropolis shakes. The air crackles with screams, pulses with drumbeats, and splits at the barrels of black war horns. The dead writhe underground. Enticed by the new spill of blood into the dirt, they rise like sharks, pushing up the walls of the city until towers topple and gates break open. Nothing sates them anymore;

they have forgotten their immateriality. Their madness runs shrieking through the alleys until Alan quiets them.

"Be still," he whispers, and they are still.

"Go to sleep," he says, and they sink back to the pits they have made for themselves near Midion's core — at the bright and haunted edge of formlessness.

The sounds of battle drain away. The world becomes small, steady, and hollow. Alan enters Winter White, and a hammer-shock of ecstasy shudders through him. Her spirit is deep in the folds of a healing bloom, wrapped in years like showers of fire. Her sadness stretches far behind her physical body. Pain rings through her constantly, but she has made her damage into something beautiful. Alan struggles to make sense of her. The draug is nowhere in Winter White. At the heart of her rose, there is only she in her flames, sleeping dense as a star.

"Wake up," Alan says, gently pressing her petals apart. "Death has come for you."

"I don't want to go," Winter says, "without taking everyone and everything with me."

"They will always be with you," Alan replies. "That's the point of the draug. You return to everything, and you disappear. When you shrink into being again, you'll be new, and you won't be alone. You never were."

"Maybe I want to be," Winter sighs. She puts what could be her blushing cheek on what might be the flat of her fist. Every form she takes dissipates or is shocked apart as the blossom blows. She is unstable. "Do you think this is the best of all possible worlds? I can make a new one. There's no such thing as obliteration. *That* is the point of the draug: death and rebirth — all I've known since the glow of the sun was young. Reincarnation, Alan. To make the world again, better for all its suffering."

"This isn't your world to destroy," Alan says, "and I have debts to pay — a job to do. Just relax. I'm sorry you've suffered so long. Wherever you go now, I hope you'll be happy."

With this, Alan wraps himself around Winter White and starts to pull her toward the draug and the black gulfs of life and death that lie behind him. He speeds her through his garden, and she plucks a bloom from the Kingwatcher's flower. At the edge of the draug, she looks up at him, her eyes like windows into golden Heaven for a moment. She is Allison, she is Hannes – she is a bolt of lightning trapped between the ground and the sky.

"I'll see you again," she says.

"I know," says Alan, and he lets her go.

The draug takes Winter White in a flash of fairy fire so bright that Alan can't look at it. He returns to himself, feeling bone-thin and lead-heavy, but he is still fast enough to catch Winter White as she collapses. He lays her empty body down on the floor of the tower and brushes her eyelids closed under his thumb and forefinger. Her lips curl in a curious smile, as if someone is telling her an amusing secret.

Alan stands, his heart heavy. This is grim work to do yet. He isn't eager to start, but knows how, and he can't dally. He turns to look at his robe-tangled corpse.

"You first," he says.

Slipping from the dead goblin flesh is easier than he expected it to be. His new body folds itself onto the floor as he leaves it, and his old one starts to twitch as he squeezes in. It is cold and shattered, but he hasn't been gone for too long. It still remembers him.

Alan fills his old skin like a gas, stretching the bones back into place and pulling their splinters back together. He closes his exploded ribcage and tugs his shoulders back into their fragmented sockets. As pain returns, he retreats into his garden to watch the last of the long, delicate process from the bank of a black river.

"I never thought I'd miss this," he says to Theia.

Theia looks up at the sky and wriggles her pretty toes in the grass. A wind lifts the single lock of hair that falls across her brow. Her face looks huge in the constant light.

"Of course you didn't," she says. "Look — you're almost done now, but you have no weapon. And you have no head."

"Not yet," Alan replies. "But that hasn't stopped me before."

"Make the best of what you have. The mind moves flesh as easily as anything else. Bone and blood respond more readily to the touch of the Aethereal Hand than to the hands of mere healers."

Alan stands, repaired. For all that it aches, his body is his again. His strange awareness returns, and he hears Calushar's voice outside. He looks out from the non-space toward the blazing Chodash gem on the table. It looks back at him, almost seeming to move.

"This is mine," he says, lifting the gem and lowering it down over the bare stump of gristle that is his neck.

The skull fits there exactly as it was meant to. Alan's flesh and bone grow into it, and his magic leaps up his spine to hold the skull in place. Power swells inside him, pushing all the pain of his latest resurrection away. Life light grows beneath his flesh, and he pulses transparent for a while. After a long moment's concentration, Alan finds that he can move the skull on his neck with no trouble. It is his — it is him. He is complete, but he isn't finished.

Alan goes to Hogar's body. It is folded like a puppet, far from life now, a thing. It's as cold as stone when he grasps its chin. He turns its head so that its star-white eyes are looking toward the ceiling. The new seal sits black above them - the Seal of Mawn. He places his hand over it and can feel its living power. It squirms under vacant flesh, responding to him as he hoped it would. As he hoped or knew. He knows that it will burn into him again and it does after a long moment. It kindles, glows, rises from the corpse, as spirits are wont to do. He takes it into his hand as he had before, and as it burns lambent across his palm, knuckles, and fingertips he presses it against his new jeweled skull. Alan trembles as the Seal of Mawn sears itself into his forehead. He feels it stronger than ever. Stronger than Aiwass. A true bulwark, not like Toven's design, containing a power of purity that Aiwass itself, whatever it was, certainly never had. Alan sinks to his hands and knees for some time after the seal stops blazing. Then he marshals his strength, such as it is, and stands again to continue. There are yet more miracles to perform.

Alan goes to Winter White's side again. He rolls her onto her stomach and splits her filmy, white dress from its collar to her Venusian dimples.

"Graveworld will always be with you, Winter," Alan says, "and you'll always be with us. I'm honestly sorry to do this, but you know how it is. There's a war on. I'll try to make it quick."

The battle roars on outside, loud as ever. Flames lick the tower, teasing into the windows and browning the purple curtains swinging over them. Alan puts his hand flat between Winter White's shoulder blades and pushes his magic into her sun-missed skin. He imagines the blade of a scalpel extending from the heel of his palm to her spinal column.

"Split," he says, moving his palm down her back. Winter's skin opens to the bone, and Alan moves his hands to stop the spurt of blood. When her back is peeled wide, he coils his magic around Winter's spine and disarticulates it from the rest of her skeleton in a long and ugly process. He fuses the vertebrae together, retching a bit every time he feels a disc bursting. At last, he lifts solid bone from the mess. Then, with Winter's spine in hand, he coaxes her closed again and turns her over.

"Forgive me," he says, stroking her dead cheek with his left hand to avoid leaving streaks of blood on her face.

Winter says nothing through her curious smile. Her eyes remain closed. Alan stands and straightens her spine in his hand, turning it a bit into a stable corkscrew. Remembering the night he and Brattle spent encamped in Pwysh's doorway, he sparks a murmurous, amaranth flame to the bone and burns the last of the tissue away. The spine is an awful thing to look at, but he is already filling it with his power. It will serve him well, and he will remember Winter White's infinite expanse of sorrow as long as he carries it.

The tower begins to tilt, but Alan isn't done. He hurries to finish his grisly work, performing the same procedure on Winter White's goblin guards. Even with the foundations of the tower audibly breaking, he makes sure the last lights of their lives are dark before he slits them open. When his gruesome task is finally done and the gore-slick floor of the tower is tilting crazily toward the ceiling, Alan wrenches all his trophies together into a three-foot shaft of bone. He bends a flare into the bottom and stretches it into an open circle as he hurries out the door and down the stairs. The tower leans over its buckling middle and waits, poised like an old man looking down at a dropped penny. The second balcony dips low enough for Alan to leap to the ground, and then the tower breaks apart backward. Something groans apart just above its base, and the upper room tips off like a hat. The one flag snaps from its pole and vanishes in the blood-hot breeze.

Towers crumble all over the Necropolis. The streets crack, and doors rattle off their hinges. Welkinbright holds no horror back. Its wrath is huge and black — the battle has come not just for Winter White, but to everything she ruled at the end. The sky is dark with monstrous crows. Calushar cuts among them like an eel. It beats its body through the air in great loops and rakes the Necropolis with sheets of flame.

Who am I sparing? Alan wonders. *This is a worse evil now that Winter White is dead.*

Alan slips away from the tower's ruin as a shadow, skimming over the walls toward the splintering south gate. The Bleeding bulges against his new seal but those warring spirits drive it back. He stops against what remains of the south wall as Winter White's army retreats into the city before a tide of sylves and spirits. Alan lifts his new weapon and makes one last twist, completing the oblate ellipse that makes it an exact copy of his trash masher in flame-cleaned vertebrae.

Dead-waker, tide-turner, he thinks. *Necromasher.*

It thrums with baleful power, full of a familiar spirit and happy to see him despite the new sorrow it contains. Alan gives it a twirl, and it sings a rattling song.

"Spare the city!" Alan cries. The dead carry his voice into echoes. The ground heaves, and the fighting stops on both sides of the wall. The valravn turn, following the dragon as it descends to wrap itself eight times around one of the Necropolis's few remaining towers. It dips its head to glare at Alan, one eye white and bleeding. Its flanks are bristling with spears and arrows.

"Destructor," Calushar says, "usurper – the deathless one is dead?"

Alan nods and holds up his new masher.

The battle hangs, pendent on the next moment. Hobs stare at Alan over the points of their polearms. A mire-og oozes nearby, its dumb eyes burning as it tries to decide what to to do next.

"No more," Alan says with his deadvoice. "This is over."

The dragon roars, wings high and tail unfurling from the tower to flow above it like a new banner. "The Wraith King lives!" Calushar bellows. Several hobs fall dead of fear. "Fall back to the gate, and drag the last ragged host of the enemy out with you!"

The misfit horde breaks. Scours fall from the bird-loud sky, their riders swallowed midfall by Calushar. Alan presses himself against the sagging south wall of the Necropolis and watches as his army pulls back through the city like a grasping hand. Dregs flood up from the lower city to meet a wall of swords. Alan dispatches them when he must, putting them down hard and fast beneath the head of his new weapon. His heart breaks for each one, though they are already dead. The last of the hobs try to flee, but they are trapped in the maw of the south gate. They meet no mercy there; the sylves crush them in the street from both directions and spread their blood in stripes on the walls of the gatehouse.

"No more killing!" Alan cries.

He pushes his voice through every dead spirit he can reach, but wrath explodes unchecked beyond the gate. The sylves and dradtails swell together, surrounding the last of the misfit horde. Winter White is finally dead, but her wrongs live on at the tips of glittering blades. Alan sees fury bright in every face, and he is afraid of it. He knows its slow, cold bite and the pull of its teeth inside. It has been his quiet power, his second heart, for far too long, and he still feels marred. He has finally evicted it, but there is no stopping it here. Lost in bloodlust, this fury will not be bound. Death sweeps down over the city, huge and quiet, and there is no order to surrender.

Alan's army obliterates Winter White's and pushes forward into the city to flush out any survivors. Then they dig Winter's spineless corpse from the wreck of her tower and hoist her up on a pole with her goblin generals. Alan rejoins his friends on the field of corpses; Stag's Blood rears up to great him with a huge embrace, draping his paws over Alan's shoulders and purring to shake the ground. Brattle shakes his hand for a full minute. Then they follow him up the hill toward the great table of bare rock where the valravn set their cages. There, the Mercy Gale bobs, her engines humming. The last of the day's light pours over her curves, and she looks cut out from the world behind her, like an ornament hanging in a window.

"I'm so relieved to see you, Alan," Stag's Blood says, pacing around Alan's legs. "Far moreso than I expected I'd be, actually, considering I was certain you would be all right. I should be smug: my faith was rewarded."

"There are better times and places than this for self-satisfaction," Alan says. "I'm sorry if you worried. I haven't exactly been your good luck charm – or anyone's – but you're here, and nothing means more. Thank you for sticking with me."

Sophia lands on Alan's shoulder. He raises his hand, and she gives his fingertip a dry, crystal kiss. She is dawn-warm and bright as a lantern. Her light fits perfectly where fury used to live in Alan's mind.

"The Sisters of M do not submit to hopelessness," Sophia chimes. "I knew the Framer would lead us back to you somehow."

"We ain't all so loyal," Brattle says. "Nora cut off after you left, heading the opposite direction: west. She said naught like 'goodbye' and we didn't stop her. She was false, Alan. You heard what Nex said."

Alan looks west. A great shape stands in darkness where the suns are setting. It seems to be some kind of statue, and it's terrible to look at. The surrounding mountains are shorter near its base, as if they've been flattened by the great shape's monstrous power. Alan tries not to think about what it must look like in the light.

"I figured she had her own road," Alan says. "It got on ours for a while, and now it's headed down that way — maybe toward whatever that is — but it'll lead her back again. Either that or we'll hunt her down. She's carrying my daughter."

"Oh, Alan," Sophia says, drumming her wings, "I am not sure how to congratulate you without being disingenuous. As always, I shall settle for frankness: she is a villain. This is a tragedy."

"I can't hate her as much as I should — maybe because I now she's a scared little fire," Alan says. "She won't lose me no matter how far she goes. I'm inside her, and we're bound. She hasn't taken from me. All she's done is borrow wrath. I almost feel sorry for her."

"Rain long foretold," says Brattle.

Stag's Blood adds, "Ever more storms."

Brattle continues. "You can only take the rain that comes, and a hard one's coming for her once this one's ended. As for me, I made my home, and I do what I want. It just happens that I'm tempted most often to be good."

Alan thinks about his night with Nora. The magic she used on him was strong, and he has held onto it. Their connection is still so deep that he can almost see her across its mists, running nude into the great, black west. He wonders if she can feel his profound disappointment kicking in her womb.

"How did you know where to look for me?" Alan asks. "The last time we talked about where Winter White might be, we mentioned the Meadowshores. Is that nearby?"

"Not in the least," Stag's Blood replies, "and we almost set out in that direction. It's only by a special grace that we found you here."

"What grace?" Alan asks.

"Bua's," Sophia replies, her heartlight pulsing a fearful green.

"The dark walker," Brattle adds. "The Cuco. He led us all the way here at a crawl, far ahead the whole time, because we were afraid to get too near."

Alan tries a chuckle, but his voice feels distant. Something squirms in his chest. "You said the Cuco was a luring flame."

"Look where he led us," Stag's Blood says. "This was a shameful massacre. Who knows what the Cuco wanted beyond blood and war – if anything?"

"If I may interject," Sophia says, "there must be facets to Bua that we do not know. Our legends hold that he is the ghost of great power that died with the last world, but I suspect there is more to him than even that. Truths have no shoals. They are invariably deep."

The group moves on across the field of cages. Alan mends and revives as many of the fallen as he's able to – friend and foe – far from the sight of any other healers. Unafraid of his new master, he brings many back from the dead side of the draug. His magic flows freely. His spirit feels huge and infinitely distant from his body. Spearbacks press grateful purrs into his hands when he restores them. Mire-ogs thank him in muddy voices, their knees bent and their heads bowed. Soon, a large crowd of fairies is following Alan, and he gives up on secrecy.

At the brink of midnight, Alan, Brattle, Stag's Blood, and Sophia finally return to the Mercy Gale. There, they curl up together in the heat of the orlop deck, and Alan slips easily to sleep. He dreams of great owls moving hooded through snowy forests, and he wakes the next day just as noon is rising above the point of the mast. Brattle and Stag's Blood enjoy a long breakfast of some dark and stringy meat, and Alan tells them about his meeting with Death in the garden of his magic. When Alan is finished with his story, Brattle explains as much about what happened in Nex's prison as he can remember.

"You pushed me," Brattle says, "but I held on tight. I got an iron grip on this world, you know, now that I been out of it and back. I clawed my way back up from the dark and the draug, and I knew it was Nettle'd taken you. I felt him too late, or things might have been very different. Some could say they'd have been worse."

"I'm sorry, nonetheless," Alan replies.

Sophia circles Alan's new head, letting the impossibly tiny tips of her fingers skim across the knob at his saggital crest. It glows in response, and Alan feels little pricks of heat on his neck.

"This gem is worth a million more journeys through worse trouble," she says.

"Let's hope not," Stags's Blood chuckles. "I feel rolled flat, and I'm due a long rest."

Forty-Seven

With midday failing behind a rumpled sheet of clouds, Alan and company return to the Necropolis. The open slope toward Suttea has been picked clean of corpses. The sylves took their dead into the sky, while the dradtails sealed theirs in wax and glued them to the boles of trees. The sparse woods sway with ghosts, and every puff of wind is heavy with mixed whispers: the Dead in Disgrace race ahead of Alan like hunting shadows. On the scarred field beneath the wall, they gather to receive him with the other generals of his army. Faro is there, scarred and beaten, sagging as if to spite the warmth of his smile. The dradtail chiefs stand shoulder to shoulder, their arms interlocked. Color blows around them like dust. A tall, homely uman joins them — the Drowned Queen in chlorine blue splendor with a white crown all but lost in her short, henna curls. Alan and Brattle bow to her. Stag's Blood lifts his rump and puts his nose into the dirt beside his outstretched forepaw. The Drowned Queen stands them all up again with a wave of her foam-white hand, and the beetle-shelled Red Guard surrounding her bows instead.

"Alan Shade," says the Drowned Queen in a voice like a cemetery full of ringing signal bells. Alan is struck by the depth of beauty in her plainness. Her eyes are dim behind rimless spectacles, and her lips are pale folds bracketed by deep marionette lines. "The man himself: the Man Who Returned. Firstborn of the Dead. Secret-keeper. I'm Morgan, the Drowned queen of Midion, and you needn't bow to me. You serve a preeminent power now."

"How do you know who I serve?" Alan asks. Brattle and Stag's Blood look at him, each wearing his own species of quizzical expression. Stag's Blood's cheeks tighten, and his whiskers prick out in tight little fans. Brattle raises an eyebrow and hitches a crooked smile beneath his ear. On Alan's shoulder, Sophia grows warm.

"We'll discuss that," Morgan says. She swings a hand toward the others waiting. "First, these vagabonds have words for you.

They would not leave until you appeared. Satisfy them. Receive your congratulations."

At this, Faro steps forward and wraps Alan in a firm but tired embrace. Pain rings his head like a halo. The flame on his head has dwindled considerably since Alan last saw him, and he was haggard then.

"Shade the Fortunate," he says. "Heroes of the Flame. I never doubted any of you. You don't belong in savage Kur. You were made for the sky. Come back to the Empyrean City with me – even you are welcome, death-eater. There is a reward of power waiting."

"Faro of the Feather," Alan says. "I will return to Welkinbright. There are still opportunities here to prove myself unworthy of your generous offer. But wait for me. I want to see you when I arrive. I want to know that you're going to recover from this."

"If only my health were my city's," Faro smiles. "I'll bear this hurt for her as long as I have to. Pain for the life of the Flame is an honor." He stoops a bit to look at Sophia. "Don't think I don't know what you took from us, Sister. Kelen tells us everything."

"I am sorry," Sophia says, fluttering. "I cannot help what I catch, you know, and I do not know how to give it back."

Faro lets go a weak laugh. "Use it well, little queen. You deserve it."

After giving Alan another, stronger hug, Faro turns away and heads east. The last crow is waiting atop its cage. Like a dark god, it broods down over the wild and blighted lands of Kur until Faro arrives, and then it lifts him into the cloud-crossed sky with a series of disapproving croaks.

"Power in the sky," Brattle muses. "Even the death-eater is welcome – what a gut-popping honor. I'd sooner choke."

"Kind of you to keep that behind your teeth while he was within earshot," Stag's Blood laughs. "Kind and strange. If you're not careful, you'll degrade into politeness."

Three dradtail chiefs approach next. One of them holds a flower in his hand. Its large, bell-shaped bloom is lit blue from inside. It droops like a new widow, its leaves swinging futilely to the foot of its stem.

"Your key show us nowhere," says the wasp, "but Lashaseph grateful for you, Ellen Shade. You risk yourself for us. We have no gifts. Queen is sorry, but here is this."

The dradtail hands the flower to Alan. It trembles as he takes it, and its bloom begins to sing. The melody flows of it in in a plume of color.

"What's this?" Alan asks.

"Death gift given to Anacadeshisemta, who you bring back from the Farhives," says a second chief. This one is wearing a headdress of quills and has his face painted like Shuni's. "Never see such a flower before. Anaca give it to you – say it should be yours. It make no pollen, but only sing. Lashaseph have no use for it."

"A lethebell," says Morgan. "There are pale shores full of them far away – beyond these goodly stretches. Don't smell it. I can give you a jar to put it in."

"Smelling that flower ain't gonna be a problem for Al," Brattle chuckles.

"Then you *are* fortunate," Morgan smiles. "Listen to it only when the moon is setting. It will sing you dead secrets."

"Thank you," Alan says, bowing to the chiefs. They buzz and bow in return. "Where is Shuni?"

"Safe and well," says the third chief. "She will remember you for us, when our memories dim. She have a new way in the Mind. You change what you touch. Know that and watch yourself, Talmashul – Magicman. Power is weight."

"Wise words," Alan says. "What about your stores of honey from the nectaries?"

"That is being returned," Morgan replies. "White's virgin troves are open now. Many have plundered them and are gone, but the Lashaseph are thorough. They remain in that chamber, working hard at scooping every last drop of their treasure away."

"Nectaries fill again," says the first chief, "but not fill complete. Not full. White take much from us. We leave now to oversee the recover. Be well, Outlanders, until your griefs find you again."

The chief in the quill headdress says, "They always do." Then, the dradtails flick their wings to speed and rise over the bowing wall. They disappear above the western quarter of the Necropolis, where Calushar lies coiled asleep across gilded roofs.

Finally, the Dead in Disgrace assemble. They crawl from nothing into a wavering throng, and it takes a long time. The sky clears while Alan waits for them to fully gather. Free from the prison's oppression, they have begun separating from each other. A proud, bright spirit pulls away from the others, her star-eyes blazing. With some shimmering effort, she makes a shape for herself. Curls form atop her head, and freckles shine across her cheeks like comets to disappear.

"Theia," Alan says.

Theia's ghost tilts a wild, meteor smile. Then her features warp away, scattered by the last lances of sunset as they shoot through her.

"This is goodbye," Theia says in Alan's head.

"No," Alan replies. "I don't want you to go. I need you to face the Bleeding."

Theia says nothing. She is gone, and the garden of Alan's magic darkens around the space she left. In Graveworld, Theia's ghost addresses Alan in a dripping whisper.

"Thank you," she says. Then the wraithmass scatters and leaves Suttea like a wind-spread thunderhead. The stars come out as they wheel away — old eyes watching from distant furnaces. Their lights reach out from ancient graves: wraithclouds of gas and color. Alan wonders if dead stars remember shining. What new lights will be born in Theia's nebula now?

"Some of those prisoners were very guilty," says Morgan. "You have unleashed your share of atrocities, Alan the Fortunate, for all the good you've done."

"I imagine you won't be thanking us," Stag's Blood says. Alan runs his hand through the basteta's fur. It is softer and thicker than ever; Stag's Blood wears strife surprisingly well.

Morgan considers a smile but thinks better of it. "One can't bowl down the towers of evil without freeing some monsters," she says. "You don't need my gratitude. What would you do with it? In lieu of thanks, I will show you to the end of your journey. Then you can thank me."

The Drowned Queen leads Alan and company into the Necropolis at a worried clip. Her Red Guard follows, their wings buzzing a marching beat. Fae are finally emerging onto the streets from barricaded safehouses. Fear hangs spider-eyed in every corner. Gloaming blooms through the city in strained silence.

"I've heard naught but ill of you," says the Drowned Queen. "I was expecting a barbarian, but look! Not one ruthless light in you. Vengeance is dead in your mind. I hear you healed even your enemies on the battlefield. Why?"

"Because it was right," Brattle sneers, "and because 'right' is what Al is."

"If you look deep down," Alan says, "as deep as you can, past the million little things that keep us apart, you'll see that there are no enemies. As bulwarks against suffering, we have only each other. I'd have brought everyone back if I could have, even if it would've started the war again. I had more power, but I was selfish. I should have pushed myself until I couldn't come back. That would have made it right."

"Great Gales — how obnoxious," Morgan laughs. "Did you really think we expected you to conquer Death itself? One flame in that dark is a miracle, and you are a candle-lighter."

The Necropolis is built on strange angles. Houses bulge toward the street, swollen as if gravid, and some are cornerless. Waves dance across the upper architecture. The paved roads flexes against their cambers like caught serpents. The city looks brighter wherever Morgan goes. She drags hope in a train over trauma's dust, blowing it away beneath her heels. The city loves her, and Alan is almost embarrassed at the way it pines for her every step.

"Winter White is entering the exchange," Morgan says. "Can you feel her, Alan?"

"No," Alan says, looking down into the draug. Winter White isn't there, but Theia is, shining like an illusion of glass in the desert. Alan can't reach out to her. She doesn't remember.

"Miracles and all, you're only human," Morgan smiles. "She is pouring out her lives. There are thousands of them. I don't know what will happen to them. Maybe she'll rise from them again. Maybe it'll be someone worse."

"Why move the Necropolis?" Stag's Blood asks. "And, if you can, why move it here?"

"This is the oldest iteration of the Necropolis," Morgan replies. They turn down a cracked-flat hill of redbrick. "What a rare gift it is to feel your heart in a stone. I have trammeled many a long, wild night here. I've kept them to milk – to remember. Now I must pull it down, and they will all go free. My cage – sweet and small. I will be empty. I would keep it, but it's been corrupted. Midion won't suffer it anymore. What will happen to my heart when the stone is broken? We'll see, but I'll have to wait.

"There is no Queen of Midion. There is only a curse for a keeper. My brother and I are twins. I am a force of thought: passive, steady and invisible. Mordred is passionate action, and passion is fire. It wasn't long before he burned something beautiful and was punished. I was made the caretaker of his torment until the end of the world, which I work to prevent. He needs his pain. Believe me."

"Forbidden stories," Sophia says, ringing eager wings. "Mordred Belfaire was an arch-heretic. We are only allowed to learn of his legendary death."

Morgan laughs. "There was no Death when we were born. Mordred can't die, but he constantly slips. His best hope is oblivion, but I deprive him of that. My brother is everywhere. In some places, he is thin. In others, he is hopelessly fractured. Here is some heresy, Sister: Mordred *is* Midion."

Night seals shut in the ensuing silence. Alan looks up to count the stars. The moons are dim mirrors in the western sky, already setting.

"Winter White wanted to end his suffering with her own," Alan says, "but you wouldn't let her. You're his tyrant — his demon."

"There's so much that you don't understand," the Drowned Queen says.

Alan tries to cross his arms, but he can't hold them in place. His body still aches terribly, and he is still relearning how to inhabit it.

"Enlighten me," Alan says.

Morgan leads them toward a squat, leaning palace surrounded by fanglike towers. She produces a key from the depths of her sleeves and unlocks the gilt-black door into its foyer. There is a purging seal on the floor there. Alan recognizes it as the Seal of Aiwass. He expects to feel something when he steps onto it, but he doesn't — it's nothing but carved rock to him anymore. His new seal has eclipsed its power to purify him.

"We have little time for long answers," Morgan says. "I will show you the simple: Winter White did not come unstuck from the wheel of death by accident."

"Then how?" Brattle asks, his voice echoing as Morgan leads them down marblke passage.

Alan knows her palace. The eyeless statues guarding the doors are identical to the ones at Toven's Gimcrack. Violets gape up at him from tubular, fulgurite vases, their blooms twisted around silent screams.

"My brother has been cultivating his reach," Morgan replies, "and he is patient. I almost didn't see him when he started working."

At the end of the hall, Morgan brings out her key again and unlocks a shield-shaped door. Beyond it is her catharsium. It is draped in black and aqua. Light discolorations on the smoke-streaked walls show where bookshelves have recently been moved, and most of the books that must have been in them are towered on the floor. A boxed bank of enormous windows looks out over the city's southern heart, where dradtails are hauling live dredges up in hanging cages and burning them.

Morgan crosses to the bare eyestone pedestal and stretches her fingers in the space where the orb should be.

"If I may ask," Sophia says, "what happened to your Framer Gem?"

"Winter White smashed it," Morgan says. "She was offensively ignorant, but she knew just enough to be destructive. She certainly knew what she wanted. A pawn to the end. I almost pity her." She turns to Alan now, asking, "How many know what you have?"

"I don't know," Alan replies. He pats the large, skull-shaped jewel he's wearing as a head. He can feel the little shock in his neck, but as his bone was, the glass-bright stone is dead to the touch. "Probably not many. I don't think anyone knows what it is."

"Ignorance best preserved," Morgan says. "Come and sit here. There are only two places in all of Midion in which the Chodash Gem may be opened. This is one – Goithion's grave is underneath. Winter White held the other – where he was born."

Morgan presses something into Alan's hand. It's his phone – cracked, cold, and blind. He turns it over, tracing the damage on its screen with his fingertips.

"Pwysh sent you this," Morgan explains. "Now it's as dead as he is, but you found your way without it. You are remarkable, Alan. What will you do now that you have the key to Midion's heart?"

Alan searches his friends' faces. Brattle wears a grim scowl. Stag's Blood's eyes are wide, and they are so much like Allison's

311

that Alan has to clutch his stomach against a sudden pain. Sophia glows a healing blue, burning the shadows away from the floor tiles.

"I don't want Nudd," Alan answers. "I want to keep it safe. I hope you see why I can't trust you with the truth."

"There is no truth, Alan the Incorruptible," Morgan grins. "You haven't decided what to do. Innocence is a kind of sickness. You love so much you cannot lead, but I am a motivating power."

"And now you'll tell us we gotta use the rock, go to Nudd, and we gotta take you with us," Brattle says. "We're wise, Queenie. We're looking for tricks now. You got us here with your guard behind us, practically driving us. We're prisoners just like we was of Toven before. And even if I hadn't seen this kind crazy already, I can smell it on you. It's in your blood like consumption, isn't it — greed's disease?"

Morgan smiles and folds her hands together while she measures her response. The room waits, spread like a lightning seeker, hairs pricking up in anticipation of singed clothes, blown out shoes, and memory loss.

"Brattle Busaw," the Drowned Queen begins in a simmering whisper, "you *are* wise to fear, but you needn't fear me. To most, Nudd is paradise. To me, it is lethally inhospitable. I've always needed champions to preserve the Gardens Arcane for me."

Alan looks into Morgan and finds nothing inside her. Her flesh is a cold, dead lie — a golem full of non-space. The real Morgan is a force like the pull of the moon on the sea. He lingers awhile in her emptiness, feeling her tugging at him. He can't help but be entranced. She can't lie anymore than a storm can lie as it whips up a wave to sweep women and children away. She is something rare and old, and he knows he's unlikely to feel anything like her again.

"I believe her," Alan says. "She's telling the truth."

"Of course I am," Morgan says, smiling. "You aren't the first to seek Nudd in the last billion years. I saw the lighting of the first star — if this were a game I'd have won it by now."

"Then we obey," Stag's Blood says. "For Nudd."

Morgan folds her arms behind her back and says, "Gather now, all of you, and listen."

After a second's hesitation, Alan sits down on the podium. It creaks beneath his weight, charred almost to breaking, and he spreads his legs to support himself on the balls of his feet as best he can. The ground strains against him, trying to flip like an axle pushing against a cracked linchpin. Something terrible awakens under the palace — a deep thing roused shaking from nightmare eons — and Alan tries in vain to shut it out as it reaches for him.

Where are you, Theia? he thinks.

There is no response. The sleeper rises against all of Alan's power at once, and he is alone. He can only just contain it, but it rages. Alan shrinks and doesn't listen as Goithion calls his name across the black expanse of death.

Brattle and Stag's Blood stand on either side of him, and Sophia twines herself into Stag's Blood's mane. Morgan circles them, her footfalls silent even in this immense chamber. Her Red Guard watches from the doorway with their spears across their carapaced chests, as if guarding themselves.

"The threat is alive, Alan," says the Drowned Queen, "and it has your head."

"Power poisoned Mordred. He loved me less and less as the new world was born. In his hate, I learned him. I saw his heart fall to darkness from a place of terrible intimacy. When the new world became deep, he took me down and drowned me in it. His heart then was full of a red, roaring end to all my shining. Now, it is full again and ready to die.

"Dear little Mordred! Go to Nudd, guardians, and cut out his gloating fury. Deny him obliteration, and deliver him into my punishing hands."

"I ain't sure what I'm doing," Brattle says, reaching out to put his palm flat on Alan's glittering face.

"Think of it like sleep," Morgan says. "Don't worry about how to do it. Just relax and let it happen. You were made for this, Conservator."

Sophia brings the light of Welkinbright's Eternal Flame into her hands. She projects it at Alan's head in a wide beam, and Stag's Blood narrows it into a heavy ray. Power and pressure mounting in his skull, Alan slips into his inner darkness.

A wild wind is moaning through his garden. The rivers are dark, and the ground has heaved up to run them backwards. Alan twirls his necromasher.

This is real, he thinks. *I'm here physically.*

Alan sees Brattle standing near the bare knob of a giant knuckle protruding from the ground. Stag's Blood appears beside him. Sophia lands in Alan's palm, and he cups her to his chest to protect her from the gale.

"What's this, Al?" Brattle asks.

Stag's Blood adds, "Is this you?

"It's my magic," Alan replies. I've been growing it in my mind, but now it's real. It's here – wherever here is."

"Amazing," Sophia says. "It has no end. It goes on forever."

"Not forever," Alan says. "But far."

The wind picks up. It flogs Alan's garden until the skies bleed rain. The fields fill with water, and the Kingwatcher's flower droops to the ground. As the rivers leap their banks and the lamps blow over smoking, a door of light opens in the mouth of the storm. It expands, and Alan's flooding garden disappears into it. When it finally dims, the storm is gone. Alan and company find themselves standing under a pink willow in a circle of vine-wrapped stones.

"Here we are," says Stag's Blood, kneading the warm grass between his toes, "in the beauty at the end of it."

"Gorgeous," Sophia adds. Her heartlight explodes into a million spectra. Colors fray through her that Alan has never seen. "The Crossworlds. Like a dream of being born."

Nudd is soft with light. Love waits where shadows fall deep. Where they thin, it breaks across the little paths in bridal trains of black gossamer. Glory hangs in the air like rain. Skies pile atop each other above a hill at the end of an ivory path, weather systems warring across them with no hope of any winner emerging. There is a fountain at the top of the hill surrounded by more pink willows, and the water in it is boiling. Something dark is hunched in the fountain. It stares down at Alan, its eyes pools of molten stained glass. It has Alan's skull in its flaming hands. They are paddler's hands, strong and broad.

"Rotbag," Brattle growls. "Blood-spitter. There he is, in the sacredest place: my muck-sucking brother back for one last fire. Come down here Nettie! Come down, worm-guts! It's been a long walk measuring the world by your shadow. Come down and see how much wider it's going to be without you."

Forty-Eight

Nettle rears up and lifts the skull above his head. For a moment, he looks traced in lightning. Gold light slants through him, and Alan realizes that Nudd has no sun. Fire fills the skull in Nettle's hands, and Nettle hurls it down the hill. It bounces into a nodding patch of lethebells, and Alan crushes it with his necromasher.

Then Nettle comes bounding down the hill, fire fanning out from his spine to envelop him. He howls, and his voice is the Bleeding, pushing in to penetrate Nudd from the outside. Alan reaches out to subdue him, but there is nothing in Nettle's spirit anymore that Alan can touch. Nettle is a walking wound — a tear across the draug through which armies of burning spirits are falling.

Like a one-ghoul ghost patrol, Alan thinks, *protected from me by his perverse connection to the source of my power.*

Sophia projects a heartlight beam, and Stag's Blood growls through gritted teeth as he hardens it into a spear. It penetrates Nettle, hitting nothing, as if he were made of smoke. He may be, for all Alan knows. At the foot of the hill, Nettle bends into a waist-high thatch of thorned vines bursting with sunny flowers. He trembles like a tighetning line as he gathers himself, the flames he wears scorching none of the greenery around him.

"Alan," Stag's Blood says, measuring his concern.

"I'm trying," Alan says. He reaches again, grasping for anything with which he might pull Nettle's spirit back into the draug. Nothing works. Nettle is death's orphan, like Winter was, but there is no darkness left that will take him now. Alan is confounded by the universe of secrets of the draug he has yet to penetrate.

"I'm done with this," Brattle says, springing forward. Light grows in him, paling his flesh like glass. His eyes go ice-black. "You been bad from the hatch. You still got that green yolk in you."

Judgie-birds start from the trees, crying fear in clacking honks. Nettle drives his fire wide, and Alan turns his back to the roaring fan. Flames rake the Gardens Arcane, burning the willows' branches to flailing whips. The soft grass browns to spikes, blooms disintegrating. Nudd screams, great and terrible, and the warring skies fold into themselves to form a sucking funnel. Alan feels his skin contracting beneath his robe. The fire licks up his shins, chest, and arms, and falls on his face in agony. There is something in the fire that reaches his spirit. The garden of his magic begins to blacken, and Theia isn't there to stop it. Alan retreats into his inner darkness, desperate to heal himself, and finds the Kingwatcher's bloom curling back from the heat.

"I'll burn your magic out," says Nettle's furnace whisper. "You ain't gonna stop it. It's just a matter of time, bony. You gotta feel — you gotta know."

Alan stands in the center of his garden and pulls all his power together to push Nettle's fire away. Even after Nudd's cyclone sky has sucked all the flames from the ground, Alan's agony persists. He hears Brattle shouting in a new voice and feels a rush of giant wings across his body, but he can't look up. When the fire in his garden suddenly dissipates, Alan is left twisted tight inside, dense as a collapsed star, squeezing his power for everything to roll back the damage.

"Depart," Brattle cries. "Go back to your ovens!"

"I'm king of those ovens now," Nettle laughs. "There's nothing to go back to, Brattie. I'm all of Avernus, and you're nothing."

Alan struggles to his feet. He feels made of pain. Brattle is driving Nettle back up the hill toward the emptied fountain. Both are blazing white, crowned with golden horns, and wrapped in flowing dove's wings. Stag's Blood is lying like a shadow across the foot of the hill, half his lush coat burned away. Before he's sure he has the strength to do so, Alan rushes to Stag's Blood's side.

"Stags," Alan says. He can't feel his friend's light. The draug is so far away that he can barely see it. The threat of its absence is terrifying. "Don't be dead. Give me a paw."

"It shall take more than that," Stag's Blood says, twitching his legs and tipping his head up to try to look in Alan's direction, "but not much more. Can we face this danger?"

"Brattle's doing his best," Alan replies. "Look at him. Show me you can."

Stag's Blood opens his crossed paws and lets Sophia crawl out from between them. She is unhurt. Her heartlight pulses sorrow.

"He intended to die for me," Sophia says, pressing her hands against Stag's Blood's cheek. "I do not know whether it is worse to see him like this. We are in the open here. Tell me there is hope left, Alan."

"There's hope left, Alan," Alan says. Sophia doesn't laugh. She flutters as if to keep herself from the brink of devastation.

Alan puts his hand on Stag's Blood's singed flank. The skin there is burned rough in large, angry patches, but it's intact. Alan's magic is returning too slowly. He reaches into Stag's Blood and can't feel the damage that must be there.

"I don't hurt," Stag's Blood coughs. "I dove low and didn't burn long. Let me stand. Don't fuss over me."

"Stay there," Alan says. "Let me fuss."

Alan slips back into his inner darkness to try and find his center. In the stillness, he can hear his magic growing – a woody, creaking sound. His focus is in chaos, and he can't break into it, so he embraces it. He lets pain bang through him, bright and hot as lightning. Fear tears across his mind unfettered until it runs itself tired. He doesn't have to back away from the abyss; eventually, its floor rises and it flattens into a bridge. The gap was just an illusion. Alan crosses this bridge into calm and the full strength of his magic.

The dark never lasts, Alan remembers. *It always burns itself out.*

Stag's Blood's body is burned deep. Dying nerves cry out in electric shocks. Tissues blacken along the ridge of his spine, and his lungs heave smoke. Alan imagines that his healing power is pure spring water and floods Stag's Blood's injuries with it.

"Knit," Alan says, thinking of Pick, Brattle's Da. "I'm here now. I'm strong. Knit for me."

"Two Conservators in mortal combat," Sophia moans. "This should not be. It is ugly. Nudd will break apart."

Above the garden, Brattle shines against his brother in righteous fury. The gaping funnel disappears from the skies as they swell with light, grass springs back to rich, green life. Flooded with healing energy, Nudd trembles like the lips of a lover in ecstacy. Stag's Blood's flesh grows anew, and Nettle falls to a knee beneath Brattle's onslaught. As Stag's Blood sucks a deep, clean breath, Brattle draws a white-hot lance from the air and drives it into Nettle's chest. Nettle shrieks, and then the star-white humors of his body disperse. Nudd falls silent again, and the judgies return after a while to watch beauty come back to the garden.

Brattle comes down the hill wreathed in color. Brilliant sheets of pearly light swirl above his head. They remain as he shrinks, his great wings dwindling. When he reaches the hill's gentle foot, Brattle is his dark, knuckle-walking self again, though there is a new power awake in his eyes.

"Everybody good?" Brattle asks. "I didn't act quick enough. I'm sorry, but it's done now – I hope it is, at least. Can't be sure."

Stag's Blood is able to stand to greet Brattle. His fur is lighter where it has grown back, and the whiskers on the left side of his face are uneven.

"I've lost my faith in endings," Stag's Blood smiles. "What happened?"

Brattle shrugs. "I cut loose. Nettie was at a disadvantage: he thought he couldn't be bossed."

"You remembered your place," Sophia says, "and Nudd remembered you. I felt it rejoicing in our return even while you were defiling it with your brother's dead blood. I am sorry for your loss, Conservator. Know that it can only have been for the good."

"Your strength fed mine," Alan says. "I'm going to say that mine fed yours a little, too, because it feels good."

"I lost sense of what sounds right anymore," Brattle says. "Say what gets you through, Al, but after you say what's next. Is this over? I never missed my swamp so much."

Alan looks into Brattle and finds his spirit completely changed. He heals the few wounds on Brattle's body, but he cannot touch the new, terrible light Brattle has inside him. It's above death, and beyond Alan's reach.

"Let's wait and rest," Alan replies.

"More coming," Stag's Blood says.

Brattle sits down crosslegged and rolls his eyes. "I knew it."

Forty-Nine

Nudd's day goes on and on. Some of the skies above it darken and show stars, but most are perpetually bright. The garden grows back until all traces of Nettle's fire are gone. Butterflies puddle up the path to the fountain, and lethebells open their azure mouths in the tall grass. The fragments of Alan's old skull disappear into a mat of creeping vines and lichen.

Sparkling peace settles over the Crossworlds. Alan, Brattle, Stag's Blood, and Sophia sit together in the rolling quiet at the bottom of the hill. Bird voices drift into the garden from far away. The lethebells whisper melodies to each other like choir singers discussing their parts.

After a while, Alan and the others start to hear the clinking of a swinging chain. Finally, a shape appears on the crown of the hill. Alan and company climb up to meet it beside the fountain, which they find full of long, green fish. The shape shimmers around its owlish eyes. It swirls itself into something solid and the garden air seems to bend around it. A great black bag with a pinched-shut mouth is at its feet. Its scar-white robes fold over a darkness that seems to go on forever, away from this world. It's the Cuco. It pushes back its red-lined hood and bows in greeting.

"I knew it'd be you," Alan says.

"Just a shade," Stag's Blood purrs, "a lying emanation."

Brattle chimes in, "Real deal ain't pure enough for this pretty place."

"One more shadow," Sophia says, "in a war of shadows that will never end."

The Cuco gives a high, small hoot that may be a laugh. Smoke from its censer rises around it. Alan sees faces moving in the smoke – lit lamp eyes blinking in fleeting coils before they curl away. Iscela is there, her hair yanked up into its signature *moño*. Alan's father is there, too. His soft, sad features spin away on Nudd's aimless, crossing breezes. A little pain sinks its teeth into Alan's abdomen and stays there, sucking.

"Those things and worse," the Cuco says in a voice full of funeral thunder. "Shadow, shimmer, sluagh – I am all but equaled in Graveworld."

"It's real," Alan says. "I can see into it. It's like a mouth opening from space into a grave pit full of stars."

The Cuco nods. "You have arrived," it says. "You have served your purpose. It has been so long, I was surprised to find room in myself for doubt, but here you are."

"What purpose was that?" Sophia asks.

"Not yours," Alan says. "Your sister Morgan's. Yours was to die, wasn't it? You're Mordred."

"Do you think yourself especially perceptive, Alan Shade?" the Cuco asks. "You are on the frontier of horror. Your way from this is longer than you will ever walk – all you will see for the rest of your life are black horizons. "

"Are you too vast a spirit to answer, then?" Sophia says, crossing her arms, a light of frustraton on the crown of Stag's Blood's head.

"Show me my limits," Alan says. "Draw the lines for me, and I'll cross every one."

Mordred stares motionless for a moment. Alan feels its presence vivdly. Its boundaries are like the red edges of a forest fire.

"Listen," the Cuco says. "This is the truth. At last, I can slip its weight and be finished.

"There are many of us. We are the Prime Mover stretched out across itself: the living aspects of a gestalt consciousness. I am action, and Morgan is thought. This you know. I saw her tell you, but she was negligent. It needn't take eons for thought to become thoughtless. You must know this as well. In Morgan's case, I have worked to make her less than she is.

"I rebelled when this world began and was imprisoned within it. Morgan is here to ensure that I continue to suffer, and she does so with relish. At first, I wanted to die. I let poison into my heart, but Morgan sucked it out. In the depths of my agony, I had a vision: there are *better worlds*. There are universes of green hills and fields and beaches that run on forever from the arms of deep, stormless seas. I made up my mind to escape.

"I made new threats for Morgan to face, and I let her defeat me time after time. She has been defeating me for millennia, and now she is blind with certainty that she cannot fail. Know that I wake every bird in the morning, and that I drag the suns across every sky with my bare hands. I push trees from seeds, and their lives are moments to me. The storms that bend them, the bores that gird them to their deaths – I am all these things, and my sister is nothing. She presides over ruin, the scope of her power collapsed, and now you will cripple her. Free me. I made you. Tear me from this world-prison, and I will remember you in paradise."

"What makes you think I have that power?" Alan asks.

"I gave it to you," Mordred replies. It looks from Brattle, to Sophia, and then to Alan. "You are my champions: the bell of the law, the light of the star, and the spirit of destiny."

"What of me?" Stag's Blood asks, kneading the ground to score the stones around the fountain.

Mordred approaches Stag's Blood and puts a willow-thin hand on his cheek. Stag's Blood looks up into its owl face with wondering eyes.

"You are my guide," Mordred says. "The bastethai are exotic interlopers – aliens here from hunting lands beyond the Prime Mover's brutal spheres. Feeling my imminent freedom, they are returning home. You are one of the last to remain. You will fade and take me with you far from here."

"And if I don't want to?" Stag's Blood asks.

"Then I will be free in Midion," Mordred says, "and there will be a war."

"Threats," Brattle grumbles. "He's leanin' on us. Don't listen. We done the good. Let's burn."

"Prescience, dear ghoul," Mordred croons. It starts toward Brattle, and Brattle bats it away. It trills a woody laugh and clacks its beak. "Augury — and I know my sister. There is a terrible, gray power behind her. Do you want to see how strong she is with all that power marshaled? Love and terror mixed in blood — great seas of it, shored in fire. This is Morgan's threat. Not mine."

"What happens to Midion if we release you?" Sophia asks. "Will it dwindle? Will it vanish?"

"Not in the least," Mordred replies. "In my absence, its true spirit will emerge. I have seen it lying green and asleep, waiting to be born. The wasting will roll back. You will see. Free me, and you will see."

At this, a wave of light and warmth riffles through Nudd from the west. Buds open in its wake, and trees strain up to gain a few inches in height. Judgie mothers flutter and squawk as eggs hatch beneath them.

"Only good can come of this," Mordred continues, "especially for me — I am honest. I have given much of myself away to this enterprise. In the end, I can only argue. That is how much I have lost. The decision is yours, Alan, Spirit of Destiny, Drudge of Death. That is your purpose — not mine or Morgan's. Speak it, and end this."

"You're gonna do it, aren't you?" Brattle asks Alan. "You're gonna listen to this hisser. I know you, Al. You can't resist a sob story. You're a compulsive liberator."

Alan says nothing. He has been reaching since he realized who the Cuco was. He is down in the formless prison, wrist deep in ancient cold and darkening sorrow. Like Morgan, the Cuco is a husk, though it has been lived in longer and retains more life. The real Mordred is a great weave with bright spiders of thought pulsing across it. The weave goes on for light years, touching alien worlds. Minds emerge from it like drops of rain, bulging clear before they fall and are caught up by spirits emerging from the exchange. Daemons dream in Avernus, the wars of their fantasies shining huge and red above them while they sleep. Malakeen watchers scour the Coma for the traitors who served Winter White. Alan glimpses Animus only briefly: a rainslick flash of headlights on a forested road, a girl at the wheel, her baby in the car seat beside her. Alan thinks of Nora.

What new era of light will our progeny see?

"No more war," Alan says.

"I make no such promises," Mordred replies.

Mordred's prison is locked with a seal. Alan sees it in his mind as clearly as the draug. It's a round mass of points glowing gold — the Seal of Aiwass, which Alan will always associate with Toven. He reads the words upon it, remembering the night he was branded with them: *Gnosis Egregore*. In no great flash and with no bone-shaking roar, the seal dissolves. Mordred's sprawling weave retracts, leaving pregnant emptiness behind it.

"You're right, Brattle," Alan says. "You can yell at me about it later."

The Cuco lifts its shoulders and closes its eyes. Its feathers quake from their tips to their anchors in its purple-black flesh. When it opens its eyes again, there is nothing behind them. They are ghost-empty.

"I thought it would be more," says Mordred. "Such small joy after my long torment. Subtle and sweet — the better to savor, I suppose. I feel the world rising. Time is moving again. Morgan, may you wither with your dead things forever."

Nudd shimmers. The water in the fountain ripples and blows away. Pink willows start to sag.

"It's time to go, isn't it?" Stag's Blood says.

Mordred nods. Stag's Blood turns to Alan and Brattle. Sophia hugs the bridge of his nose from its tip, her heartlight pounding, and he curls his whiskers around her.

"I am awaited," he says, an irrepressible smile hitching up his cheeks. "Keep a warm place on the Gale for me, friends. Brattle, Alan, Sister Sophia, thank you all for a wonderful adventure."

"Take care of yourself, Stags," Brattle says. "Watch this one. Don't trust him."

Mordred levels a glare at Brattle. Nudd trembles again when Stag's Blood and Mordred fade from the world. Sophia lands in Alan's palm, her warmth like weight.

"How do we get back?" she starts to say. Then Nudd is quietly gone. The trees and the judgiebirds disappear like shadows in the rising dawn. The fountain stones with Stag's Blood's claw marks pale away to Suttea dust. The walls of the Necropolis rise with its towers in the north, and Calushar is still sleeping across the far rooftops. Gimcrack leans nearby in the glittering ruin of its mechanical mountains. Its roofs have fallen in – it is little more than a heap of rubble with ghosts circling hopelessly around it. Rustic ghouls look down the hill from the edge of the woods, their eyes like creeping lamps.

"Nothin' feels over," Brattle says. "The world don't feel saved."

"What now?" Sophia asks.

"Back to the Mercy Gale," Alan replies. "It might be best to get as far away from here as possible. Morgan probably isn't going to be too happy with us."

The night is deep and cold. The stars sleep under cloudy blankets, their mother moon watching them in secret from the mountains. Suttea waits beneath a witching hush so charged and full that it feels sacred. Alan remembers lonely nights at church bonfires, his faith hanging on nothing, wondering if he might see God staring down through the smoke. There are no more Shades of his blood. Animus is blasted bright now, and no corners remain for his kin to shadow. Only Graveworld is haunted enough to hold him.

The Mercy Gale waits at the stone-bald crest of the hill that leads out of Suttea. She is dark and tugging her anchor, eager to run. The wraiths roll down her sail as Alan and Brattle climb the rope ladder to the main deck. There, the chief mate greets Alan.

"The lady is aboard," it says. Alan is surprised to find that he's missed this wraith's shining, clustered eyes. "She waits abaft. What's our heading?"

Alan looks toward the new light on the quarterdeck. Lady Nightjar stands at the podium, her hands above the eyestone, an unfelt wind tugging her dress.

"Marmorea," Brattle replies as he climbs over the gunwale. "When'd she arrive? What's she want?"

The chief mate shivers, stirred by the same phantom wind as Lady Nightjar.

"She waits abaft," the chief mate repeats. "Are we all aboard?"

Brattle sighs and looks over the port side at the swaying forest. Sophia lands on the rail beside him, her heartlight burning from black to violet and back – the colors of Stag's Blood's coat.

"All aboard and ready to get underway," Alan says. "A little hurry would be nice, too, chief."

"Marmorea," the chief mate says, "full speed."

The wraiths haul anchor, and the Gale's sail fills with a chalk-heavy wind. Alan mounts the stairs to the quarterdeck to meet Annun, who tips him a little bow. She looks much stronger than before. She's almost solid, but she still seems weightless. Light strains through her as if through glass, splintering into faint rainbows at her feet.

"Welcome aboard," Alan says. "You're not on some infinite beach by now? What do you want from me?"

"The sylves have not been my people for many years," Annun says, "much to my surprise. They had written me off as lost. There's no place for me in Welkinbright anymore. A dead queen ruling the Empyrean City? No. And Gimcrack is gone, but I still have my ship. I have the Gale and you. That's all I want."

"I thought you might pass on. What made you stay?"

"All in time, thanoturge. And I might not be the best one to explain it anyway. Ask your new master. He will know."

327

Alan nods. "So you're here and you want me – how?"

Annun smiles. Her cheeks move like flesh, twitching up against deep laugh lines. "As you are, Hero of the Flame," she says. "I am in your debt."

With this, Annun takes a small glass case from beside the eyestone's pedestal and hands it to Alan. Inside is the lethebell that the dradtail Anaca brought back from the shores of death. The heart of its bloom glows pink and warm.

"Morgan meant to steal it," Annun explains, "but I pulled it from her bedroom. Those walls mean nothing." She nods down the hill at the Necropolis. "It must be special if she wanted it, but I don't know how."

Alan holds the glass against his forehead. The flower sings softly, its bloom swaying. The words of its song run together like mud. All the same, Alan feels a knot forming in his chest as he listens. Sadness warms there with a heart of fear.

"It's the last piece of Mordred in Midion," Alan says. "I thought it would fade. I wonder why it didn't."

"Mordred," whispers Lady Nightjar. The word is like an ancient promise, unfulfilled and long-forgotten. "The world seems a little emptier now. It was a subtle thing at first, but now it is all I feel. Do you feel it? What did you do in the Gardens Arcane?"

"Did you speak with Kelen in Welkinbright?" Alan asks. "He gave his spirit for the city. Did they tell you? Did you see him?"

"He is quiet," Annun says, "but he's there. And he's strong. You've done well, Alan. You could not have done better."

Alan puts his hands on the eyestone. It is awake and watching him. He feels the life of the Mercy Gale pulsing through it – fire like blood surging to push the ship out of Suttea as fast as she can go. A falling, green steppe opens before her, night sitting on it like a funeral pall.

"I opened the ultimate prison," Alan says, "and freed a fallen god. Morgan was his jailer. She's coming after me. I can see her

Red Guard moving in the city, making ready, scrambling. Maybe there's going to be another war after all."

"Dangerous business," Annun nods. "Fallen gods accounted for, I can't think of a more dangerous enemy than Morgan Belfaire."

"Not even Winter White?"

Annun gives a little chuckle. Her laugh is like the call of a Poorwill waking in the North Dakota scrub. Alan tries to ache for his old sphere, but he can't find the longing in him anymore.

"Are you certain," Annun asks, "that Morgan and Winter White weren't one and the same?"

With this question niggling at him, Alan bids Annun good night and retires below. Death follows through the gloom, its wings wide and not altogether silent. Alan feels its claws close hard around his heart.

Well done, it whispers with Allison's voice, *my good and faithful servant.*

Alan stows the last lethebell in his cabin with his knapsack. He hangs his necromasher on the wall and stands looking at it for moment, trying to see Winter White in the twist of her spine. On the orlop deck, he finds Sophia propped against a barrel watching Brattle sleep in the heat of the engine. Alan pulls off his basteta-fur robe and drapes it across Brattle's sprawling form. Though he cannot be cold, Brattle immediately hugs the robe and presses his face into it to fill it with whimpering snores.

"I feel as tired as he must have been," Alan says to Sophia, "but I don't have much hope for sleep."

"I miss Leadlight," Sophia says. "I need to go back, but I am afraid. I do not know how it might have been touched by this strife. Maybe not at all – or maybe it has been gutted like Cheel Gar was. I cannot bear to find out. I am not made for such trials. That is what I have learned on my first pilgrimage."

"You proved yourself," Alan says.

"Stag's Blood called this a wonderful adventure. *He* proved himself. I was along for the ride like a leaf in the wind, every bit as fragile as I look. I was not brave. I was only lucky."

Alan puts a comforting fingertip between Sophia's wings. She turns to embrace his finger and then mimes dancing with it for a moment.

"Why didn't we go with him?" Alan says. "That's what I keep asking. Why did we let him leave us here?"

"We do not belong in his Wildlands," Sophia replies. "At least not yet. Who knows anymore what waits beyond the veil? I certainly do not."

"Maybe we belong more than Mordred."

Sophia pumps up her heartlight until the Eternal Flame flickers into it, filling the deck with great golden rays. Brattle pulls Alan's robe over his face.

"Maybe," she says.

That night, sleep comes creeping into Alan's cabin like a sorry dog. He takes it into his arms and loves it, letting it pull him into a long and aimless dream. In it, he sees human shades standing on the Plutonian Shores. Many are knee-deep in dark, airy water. Most roam the beach with their heads bowed, shouting nonsense in gull-like voices. Something moves among the spirits, selecting some for reincarnation. Winter White is there for an instant, a sought smile's glimmer going the wrong way through the madding throng. Then she vanishes, leaving the whole complexion of the dream changed. When Alan wakes, he can't remember how the dream ended.

Morning pours through his cabin windows. It falls soft and eager across the chairs, its voice the warring titters of birds outside. Its breath is a warm, insistent breeze wheezing beneath the windowsill, blowing dust up to dance through the white-gold shafts of light. Alan stretches and pulls on a threadbare kersey jacket he finds hanging in his armoire. Then he slips on his shoes and goes topside to find Brattle and Sophia far afore.

Brattle swims in Alan's robe. Sophia walks the bowsprit with her arms out, flapping her little wings for balance. The Lady Nightjar stands nearby, watching over the starboard side as still as a gravestone. The Mercy Gale creeps over sandy ground toward the edge of a dune sea. Gray towers rise beyond the dunes, flying shreds from their flagpoles. Dead rise from the sand like frozen curls of black smoke.

"Where are we?" Alan asks, resting his elbows on the gunwale.

"Keimai Terion," Brattle replies. "That's Charnea ahead. The wraiths're takin' odd ways out. Worried about followers."

"Let's hope we've got enough of a head start," Alan says. He casts his deadsight behind them, through the spirits of sylvan kings trapped in their buried remains, and sees nothing. The dead voices in his mind hum together, distracted.

"I dreamed of Nora last night," Brattle says. "Wonder where she is — who she had waitin'. Nex was still in his cell when I squirmed out of that pit in Sepulchra, but, now Calushar's gone, who knows what's happening with him?"

"I plan to find out," Alan replies. "First we need to rest. I want to go back to your meteor and put it in order. It's been too long since you were home."

Brattle crosses his arms. "I thought you'd wanna go back to the gate. It might open for you now. Ain't your purpose here served?"

"I decide my purpose," Alan says. "That's what I've learned. I want to see my sphere again, but, like you were saying last night, Sister, I'm not sure how I'll find it. There's more to be done here still. I remember when all I wanted to do was go back, but I wasn't me then. Now I'm more me than I've ever been, and there's nothing to be done anymore."

"Ever more storms," Sophia chimes. "I will follow you into whatever is next."

Alan opens his palm and lets Sophia fly up to land on it. Her heartlight beats a strong, hopeful red. "I'm glad to have you, Sister."

"What *is* next, Al?" Brattle asks, rising onto the tips of his toes to lean far over the gunwale.

A tailwind whips up, tossing Brattle's faint strands of hair over the crown of his head. The sky is clear sapphire for miles. Alan looks across it into the wavering distance.

"What's next?" Alan says. "Everything."

www.ingramcontent.com/pod-product-compliance
Lightning Source LLC
Chambersburg PA
CBHW030416180626
46812CB00005B/2029